THE
PHOENIX
CODEX

THE PHOENIX CODEX

KNIGHTS OF MANUS SANCTI, BOOK ONE

BRYN DONOVAN

This book would not have been possible without the support of my family and my friends, especially my beta readers. Most of all, I am so grateful for the encouragement and the help of my wonderful and brilliant husband and the love of my life, Gill Donovan.

—Bryn

Copyright © 2017 by Bryn Donovan
Published by Almeris Press.

ISBN 978-0-9967152-4-9 (paperback); 978-0-9967152-3-2 (eBook)

To learn more about the author, visit her blog, bryndonovan.com.

Dedicated to J.R. Boles

CHAPTER ONE

CASSIE CAME HOME late from her dinner with Ana. Her friend had assured her that she'd find another job soon, this time at a place where she felt like she belonged. For the first time in a few weeks, Cassie believed everything would be all right.

When she flipped on the light, the room remained dark. Weird. Hadn't she just changed that bulb?

Someone grabbed her around the shoulders from behind.

She squeaked, trying to yank away. He dragged her a few steps backward and set her down on a chair. Her kitchen chair, moved to the living room. Terror streaked through her. *What is happening?* The next thing she knew, he was half kneeling on her, pinning her down where she sat, his shin pressed across her thighs.

Fuck! She swung a fist at him. He grabbed her wrist, held it down to the back of the chair, and tightened something around it. A zip tie. She'd never seen one in real life. *Do something. Gouge his eyes out!* She tried, but he caught her left hand and secured it to the chair as well. He was so fast, so efficient. Like he'd done this a hundred times.

Her loaded gun waited in the drawer of her nightstand, but a lot of good it did her now. Years of target practice with her dad and her sister, not to mention hunting with Uncle Charlie, all going to waste. *Scream. I should scream.* She turned her head toward the door. "Help! *Help!*"

"No one's going to hear you out here." His calm, baritone voice suggested that she was being unreasonable.

In her small ranch house in the desert, her closest neighbor was almost a mile away. That was one of the reasons she'd rented it—all that wide, open space made her feel free. *I'm such an idiot.* She doubted anyone had seen him on her side road with no streetlights. If they had, he wouldn't have stood out much—nondescript in a black T-shirt and jeans. She leaned her head closer to his ear and shrieked, wordless, at the top of her lungs.

He got off her and crouched near her leg. She tried to kick him, but he was too far to one side, out of her range of motion. He bound one of her calves, and then the other, to the chair legs with plastic ties.

"Who are you?" Stupid. Like he was going to hand her a business card. A robber with any sense would've chosen a nicer house. She didn't like the other possibilities.

He stepped behind her and tipped the chair back. More panic sparked through her nerves—the primitive fear of falling. He dragged the chair to the kitchen, set her next to the table, and took a step back to look her in the face.

He was white, with narrow, steel-blue eyes in a rawboned face. She would need to describe him to the police. Hopefully. Over six feet tall, broad shoulders. Light brown hair buzzed almost to the scalp on the sides and a little longer on top. Military? Around her age, maybe, thirty-two. His nose bent slightly in the middle, as if he'd broken it once.

Why didn't he care if she saw him? Because she wasn't getting out of this alive? Her mouth went dry.

He walked to the front door. *He hasn't really hurt me yet.* But that was no reassurance. As strong and deft as he was, he hadn't needed to. Maybe he was just getting started. He locked the front door, turning the double bolt with a click, and strode back to her. Images flashed through her head. Torture, sexual violence. Her pulse slammed in the side of her neck as though the vein might explode.

"Please don't kill me," tumbled out of her mouth. "Or rape me."

Did he flinch? No, he couldn't have. "I'm not a rapist."

Just a killer, then? A fresh current of anger surged through her. "Is this how you get off?"

He crouched down next to a black backpack in the corner of her kitchen. "I'm going to cover your mouth so you can't cast a spell."

"A spell." He thought she was a wizard, or a witch? If only. She could wave her wand and have the next rent payment, or better yet, a job. "You're insane."

He leaned close with a length of duct tape. Cassie jerked her face away, but he pressed the tape hard over her mouth. A strand of her long hair got caught in it, tickling the corner of her lip. He said, "Of course, for all I know, you don't need to speak words out loud."

She struggled hard against the zip ties. Although she wasn't particularly strong, five-foot-five and average-sized, she hoped adrenaline would give her the strength to pull through them or break the chair. They only bit into her skin. Stupid well-made furniture.

"Looks like you're breathing fine." The impassivity in his shadowed, sculpted face made him look like an angel of death. "Cassandra Rios, you are accused of using deadly magic against your enemies."

She stopped struggling. Nobody called her Cassandra, except her dad, when she'd gotten in trouble as a kid. She was in trouble now. This guy was out of his damn mind. Would the cops tell her parents they'd found her body? Would anyone find it, or would he hide it somewhere? Her heart pounded hard and fast. Maybe she'd have a cardiac arrest before he had a chance to murder her. "A jaguar killed your ex-husband six months ago."

Shit. The animal attacks. She wanted to scream, *They weren't my fault!*

Rick's death had horrified her, and it had panicked everyone in Phoenix. Jaguars had only just been discovered in Arizona again. This one had ambushed her ex in his driveway in the middle of Scottsdale, leaping from the top of his SUV to tear out his throat.

"Your coworker was seriously injured by a coyote two months ago." She cringed at his words. Coyotes usually avoided humans. They didn't go after them in populated places any more than jaguars hung out in cul-de-sacs slaughtering people. "And last Tuesday, not long after he left your mother's house, your uncle was attacked by a javelina." His eyebrows rose. "In a parking garage."

A few hours before it had happened, Cassie had seen Uncle Charlie at her parents' house. He'd tried to get her mom to loan him more money, although she didn't have it to loan. Almost no one got rich running a stable, and in the last few years, business had slowed. Her dad hadn't been home. Cassie couldn't hear most of the conversation, but after he'd left, her mom had been crying.

The blurry security camera footage had made the evening news. A big, black, hairy desert pig had come out of nowhere, tusks bared, and slashed Uncle Charlie's shins. The uncanny coincidence—three attacks against people she'd been mad at—had made her feel guilty, even though there was no way, logically, she could have been to blame.

"Since you've killed with this spell once, we can only assume you will again." His voice carried no emotion. Who the hell was *we*? He pulled up another chair for himself and sat down, so close that his knee grazed her thigh. "I'm here to go into your psyche, verify your guilt, and learn what I can about the magic you're using, because we haven't seen it before."

Cassie struggled against her bonds again as he reached down into the backpack. A faint smell emanated from it—incense, of all things.

He took out a gun.

Cassie stared at the Glock with its dull gleam. Her blood chilled. *I am going to die. I am really going to die.*

"You'll have one minute after I release your mind to prepare yourself, and then you'll be killed with one shot to the head." He laid the weapon on the table, right next to a pile of junk mail and an empty drinking glass. Her stupid, messy life, finished before she'd even done anything with it. She started shaking, but she willed herself not to cry. Instead, she glared at him. He could remember the look in her eyes when he was burning in hell.

A bullet to the brain. At least it would be quick. She imagined her blood on her dirty kitchen tiles. Was that why he'd dragged the chair in here? So the mess would be easier to clean up? No, he'd probably done it because the kitchen couldn't be seen from the street. Maybe no one would even hear the gunshot.

She jumped when he gripped her right hand where it was tied to the back of the chair. Her fist felt tiny and cold in his. He bowed his head.

Raw force pushed up against her brain, her heart, her *self.* Behind the duct tape, she whimpered, squeezing her eyes shut. It pressed from all sides and sucked at her at the same time. What the hell was happening? *Go into your psyche,* he'd said. He could do that? Gritting her teeth against the pain, she willed herself to stay intact. Something was trying to crack her skull open like an oyster shell to inhale the quivering morsel inside. She thrashed and shoved against it with all her strength.

The invisible walls separating her self from him and the rest of the universe tumbled inward. Her eyes flew open.

CHAPTER TWO

JONATHAN STOOD FACING Cassandra Rios. The scents of creosote and ozone, smoky and fresh, startled him. He was in her psyche, and she was a murderer. He'd been prepared for the smell of blood or rotting flesh, not the desert after rain.

Every person had a unique inner world that reflected their character and their experiences, their pain and their dreams. He looked around him at Cassandra Rios's psyche. Many-armed ocotillo cacti, fuzzy teddy bear cholla, and rough shrubs dotted a rolling plain. No roads, telephone poles, or other signs of human habitation marred the landscape. No sound intruded upon the silence. Cobalt blue and bright pink streaked the sky, and near the horizon, the clouds glowed orange. Near his feet on a prickly pear cactus, pink-red fruits ripened. They reminded him of hearts.

Doubt coiled in his gut. This wasn't the soulscape of a killer. At least, it wasn't like any he'd ever seen. He'd expected ugliness inside her, even if it didn't show on her outside.

In her photograph in her file, she'd struck Jonathan as more attractive than the usual target. She had big brown eyes, a prominent nose, and long, dark hair, and in the picture, she was laughing and full of life. *A pretty woman is just as likely to be evil as anyone else.* He'd reminded his younger brother of that on the drive from the middle of New Mexico to Phoenix.

Of course, it had been an imagined conversation, the only kind he could have with Michael now. His brain kept playing tricks on him, though, making him think he would see his brother again, as if he were merely posted in Manila or D.C.

Her soulscape wasn't perfect. Scarred black trunks of trees covered one mountain. A wildfire had blazed through. But even that looked like damage, clean and simple, more than anything else. What had hurt her?

Wrong question. He had to find out how she'd caused the animal attacks. They couldn't be a coincidence.

Far in the other direction, about a dozen horses grazed. No saddles, no bridles, some of them tawny, others extravagantly spotted. They threatened no one.

She's a bruja. *This is a trick.* He'd never heard of anyone being able to conceal the truth of their own psyche before…but after hundreds of years' worth of carefully documented missions and the study of ancient and obscure lore, Manus Sancti still occasionally encountered something new.

"You killed me?" Cassandra demanded. "This is heaven?"

"If this were the afterlife, I wouldn't be here. I'd still be alive."

"True. And I'm pretty sure serial killers go somewhere worse than this." If she'd been innocent, he would've admired her spirit. "How did you get me out here?"

"It's not out anywhere. We're inside you."

"What?" She closed her eyes as though willing reality to return.

"This is your psyche. It feels familiar, doesn't it?"

Her brow creased. "You drugged me."

"You know I didn't." This conversation was pointless. With most targets, simply asking them a few questions while inside their psyche proved their guilt. In her case, he'd been assigned to go through her memories first to understand exactly how she was doing the spells.

One of the horses spooked and ran away, and the others followed him in a panic, rumbling toward the far hills. The saturated colors in the clouds tumbled and shifted in a rhythm like music: sapphire, tangerine, fuchsia. A dark hawk cut across the swath of color, not hunting, just flying. He couldn't remember when he'd been in a more beautiful place.

She said, "You have no right to be here."

Maybe she was right. He couldn't shake the feeling that he was trespassing on sacred ground. "It isn't what I expected."

"What *did* you expect? Oh yeah, you thought I was a witch. Did you think I'd be in some kind of cave? Or some, like, scary castle with flying monkeys?"

"Something like that." He took a step closer to her. "You're not able to lie to me now. You can't even avoid answering me. Let's watch the coyote attack. You saw that one." He raised his hand in a slight, beckoning gesture. A huge image appeared on the sky above the mountains, like a giant movie screen. The company picnic at Arroyo Park. Dozens of employees wearing bright blue T-shirts with the corporate motto.

Cassandra said, "I don't want to watch." She shouldn't be able to feign emotions in here, but misery clouded her features.

"You have to." His voice came out hard. He knew from having his own memories reviewed, perhaps a hundred times in the past, that she could feel herself in the recollection, even as she watched it.

The coyote ran toward the group. A middle-aged man looked up and asked, "Hey, whose dog is that?" Its silver-bronze fur glinted in the sun as it rushed them.

"Run!" a young woman screamed, vacating her spot at the picnic table—Ana, Cassandra's friend. Jonathan recalled the name and the face from the briefing. Others scattered, including Tiffany

Daly, but the coyote went right after her, ignoring everyone else. His jaw clamped down on the woman's calf, and she fell flat on the ground.

Next to Jonathan, Cassandra cringed at the scene. Tiffany's leg soaked in blood, and her awful, high-pitched screams. She tried to push the coyote away, and it bit her hand, its gory teeth sinking into the flesh. In the memory, Cassandra ran toward Tiffany and the enraged beast. Jonathan straightened. No one had told him she'd done that. Why would she? A show of trying to rescue the other woman so no one would suspect her as a witch?

Cassandra yelled at him, "Make it stop!"

He lifted a finger and the screen abruptly disappeared, leaving only sky.

"What the hell is happening?"

"Not sure." He folded his arms across his chest in a pretense of detachment, as if he didn't have a growing sense of dread telling him that he'd made an unpardonable mistake. "Let's talk about your ex. Why did you two split up?"

The screen materialized again. Richard Belton was driving, and she was in the passenger seat, wearing a red sequined dress that revealed a lot of smooth, golden skin. It was a contrast to the plaid shirt, jeans, and cowboy boots she wore tonight, though that looked great on her, too.

"Not this." Her voice had taken on a pleading tone that cut through his defenses.

Not trusting himself to look at her or reply, he shook his head, touching a finger to his lips.

On the screen, she kicked off her stiletto sandals and flexed her feet. As the SUV passed a trio of saguaros with upraised arms wrapped in twinkling colored lights, she said, "That was so much fun." Glowering at the road, Richard Belton didn't answer. "What's wrong?"

"How many beers did you have?" he asked her.

"Three." He said nothing, and she spread her hands. "What?"

"I thought you had more than that, with the argument you got into."

"It wasn't an argument," she protested. "Your friend's wife kept telling me how much she loved Mexico and how she's been to Cancun five times. All I did was tell her I've never been to Mexico in my life."

"It was your tone. You made her uncomfortable."

Jonathan had to stop himself from shooting Cassandra a look of sympathy.

In the memory, Cassandra said, "That's not my fault!" She turned the heater down.

Richard Belton dialed it back up. "Don't you get it? He's not a friend, he's a colleague. I have to present a certain image every single day, and it's like you're trying to ruin it."

"All you told me was not to use the f-word. And not to argue with his political views, which, by the way, are completely fucked up."

Jonathan started to smile at that and caught himself.

"You rolled your eyes at him!"

"Oh, come on," she said. "You knew when you married me I wasn't this perfect, polite lady."

"I thought you would change."

She threw her hands in the air. "You don't marry people and then try to change them. I'm just being myself!"

"Well, could you not?" He almost missed the exit, swerved into the right lane, and clipped the car behind them in his blind spot. "Damn it! Look what you made me do!"

The memory wasn't showing Jonathan anything helpful, and he cut it off. The image flickered and faded to blue sky. He needed to ask more specific questions, like he usually did, instead of indulging his desire to know more about her.

"He was nice to me when we were dating," Cassandra said.

"Just the way he's nice to his coworkers. But it was all fake. And he wanted *me* to be fake. And meanwhile, I kept thinking maybe he'd get used to me and—love me for who I was." She looked away. "Shit. Nothing like a good therapy session with a guy who's going to blow your head off."

The words made him wince. "You can't help but say what you're thinking in here."

"I'm not good at that anyway—not saying what I think. That's why he didn't love me."

"He was a jerk," Jonathan acknowledged. "That didn't give you the right to murder him."

"I didn't!" Her beautiful brown eyes filled with despair.

Jonathan's heart twisted in his chest. *There's no way that's an act.* They'd been sure she was a murdering witch. Verifying her guilt had been not much more than a formality. Now he didn't know what to think.

She swallowed. "You said yourself I couldn't lie here."

"You shouldn't be able to. Unless it's some kind of psychic defense I don't know about."

"The only thing I did the day he died was get mad at him."

Focus. Do your job. "Why?"

"I was mad at him pretty much every day." That definitely sounded like honesty. "But that day I was especially pissed."

He lifted a finger to draw another memory out of her. The screen over the mountains showed a picture of Richard Belton, wearing a suit, with his new fiancée, in a fancy courtyard. "This is a photograph?" he asked. "When did you see it?"

"Facebook," she muttered. "We still had friends in common."

The photo receded, showing the caption beneath. *I asked the beautiful, amazing woman of my dreams to marry me and she said YES!! I've finally found "the one"!!* It had gotten over two hundred likes.

"Ouch," he said.

"It's worse than that. Look at the date." She pointed. "That's the date we got married. On our last anniversary, I said we could go there. Milagro—it's the fanciest restaurant in Scottsdale. I didn't really want to. But we'd been fighting a lot, and I wanted to make things better. He liked fancy places." She gave a bitter laugh. "And I thought maybe our marriage could use a miracle." Her file had said she only spoke English, but most people in Phoenix knew some Spanish words here and there, like *milagro* for miracle.

Cassandra wrapped her arms around herself despite the desert warmth, as though she needed a hug and she was the only one who would give it to her. "He said he was too busy at work to go out on a weeknight, and we could figure out what to do that weekend. But then we had another fight. We never did anything for that last anniversary."

"But he took his new girlfriend there on your anniversary and proposed to her."

"On a Tuesday night." Her cheeks darkened in a humiliated blush. "I found out later from his sister that he had, uh—he started seeing her while we were still married."

Jonathan's blood boiled. "I can't stand cheaters."

Her eyebrows rose, as if he'd said something crazy. "Me neither." Of course she was confused. A few minutes ago, he'd been declaring his plans to execute her, and now he was angry on her behalf.

"Were there any incidents with animals while you were still married to him? Things that he knew about?"

"No," she said. "Nothing like that."

"And you didn't send a jaguar after him?" He lifted two fingers with a harder psychic tug. The screen in the sky fuzzed, but nothing appeared. He stared at her, sure now of what he'd suspected ever since he'd entered her soulscape. "You're not causing the attacks on purpose."

She threw her hands in the air. "That's what I've been telling you, you fucking psycho!"

"But you are doing it," he said, more to himself than to her. The stricken look on her face made it clear that she believed him. *Christ help me.* This mission was a mess. He'd taken it too soon after the last, disastrous one—to distract himself from it and to begin to atone for it with a job well done. Not that he would ever be able to atone for it, as long as he lived...

And now he'd attacked an innocent woman. She was courageous, with the most breathtaking soulscape he'd ever visited—pure, wild, and free. Life hadn't treated her well lately, and then he'd come along to make everything truly terrible. He'd tied her up, threatened to kill her, and crashed into her psyche. Yes, he'd done what he'd been sent to do, but that didn't matter. She'd needed his *help.*

The best thing he could do for her was stay calm and solve the problem. Even if it wasn't her fault, they could hardly allow animals to keep attacking anyone who crossed her. If it wasn't fixed soon, who knew what Capitán Renaud would suggest as a solution, but it might not be good. Jonathan wasn't sure how he'd convince her to work with him, but he had to try.

"Cassandra," he said. "I'm sorry."

CHAPTER THREE

CASSIE DIDN'T LET down her guard. "Who are you?"

"My name's Jonathan West. Listen, I know I scared you—"

"You fucking assaulted me!"

He held up a hand. "We need to figure this out. Your coworker, Tiffany Daly. Did you get mad at her, too?"

Even though she didn't trust him in the least, she couldn't avoid telling him whatever he wanted to know. "I got mad at her that morning. She was bullying Ana again. Tiffany made her cry, and it was totally uncalled for."

"This is Ana Quintero you're talking about."

She stiffened at the mention of her best friend's name. "What are you? FBI, freak division?"

"Something like that." He took a step toward her. "And you got angry with your uncle."

"He wanted another handout from my mom. And he got her all upset."

Jonathan West nodded. His thoughtful, steady gaze should have disturbed her less than the cold glare it had replaced. Instead, it registered as a different kind of danger, one she couldn't name. "The attack on Charles Warner was the mildest of the three. The javelina slashed him in the legs, and he got a few stitches. Would you say you were less angry with him than with your ex?"

"Probably." Uncle Charlie had been nice to her when she was a kid. "I mean, he is family, even if he can be a dick."

"And you were angrier at Tiffany Daly than your uncle?"

She could see what he was thinking. Tiffany's attack had been worse than Uncle Charlie's, though not fatal, thank God. "Yeah. I never have to work with her myself, but she pulls that kind of shit with her staff all the time." She looked down at the ground. A tiny lizard scuttled from one rock to another.

"And in each case, there was some time between when you got really mad and when something happened."

"I guess so," she said.

His forehead puckered. "I'm surprised nothing happened to your ex-boss."

Shame prickled along her scalp. It was stupid. There were more embarrassing things than losing your job. Going around attacking innocent people, for instance. "You know everything about me."

His rueful laugh surprised her. "I wish. Why were you fired?"

"I don't know. I feel like some people blamed me for the coyote attack on Tiffany." She shoved her hands in the front pockets of her jeans. How strange that she'd be wearing the same clothes here as in the real world. "Someone mentioned that it was weird, after what happened to Rick."

"So your boss fired you for hexing someone?"

Cassie could just imagine the HR people putting that down in their paperwork. "He said I wasn't a good fit with the corporate culture." Her shoulders sagged. "Which was probably true." She cursed too much. She wore cowboy boots.

"Your ex-husband's new fiancée... You must have been mad at her, too. Why didn't anything happen to her?" His eyes flicked up at the sky, maybe expecting it to reveal a lesser attack on her—a hornet sting or a Chihuahua bite.

"She's not the one who made wedding vows to me."

Jonathan tilted his head, conceding the point. He paced a few steps. A jackrabbit bounded out of his path, narrowly escaping the bottom of his boot, and he froze. As he watched, it scampered maybe fifty yards and then hid behind a lone palo verde tree. Frowning, he turned back to Cassie. "I'm going to get out of your head now. But you have to keep answering my questions."

"I'll call the police." Shit. She hadn't meant to say that out loud. And how the hell could she do that, anyway? In the real world, she was tied to a chair.

"Calling the police wouldn't help. I'm not easy to catch." He sounded sympathetic. "You need to work with me, or you'll be in trouble with people who are a lot scarier than the cops."

"Whoever sent you to kill me could send someone else." Dread trickled down her spine.

"They won't." Reassurance warmed his voice, and she wanted to believe him. "It's going to be fine as long as you cooperate." He flicked into transparency. "When we're back on the other side, stay calm."

Black clouds rolled in from the low blue mountains. Darkness ate up the landscape from all directions. The breeze ceased, and Cassie felt the chair under her. She opened her eyes.

They sat in her kitchen again. Jonathan's hands still enveloped her fist where he'd bound it to the chair back.

He raised his head. "Your hand is freezing."

A wave of nausea roiled through her. He eased the duct tape off her mouth, although it hadn't been on long enough to really stick. She tried to wipe her wet mouth on her shoulder. He grabbed a bandana out of his pocket and blotted off her lips. The overly intimate gesture made her uncomfortable, and she wanted to say something smartass but couldn't come up with anything.

He unfolded a large black knife, and she recoiled. He held up his empty hand. "I'm just cutting the ties."

She had pulled against them as hard as she could. When she inspected her freed hands, she saw red streaks marking her wrists, front and back, with a few thin smears of blood.

"You're a fighter," he muttered, sounding angry. He took a metal box out of his backpack and she stared at it. What the hell was he planning now? He flipped it open to reveal bandages, vials, needles, and gauze.

"You have all kinds of things in that bag," she said. "You're like a...scary Mary Poppins." The room tilted and spun, making her dizzy.

He rubbed some kind of salve on the flayed skin of her wrists. She winced at the sting, and he mumbled, "Sorry."

Did he think she'd forget about the fact that he'd done this? She would have punched him, except her feet were still tied to the chair legs. Gently but quickly, he wrapped one wrist and then the other with gauze. Then he kneeled down and cut through the ties around her legs. This time he didn't take care to stay out of the range of her boots. She aimed a vicious kick at his face.

He jerked back and to the side, and her toe barely connected with his ear. She jumped to her feet and hoisted up the chair, intending to swing it into his head. He caught one of the chair legs and yanked it away from her with little effort, tossing it over his shoulder. Even as it clattered to the floor, she was darting toward the gun on the table.

She almost made it. From behind, he pinned her arms to her sides, hauling her in against him. She struggled, stomping the heel of her cowboy boot down onto his toes as hard as she could. It hit something hard—steel-toed boots, she guessed. Why did she even try? Maybe she'd seen one too many action flicks. His chest pressed hard against her back. Her ass was shoved right up against his crotch.

He adjusted his stance, putting a little space between them

there without loosening his grip. "I'm not going to hurt you. Even if you keep trying to hurt me."

She stilled. He hadn't retaliated when she'd tried to kick him in the face. Hell, he'd just taken care of her skinned wrists.

He spoke into her right ear, a distracting imitation of tenderness. "You need our help. What if you got mad at your parents? Or Ana?"

Terrible images flashed through her head. Her mom and dad, lying on their living room floor, their throats ripped out like Rick's had been in the graphic pictures leaked to the internet. Ana opening a sock drawer and finding it full of scorpions, the small, most dangerous kind. She had managed not to cry before, but now tears sprang to her eyes.

He relaxed his iron grip and turned her around to face him, still holding her upper arms. When he saw she was near tears, his controlled expression melted into concern. "Hey. You're going to be okay."

It caught her completely off guard. A connection flared between them, as though she'd known him very well, long ago, and just now recalled it again.

No. None of this made any sense, and she shoved the feelings aside. Who the hell was he, even?

He closed his eyes briefly. "I haven't given you any reason to trust me. I'm asking you to trust me a little anyway."

Cassie had never heard a less sensible proposition, not even in biker bars, but the sincerity in his deep voice swayed her. "I won't hit you again." She felt too weak anyway, and for some reason, very cold.

He let go of her and inclined his head toward the couch. "Go lie down."

"I have to go to the bathroom." And she wanted to change her shirt. She stank, with that awful, panicky stench one only got in truly terrifying situations, like when one was about to be murdered or about to speak in public. Her thoughts darted to her gun, still waiting in the nightstand drawer.

Maybe she didn't need to protect herself from him anymore. He hadn't picked up his own gun again, and she vaguely wondered why. Anyway, he wasn't stupid. He followed her into the bedroom, and when she reached for the dresser drawer, he put his hand up against it.

"I just want a fresh shirt," she snapped.

He paused and then let go of the drawer, watching her as she opened it and grabbed one. As soon as she did, he pushed the drawer shut again. His gaze flicked to the adjoining bathroom and back to her in what must have been a rapid risk assessment: one high window over the shower too small for a person to squeeze through, one door that locked but that he could probably kick in if necessary, and one freaked-out woman. He nodded.

She locked the door behind her and took the opportunity to pee. It was a wonder she hadn't peed her pants already, considering. She raked a comb through her hair, wanting to feel less disheveled, more in control, and then scrubbed under her arms. Maybe she could call the police now. But her phone was in the living room. She put on the plaid Western-style shirt and fastened the snaps up the front.

Nausea still swirled through her. She emerged from the bathroom and wanted to collapse on the bed, but she didn't like him being in such a personal space. "My head hurts. I'm going to lie on the couch." Exactly as he'd suggested—no, ordered—a minute before. He followed her, like her horse, Layla, when she knew Cassie had a granola bar in her pocket.

She tossed the purse and newspapers from the couch onto the floor. Since she'd moved out on her own, she hadn't kept up as much with the cleaning. She stretched her body out and appreciated the softness of the cushions.

Jonathan picked up the quilt wadded at the end of the couch.

Her great-grandma had made it out of scraps. It was ugly, to be honest, but she liked having something that had belonged to an ancestor. He spread it out on top of her. One minute, he was going to blow her head off, and the next minute, he was doing this? The contradiction disturbed her—and allured her, which was all the more disturbing.

"I'm going to check your pulse." He lifted her hair, damp with sweat, away from the side of her neck and rested two fingers beneath her jaw. The light touch made her quiver. "Still strong," he said, as though to himself.

"I'm fine," she muttered, just to get him to leave her alone. He ignored her, holding his fingertips there for several seconds. Then he looked straight into her eyes, maybe checking for some other kind of symptom. His scrutiny embarrassed her, and she looked away.

He withdrew his touch. "Heart rate's not bad. Considering." Anger edged his tone again—why? She peered up at his face. Was he mad at himself?

She resisted the urge to pull back when he picked up her hand, studied her rough, short fingernails, and then set it down exactly in the same place as before. He grabbed a pillow from the other end of the couch, lifted her feet, and tucked it beneath them. "If you're in shock, it's mild."

"No thanks to you. You scared the shit out of me!"

With an enormous crash and explosion of shattering glass, something huge barreled through the sliding door off the kitchen.

They both leaped up. Jonathan stepped in front of her, planting his feet wide.

A black bear snarled at them. A fucking bear, in her house. Huge and pissed off.

A rancid locker-room smell filled her nostrils. *So that's what bears smell like.* Cassie stood frozen.

"That didn't take long," Jonathan muttered.

The beast shook shattered glass off his pelt like drops of water and advanced into the living room toward him, blocking his path to the gun on the table. Long, sharp canines glistened as he drew back his lips and let out a throaty growl that vibrated through Cassie's shoes.

Of course this would happen. Cassie had gotten as angry with Jonathan as she'd ever been with anyone. And now a bear, who had no interest whatsoever in harming her, was going to tear his head off right before her eyes.

Jonathan stepped away from her. The bear bounded toward him, fast and graceful despite his massive size. He rose on his hind legs. Jonathan crashed his fist across his mottled brown snout. *Holy shit.* Who punched a bear in the face?

The massive animal staggered and went back down onto all fours. His nose was probably more vulnerable than the rest of him, padded with thick hide and hefty muscle. Jonathan only got a step closer to his gun before it charged toward him again.

She picked up the floor lamp and smashed it down on the bear's head.

He turned to her. *Oh God. Now he's pissed at me, too.*

His face reflected hurt and bewilderment. He was only trying to protect her from this intruder. Confusion swirled in her brain. Maybe she should have stood back and let him.

Jonathan sprinted for the Glock. The bear launched himself after him and reached him with one swipe. Claws slashed red lines in Jonathan's back. Pivoting, Jonathan delivered a hard-booted kick to the creature's other front leg, right at the knee joint. The animal let out a high-pitched howl. Jonathan made it to the kitchen table and picked up the gun.

"Don't shoot!" Cassie screamed.

He froze and looked over at her.

The bear ran away. This made no sense—animals didn't know about guns. It was as though he'd picked up on her fear for his safety. Even with the limp from the damaged leg, he moved fast, disappearing through the shattered sliding glass door.

Jonathan took a step after him, still aiming. Then he lowered the weapon, panting.

"Is he gone?" she asked.

He nodded once, his mouth slightly open. "Why'd you tell me not to shoot?" The tone of his voice implied she was crazy, which raised the question of why he'd obeyed her.

"It's not his fault! He was trying to protect me." A sad thought occurred to her. "But I don't know if he'll survive with a broken leg."

"Didn't break it. Tried." He craned his neck around, trying to see his back. She came over to get a closer look and sucked in a breath.

Blood soaked the back of his shirt, or what was left of it. The claws had ripped it into long ribbons that revealed torn, glistening furrows of flesh. *Oh, God. My fault.* She couldn't believe he hadn't screamed in agony.

Maybe she should try to run now, while he was injured and distracted. Drive away, call the cops.

But what if he were the only one who could help her? Like he said, she couldn't let this happen to anyone she cared about. She didn't have the worst temper in the world, but she wasn't a saint, either. He'd been trying to protect people, just like the bear.

She said, "I'll call 911."

"Don't." His scary voice had returned. She straightened. "I know someone who can stitch me up," he added in a more human tone. "You're staying with me."

What if she said no? He'd said he wouldn't hurt her. Hell, when the bear had charged toward them, he'd jumped right in front of her, instinctively shielding her from the threat. Of course, she hadn't been the one at risk. Even if he'd really made the switch from executor to protector, she didn't like the thought of one of his friends showing up, whoever they were.

"We're not going to a crowded hospital." Pain tightened his words. "You're too dangerous." He bent down to grab his backpack, swayed, and almost fell on his head.

He was in no shape to drive. Hell, he could pass out behind the wheel and run somebody over. "I'll take you. Let me get some bandages." She didn't want him bleeding out in her living room, and he'd need something sturdier than the gauze in his first aid kit. She ran to the linen closet, grabbed an old sheet, and after scrabbling for scissors in the kitchen junk drawer, she cut and tore a few long bandages. When she rushed back into the living room, he'd stripped to the waist and was tying the T-shirt around his middle.

He was seriously ripped—in the muscle way, in addition to the clawed-by-a-bear way. A thick purple scar slashed across his collarbone, shiny against pale skin. A concave gouge marred his side. A bullet wound? Brown hair smattered his chest and traced the trail from his navel downward. A small silver crucifix hung near his heart from a cheap ball chain. He gave her a bemused look as he took a makeshift bandage from her. "Surprised you're helping me."

"So am I," she muttered, but she cringed as she caught another glimpse of the slashes. This was what she did to people. He gritted his teeth, knotted the second strip, and then picked up the Glock again. She froze. "Give me the gun."

He gave a short laugh. "No."

"Otherwise, I'm not going anywhere with you."

"I'll make you go with me if I have to." He sounded resigned rather than hostile. With his injuries, could he force her to do anything? Maybe.

She looked him in the eye. "You really want to piss me off again?" She was pretty sure he wasn't up to a second bear fight.

His eyes darted down to the Glock and back to her. "They said you're a good shot."

"Damn right I am—Who said that?"

This elicited a chuckle from him despite his clenched jaw. He unloaded the gun and handed the magazine to her. "Good enough?" She nodded and shoved it into her giant purse. Once they were both in her truck, she asked, "Where are we headed?"

"Southside." He gave her the address. Not the safest neighborhood in the world, but not the worst, either. Her parents lived in Mesa and volunteered at a food bank not far from there. She'd gone with them as a kid.

Gravel sprayed as she sped out of the driveway. "So who the hell are you? How did you know about the animals?"

"Can't explain that."

He could if he wanted to. "How can you get in my thoughts?"

"Uh. Natural ability. And practice."

"You do that to people a lot?" She took a sharp turn, and he grunted.

"Only when someone's murdering people with magic." He laid his head back on the seat. A couple of days' worth of stubble covered his jaw and upper lip.

This is crazy. It can't be real. She asked him, "How many people have you killed?"

"Not people. Witches, demons. Monsters."

She shook her head. "You expect me to believe that?"

"Would anyone believe you? About the animals?"

Fair point. Still, her temper rose. "Who gave you the right to decide?" Her tire hit a pothole with a thump, and he took in a sharp breath.

"Try not to get mad. You don't want a bear coming through your windshield."

"They don't show up right away." Nonetheless, she forced

herself to calm down, fast. She couldn't afford car repairs. "There's no way you work for the government."

He shifted in the seat, his long legs sprawling, and said nothing. Maybe he wasn't part of a bigger organization. Maybe he was just an insane, violent man.

"Jon!" A loud, male disembodied voice in the truck made her jump. "I've called you ten times. What the hell's going on?"

CHAPTER FOUR

J ONATHAN WINCED. THIS was a bad time for his mission
runner, Dominic Joe, to break through. Nic was tracking his
vitals. He would have gotten an alert on the inevitable surge
in heart rate and the adrenaline dump when Jonathan had started
fighting a bear. Depending on how much he was bleeding, his
blood pressure might be dropping, too. He yanked his phone out
of his pocket. "I'm fine."

Cassandra's head swiveled over to him, eyes wide. She clearly
believed he was nowhere close to okay.

"The hell you are. I'm sending Gabi."

"No!" He said it loud enough that Cassandra jumped. Nic
was overreacting, not that Jonathan could blame him after the
last mission.

"Why?"

"I can't talk now." Officially, a mission runner made the decisions. In reality, the runner and those in the field usually came
to agreements together, and this was especially true if they were
friends. He knew Nic would back off, even before he heard his
frustrated sigh. "Call me soon," he said and hung up.

"How did he know you were hurt?" Cassandra demanded,
and Jonathan shook his head. Almost too late, she saw a stop sign

and jammed on the brakes, making him lurch forward in his seat. "*Christos*," he muttered under his breath.

She gripped the steering wheel more tightly. "How hurt are you? Are you going to die in my truck?"

"No. Turn here." He directed her past an old building, covered with graffiti—elaborate, unreadable letters, disgruntled green skulls—and down a block of small houses in disrepair.

When they walked up to the driveway to the stucco house, he staggered. He pounded the heel of his hand against the door a few times and then braced a forearm against the frame. They waited.

"There's a hospital not too far from here," Cassandra said.

Jonathan banged harder.

The door opened. Morty Silva stood there, his slightly hunched, stout frame wrapped in a shiny maroon bathrobe. He looked the same as ever, other than grouchier than usual, the way most people would be if you rousted them out of bed in the middle of the night. Although he was sixty-five or seventy, he had a full head of dyed-black hair, slicked straight back like Elvis or an Italian gangster in a movie. "What's going on, Ace?"

"My back needs stitching up."

He stood aside and invited them in with a jerk of his head. Scents of cinnamon and incense filled the dim and cluttered room. Morty gave Cassandra a keen look and then turned on Jonathan as he slammed the door shut. "What did you do?"

"Messed up."

The older man glared, his head lowering like a bull's. "Why do I get the feeling I should be calling the cops on you right now?"

Cassandra's eyes went wide.

Jonathan clutched a low bookshelf for support. "Sew me up first?"

"Go in the bathroom before you bleed on my rug."

Jonathan lurched down the hall while Morty introduced himself to Cassandra as though he had all the time in the world.

The older man wasn't Manus Sancti, but an occasional consultant. Jonathan sat down on the lid of the toilet, rested his folded arms on the sink, and laid down his head.

When Morty came in and peeled back part of the first make-shift bandage, he said, "God damn. You should have gone to the ER." Good. His wounds might at least make Morty forget he was mad. "'Course, I know you guys avoid them if you can. What the hell did you do?"

"Fought a bear."

Morty dug around in the medicine chest. "You win?"

"Does it look like it?"

"You're still breathing." He dabbed a wet washcloth on the exposed part of the slash, and the smell of rubbing alcohol hit Jonathan's nostrils. "Where was your gun?"

Jonathan let out a harsh exhale and turned his head to see what Morty was doing. "I set it down." He could've picked up the weapon right after Cassie's unsuccessful struggle with him, but he'd been trying to get her to trust him.

Morty flipped open a first aid kit. "Not like you to leave it lying around." He threaded a needle and swabbed it with more rubbing alcohol. "I'd give you some whiskey for this, but I don't have any in the house."

"Good for you." The last he'd heard, Morty was giving Alcoholics Anonymous a second try—which had probably taken more courage than trying it the first time. Empaths were natural addicts. They sought out ways to dampen the onslaught of emotions from others in addition to their own. As the needle bit into Jonathan's skin, he wondered if Cassandra had gone home. He couldn't think of a reason why she wouldn't.

He woke up on Morty's bed without any recollection of lying down there. Sunlight streamed in through the small window, and his Glock—unloaded, he recalled—lay on the nightstand next to him. The jagged pieces of the night before reassembled themselves in his head.

"Morning, babe." Morty's greeting in the living room was definitely not directed at him. He heard Cassandra's voice, though he didn't catch what he said. *She's still here.* His heart sped up.

Last night, when he'd wrapped his arms around her to stop her from grabbing his gun, the feel of her body pressed against his had triggered a lust in him as extreme as it was inappropriate. Remembering it now, a fantasy took over his mind. He imagined restraining her, but not against her will this time. Tying her up and kissing and stroking her, discovering all the secrets of her body and making her beg for more until she finally came undone.

There was something wrong with him, thinking like this. He had no business wanting someone he'd assaulted. He started to get up, and pain sliced across his back. *Try that again*, he told himself, and rolled to his side before sitting up. He moved to the closed door to listen.

Cassandra asked, "How long have I been asleep?"

"It's about six in the morning."

"Jesus." She gave a rueful laugh. "I haven't crashed on anyone's couch since college."

"You needed the rest. He got in your head, didn't he?"

The visceral memory of forcing his way into Cassandra's psyche made Jonathan feel sick. The recent injuries probably weren't helping. He rested his forehead on the door, and his mind flickered back to the beautiful sky of her soulscape, the sunset more colorful than any he'd ever seen in real life. Or was it a sunrise? He'd never see it again. Finding goodness when he'd expected evil, after seeing so much evil lately, had affected him in some way he couldn't even name.

She asked Morty, "Can you do that, too?"

"Nah, nothing like that. I get a sense of people's feelings, mental states."

"Oh." She didn't sound surprised. Maybe she'd already reached the point where nothing would surprise her. "You must be part of his secret group."

"They wish." Well, he wasn't wrong. There had been talk of recruiting Morty, although no one had ever approached him directly, as far as Jonathan knew. Between the ex-priest's empath abilities, his ghost talking, and his expansive knowledge of lore, he would have been a worthy addition.

"Are you a doctor?"

"Not that kind of doctor," Morty said. "I've just had practice. So has he, but you can't sew up your own back."

"Where is he?"

"Still out for the count, on my bed."

"Is he going to be okay?" A note of worry strained her voice. Strange. She shouldn't be concerned about his welfare.

"I think so. He bled a lot, though. Passed out once before I was done." Did Morty really have to tell her that? Not that there should have been anything embarrassing about blood loss.

Jonathan remembered now that after Morty had made him drink a full glass of water, a second glass of orange juice, and left him to sleep in his bedroom, he'd texted Nic, filling him in on what had happened. Nic had again suggested sending Gabi Bravo to join him. Jonathan had convinced him not to, pointing out that a second Knight might make Cassie feel more threatened, which would increase the likelihood of another animal attack.

A few hours later, when Jonathan had gotten up to go to the bathroom, he'd seen that Nic had texted him orders from Capitán Renaud. Under no circumstances was he to leave Cassandra Rios by herself, and he was responsible for making sure no one else got hurt. He'd have a couple of days to investigate the animal attacks, and if he couldn't solve the issue, he'd bring her in. At El Dédalo, with its staff of trained Mages, she could be controlled and contained while a Scholar worked on the problem.

Jonathan couldn't fathom anything he wanted to do less than drag Cassandra Rios against her will to a compound in the middle of the New Mexico desert. The solution had to be close at hand, and he would find it.

He scanned the little bedroom—austere but with posters, book pages, and flyers covering the walls—and spotted his backpack sitting in the corner. Either Morty or Cassandra must have put it there. When he bent over to dig through the backpack, the stitches felt like laces of fire. He found the extra magazine, loaded his weapon, and shoved it back into the concealed carry holster inside his belt. Then he pulled out his spare shirt, a black button-down, and eased into it, only doing two buttons at the bottom so the fabric wouldn't rub against his wounds. Had he taken off his shoes and socks? Morty had done it, probably. Embarrassing. Barefoot, he emerged to see the man handing a mug of coffee to Cassie, who sat on the sofa.

She must have crashed there. It had nothing to do with him. After getting attacked, she'd been exhausted. Was she all right?

Morty saw him and straightened up. "He lives."

"Hey, Morty," he said, not looking at her. "Thanks again. I'll have them—they can pay you."

"She's all right," Morty said. "No thanks to you, barging into her head. You scared the living daylights out of her. I felt the aftershocks on her last night, as soon as she came in."

Cassie said, "It wasn't just the…mind-reading thing." From the tone of her voice, Jonathan guessed that she didn't want to be taken for a weakling, though anyone would be shaken by a psychic invasion. "He tied me up and threatened to blow my brains out."

Morty's mouth fell open. He gave Jonathan a look of utter disgust. "What the hell is wrong with you?"

There was no good answer for that. Jonathan stared down at the rug.

Morty must have felt his shame, and he said in a less hostile tone, "You're going to need to explain this to me."

"Actually, I'd like to hear your opinion." Still avoiding her eyes, he ventured into the room. He winced at the pull on his stitches as he sat down on the opposite end of the couch from her, leaving as much space as possible between them. "When Cassandra gets mad at someone, a wild animal attacks them."

"Huh." Morty's lower lip jutted out thoughtfully. "That's a new one. A wild animal like, say, a bear?"

"For instance," Jonathan said dryly. "There's also been a jaguar, a coyote, and a javelina."

"I'll try not to piss you off," Morty said to Cassie.

"The jaguar killed her ex," Jonathan said.

Morty sobered. "Ah, yeah. I heard about that."

"But she's not doing it on purpose. Any idea what could cause it?"

"Not offhand, no. It's strange that they're different animals."

"Really?" Cassandra interjected. "That's the strange part?"

"They're all from the desert, except for the jaguar," Morty commented.

"The jaguar is, too." Jonathan respected Morty and didn't like correcting him. "They used to be common in this part of the state, just like in Mexico and further south. People thought they were extinct, but recently, a few of them have been seen north of the border."

"Good for them," Morty said. "So you're thinking they're regular animals? I talked to an expert last year about all the local lore, right when I first moved out here. She said no one she knew had seen a skinwalker in a while."

"We haven't dealt with one for over a century," Jonathan said. Cassandra lifted her eyebrows. "Which isn't to say they aren't out there. But we were sure these were regular animals controlled by a witch—Cassandra."

"I go by Cassie," she interjected.

"Cassie," he corrected himself. "Given the time delays between when she gets mad and they attack, that theory still makes sense. It takes a jaguar some time to get from the desert to Scottsdale. A little less time for a bear to get to her house on the outskirts of town." Jonathan shook his head. "But it just started happening recently, and she doesn't know why."

"Right." Morty stood up. "You guys want pancakes?"

Cassie said, "Oh my God, yes, I'm starving." Their host disappeared into the kitchen.

Jonathan rubbed his shoulder, although it wasn't sore. The gashes in his back, on the other hand, throbbed in pain. He asked her, "How are you feeling?"

"How are you? You're the one who got mauled."

"I'm fine."

She looked him up and down, making him aware that his shirt hung open. No doubt she noticed how scarred up he was, which probably didn't make him seem any more trustworthy.

He searched his brain for something else to talk about and cleared his throat. "Sorry you lost your job."

She blinked. "I'll find something else."

"What did you do there?"

"Nothing important. It was a mining company—you probably knew that much. I dealt with the clients."

This was good. A normal conversation. "You liked it?"

"I liked some of the people." She shook her head. "They, um… The company said they had these high environmental standards, but I think it was bullshit."

"Do you know what you want to do next?" He felt strange asking the question. All his life, he'd known what he was meant to do.

"I don't know." She sighed. "I texted my sister, Sam, yesterday—she's a park ranger. I thought that might be fun. Sam was at Organ Pipe, and there were a lot of problems with the drug cartels, but she's at Bryce Canyon now." Interesting that she'd describe the job as *fun*, even knowing it could be dangerous. "Anyway, Sam said it takes a long time to become a park ranger, but on the upside, the pay is crap." She shook her head. "I don't know why I'm telling you all this."

He doubted it was a reflection on him. She was the kind of person who said whatever was on her mind. He could appreciate that. In the past, he'd dated more than one woman who'd made him feel like he was always guessing about what they were thinking and feeling. He'd always felt like he offered all of himself and had gotten thin slivers in return. Not that there could ever be anything romantic between him and Cassie, but if they were going to figure out this curse together, her openness would make it easier.

"I can see why you thought I was an evil witch, though," she admitted. "I mean, if witches and demons are real." She peered at him. "They really are?" He nodded. "What else is there? Vampires?" Most people in her position would have been significantly more freaked out than she was by this conversation.

"They're extinct."

"So you're not one."

He straightened, offended despite all he'd done. Vampires had been disgusting creatures. "Why would you think that?"

"Because you can read minds? Not to mention you fight like a...like a person who's super good at fighting."

Well, that wasn't so bad. He reminded himself that *sonámbulos* had the wrong idea about vampires. "If I were one, I'd bleed a lot less. I'm a hundred percent human."

She shifted on the sofa to face him. "And you said there were shapeshifters? Like werewolves?"

"Hundreds of little packs. There are wolf Shifters in Arizona, in Springerville."

"No way. I've been to Springerville! I might've met one! Wait, do they look different?"

Her astonishment amused him. "When they're human, they look like anyone else. And they're not just wolves. There are others close to here—coyotes in New Mexico and elk in Colorado."

Her eyes narrowed. "Are you lying to me?"

"I'm never going to lie to you." He knew he sounded too earnest, but he meant it.

"They're all over the country?"

"All over the world. Foxes in Osaka, tigers outside Wuhan, lions in Nairobi, seals in the Shetland Islands. And lots more. Mice in Chicago."

She burst out laughing. "Mice."

Jonathan remembered the skinny teenage boy who'd helped him track down a banshee. "They're really nice."

Cassie gave a little smile, as though she found this adorable. "Are all shapeshifters nice?"

"Ha, no. Every pack's different. And every individual." He shrugged. "Like people."

"And your whole job is to fight evil, magical things?"

After a moment of hesitation, he nodded. He was saying way too much, but he needed her to understand him.

She traced the rim of her coffee cup with her thumb. "That sounds hard."

Of course, he thought of Michael. Silence hung between them, broken by a clatter of dishes in the kitchen.

"Fine. You don't want to answer questions about your creepy-ass fraternity. What about zombies?"

"Brain eaters, no," he said. "Animated corpses, yes."

"Jesus."

"Real," Jonathan said. "Definitely tortured and executed.

Everything else is a matter of faith—" He registered her bemused look and stopped. "You weren't asking about that one."

"That's okay. Go on."

He shrugged. "Morty's a better person to ask about religious stuff."

"How come?"

"He used to be a priest."

"'The Lord hath sworn, and will not repent, Thou art a priest for ever after the order of Melchizedek.'" They both looked up at Morty, standing in the doorway. "It's too early for theology," he said. "Come eat."

They squeezed around the small table in the cramped kitchen drenched with the smells of coffee, butter, and syrup. Morty had sliced up bananas to go with the pancakes.

Cassie shoved a bite into her mouth at once. "I never have anything for breakfast but coffee. But I really should."

Before Morty sat down, he put a black pill and a glass of orange juice in front of Jonathan. "Iron. You need it."

Jonathan washed the pill down. The syrupy pancakes were probably a good idea, too.

Morty began cutting his up. "So. You all thought Cassie was a badass witch, and they sent you to deal with her in your usual civilized way." He paused and looked at her. "How much does she know?"

"Too much," Jonathan said at the same time she answered, "Nothing."

"And I've given my word not to say more." Regret tinged Morty's voice. "There's no use telling you anything anyway. They'll wipe your memory if they have to."

"What?" Cassie whipped her head around to stare at Jonathan. "Are you going to wipe my memory?"

"No." Capitán Renaud might order a Mage to do it, though.

He truly didn't know what was going to happen to her if they didn't solve her problem quickly. Cassie's eyes narrowed.

"He doesn't have that talent," Morty informed her. "Not personally, that is. His job is judge and executioner."

Jonathan bristled. "Do you know what this world would be like if it weren't for us?"

"You know I do. It's when you have human targets that I get a little cranky."

Jonathan stabbed at his pancakes. "We don't have much choice with witches who kill. They can't be convicted in courts, and historically, they can't be rehabilitated. They always get worse."

"Historically," Morty repeated.

"The last witch I dealt with? In less than a month, she went from giving people nosebleeds to drowning them in sinks full of their own blood."

"Ugh." Cassie grimaced.

Morty said, "Come on, Ace, we're eating here."

"I'm just saying. Once witches start doing harm, it gets worse fast."

She asked, "You knew she did it because you mind read her, or whatever you call that?"

"Yes."

"What's it like? Going into the psyche of someone really evil?"

"You don't want to know." Some images stayed with a person forever.

Morty asked, "If you all thought Cassie was so dangerous, why didn't Michael come with you?"

"Michael—" A wave of grief rolled over him, and he couldn't continue.

This had happened a few times since the memorial service. He'd be fine, and then sorrow would come out of nowhere and blind him. Tears and revenge both honored the dead, and Jonathan had already offered up both, even if the latter hadn't given him satisfaction. Now wasn't the time for this. Deliberately, he set down his fork.

"Ah, kid." Pity filled Morty's voice. "I'm sorry."

Jonathan didn't look at either him or Cassie. "The Taos possession. You must've read about it." His voice came out tight but steady.

"I did. I figured possession, anyway. The victim had been to the Urraca Mesa portal?"

Jonathan nodded.

Cassie asked, "He was someone you worked with a lot?"

"Yeah. My younger brother."

She put her hand over his. Jonathan flinched as though her touch burned him and looked over at her, startled. She withdrew her hand. Her eyes were filled with sympathy, her mouth slightly parted. How could she be so soft to someone who'd been so hard with her?

Capture bonding. The thought gave him a heavy feeling in his gut. She was a natural fighter, but she'd lost, and now she was emotionally identifying with her abuser. It was a survival instinct, one he'd been taught to resist as part of his interrogation training, but she was a *sonámbula* with no training at all.

"Your boss had no business sending you out this soon." Morty's voice was a growl. He'd never liked Capitán Renaud.

"I wanted to go." Being idle at the headquarters, El Dédalo, had nearly driven him out of his mind. Most people spent a week or two with their family after a loss, but that only consisted of Jonathan's father, whose company wouldn't have been much of a comfort in any circumstance, and who now blamed Jonathan for his favorite son's death. "We should, um. Focus on the mission. I mean, on Cassie's situation."

Morty pressed his mouth into a grim line. "All right. Cassie, he said this started not too long ago?"

"Rick was the first time." She looked ill. "As far as I know."

Jonathan asked, "Did you do anything unusual in the weeks before that happened? Visit a psychic, take part in any rites or séances?"

"Rites? I went to Mass with my parents once. That's it. Unless you call signing divorce papers a rite."

"Did you come into possession of any unusual objects lately? A piece of jewelry, any kind of antique?"

"Hardly. I was trying to get rid of stuff, not get more." She took another bite of pancake.

"Get rid of things?" Morty chimed in. "How come?"

"Rick kept the house. I moved out. I had to box up my stuff, and I threw things away right and left."

Jonathan leaned forward. "Did you throw away anything unusual?"

"No, just a bunch of crap. You wouldn't believe how much garbage I accumulated in only five years of being married." She shook her head. "I moved in with my folks for a month with all my boxes, so I wanted to pare down." She froze. "Oh, God."

"What is it?" Jonathan asked.

She wrapped her arms around her middle. "I think I know what happened."

CHAPTER FIVE

CASSIE HAD THOUGHT of this once before, after the coyote attack. Because the idea was so ridiculous, she'd pushed it out of her mind. Last night, a box full of curiosities on Morty's coffee table had pricked at her memory again. Now, she told Jonathan and Morty the story.

While she'd been finalizing the divorce, she'd moved out and stayed at her mom and dad's house for a while. It had hardly made her feel like a success in life, doing that in her thirties. They'd been nice about it, mostly because her dad had loathed Rick all along.

She'd hauled all of her boxes of stuff down to their basement, and her mom had suggested that she go through some of her old things already down there. Most of it she'd pitched, except the equestrian trophies.

In one unmarked box, she'd found someone else's belongings. A blurry gray photo of a woman standing in the middle of a jungle. A large toy army tank, its tin mottled with rust and chipped paint. A key.

She'd pulled out a book with a worn, black leather cover. Small, slanted handwriting, in Spanish, filled the pages. The ink had faded, and she hadn't known much of the language anyway.

Her mom had never spoken it, and her father had never spoken it with them.

Her mom hadn't recalled seeing either of the photo or the journal before, but she'd told Cassie the woman was her great-grandmother, and the journal must have belonged to her great-grandpa.

Cassie had asked, "Did you know Grandpa De La Garza?"

"Well sure, sweetie, he only died a year before you were born. I've told you about him." She sounded impatient, as she often did when Cassie had a lot of questions. "He was in Mexico, and we only went down there the one time." Her mom was more Anglo than Mexican, though her dad was Mexican on both sides. "He was an archeologist. And an anarchist."

No way had she ever told Cassie this. Cassie would have remembered. "Why didn't you see him more often?" Her dad's side of the family loved getting together. She'd spent a good portion of her life in crowded relatives' houses and pavilions at parks, drinking Coke as a kid and then beer as a grownup, playing with somebody's baby or listening to an aunt's long story about her last surgery. Cassie's mom not seeing her grandpa was weird, even if he was far away.

"He wasn't sociable," her mom had said. "After my grandma died, he kept to himself more and more. He would go off to different places, and nobody would even know where he was."

"Wow." To Cassie, he'd sounded crazy.

"He was a very smart man, though," her mom had insisted. "Just an eccentric. An *eccentric*."

Cassie had returned the photo to the box in the basement and flipped through the journal. On a page near the back, the writing looked different: in larger block letters and short lines, like poems. Dashes separated them into syllables. It hadn't looked like any language she'd seen before, although that wasn't saying much.

She'd pronounced the first word aloud and liked the sound of it, the feel of it in her mouth. Slowly, she'd read on, for some reason wanting to get all of it right. In a few places, he'd written two a's together, or two i's, and she'd drawn out the vowels. When she'd reached the end of the page, she'd stared at it for a moment, and then muttered, "Huh. Weird." She'd shut the book and put it back into the box.

When Cassie finished telling this story, Jonathan pushed away from the table. "Where's the journal?"

"Still in my parents' basement." She took her dishes to the sink, ran her sticky fingers under the tap, and then wiped her hands on her jeans. "But there's no way you'll know that language."

"I'll find someone who does. And they'll figure out a way to reverse it. Let's go to your parents' house." He stood up.

He really could be bossy sometimes. "How am I supposed to explain you to my parents? I'll get it and bring it to you."

Jonathan shook his head. "I can't let you out of my sight."

She stiffened. "Excuse me?"

"I talked to my…coworker this morning." The guy who'd called yesterday, Cassie guessed. "I have orders."

"Well, fuck your orders," she snapped. Morty gave a broad smile at this.

She half expected Jonathan to yell at her. Instead, he said in a low voice, "Look, I'm sure I'm the last person you want to be joined at the hip to." Unexpectedly, an erotic image flashed through her brain. "But there's no telling when you're going to get mad at someone. If I'm close to you and that happens, I can save whoever the animal goes after." He moved closer to her, looking into her eyes. "Think of what that jaguar did to Rick. What that bear tried to do to me. You really want to go to your parents' house alone?"

She sagged back against the kitchen counter.

"He's right," Morty told her. "Sorry to say."

"I get annoyed at people every day," she said. "I think I have to be seriously pissed for it to take effect."

"Good to hear," Jonathan said.

"But aren't you afraid I'll get angry at you again?"

His shoulders lifted in the slightest of shrugs as he fastened the rest of the buttons of his shirt. "If you could try not to get mad, that would be great."

When she turned onto the freeway on the way to her mom's, the sun streamed into her eyes. "Ugh. Wish I had my sunglasses."

"Take mine." He picked his backpack up off the floor of her truck and unzipped the front pocket. Something tumbled out into the coffee cup holder. She reached in to pick it up at the same time he did, and the backs of their hands touched. The contact, slight and accidental, electrified her senses.

Cassie hated the way her heart stepped up its pace. She could not be getting a crush on this stranger. Yes, she was forming the strong impression that he was a good man doing a hard job, but really, she knew nothing about him. Even in her impressive history of sketchy-as-hell decisions, this would achieve a new height of idiocy, like a misspelled forehead tattoo. Or would it? Having no experience with mysterious monster slayers, she didn't really know.

He wasn't handsome, she told herself. Definitely, there was nothing *pretty* about him—a face composed of hard angles and a muscled neck nearly as wide as his head. The bend in his nose added to an impression of raw strength and a certain lack of self-preservation. There was no reason for adrenaline to go skittering through her at the touch of his hand or the intensity of his storm-blue eyes.

He returned the object, a small, maroon stone sphere, to the backpack and gave her a pair of men's aviator shades.

She put them on, noticed him staring at her, and grinned. "I bet I look ridiculous."

"You look great," he muttered in a grim tone that perplexed her. Probably the gashes in his back were hurting him, although he refused to say so.

When they got to the house, her parent's truck was in the driveway. Cassie and Jonathan walked in the front door, and she called out, "Hello?"

"Cassie?" Her mom emerged from her office, wearing a top with a sunflower print, baggy capri pants, and flip-flops. She and Cassie had the same dark, straight hair, though she kept hers short. "Hi honey, I didn't know you were coming! Who's your friend?"

"David Ramirez," Jonathan said. "Nice to meet you, ma'am." He inclined his head as he stepped forward and held out a hand.

She raised her eyebrows, either at the formality or at the name. He didn't look like a David Ramirez, but then again, one couldn't always tell. As they shook hands, she asked, "How do you know Cassie?"

"From ASU." He didn't miss a beat. Of course, he knew where Cassie had gone to college. He knew everything about her. "I moved back into town a couple of months ago."

Her mother's eyes lit up. From the day Cassie's divorce had become final, her mom had wanted Cassie to date again, find someone better than Rick, let the whole world know it…and maybe produce a grandkid or two. Cassie's sister, Samantha, showed no interest in actual relationships, let alone marriage, so she was no help.

"Isn't that nice," her mom said. "Cassie, you should have told me you two were coming over. Your dad will be back soon. Are you staying for lunch?"

"We can't," she interjected.

Her mother gave her a puzzled frown. "What did you come all the way out here for?"

"I'm getting my PhD in archeology," Jonathan said. Cassie

stopped herself from looking at him as though he'd lost his mind. "Cassie said her great-grandpa had a journal that might help with my dissertation."

"Oh." She looked doubtful. "If there's anything interesting in there, you're welcome to it. Do you speak Spanish?"

He smiled, and Cassie felt a flutter in her stomach. Had she even seen him smile before? "That's how I talk to my family."

Cassie's mom said, "Well, good luck, though that basement is a horror. A *horror!*"

Cassie shut the door to the basement behind them and led him down the stairs. "You're a good liar."

"Thank you."

"It wasn't a compliment."

"Didn't think it was. Where's the journal?"

She found it, but hesitated before handing it over to him. It was her family's private property, even if they had ignored it.

He flipped through it carefully. "Where's the spell you said aloud?"

"Here." She leaned closer to flip the pages to the back. Then she realized she was too close and stepped away. "I wish we could read the rest of it. Maybe it says what that part is."

"I can read the Spanish."

"Are you really fluent?"

"Yeah."

Cassie felt a stab of jealousy. She looked Hispanic enough that sometimes a lady on the bus or a guy in a store would try to talk to her in Spanish. She would shake her head because they spoke too quickly for her to pick up even the words she did know. It always embarrassed her, feeling like a white girl in Mexican skin, though not enough to prod her to learn. She'd done all right in two years of high school Spanish, but the classes hadn't been particularly challenging. Even if she tried to learn to really speak it, she wasn't sure she'd be able to. "Do you speak any other languages?"

"Egyptian Arabic."

Cassie hadn't even known Egyptians had their own brand of Arabic. And why that language, of all of them? He found bubble wrap in a box of Christmas decorations, wrapped the journal in it, and put it in his backpack. On impulse, Cassie tossed the toy tank and the grainy photo of the woman in the jungle into her purse.

When they came upstairs, Cassie said, "We found it."

Her mom looked up from her knitting. Once, when Cassie had been young, her mother had tried to teach her how, but the lesson had only lasted about five minutes. She hadn't been a patient child. "Oh, good. Just bring it back when you're done."

"Of course," Jonathan said. "Your grandfather sounds like an interesting person, Mrs. Rios. Can I ask you a few questions about him?"

Cassie suspected his polite, earnest manner came naturally when he addressed people who were much older than him. He'd spoken to Morty with the same kind of respect, even if he'd gotten defensive about his secret monster-hunting club.

Her mother set her knitting needles aside. "Call me Patty. I don't know a lot about him, but he was very interested in languages. And very political."

"Did you ever hear any strange stories about him? Anything unusual?"

"Oh, I don't know. He was smart, I know that. Taught at the university in Mexico City, and then at one further south. I bet you would have enjoyed knowing him, given your field."

"I'm sure," Jonathan said.

"But people thought he was a bit off. My grandma died when she was still a young woman—I want to say malaria? Anyway, after she died, he turned into kind of a hermit. My dad came to America and tried to stay in touch with him, but my grandpa got bad about writing back. He couldn't get him on the phone at all."

Jonathan nodded. "Would there be any way I might be able to talk to your father?" Inwardly, Cassie cringed.

Her mother said, "He passed away a few years ago." It had been very tough on the whole family. Cassie's grandpa had been a great guy.

"I'm so sorry for your loss."

"Thank you," her mom said. "Do you want to see a picture of him? He looked a lot like Grandpa De La Garza." She retrieved the big group photo from Uncle Mike and Aunt Linda's fiftieth anniversary a couple of years back. Rick had been in this photo, but after the divorce, Cassie's mom had put her father in there instead. Except she didn't know how to use Photoshop, so she'd made a color copy of a picture of him, cut out his face, and pasted it in there over Rick's.

"Here he is. He'd already passed when we took this photo, but I, uh, thought he belonged in there." Jonathan took the photo from her as she pointed out, "See, he and my grandfather had the same dark hair and the same nose. Cassie has that nose, too."

Cassie fought the urge to cover her large nose with her hands. "Jesus, Mom."

"I'm embarrassing her," her mother said to Jonathan. "I don't know why she gets embarrassed. She's such a pretty girl. She's got those huge, gorgeous brown eyes… Of course, I'm biased."

"No, you're right. She's beautiful." Cassie knew he was only playing a part, but heat flooded into her face. He handed the picture back. "You said your Grandpa De La Garza was interested in languages. Do you know which ones he spoke?"

Her mom exercised a lot more patience with his questions than she ever did with her daughter's. "Just Spanish and English, But he studied old, what do you call them, hieroglyphs and things. I don't know much more."

"That's really helpful," he said. "I can't tell you how much I appreciate it."

"Oh, it's no problem. So did you meet Layla yet?"

He looked baffled. "No."

"You should go say hello to her." Mom picked up her knitting needles again. "She's such a good horse. Do you ride at all, David?"

"No, never." Well, there was one thing he didn't know how to do, if he were telling the truth.

"That's a shame. I'm sure Cassie will try to forgive you. She's been riding since she was about four."

Cassie doubted Jonathan was really interested in this, but he did a good job of faking it. "She wasn't scared?"

"Cassie?" Her mom laughed. "She's never been scared of anything. Neither of my girls were. When Cassie was about—how old were you, nine? We were boarding this beautiful, big thoroughbred, and she tried riding it. Well, you know, this was a high-strung horse, and he threw her off. She broke her arm in two places. Lucky she didn't break her neck. But common sense has never been her strong suit."

"Thanks, Mom," Cassie said, her voice dry. She stood up, and Jonathan did the same.

Her mother said, "Oh Cassie, I almost forgot, there was something I was going to show you on the computer."

"What?"

"Come on, it'll only take a second." She added to Jonathan, "Excuse us for a minute." She shut the office door behind them.

Cassie asked, "Something about Christmas?" It was October, which meant she'd already be shopping for gifts. She liked to show Cassie what she was buying for everyone else.

"No. I wanted to tell you I think you should hang on to this one."

"What?"

Her mom nodded in the direction of the living room.

Cassie rolled her eyes. "He's just a friend."

"He'd like to be more, then. Have you seen the way he looks at you?"

Like she might kill someone with a bighorn sheep? "He doesn't look at me in a way."

Her mom sighed. "Cassie, open your eyes."

This wasn't like her. "You only just met him."

"He's a good guy. I can tell." Cassie could imagine her mom's reaction if she found out how Jonathan had really met her. When they returned to the living room, her mom insisted again that he should meet Layla. He agreed, which surprised her. He was in a hurry to figure things out, and being around her and a big animal at the same time wasn't exactly the safest thing.

Layla's ears pricked up and she nickered as they came up to her stall. As Cassie scratched her neck, she talked to her in a high-pitched voice, as if she were talking to a baby. She didn't care if he thought it was stupid. "Hi, sweetheart. Did you have a good week? Was everybody nice to you?" The horse nuzzled at her jacket.

"She really loves you," Jonathan said.

"And she figures I have a treat. You can pet her if you want."

He took a step closer. "Is she—what you call those blond horses?"

Cassie laughed. "Palominos. Layla's a mix, palomino and quarter horse and something else. She's not fancy."

He raised a hand, hesitating before patting her on the neck. Had he ever touched a horse before in his life? "She looks fancy."

Cassie couldn't help the warmth that blossomed inside her at that. A surefire way to become her friend was to say something nice about her horse. "Do you want to give her an apple? She's really good, she won't bite your fingers." She handed him the one she'd grabbed from the kitchen counter.

Jonathan held it under Layla's nose, and she turned her head away. "She's not hungry."

She'd forgotten to tell him. "You have to take the stem off first. Otherwise she won't eat it."

He looked from the apple to Layla. "You're kidding."

"I know. She's a dork."

He twisted the stem off the apple and offered it again. She bit off the top half of it, chomped it down, and took the rest.

Cassie stroked her mane. "See, she's really gentle. They put new riders on her. You should try riding sometime."

"I doubt that's going to happen."

After they pulled out of her parents' driveway, Cassie asked, "You didn't really go to ASU, did you?"

He shook his head. "West Point. Then Army Ranger school."

Wow. She'd guessed he might have a military background, and she congratulated herself on being right, but West Point and Ranger School were pretty hard core. "Did you like them?"

"West Point—not usually, but sometimes. Nobody likes Ranger School."

The sunlight made her squint, and she remembered to put on his sunglasses again. "At least you learned how to fight."

"Not there so much. I did MMA training since I was a kid."

"The cage fighting?" He nodded. She'd seen it a couple of times on TV, and it looked brutal. Why had his parents allowed him to do it? Maybe it had been their idea. For all she knew, they hunted witches, too.

"If I did a spell, does that make me a witch?"

"Sort of."

Cassie swallowed. "But you don't think witches are human."

"I misspoke," he said quickly. "A lot of people use magic, and most of them are good. But very rarely, one of them uses their powers to hurt or kill. That's when they give up the privileges of humanity."

The privileges of humanity. This sounded like an official doctrine. "Who are you people?"

She didn't really expect him to respond, but it still rankled her that he didn't. Who would he give her great-grandpa's journal to? She didn't even know. Maybe she should find a way to take it back.

As she pulled into her driveway, dread clouded her thoughts.

Once inside, he inspected the smashed sliding door to her kitchen. Glass crunched under his feet. He found her broom and began cleaning it up.

If he thought he could avoid her questions that way, he was wrong. "You say you're going to help me, but if you're going to take the journal, I need to know more about who you are." He held the dustpan with his foot, and the glass shards clinked into it. After a few moments, she continued. "It's not fair. You know all about me. The least you could do is be more scrutable."

He looked up. "Scrutable?"

"Yeah, as in the opposite of inscrutable?"

"I don't think scrutable's actually a word."

"I don't think I actually care!" Cassie threw her hands in the air in frustration. "What's the name of this group you're in? How many of you are there?"

"The only thing I can tell you is that you don't want to be on their bad side."

"Well, apparently, it's not a great idea to be on *my* bad side, either," she pointed out. "Tell me *something*. Tell me about your last mission." He'd used that word, *mission,* before.

His jaw flexed. "Why?"

"So I can know more about you. So I can trust you!"

He let go of the broom suddenly and it clattered to the floor, making Cassie jump. "You want to hear about my last mission? Fine. It was in New Mexico with my brother, Michael."

Shit. She hadn't thought about that. "When?"

"Three weeks ago."

"Three *weeks?*" She searched for something else to say.

He sat down on the kitchen chair, the one he'd tied her to the night before to interrogate her. It seemed as though he wanted to tell the story just to make her sorry she'd asked. "We were in New Mexico to banish a demon."

A chill snaked through her. She could no longer doubt these

kinds of things existed, and she couldn't imagine what it must be like to go up against them. She sat down in the chair next to him. "How did you know there was a demon?"

"Do you remember a news story about a man in Taos who killed his wife? He cut off her finger and—"

"Oh God. Yes." She shuddered.

The man had eaten his wife's finger and posted a picture of the bones online. The gruesome news story had especially disturbed her because the guy had no history of violence. He was a nice husband and father who'd managed a restaurant.

"He'd just gotten back from a scout camp at Urraca Mesa, which is an old gateway to a demon realm."

"Holy smokes. How do you know this?"

"There are stories going back for centuries. There used to be Pueblo people in that area—some people call them Anasazi. But they all disappeared and left behind evidence of torture and cannibalism." She nodded. She'd heard about them. "We believe the demon possessed the ancient people there, making them do terrible things, and that's why they fled. They say a Navajo shaman set a powerful spell to keep the demon on the other side, centuries ago. But banishments never last forever. Whether it was physical change to the portal or someone tampering with magic, something finally broke the binding."

"So the guy who killed his wife was possessed, too," she said. The police had shot the man dead after a short standoff. "How were you and your brother supposed to fight this thing?"

"First, we went to the place it crossed over."

"Wait," she said. "If it's a Boy Scout camp, didn't you kind of stand out?"

He gave a mirthless chuckle and told her the rest of the story.

CHAPTER SIX

IT HADN'T BEEN peak Boy Scout season at the camp. Jonathan and Michael had gone to the top of Urraca Mesa, where no one was officially allowed.

The place had more lightning strikes than anywhere else in the state. Compasses didn't work there because the ground was full of lodestone. The entire area was shaped like a skull. Two different legends claimed the eye in the skull, a depression in the earth, was a gateway to the demonic plane.

Cassie interrupted Jonathan to ask, "Why does a demon want to hurt people? Just for fun?"

"That's how they survive and grow. Demons start out as ghosts of evil men and women, and they become more powerful by turning others evil and absorbing their life essence. It's like how a dust storm gets bigger when it rolls over the desert."

"I thought demons would be totally different from humans."

"Some of them are centuries, even millennia old. This one, for instance. There's nothing human left in them anymore."

He explained that local stories called the Urraca Mesa demon "Dakos." The name was a bastardization of the Navajo word for a bunch of clouds. For as long as anyone could remember, people had seen clusters of glowing blue clouds on the top of the mesa.

When Jonathan and Michael had arrived at the site, everything had been quiet. It had been September, and the cottonwoods had been turning gold down by the creek.

Once they faced Dakos, they'd say an incantation over a fire of palo santo wood. That would send it back into the abyss. Their boss could have sent another Mage with Jonathan, but a demon in a human body commanded brutal strength, and Mages weren't trained in combat. Jonathan's powers allowed him to maintain a psychic barrier around himself and another person. He'd done it several times before, most recently with Michael a few months ago on a mission in Oklahoma where a malevolent spirit had been persuading drivers on a particular stretch of highway to crash into one another.

On Urraca Mesa, dusk was a few hours away, and demon and ghost spell work rarely succeeded in daylight hours, so they waited. Michael complained about missing the qualifying football match between Mexico and the United States. Several of their friends were watching it on the big screen in the cantina at their headquarters. Michael found a deck of cards in the glove compartment, and almost as a joke, they played gin rummy, which their grandfather had taught them. They hadn't played it since they were boys, but they wound up really getting into it.

As dusk gathered, they found a big, flat rock near the portal, which looked like a small cave. Jonathan painted the summoning circle with the proper sigils. He used rust-colored oak gall ink, to which they'd added a little powdered bone from the demon's victim in Taos, because a body that had housed a demon became connected to it. The complicated symbols took longer to render than he'd expected, and by the time he painted the last one, the night had deepened enough that Michael held the flashlight so he could finish.

Michael crossed the sticks of palo santo wood in the middle. He sprinkled them and each symbol around the circle with oil of frankincense from the lost city of Ubar. He straightened up again and gave Jonathan a grim, amused look like, *Well, here we go.* They'd been going on most of their missions together for almost two years by then, so Jonathan knew the look well.

Jonathan closed his eyes and pulled up the energy and power from within his mind. He was aware of Michael's psyche, like something shimmering in his peripheral vision. Although he didn't venture into his brother's consciousness, the link brightened and strengthened. When Jonathan opened his eyes, Michael was cutting his forearm with his black tactical knife. He sprinkled blood over the frankincense on each of the symbols in turn. Jonathan held the psychic barrier over them both. Until they banished Dakos, he needed to keep his concentration steady so the shield didn't slip.

Michael wrapped up his arm. As he recited the incantation, he flicked his lighter and set fire to each symbol. They burned because of the oil mixed with the blood, but only for a few seconds. When he said the last words and lit up the last symbol, however, the flames shot up higher than his head before they burned out.

A sharp sideways wind cut through Jonathan's clothes to the skin. The dark trees above them hissed in the sudden gale. Horror dragged through his body like a heavy chain. It knocked against his bones, twisted around his brain, and then pulled tight, trying to strangle his thoughts. Jonathan forced himself to keep the psychic barrier smooth.

Dakos arrived, not in a human's skin, but as a shadow in the shape of a man's body—faceless, ten feet tall. Glowing blue clouds gathered where one might expect a head to be. Lightning slashed to the ground from one of the clouds, and everything went bitterly cold.

Humans. You are disgusting.

Jonathan wasn't sure whether he heard the demon's words, or

whether they resounded directly in his mind. Either way, the voice threatened to deafen him. He covered his ears.

Walking bags full of blood and shit and piss. At best, you are meat.

No demon he'd ever faced before had emanated this much power. The iron chain of terror pulled tighter, about to crack his skull. Michael must have felt the same thing. They stood welded to the spot.

You scarcely live longer than insects. Your only hope of greatness is being subsumed into myself.

Jonathan struggled to keep his defenses in place. He drew on more power to strengthen the shell around them. Michael shook himself and lit the palo santo wood in the center of the circle. The demon's hand reached for his head.

Lightning struck Jonathan, crackling through his head and down his spine, and the pain—

But no. Nothing had struck him. Michael had stopped speaking. Jonathan had let the barrier slip, for a moment, but surely not long enough for a demon to slither into his brother's skin. He wouldn't be able to hold it much longer, though. He screamed at Michael, "Finish it!"

His brother turned around and smiled. Jonathan could barely see his face in the light of the burning wood, but it wasn't a smile he'd ever seen before. Michael spoke, and he wasn't Michael. "I will never go back."

Jonathan felt like his insides had been ripped out. *My little brother.* The one person he'd always been told to protect. The one he loved more than anyone else alive. This was the moment he had to kill him, because he'd failed him.

That was the protocol. Kill a possessed person immediately. Attempts at exorcism almost never worked, and the possessed human became a powerless witness to the demon's depravity. *A bullet is a mercy.*

No. He would finish the spell. Save his brother. To protect himself, he drew his knife—not the gun, not while Michael housed the demon—and opened his mouth to speak the next words.

Michael exploded. The bright shimmering cloud dissipated and fell like dust and disappeared into nothingness.

Jonathan had shouted his brother's name. There had been nothing to shout at. Invisible now, the demon had pried at Jonathan's psyche like a locked trapdoor in the top of his skull. Jonathan had slammed up an extra barrier and roared the final words of the spell that Michael had begun. A burst of energy and a huge flash of blue light had blinded him and knocked him to the ground. His head had smashed against the big stone with the circle. All had gone dark.

"When I woke up, there was nothing," Jonathan told Cassie. His eyes were burning, his throat tight. "Just darkness, silence. Dakos gone. Michael gone."

After a long moment, she told him in a low voice, "It wasn't your fault."

He'd heard that before, and it didn't mean a thing. "When one of your own falls, it's your job to recover the body, even if you risk your own life. I—I scrambled around on the ground, trying to find anything that had been him. Everything looked the same. Just dirt." He tightened his hand on his knee into a fist.

She took his hand like she'd done once before, and he wrapped his fingers around hers. "If you guys go on these dangerous trips and fight evil demons, terrible things must happen. This couldn't have been the first time."

"No," he admitted.

"And if someone gets hurt or killed, do you blame the people who were with him?"

"They weren't me."

She frowned down at their joined hands. "Why did you tell me this story? It can't be easy to go over it again."

"To shut you up, I guess." His voice was wry, making fun of

himself more than her. "I don't know." She didn't say anything. The story had succeeded in making her a lot quieter than usual. "I didn't see Dakos get pulled into the void, since I got knocked out." This fact still troubled him.

"How many demons have you killed? Or...sent back, I guess?"

"Seventeen. Eighteen, counting this one. It must have worked. There haven't been any signs of possessions since."

"Thank God for that, at least," she murmured.

When Nic had heard what happened, he'd directed Jonathan to a nearby motel, saying he shouldn't be behind the wheel. He'd met Jonathan there a few hours later and had driven him home in silence. Jonathan had been numb, staring out the window. They'd been maybe a half hour from home when Jonathan had broken down. Nic, who wasn't one to share his own feelings, had kept driving. Then after a minute, he'd pulled over to the side of the road, stopped the car, and hugged Jonathan close to him, and Jonathan realized that Nic was crying, too.

Jonathan shifted where he sat. The memories were fresher and more painful than the wounds on his back. "I have these dreams where...in the last one, Michael and I were at this place we went to sometimes, outside of Albuquerque. He always said their pork back was good for a hangover." He smiled briefly. "And I'm eating my eggs, and I think there's too much pepper on them, but then I realize it's...that sparkly dust. That he was turned into." He hadn't told anyone about this, not even Val, to whom he told almost everything because she'd been his friend since childhood. She had regular and official access to his psyche, anyway. "My whole plate is full of it, and my mouth. And then there's nobody else in the whole restaurant. Just the sound of the wind, like up at the mesa. That howling wind."

"It's horrible. I'm sorry." The sympathy in her voice soothed the raw places inside him. She squeezed his hand. "You were a good brother."

The words meant more to him than she could know.

After a few moments, she asked, "It sounds like it bothers you that you couldn't bury him."

"Yeah. He doesn't have a memorial. Though I made a stack of stones above the portal." The cairn might have been knocked down already.

She said, "When my grandpa died, we did cremation."

"We do that, too, a lot of times. But even then, the night before the cremation, the body is laid out in a room full of candles. The people who were closest to the person—husband or wife, family, whoever—they each get at least a few hours alone with the body. The body's not left alone all night."

She pursed her lips, considering this. Maybe to her, accustomed to typical American funeral services, it sounded creepy. "Do you stay with them so you can pray for them?"

"If that's your tradition. Yeah, that's what I would have done. A lot of people believe—*I* believe—the spirit is still hovering close by during the vigil. But I didn't get to have the vigil for him."

They were still holding hands, and she stroked his with her thumb, a gentle touch that both comforted and alarmed him. "If what you believe is true, his spirit would have been there with you anyway, before the funeral."

"I don't know." Because there had been no body and no vigil, he'd gone to *el huerto*, the level where they grew fruit, rice, and vegetables, out of some primal instinct to be surrounded by life. In the long hours he'd prayed, he hadn't sensed Michael's presence. He'd never felt so alone. "I didn't mean to talk so much." He felt almost as depleted as he had after fighting the bear.

Her eyes glistened, reflecting his sorrow and lessening it. "Thank you for telling me."

"Uh." Jonathan was trained to deal with all kinds of unexpected circumstances, but she could throw him off with a few words or a gesture. "Why would you thank me?"

"Because it's personal, and you trusted me with it." He'd burdened her with his pain, and she talked about it like a gift. "And I was your first mission after that... You must have been ready to kick some evil ass. I'm lucky you didn't just shoot me in the head."

He tensed. "We never kill humans without being absolutely sure they're guilty. They sent me because I can Read people. So there would be no question."

"Thank God for that." Her thumb traced his hand again. He should tell her to stop doing that, though he struggled to remember why. "Was Michael a lot like you?"

He considered the question. "In a lot of ways. But he's...he was funnier than me. And he, uh, flirted with people a lot."

She smiled. "So he was pretty popular with the girls?"

"Yeah. Some guys, too. And he was a smartass. Always questioning everything, even as a kid."

"He must have been a handful for your parents."

"He was really their favorite." She stopped smiling at that. "It's, uh... My mom isn't with us any more."

She cringed. "I'm sorry."

"It's all right." It wasn't, at all, but he didn't want to discuss it. "Was your brother psychic like you?"

"No. He was just a warrior— I shouldn't say *just*. He was great." Michael had been the best fighter Jonathan had ever seen, except for Samir and Freya, who both had telekinesis. They'd started training even younger than Jonathan and Michael had, because as far as Manus Sancti was concerned, children who could move objects with their minds were destined to be warriors. Michael's secret weapons weren't psychic gifts, but speed and fearlessness. Guilt cast long shadows over his mind again. His brother wasn't only a loss to him, his father, and to everyone who loved him. He was also a loss for the cause, for humanity...

Cassie dipped her head to meet his eyes. "I think you're pretty great yourself."

A force like gravity pulled them toward one another, difficult to resist, impossible to ignore. He stared at her mouth. God, he wanted to kiss her, just once. She leaned closer, laying her hand against his cheek. *Yes.* At the simple touch, his instincts roared to life, every part of him straining for more.

No. This isn't right. He'd indulged himself and drawn out her sympathy, and he was a heartbeat away from taking advantage of an unfair situation. Gently, though it almost physically pained him to do it, he removed her hand and detached himself from her, standing up. "We shouldn't."

"Why?— Oh, God." She scrunched her face up and pressed it into her hands. He turned his back to her, waiting for his body to get itself back under control. She said, "Sorry, I was married a long time. I don't know how things work anymore." She forced a laugh. "Maybe I didn't ever know. Anyway. It's been a weird couple of days."

She thought he was *rejecting* her. "Cassie, it's not—"

"Let's forget it. No big deal." Her voice rang with false cheer.

"No, listen." He turned around to face her. "You are—so beautiful. And you're brave, and I… But it wouldn't be right."

"You have a girlfriend." Horror passed over her face. "A wife."

"Neither. Cassie." His kept his voice deliberate. "You have Stockholm Syndrome."

"I do not! I forgot what that means."

He felt the corner of his mouth tugging up at that, but then he sobered. "When someone gets captured, or abused, sometimes they get emotionally attached to the person who did it to them. It's a classic coping mechanism. They want to give the person in power whatever he wants." She frowned, processing this. "I guessed before. At Morty's."

Her cheeks darkened in a blush. "I felt bad about your brother."

"It's not normal to feel bad for someone who threatened to kill you." Self-reproach barbed his voice. "Nobody's that nice."

He didn't like standing at a distance, and he didn't want to sit too close to her, either, not while he was barely managing restraint. He came over and dragged the chair a short distance from her before sitting down again. "I terrified you, hurt you, forced myself into your psyche. And I am so sorry."

"You already apologized. I get why you did it. These people getting hurt, Rick getting his throat ripped out...you had pretty good reasons." She gestured toward his back. "And you paid for it." He didn't see it that way and didn't want to argue. She hugged her arms. "Okay, let's stop talking about this. When people are telling me why they don't want to kiss me, I like to keep the conversation short."

Frustration rose up in him. "It's not about what I want!" She jumped. He was scaring her again. In a quieter tone, he explained, "Whatever you're feeling right now is a response from trauma. Trauma I caused."

"Right." Her eyes flashed with annoyance. "It has nothing to do with you turning out to be this good, caring person. Who doesn't mind when I say what I think. And oh yeah, who can speak a bunch of languages and beat up bears." He smiled before he could stop himself. She said, "I know how I feel."

Maybe she did. Maybe she genuinely liked him. His resolve was slipping, but he made a last-ditch effort to resist her. "You'll feel differently later."

His phone buzzed.

CHAPTER SEVEN

CASSIE MENTALLY CURSED whoever was calling for their shitty timing.

Jonathan gave her a pained look. "I have to take this." He answered it, saying, "*Salaam,* Nic." After listening for a moment, he said, "Yeah, I know." He got up and strode into the living room.

Should she give him more privacy? No. They were talking about her, and she didn't know nearly enough about them. He stood with his back to the kitchen, and she slipped out of her chair and stole over to the doorway to listen.

"She's an innocent *sonámbula,* and I attacked her— No. *Actus non facit reum nisi mens sit rea.*" God only knew what any of this meant, but he sounded defensive.

"No. I can persuade her…" He paused to listen. "That'll just set her off. I've got this—" Nic cut him off again, and he let out a harsh sigh. Cassie didn't catch his next sentence, but he sounded more subdued. After a few more moments, he said, "Okay. She can meet us at her house." She bristled. More silence. "*Obedezco.*" As he hung up, he turned around to face her.

"Who can meet us?" she burst out. "What's going on?"

He shoved the phone back into his pocket and took a deep breath. "I told the people I work for about the spell, and they think you're a clear and present danger to everyone around you. Which is true," he added. "I sent them pictures of the journal pages, and they think the journal may be all they need to figure out your problem."

Cassie's temper rose. "You didn't tell me you were going to do that."

"Listen, now that we've found the journal, they want me to take you to headquarters so that until we find a solution, the threat can be contained."

Headquarters? She thought of Washington D.C., and then Quantico. "That's crazy. Who are you people?"

He didn't answer. She hadn't really thought that he would. "Contained how? Don't they know I'd be pissed off at all of them? They bring me in, they'll have to deal with a herd of bears." Maybe one didn't call that a herd. "A horde of bears."

"The location minimizes the danger of attacks."

"What location, outer space?" Guantanamo Bay, maybe, or someplace like it. Fear wrung her heart.

"And if they need to, they have much more powerful psychics than me who can neutralize your consciousness while we work on a solution."

"Neutralize my— What does that mean?"

His forehead wrinkled. "Put you in a suspended state, not exactly a coma—"

"Jesus!" She turned her back on him and stalked back into the kitchen.

"Not for long! It could be a few days or a week."

Or the rest of her natural life, for all she knew. Maybe she should bolt through the jagged hole that had once been her sliding door and make a run for her truck. But no, she wouldn't get very far. This was unreal. One minute, she'd been trying to kiss him, and the next, he wanted to haul her off to God knows where and put her in a vegetative state. Maybe an outright execution would've been better.

He followed her, talking to her back. "They're not seeing a lot of options. They can't let other people get hurt, or even killed." His hand came to rest on her shoulder. "If there's a way you could calm down—"

She spun around. "Don't you fucking tell me to calm down!"

He gave a tight, ironic smile. "Guess that wasn't the way." Deliberately, he took a seat at the kitchen table.

She could almost taste her own bitterness. "I'm not going anywhere with you."

"Cassie, you're not understanding me." His gaze locked on hers. "I can take you whether you want to go or not."

Cold fury rooted her to the earth. "You're threatening me?"

"I'm begging you." The vulnerability on his upturned face began to thaw her anger. "I do *not* want to drag you in."

"Then don't."

"I have orders," he said. "I have *vows*."

"Vows? Is this some kind of cult?"

"I've failed them before." Did he mean his brother? Despite her anger, this tugged at her sympathy. "I'm doing the best I can here." Cassie picked at one of the scrapes on her wrist. A little bit of the scab came off, leaving a red line but no blood. "I've told them you're not to blame," he said. "I'll do everything I can for you."

She sat down. "What was that you were saying on the phone?"

He shook his head, uncomprehending. "Something like, *Act us non?*"

"*Actus non facit reum nisi mens sit rea.* It's a saying. It means, what you've done doesn't make you guilty if you didn't know you were doing it."

"That's a pretty good saying," she muttered.

He set his hands on his knees, palms up. "Please come with me voluntarily. You don't want this curse on your head. Your ex-husband is dead, and even though you didn't like him, I know it's weighing on you." He was right. Sometimes she thought of Rick's family, or how he must have screamed before the jaguar tore out his throat, and she could hardly stand it.

"I don't even know where we're going."

"It's about nine hours away." He looked wary. "They're sending someone else out to drive with us. She'll be here early in the morning."

Cassie wrapped her arms around herself. "How can I even trust you?" An answer came to her. "Can I go into your psyche, like you went into mine? So you can't lie to me?" Her curiosity spiked. What would his look like?

"It doesn't work that way. You need a certain kind of psychic talent to go into someone else— Ow." He jerked his hand up in the air.

A snake was clamped to it, its fangs sunk into the flesh between his thumb and wrist. It was skinny but at least three feet long, and banded in red, black, and yellow. Cassie screamed as Jonathan jumped to his feet, shaking the thing off. It fell to the floor and wriggled away behind the refrigerator.

She said, "I'll get the broom!" She could bludgeon it to death.

He stood, looking at his hand. "Let's go out to my car." He seemed unnaturally calm, almost robotic.

Jogging a little to keep up with his long strides, she followed him to a black SUV parked a little ways down the block. She grabbed his hand to inspect it and saw little more than a scratch. "It doesn't look that bad."

"It's venomous." He popped open the back of the car, retrieved a large steel case, and flipped it open. Blue velvet lined the interior, reminding her of her clarinet case in fifth grade. A couple dozen hypodermic needles, the sharp ends encapsulated in plastic, nestled in compartments.

"Whoa," she said. He pulled out a small booklet held in the elastic of the top part of the case. Then he grunted, gripping the bridge of his nose. "What is it?"

He gasped. "Head hurts. Trouble breathing."

"Oh my God." She pressed her hands to her face. "I'm sorry."

He pushed the book in her direction. "Look up the snake. Yellow and black—"

"Red and yellow and black." The cover of the manual was in Spanish. She flipped it open and saw it had pictures of scorpions and gila monsters and such. "Here!" She stopped on the picture. "Coral snake."

"Okay." He half sat, half fell onto the back of the open SUV. Sweat glazed his chalky face. *Oh, God.* He looked bad. She skimmed the description of the bite. *Neurotoxin*—that was an English word. *Respiración artificial.* Artificial respiration. *Muerto.* Death.

Fuck.

"Get the antivenin." His speech slurred so badly that she stared up at him. His mouth hung open. "Swollen tongue," he said. "Anti—"

"Right, okay." With shaking hands, she searched through the needles, each in its own wrapping. Someone had affixed labels to them with tiny handwritten words. *El escorpión.* No. The second needle said the same thing. *Araña reclusa parda.* That had to be a brown recluse spider. *La serpiente de cascabel.* Shit, was that it? Why the fuck couldn't they use English? *La serpiente coral.*

"Yes!" She got the syringe out of the plastic and grabbed his bitten hand.

He made a move as though to stop her, and his words came out thick between labored breaths. "Have you done this before?"

"No." She stabbed the needle into the top of his hand. It sank into the flesh between his thumb and finger, an inch from the bite mark. She hoped it was in far enough. Slowly, she injected the full dose of clear liquid into him. She pulled the needle straight out. Still, blood welled up. "Fuck, fuck," she muttered. She tossed the syringe aside and pulled up the hem of her shirt, pressing the fabric against his hand. "It's swelling." One of her thumbs came to rest on the inside of his wrist, and his pulse galloped beneath the skin.

He still fought for breath. "Wrap it up." He mimed winding a bandage around the hand. Gauze. He had gauze in his backpack. She scrabbled through the bag, found the roll, and began wrapping up his hand. "Tighter," he said, and she pulled the strip as hard as she could, winding it well past his wrist until she ran out of gauze and then tucking it in at the end. "Good. Hospital."

He and his friends didn't like hospitals, and he didn't like her being in such a populated place. If he wanted to go anyway—

Shit. He's dying. A tear splashed onto her cheek, startling her.

Even in his weakened state, he noticed it. His expression softened. Concern for her, maybe, or surprise at how much she feared for his life. If he doubted the genuineness of her feelings for him, he only deluded himself. Anyway, he shouldn't be thinking about her right now. He should spend every ounce of energy staying alive.

She helped him into the passenger seat. His legs wobbled beneath him. "Keys," she said.

"Front pocket." She thrust her hands into both of his jeans pockets at once, no time to be polite, and found them. After she yanked the driver's seat forward so she could reach the pedals, she buckled him into the seat and zoomed off.

As she drove, he said, "David Ramirez."

"What?"

"In my wallet."

It took her a moment to put this together. "You have a fake driver's license?"

He laid his head on the back of the seat. "And insurance."

From the cup holder, his phone vibrated. She ignored it. It wouldn't stop. At a red light, she picked it up.

When she pressed the button at the bottom, the screen remained blank. She tossed it back and concentrated on the road. His short breaths rasped in his chest, and his eyes glazed over. At the next red light, she looked both ways and then sped through.

A loud, disembodied male voice made her jump. "Jon, you there?" The same voice as before, after the bear attack.

"Call me later," Jonathan said, almost unintelligible.

The man snapped, "What?"

Shit. She'd gotten him hurt for a second time, and his group was going to kill her. "Hi," she said. "He got bit by a coral snake, but I gave him the, um, the shot."

"Cassandra Rios?"

Her heart sank. "Yeah. I'm so, so sorry. I'm taking him to the hospital."

"Jon, is all this true?"

"Yes," Jonathan said.

"*Christos.*" A few moments of silence. "Jon, call me back when you can."

Jonathan didn't look or sound any better by the time they got to the emergency room. *Fuck. I didn't do the injection right.* Cassie helped him stagger inside, and the woman behind the counter said, "Take a seat over there, and we'll call your name."

"No!" Several people looked up. "He needs a doctor right now! A coral snake bit him, and he's dying!"

Jonathan gripped her arm hard. "Don't. Get mad."

He was right. She took a deep breath and said calmly, "I think he's dying."

A man in scrubs came to take him back to a room. He said she could wait in the waiting room. She told him no and followed them.

The nurse guy had Jonathan stretch out on a bed with gray curtains on either side, separating him from other patients. "Sir, if you could lie on your back—"

"On his side," Cassie interjected. "He has stitches." The nurse looked startled. The ER doctor, a short woman with silver threads in her dark hair, strode in saying, "Okay, Mr. Ramirez, how are we doing?"

Cassie said, "He can hardly breathe!"

The doctor ordered the nurse to get him into a gown and hook him up to an oxygen tube. Cassie remembered the phrase from the manual: *respiración artificial.* Out of respect for his privacy, she retreated into the doorway and looked out at the hall.

"Who stitched up his back?" the doctor asked.

"I did," Cassie said. She glanced back and saw the side of his naked torso and hip as he put on the thin hospital gown. She didn't mean to gawk. As strong as he was, her spell had humbled and incapacitated him, and it wrenched her heart. "A bear attacked him."

"And then he was bitten by a coral snake?" Cassie nodded. "Are you sure that's what it was?"

"We're biologists. We, um, specialize in snakes." She didn't know where that came from, but she couldn't have the doctor messing up his treatment somehow because she didn't believe her.

She looked grim. "Then you know we no longer produce an approved antivenin for this."

Holy smokes. "I gave him one." What if it hadn't worked?

The doctor's head bobbed back in astonishment. "Where did you get that?"

Jonathan said, "Mexico." He stretched out on his side on the hospital bed.

"Hopefully, one dose will be enough." The doctor sounded doubtful. "Did he take anything for the pain?"

Cassie shook her head, watching the nurse put an oxygen tube in his nose. "Do you think he needs to?"

"A coral snake bite will make your head feel like it's going to explode." She narrowed her eyes. "But you should know that."

"I'm a little freaked out." That much was true.

The doctor ordered the nurse to hook up an IV with Demerol and inspected Jonathan's back. Cassie cringed at the ugly gashes and the puckering, purpled skin. He'd coped with the wounds so stoically that she'd almost forgotten how bad they really were. The doctor said, "I can't believe you didn't get medical attention for this."

"We were out in the middle of nowhere," she lied.

The doctor pointed out a place where the skin was hot and red, showing signs of infection, and swabbed at it with something that made Jonathan twitch. "I'm going to give you an antibiotic, and we'll re-stitch this area a little later, once you're stable," she told him. "Your heart rate's slowing down. That's good."

He didn't answer. Cassie's hand flew to her mouth. "Is he all right?"

"Unconscious for now. Just as well." She said they'd done all they could do for the time being, and she and the nurse left.

Cassie went out to where she'd illegally parked near the entrance and moved the car to a more suitable spot. Then she dug through the metal case full of syringes and found another dose of the coral snake antivenin. It was still wrapped in plastic, and she put it in her purse. As an afterthought, she grabbed his phone.

When she came back to the ER, she couldn't find him, and eventually someone pointed her to another wing of the building where he'd been transferred. He was still asleep, or unconscious. They hadn't stuck him in with a roommate, and she was glad of that. The hospital gown revealed most of his bare ass, which was a magnificent sight—something she shouldn't be noticing when he was hurt. Once she sat down in the chair next to him, she couldn't really see it.

Although she wished someone would check on him, no one came by. Maybe they were too busy. Strange to think about how people were sick and hurt and dying all the time, night and day, with their friends and family feeling all sad and scared, like she was feeling now.

Not that Jonathan West was exactly a friend. She didn't know what he was. But, apparently, he tried to save people a lot and often got hurt in the process. He'd suffered so much in the past couple of days, trying to make sure people didn't get attacked because of her.

On her phone, she looked up images of snakebites and then bear attack wounds. This was a terrible mistake. These things resulted in all kinds of horrible outcomes besides the obvious one, death. Jonathan could have lost his hand. Jesus, with the bear, he could have lost his *face*. She put the phone back in her purse. She'd never been good at waiting or sitting still. As a kid, her mom had joked sometimes that she would tie Cassie to a chair, although she never had, which was more than Cassie could say for Jonathan.

A reddish-brown spot near the hem of her shirt caught her attention. Jonathan's blood, from when she'd given him the shot. That wasn't going to wash out.

The nurse finally came in, writing things on his clipboard and commenting that he seemed to be doing okay. Cassie got up, wandered around, and found a coffee machine. She took the Styrofoam cup full of black coffee back to her chair by Jonathan's bed. It burned her tongue and tasted like asphalt. She drank it anyway.

He stirred. "Hey," she said softly.

His eyes opened and then his brows knitted in confusion. "Where am I?"

"St. Luke's. A snake bit you, remember?"

He focused on her, or tried to. "Cassandra Rios."

"Afraid so."

He nodded and said, as if to himself, "The beautiful and dangerous."

She felt a stupid grin take over her face. "You're high on Demerol."

He looked around himself and then up at the IV bag. "Oh, that's bad."

"Why?"

"Letting my guard down." His head lolled on the pillow.

"How's your hand?" She got up to inspect it. They had

re-wrapped it, a much neater job than she'd done. "It's not swollen anymore. I was scared I didn't give you the shot right."

"You were perfect. You just—jammed it right in there." He chuckled like this was hilarious. Even though she worried about him, it still amused her to see him a little loopy.

"That snake showed up so fast."

He nodded. "Lots of snakes and bugs we never see. In the bushes. The woodwork. They warned me." His brow furrowed. "Can you get my phone?"

"I've got it." She patted her front pocket.

He stiffened and propped himself up on one elbow. "I'm going to be sick." She snatched the wastebasket and set it next to his bed. After a few moments, he lay back. "False alarm."

"I'll get you some water. And crackers. I'll be back in a minute, okay?"

When she returned, the doctor was talking to him. "I called to my friend who's a specialist. He said you might have died without the antivenin. Did you get the dose right away?"

"About a minute after the bite," he said.

Only having the right injection on hand had saved him. If it had been anyone else, they'd be dead now. Her mom or dad, Sam. They would've been in terrible pain, unable to breathe, and then they would've died. She thought of all the different needles in that steel case. All those different poisonous things.

He might be the only one who could help her, and she kept hurting him. Her hand trembled as she put the crackers and water next to him. "Can he have these?"

"Sure," the doctor said. "Settle his stomach." She listened to his breathing, said he could go off the ventilator for now, and convinced him that he'd need to stay in the hospital at least for the night. After she left, he asked, "My phone?" He seemed less dopey now than when he'd first woken up.

Cassie handed it to him. "It might be out of juice or something."

He pressed the button, and the screen lit up with strange icons. "What the hell?"

"Only works for my finger." She got up to step out of the room, but he stopped her. "Stay." A few moments later, he said into the phone, "*Salaam,* Nic." Strange. He hadn't dialed a number. She was sure of it. The man said something on the other end. "I'm fine." Again, his definition of *fine* was much broader than hers. "Yeah, she's here. I'm at the hospital." He frowned at whatever the man said next. "Not necessary. I don't think it'll happen again." A long pause, and then and Jonathan replied, "All right— *Inshallah.*"

As soon as he set the phone down, Cassie blurted out, "How does he know when things happen to you?" She suspected telepathy.

He held up a hand, asking her to give him a moment, while he took a long drink of water. "I have a tattoo here." He hitched the hospital gown all the way up past his hip, revealing curls of male hair and a glimpse of his heavy cock past the pale blue cotton of the gown. Her face heated. It didn't seem like he even gave it a thought. The tattoo nestled inside his hipbone, the black ink tracing crisp lines against his pale skin. A star with many points, inside a double circle.

"What does that have to do with anything?"

"There are nanochips in the tattoo that communicate information back to headquarters."

"You are fucking kidding me."

"They're actually below it, deeper in the skin."

She studied him to see if he were joking. He wasn't. So far, he didn't seem like the joking type. "What kind of information?"

"Location, first of all."

"GPS? They know where you are at all times? Like, for your whole life?" He nodded, and her shoulders hunched up. "But that's so creepy. Why would you let them do that to you?"

"It also lets them track my heart rate, breathing, and other vitals."

That was possibly even more creepy. "But sometimes it's normal to have a fast heart rate or a change in breathing."

"Like every time I go to the gym." Jonathan pulled the gown back down. "The signs need to be really abnormal before they get concerned." He picked up the pouch of goldfish crackers she'd brought him from the machine in the waiting room and ripped it open. "If I'd gotten killed and my vitals had gone away, Nic would've sent a couple more people." He popped a handful of goldfish into his mouth and swallowed.

"That would have been bad."

"Very." His blue-gray eyes looked tired and sad. "Will you please come with us to headquarters? Without fighting us, I mean."

Cassie hated the thought of anyone messing around with her mind again, and the idea that someone might put her in some kind of coma still terrified her. But the possibility of one of these attacks happening again frightened her even more.

"I know it's been a horrible couple of days for you," he said.

"It hasn't exactly been your best week, either."

This elicited a brief smile from him. "Everything's going to be all right."

"You can't promise that."

He said quietly, "I'll do everything in my power to help you and keep you safe. I swear."

He'd mentioned orders—no, vows—made to people he allowed to track his every move and send him into deadly situations. But as little as she knew about him, she knew he'd try to look out for her. "Okay," she said. "I'll go with you."

CHAPTER EIGHT

JONATHAN WOKE UP with his tongue filling his mouth and his hand on fire.

As he struggled to sit up, Cassie rushed over to his side. She was still here. "Your tongue's swelling up again."

He nodded and held up his puffed-up hand. "The other shot?" Nic had packed two doses of each of them.

"I put it in my purse. I'll get the nurse to give it to you."

"He won't. Won't be sure what's in it."

She looked over her shoulder at the closed door and then took out the syringe. "I still don't know what I'm doing."

"Just do it." He preferred not to try himself with his left hand while his skull felt like it was about to break into bits. She'd gotten it done the first time.

She unwrapped his hand, removed the safety cap from the needle, took a deep breath, and gave him the shot. He watched her face as she concentrated on the task. *I should've kissed her before.* As she wrapped up his hand again, the slight physical contact and, particularly, the way a strand of her hair brushed across his arm sent a dark thrill racing through him, and his groin flooded with heat. As if a swollen tongue weren't enough to deal with. What was wrong with him? He was tempted to suspect she was a *bruja* of a very different kind. "Thanks," he said when she finished. "Ice?" He needed a minute away from her.

"I'll get some. Be right back."

He stared up at the ceiling, his heart drumming hard. It had been more than two years since he'd been with a woman, and maybe it was getting to him. His last relationship had ended badly. Honestly, though he hadn't been able to recognize it at the time, he and Sophie had been wrong from the start. On some days, she'd seemed close to him, and on others, she'd been distant and closed off. He'd had no patience for it, and they'd oscillated between sex and fighting.

Cassie returned with a cup of ice. He took it from her and thanked her. A woman who could send angry bears after him might not be an improvement over his last girlfriend. He knew this, yet a stubborn part of him remained unconvinced.

Within a half hour, the burning in his hand and the swelling of his tongue had mostly subsided. He listened to her talk about the first horse she'd ever ridden, not quite tracking, because his brain kept going off in incredibly inappropriate directions, but enjoying the sound of her voice—which, in fact, contributed to those inappropriate directions.

The nurse's voice interrupted them. "Hello? David's friend is here to see him."

"*Gracias.*" The curtness in Gabi Bravo's contralto voice suggested, *You can go away now,* and the nurse did. Gabi entered into the room and shut the door behind her. She wore an olive green utility jacket, unbuttoned to reveal a black tank underneath, khaki pants, and work boots. Her natural hair was pulled back in a ponytail, and a duffel bag hung across her back.

Now that she was here, Jonathan would have help if Cassie triggered another animal attack, not to mention the advantage of her long experience. He didn't know exactly how old Gabi was—somewhere in her forties or maybe early fifties. She'd been

Michael's mentor, and Jonathan gave her credit for helping him in many ways beyond actually learning to carry out a mission.

Cassie got to her feet.

Easing himself up into a sitting position, Jonathan said, "*Salaam,* Gabi. You made good time."

"*Salaam.*" Her thick brows drew together in a frown. "You look like hell." She strode over to the hospital bed, pulled aside his hospital gown in back to inspect his wounds, and then clucked her tongue at the sight.

Jonathan said, "Could have been worse."

"Much worse, you'd be dead." Her heavy-lidded gaze rose to Cassie, flat and hostile. "This is the *bruja?*"

Cassie bristled.

"Not a *bruja.*" Jonathan said. "Gabi, this is Cassie Rios. Cassie, this is Gabi. She works with me."

"I figured," Cassie said, stony-faced. "Hi."

Gabi asked him, "You ready to get out of here?"

"He needs at least a couple more days," Cassie protested. "And tell them to send more shots!"

Gabi held her in a level look. "Let's get something clear. You even start to lose your temper, I'm authorized to use any force I see fit."

Jonathan might've behaved in exactly the same way if a *sonámbula* injured one of his fellow Knights two times in as many days. Gabi was probably even more on edge than usual because of Michael's recent death. At his memorial service, she'd wept the entire time.

Gabi wouldn't make a move against someone without a reason. But Cassie didn't know that, and she stood as stiff as a steel beam.

Jonathan told Gabi quietly, "She's agreed to come with us."

Gabi took something out of her duffel bag. Leaning over, she pulled the IV out, and then pressed a square of adhesive gauze against the top of his hand. "He's better off with us," she told Cassie. "They'll have more antivenin by the time we get there."

Cassie's shoulders relaxed slightly. "But I didn't even pack a bag."

"Nic packed one for you." She added to Jonathan, "He brought you fresh clothes, too." She unzipped her duffel bag and set a roll of clothing on the bedside table. Jonathan maneuvered out of bed and took off the hospital gown. "We'll drive your car back. They'll come to get mine later."

As he bent forward to put on the boxers, the pull on the stitches in his back made him wince. The venom from the coral snake still pounded in his head. "I don't think I can drive."

"I'll do it. What's another nine hours?"

Jonathan felt for her. He'd had long hauls like that before. There was no point suggesting that Cassie, the only one who was healthy and well-rested, could take the wheel.

Cassie was staring at him—specifically, at his body, with frank appreciation. She met his eyes, and her cheeks flamed as she looked away. He couldn't help but feel pleased. Christ help him, he was fighting a losing battle. Maybe he'd already lost.

He asked Gabi, "Why didn't Nic come with you? He loves to drive."

"He had another mission to run. Ramon and Samir are headed to Kansas City. Somehow, a bunch of haunted houses there have started to feature real, live homicidal ghosts."

Jonathan grunted. "The most wonderful time of the year." As he eased a white undershirt over his back, Cassie was still eyeing him, a fact he tried his best to ignore. He put on a gray shirt and fastened a couple of buttons with his left hand. "Maybe you should sleep a little first," he said to Gabi.

She shook her head. "They're worried about that bite of yours. I'll manage."

Jonathan sat down on the edge of the bed and started to put

on a sock. A simple enough task, but between the strain on his stitched back, the stiffness in his bitten hand, and the dizziness that overtook him whenever he bent over, it wasn't easy.

Cassie came over and took the sock from him. "Here, I'll do it." Her eyes were filled with concern, and when she crouched down near his feet, her nearness and her position summoned vivid erotic images to his brain. Her hands on his cock, her mouth...

"No, that's—" He stopped himself, having no real reason to object. The desire and guilt intertwining in him were his own problem. "Okay." As she put on his socks and then his boots, he stared at the corner of the hospital room. When she was finished, he said, "Thank you," and his voice came out too formal. Gabi regarded them both with obvious interest.

Cassie stood up. "I have to call my parents first. If I'm going to be out of town, they need to know."

"You'll do that from the car," Gabi said.

They didn't tell anyone at the hospital that Jonathan was leaving. At Jonathan's SUV, Gabi told Cassie, "You're in back. You too," she added to Jonathan. With his orders to stay next to her, he'd been planning on it. They pulled out of the parking lot and got onto the interstate. A bus engulfed them in a cloud of diesel smell, and Gabi sped up to go around it. Gabi looked back at Cassie. "Call your mother now on speakerphone. Make up an excuse."

Cassie's chin jutted out in defiance, even though she'd just said she needed to call. It reminded Jonathan of his brother's stubbornness. Once he trusted and respected someone, he would follow any order, but it had to be earned.

"You don't want anyone worrying," Jonathan told Cassie, meaning both her mom and Manus Sancti.

Cassie pressed her lips together, turned on the speakerphone, and dialed.

Mrs. Rios picked up right away. "Hi, honey. What's up?"

"Not much," Cassie said. "No, a lot, actually."

"What is it? Your dad's here, too. I'm going to put you on speakerphone."

Speakerphone on both sides, then. Cassie said, "You know that guy you met the other day? David Ramirez? I'm, uh, taking a trip with him."

"Oh." A small silence that followed. A male voice interjected. "Taking a trip where?" Cassie's father, obviously.

Cassie scrunched up her face. "Uh, to Mexico."

Her mother asked, "Cassie, are you still saying you two are just friends?"

Gabi glanced over her shoulder at Jonathan, her eyebrows raised.

Cassie sighed. "It's complicated."

"What part of Mexico?" her father asked. "And for how long?"

"Cancun."

Mrs. Rios said, "I told you about him, Eddie. He's a very nice guy."

"All right," he grumbled. "What are you going to be doing on this trip?"

Cassie rolled her eyes, and Jonathan half expected her to say something disastrously honest. *Put myself in the hands of a scary secret gang. Keep wild animals from eviscerating my enemies.* "Go to the beach, drink some beer."

An image of Cassie in a bikini, beer in hand, flashed through Jonathan's brain. If only she could be having a good time, away from a worthless ex, the shadow of unemployment, a deadly curse—and away from him and Manus Sancti, as far as that went.

"I think it sounds fantastic. Fantastic!" Mrs. Rios said. "You deserve to take a break and have fun! As long as you don't go too crazy with the money."

"It's his treat," Cassie said.

"Isn't he in grad school?"

"He, uh, he has a trust fund."

Gabi snorted.

Cassie's mother chirped, "You didn't tell me about that! How long do you think you'll be out of town?"

"Um. I'm not sure yet."

"Oh. Well, let us know if you get a chance. We hope you have a wonderful time!"

Jonathan regretted making Cassie lie to her mother, although it was for the best. When Cassie got off the phone, he said, "Your mom's nice."

"She thinks the same of you."

He leaned his throbbing skull back on the seat and closed his eyes. They drove for a long time without talking, and he was half asleep when the chorus of a very silly pop song began playing. Gabi's ringtone.

She answered her phone with a smile. "Hey, baby. I was just about to call you."

Cassie lifted her eyebrows. No doubt she was surprised to hear Gabi speak in that tone of comfortable warmth after the woman had threatened her.

Gabi continued, "I'm a little tired, but I'll be all right." After a pause, she said with a glance at Jonathan, "He'll live. Rough couple of days. I'll tell you later. How was the Palimpsest meeting?" She listened for a while and then responded, "I'm sorry. But six months, that's not that long."

Jonathan leaned his head back on the seat again.

Gabi laughed at something. "I know, Athens. He talked to me about it before we left." Another pause. "Well, I'm not as against it as you are. I'm a *little* against it— All right. Yeah, love you, too."

She hung up, and Jonathan asked lazily, "Who was that?"

"Ha ha."

Jonathan often watched football matches with Gabi's husband, Andre, a Diviner. Sometimes, they even watched American football, because Andre had played it as a teenager in Alabama and he was a big fan. Jonathan had taken a mild interest in it while he'd been at West Point.

"Hey, I have a question," Cassie said. "How do you know if there's a witch or a demon out there? Do you watch the news a lot, look for weird things?"

Jonathan glanced at Gabi, who said, "I don't care. Capitán says they'll probably wipe her memory anyway."

Cassie's eyes widened in sudden alarm. "Don't tell me then! I don't want my mind messed with!"

"They're not going to. Not if I can help it." He ignored Gabi's look. "There are people who do nothing but monitor what's happening in the world and find cases of supernatural evil. Sometimes, it's through the news, yeah, but they watch everything. Strange weather patterns, government investigations, groups on social networks, the deep Web—"

"That can't be legal."

"It's for the best. Some cases are pretty obvious, like yours or the Dakos demon. Others are more subtle. The Diviners notice changes in patterns and find connections others would miss."

"The Diviners?" she repeated.

"They used to have prophetic abilities, hundreds of years ago." He put the sunglasses on.

"They're hundreds of years old?"

She was probably thinking about vampires again. "No. There used to be people who could divine the future. But the gift died out."

"Why did it go away? Do you know?"

He shrugged. "It was always rare. Recessive gene, probably. And a lot of people who had it… They went crazy and died young."

"Or they were burned at the stake as Devil worshippers," Gabi added, her voice tart, as she turned onto an exit ramp to head east.

"So the Diviners do all kinds of internet research, they tell you when things are going wrong, and you to go take care of it," Cassie said.

Jonathan shook his head. "They tell our boss, who sends us on missions."

"If those people are called Diviners, what are you called? Like agents or soldiers?"

"Knights."

"Both men and women? That's pretty badass. And you're all over the world? Gabi, where are you from?"

Gabi raised her thick eyebrows at Cassie's attempt to get to know her. "Brazil. I grew up in Sao Paolo."

"Oh. I guess that's a Portuguese accent."

"Guess so."

Late in the day, Cassie woke up as the car turned onto another highway. Still wearing his sunglasses, Jonathan relaxed back into the seat at an angle, probably to avoid too much pressure on his stitches. His long legs sprawled wide. The fact that she'd seen him naked made it even harder for her to ignore the proximity of his body to hers. Maybe he wasn't even aware of how ridiculously good he looked. She got the sense that he treated his body as a vehicle or a weapon—to take care of, certainly, but only so he could rely on it.

What was he like in bed? Gentlemanly? Domineering? She'd seen him both ways.

Sex with Rick had lacked a certain kind of passion. Not that it had been exactly bad. She hadn't been stupid enough to marry someone with whom the sex was terrible. But once a person got divorced, she admitted all kinds of things that she'd pretended were okay before, and Rick had always been very…calm.

She knew now that Jonathan had strong emotions. And obviously, he could be forceful. At least once again in her life, she wanted someone to just shove her up against a wall and kiss her until she couldn't breathe. To tell her what to do, which she loved during sex as much as she hated it at almost every other time.

"Thirsty?" Jonathan held a bottle of water out to her, and she shook her head. She needed to pee, and if they didn't stop soon, she was going to have to ask them to. "Open it for me," he said. She obeyed and handed it back to her. He took a long drink, the muscles of his throat contracting.

Gabi glanced back at him. "Guess you'd better drive for a while. I'm about to nod off."

"Sorry, better not. My hand's swelling up again, and my head's about to explode."

Cassie peered around him to see his bandaged hand. It was puffy, though not as bad as before.

Gabi sucked in a breath. "Why didn't you say something?"

"Nothing we can do about it."

She smacked her palm on the steering wheel. "Why didn't Nic pack more antivenin?"

"It's hard to get. I'm lucky he tracked down two." They passed a sign announcing gas stations and a fast food restaurant at the next exit, and he said, "Hey, I need to stop."

Gabi hesitated. "All right. I need more coffee."

They pulled into a convenience store, and Cassie went to the women's room and peed furiously. When she emerged, Gabi was waiting for her right outside the door. "Hurry up, we need to go."

Jonathan already stood at the entrance. She couldn't blame them for rushing because of his hand. Once they were pulling onto the highway, he asked her, "You're sure it was them?"

"I'm sure." She nodded at the rearview mirror. "Look."

A black Jeep drove far behind them. Cassie felt shaky. "Are they following us?"

Jonathan squinted back at them. "Yes." He drew his gun.

Shit. "Who is it?"

He paused before answering. "Coyote Shifters."

Coyote Shifters. She repeated these two words in her head a few times. He'd said they existed, and that they weren't all nice. Obviously, these were the not-nice kind. She glanced back at the truck. She couldn't see them well, but they were in human form, of course. Coyotes didn't drive. "*Why* are they following us?"

Jonathan ignored the question. "What are you thinking, Gabi?"

Gabi glanced back at Cassie. "Can her animals help?"

Cassie blinked. She didn't expect to be considered as an ally.

Jonathan shook his head. "She doesn't have any control of it." It gave her a pang of regret, even though it was true.

Gabi said, "Then I'm thinking we're getting off the road." She turned and stepped on the gas.

CHAPTER NINE

THEY JOLTED OVER the desert floor. The Jeep following them had no trouble with the terrain. It sped up, coming closer. "Abandoned buildings over here," Gabi said to Jonathan, and Cassie understood. Gabi had gone off the road to make sure nobody else who happened to be driving on the interstate got smashed into or shot.

After all Cassie had been through, she'd be damned if she got hurt by Coyote Shifters. Fury rose in her like a boiling tide, and a metallic tang filled her mouth. Where had she tasted that before? It tasted like blood. But it was more than that. She'd tasted it when she and Jonathan had argued, right before the snake had bitten him.

It came with the kind of anger that would trigger the spell. The anger felt different from annoyance or irritation. It required swift and dramatic retribution. She was almost sure of it...but not sure enough to tell them.

Jonathan pulled her down by the arm. "Get down and stay down." The earnestness and authority in his deep voice compelled her to obey. She kneeled between the front and back seats. He watched the back window, gun in hand.

His left hand. "You can't shoot," Cassie said in a rush. "Give me your gun."

"No way," Gabi said, taking a sharp left turn that sent Cassie flying into Jonathan's knee.

"Then give me another gun!" She had a feeling they had more.

Jonathan pressed his lips together. Then he unloaded the Glock and set both the gun and the magazine on the floor of the car next to her.

"The fuck are you doing?" Gabi exploded.

He took another gun out of the side compartment and loaded it with stiff and careful movements, telling Cassie, "Stay down. Don't do anything unless I tell you."

Gabi took another sudden sharp turn, and they passed a stone building. Cassie caught a fleeting glimpse of a hand-lettered sign that read *Sandwiches*.

How in God's name had she wound up here? If she turned up dead in Las Cruces when she said she'd be in Cancun, her parents were going to be so pissed. She couldn't cower like a jackrabbit behind a shrub. She rose up high enough to see the black truck looming closer.

Gunfire rang out, and two holes exploded in the back window. "Fuck fuck fuck," Cassie said as Jonathan yelled to Gabi, "You all right?"

"Yeah." Gabi yanked the car left and headed into a rickety wooden garage. The Jeep followed. "Hang on," she said, and Cassie let out a little scream as she drove straight into the back wall.

The windshield smashed, but they emerged from the structure, which crashed down on the Jeep behind them. Jonathan rolled down the window.

Gabi said, "That Jeep is bulletproof."

"The tires aren't." He leaned up against the window on his side and glanced over the backseat. As Gabi floored it across the bumpy terrain, Cassie rolled down her window, too.

The Jeep exploded out of the wreckage. Jonathan flung his upper body out the window and took aim. Cassie had a gun, too. She had to try to help. Jonathan fired. He wasn't going to be able to hit anything, not with that hand.

The car jolted as she loaded the gun. She leaned out the window, bracing herself on shaking legs. Front tire. She squeezed the trigger, missed. Fired again. The tire exploded into scraps of black rubber. She dove back into the car just before a bullet whizzed by.

She flung herself down onto the seat, and Jonathan did the same while Gabi crouched low. Another shot crashed through the back windshield, and Cassie sucked in her breath.

"Hang on!" Gabi's voice flooded Cassie with relief. She drove them up a rocky hill. No more shots—someone needed to reload, maybe.

Cassie unloaded the gun in her hand so she wouldn't accidentally shoot someone or herself in the face as the car bounced around. The car slid backward and she gasped. It ground forward again. The Jeep couldn't follow with its blown-out tire. Cassie peered out the back to see two men jumping out of the car.

"Look!" Gabi came to a stop, staring in the rearview mirror.

Something gold flashed in front of the men. It pounced on one of them and sunk its jaws into his neck, knocking him backward. *My animals.* The other man whirled, trying to get a clear shot. His companion must have dropped his gun. His arms and legs flailed and he screamed, high-pitched like a terrified child. The animal adjusted its hold on his shoulders, gnawing his throat.

"Mountain lion," Cassie said stupidly. Two more of the animals ran at the standing man from the opposite direction. He blurred, and Cassie blinked, trying to clear her eyesight.

A coyote stood where he'd been, larger than any she'd ever seen. It barked at the mountain lions, a croaking yell that sounded too human, and bared its teeth. One of the felines leaped at its throat. The other sank its teeth into his leg and yanked hard.

The coyote went down. Cassie cried out as it fell limp, spattered with gore. The mountain lion tore its back limb from its body. The animal let out a strangled scream, and Cassie covered her eyes.

"*Christos,*" Jonathan and Gabi said at nearly the same time.

After a few moments, she looked up again. Two men, one clothed and one naked, slumped bloody and inert at the bottom of the hill. A detached human leg lay a couple of yards away. The mountain lions, their muzzles, paws, and the fur on their chests mottled with blood, prowled slowly around the men's bodies, sniffing at them.

"They're making sure they're dead," Jonathan said, his eyes wide. Slowly, the animals walked away.

Gabi stared after them. "That was incredible," she murmured. Then she started driving again, easing diagonally down the slope of the hill toward the highway.

"They're dead," Cassie said. Just like Rick. Except this time, she'd seen it happen. That leg torn off. "Oh my God." Her insides swam with nausea and horror. She leaned over, gripping her head in her hands.

Jonathan encircled her shoulders with his strong arm and pulled her close. "Shh. Everything's fine." She melted against his body, solid and reassuring, and allowed herself the luxury of a deep breath, in and out. He stroked her hair. The over-familiarity and gentleness startled her, at odds with the violence they'd just ridden out, and she loved it. "You don't have to feel bad about this one. They were going to kill us."

She nodded. Would the police come after them? But they were far enough from the road that it might be a little while before they were found. And the men had been torn apart by wild animals.

"Well, now I'm awake," Gabi quipped as she pulled the vehicle onto the interstate again.

"Nice driving," he said to her, and they exchanged weary smiles. He turned back to Cassie. She expected him to let go, but he kept his arm wrapped around her. "I thought I told you to stay down." When she opened her mouth to protest, he said, "I'm kidding. You were amazing. The animals attacked so fast. And that was a great shot from a moving car." It had been. All her hunting and time at the range had come in handy. He leaned closer. "You scared the hell out of me."

Something inside her melted, as sweet as chocolate. He cared about her, a lot. She'd pulled her unwashed hair back into a pony-tail, and his mouth hovered not so far from her neck now. His breath heated her skin, and every nerve of her body vibrated in response. No matter what his fine-tuned sense of honor compelled him to do—or not do—he wanted her.

"I'll take that gun back from you now," Gabi said to her from the front.

Jonathan straightened and moved his arm to the back of the seat. Cassie tried to ignore her pang of disappointment. She looked down at the Glock and the magazine on the floor. It wasn't like she had any more use for it. What was she going to do, shoot Gabi and Jonathan both in the leg and run off in the middle of nowhere? Not a smart plan, and even if it had been, she wouldn't have done it. She handed the magazine to Gabi and then the gun, facing down with the grip toward Gabi, the way her uncle had taught her to give someone a firearm. Gabi put them both in the glove compartment and glanced back at Jonathan. "You're going to catch hell for letting her have that."

Cassie asked her, "How did you know those buildings were abandoned?"

Gabi's lip curled. "I've been down this road fifty times. I've taken cover there before." The ridiculous pop song that was her ringtone sounded again, and she picked it up. "*Salaam*, Nic. We had a detour."

As she explained the situation, Cassie joked with Jonathan, "It's dangerous to talk and drive." Jonathan managed a quick grin, though his face looked gray. How much pain was he in? Hopefully, his group would be able to take care of him. "Are all Coyote Shifters bad?"

"What? No. These guys are pretty bad. Though we sort of had a truce with them. They're drug dealers."

"They're, like, a gang?"

"Yeah."

Cassie shuddered. "Why would you have a truce with them?"

"They were better than the alternative. A drug cartel was becoming active in this area. Well, not just drugs. Extortion, kidnapping, lots of human trafficking."

"Are we talking sex slaves or workers or what?"

"Both," Gabi said, having just hung up.

Jonathan said, "Coyote Shifters here managed to beat the cartel out of the territory. And the Shifters only sell drugs—none of the rest of it."

"Except for the occasional magical artifact," Gabi added.

"Right," Jonathan agreed. "They're a rough bunch, but sometimes we have business with them, and mostly, we stay out of one another's way."

"It sure as hell didn't look like that to me. What happened?"

"I killed one of their buddies last month," Gabi said.

Her words made Cassie freeze up inside. Maybe she wasn't with the good guys, after all. "How come?"

"I met him at a house party to buy a certain artifact for our group. I don't know how they got their hands on enchanted Viking gold, but they did. I passed a room where people were fucking, and I saw a girl wasn't moving. I went in. She was a human girl, passed out, getting raped by a Shifter in human form." Gabi's jaw tensed. "I put my gun to the Shifter's head and told him to stand up. He did. Pants around his ankles. I told him, 'She's unconscious.' He said, 'But she's fucked half the guys here.' That's when I took out my knife and slit his throat."

Cassie's mouth fell open.

Jonathan said, "Any one of us would have done the same. Even if he were one of our own."

Cassie hardly knew what to say. Finally, she asked, "Why did you slit his throat instead of shooting him?"

"So no one would hear. I got the girl out to the car and took her to the hospital. Am I going to get the speech about due process now?"

Jonathan watched Cassie, clearly wondering the same thing.

"No." Cassie's voice came out annoyed. Yes, it was wrong, killing a man in cold blood. But she was in no mood to give someone who was more or less her captor a lecture. And most rapists never even got reported. She wasn't going to cry over one of them receiving rough justice.

Gabi's eyebrows rose. "I'm starting to like this *bruja*."

After another half hour or so, Jonathan said, "My hand's not as swollen." Color had come back into his face.

"Maybe you're through the worst of it," Gabi said.

They took an exit to apparently nowhere, and a while later, they turned onto a dirt road. After many more miles, they arrived at a tall chain-link fence topped with coils of razor wire. It cordoned off a huge portion of land, as though it surrounded a prison. A gate blocked the road, and two men in quasi-military outfits carrying automatic rifles stood on either side.

Cassie sat up straighter. "Shit. Who are *these* people?"

"It's okay," Jonathan said. "This is us."

CHAPTER TEN

CASSIE'S EYES DARTED from the closest guard to the car door handle. Jonathan reached over to squeeze her hand. To any *sonámbula*, the perimeter of El Dédalo would have been alarming, and she'd been through so much already.

Was he looking for excuses to touch her? Maybe, but he did want to comfort her, too. Honestly, after the run-in with the Coyotes, he'd also wanted to comfort himself. He'd been terrified that she'd get hurt or killed. It was bad enough when it happened to Knights, but they had chosen this life, more or less. Many of them, like him and Michael, had always been expected to take this path. But Cassie was never meant to have anything to do with it.

Gabi pulled up to the gate, stopped, and rolled down the window. "Bravo 1115," she said to one of the men.

"*Salaam,* Bravo. The *bruja* needs a tracker."

As the guard handed Gabi a box, Jonathan told her, "It gets injected under your skin so you don't show up on the security grid as a non-registered."

She swallowed. "Can I get it out later?"

"Absolutely. They'll remove it when you leave." *Don't get angry,* he added mentally. A mountain lion or bear attack as soon as she arrived would mean that she'd be put in psychic suspension, no question, assuming that a frightened guard didn't turn his weapon on her first. He didn't even know what he'd do if that happened, but none of the likely choices would be good. Cassie nodded, and Jonathan exhaled in relief.

Gabi leaned over the back seat to give her the shot in the forearm. Jonathan pressed a clean handkerchief against the drop of blood that welled up.

Cassie took it from him and stared down at her arm. "Is the chip in there?"

"Yeah, it was in the solution. It's tiny." She scowled out the window as they went through the gate and continued down the narrow road. "Hey, Cassie." He tried to keep his voice casual. "There's going to be a couple more security procedures that might seem a little weird, but try to stay relaxed, okay?" Security had already texted him detailed instructions.

She snapped, "What are they going to do, strip-search me?" Jonathan froze. She said, "Oh my God."

"You'll walk through a body scan. No one will touch you." *Sonámbulos* in most countries he'd lived had an aversion to nudity. He almost said he'd be right there, but he wasn't sure that would make it better. "And then someone will Read you."

"Mind-read me? Like what you did?" He nodded. "Shit! That's even worse.— I'm not mad at you," she rushed to add. "I'm freaked out."

"I'm telling you now so it's less of a shock." He held her gaze and tried not to think about how beautiful her eyes were. "But listen, when I Read you, you were scared out of your mind and resisting me, which made it hurt a lot. The person who's going to Read you today is an old friend of mine, Valentina Vega. She can go into people's heads without them even feeling it."

"That almost scares me more." Cassie gave an uneasy laugh. "How come you can't do that?"

"I don't have her talent. She's like someone who can walk

through walls, where I have to smash in a window. And afterward, she can erase the memory of her being in there."

"Why would she do that?"

He tried to think of how to explain this. "She doesn't do it with me, because she knows me well. But for most people, it's more comfortable. When someone's in your head, it can make you feel defensive."

"No kidding. It's like the ultimate invasion of privacy."

"When she's done, though, everyone here will know you're innocent."

That would be nice. She needed their help, and so far, they didn't look friendly. They passed rows of industrial steel buildings with arched roofs that stored cars, trucks, and a few airplanes and helicopters. More soldiers milled about, but they only glanced up at the moving car. She hugged her arms. "I'm trying not to freak out."

"I'm sorry. None of this is your fault."

"As long as they can help me fix it." She peered out at the compound. "Do regular people around here know who you guys are?"

"The only people who know about us think we're right-wing religious nutjobs."

"But no one bothers you?" she pressed. "The police, the government?"

"The last thing American politicians want to do is mess with a bunch of Christians with guns. Especially if they're not hurting anyone."

"Are you all Christians?"

"Hardly, but that's what they think. And we pay important people lots of money to leave us alone."

"Money we take out of their own assets, which they get from illegal deals," Gabi chimed in. "But they don't know that."

They pulled up to the one-story concrete block building and parked. Cassie followed them through the grimy steel door. They stepped into the lobby with a gleaming terrazzo tile floor. Cassie looked all around her, making Jonathan see the room as though for the first time. A huge red tapestry hung on one wall, covered with flowers, birds, and mythological beasts. Elaborately carved wooden chairs with leather seats and curved armrests gathered in a circle. The floor featured an inlaid metal design of a twelve-pointed star. "This is like one of those rooms in a museum," she said. "Except we're on the other side of the velvet rope."

The woman behind the desk said to Jonathan, "Take a seat. A medic's on his way." Cassie and Gabi sat down, as well.

In a few minutes, a guy showed up to give Jonathan another dose of the antivenin and something to make his hand numb. He said, "I'm supposed to ask you if you can stay on duty for a few more hours. Otherwise, another Knight can help escort the *bruja*."

Jonathan's head was pounding, the stitches in his back stung, and he felt like if he laid down, he could sleep for a week. But he couldn't abandon Cassie to people who were strangers to her, especially when she was so afraid. "I'm fine."

They passed through a side door flanked by two more armed soldiers. Cassie said in a low voice, "I can see why I'd be less of a danger here."

Jonathan nodded. A bear or a couple of mountain lions would have a tough time getting past all the guards. Gabi shut the door behind them.

In the large darkened space, a man and a woman sat at computers, and technical equipment lined one whole wall. A large metal tunnel stood in the middle of the room. "You first, West," the Mage said to Jonathan, standing up and walking over to them. She wore rimless glasses and spoke with an Arabic accent. He began to unbutton his shirt, and Cassie gaped. "Why do *you* have to undress?"

"To make sure nothing's been planted on me, or in me. And that I'm not a revenant. The clothes get screened for unfamiliar compounds and hexes." He dropped his shirt into a steel barrel similar to the kind that stored radioactive waste, handed the woman his gun and holster, and shucked off the rest of his clothes. The Mage rested her hands lightly on Jonathan's shoulders and closed her eyes, taking a couple of moments to psychically scan for any curses or abnormalities. She would do the same with his clothing. Cassie's eyes widened. It was good that she could see him going through security first. Hopefully, it would make her less nervous.

When he placed his palms on the nape of his neck so his elbows jutted out on either side, it pulled on the slashes in his back, the pain already familiar to him. He stepped into the metal tunnel. A glowing image of his body would appear on one of the computer screens, and an illuminated schema of an eyeball would show up on the other. After a few moments, lines of information would type themselves out beneath the images.

"All clear," the man at the computer said, and Jonathan stepped out of the scanner and retrieved his clothes. The woman with the glasses nodded at another steel canister and told Cassie, "You're next."

As Gabi waited behind her, Cassie peeled off her T-shirt without hesitation, then unfastened her bra and deposited it into the container. Her dark hair fell around her naked shoulders, and the shape of her breasts in the low light, graceful and inviting, stilled the breath in his lungs. His hands froze on the bottom button of his shirt.

She met his eyes. He was staring at her, making a process that was already uncomfortable for her even more so. Deliberately, he turned away.

He'd been through security many times before with women, including Gabi. Of course, he'd noticed that Gabi was gorgeous for her age, or for any age. After their first mission together, it had crossed his mind that Andre was a very lucky man. It hadn't been too personal.

He wanted to talk to Cassie and listen to her for hours, to protect her, to caress every inch of her body, to take control of it and make her come again and again. He wanted to be in her psyche, but with her permission this time. The force of his need for her shook him. He didn't look at either of the women as they went through the scan and got dressed.

"I'm off-duty," Gabi told him as she straightened from tying her boots, breaking the silence.

Jonathan smiled at her. "Get some rest."

"Yeah, I don't think that'll be any problem."

"Thanks, Gabi." As she walked away, Jonathan finally turned to Cassie, now fully clothed. "Not so bad, right?"

She glared at him. "At my old company, I just swiped a badge. Where next?"

"This way." He touched the small of her back, guiding her into the hallway.

Jonathan's controlling touch annoyed Cassie even as it sent a curl of warmth through her body. She couldn't avoid repeated thoughts of seeing him in all of his considerable glory. And when she'd been getting undressed herself, she'd caught him staring at her with a dark and distant look in his eyes as though he'd been imagining all of the terrible things he wanted to do to her. Very good terrible things, which she also wanted him to do.

But even if she did find herself alone with him here, which didn't seem all that likely, she couldn't hit on him again. It would be way too desperate on her part, and no matter what he was thinking, he'd already said no. Yes, he'd embraced her in the car, but only to comfort her after a horrible shock.

He held open a door for her. As soon as she stepped inside the room, she laughed out loud. The walls of the small, cluttered space were painted a brilliant turquoise. A fluffy flokati rug covered part of the black-and-white checkerboard floor, and a lime-green chair that appeared to be made out of the same plushy material as a stuffed animal sat next to a bright pink tufted sofa.

A young woman with a teal streak in the front of her wavy brown hair got up from another chair, a huge smile on her face. "Johnny!" she said in a soft, breathy voice, avoiding the injuries on his back as she gave him a hug.

He had to bend over to return it, as he stood several inches taller than her, a warm smile suffusing his features, as well. "Hey, *corina.*" Cassie tried to think what *corina* meant in Spanish. He'd said he didn't have a girlfriend. Still, this hardly seemed professional.

"Thank Goddess you're all right!" She glanced at Cassie and switched to speaking in Spanish, and Jonathan answered her in the same language. *Rude.* The only thing she could catch was *serpiente,* snake. The young woman was extremely pretty, wearing a red cardigan over a polka dotted dress that flared out at the knee. Her red round-toed heels matched the sweater, and so did her lipstick, outlining a curvy, full mouth. The rest of her was full and curvy, too. Cassie had always felt uncomfortable around ultra-feminine girls like this, as though her face was dirty. And she was impressed and a little intimidated that this girl was in her early twenties at most, yet she apparently had a big office of her own.

Her smile disappeared as she turned to Cassie. "I'm Valentina Vega. I'm going to debrief both of you and make written records of your experiences. Do you have any questions?"

So many that Cassie didn't know where to start. As she shook her head, she realized that as sweet as Valentina seemed, she was just as pissed at her as Gabi had been for getting Jonathan attacked.

When Valentina returned her attention to Jonathan, her features immediately softened. He sat on the couch, and as she settled down next to him, he closed his eyes, his large hands resting on his knees. She didn't touch him, but instead folded her hands and bowed her head slightly, closing her eyes as well.

Cassie guessed the young woman was in his memories now,

experiencing them as he had. Did she feel what he felt? When she reached the parts with Cassie in them, what would it be like?

He'd said Valentina could do this without people even feeling it and could erase their memory of it afterward. Thinking of that power terrified Cassie. What could she do with it, if she wanted to? Cassie looked around the room. Framed paintings of roses and seascapes, not particularly well done, hung on one of the walls in old, tacky frames—thrift store purchases, maybe. The long white shelves held teapots, teacups and saucers, tins, and dark blue glass jars filled with loose tea leaves and labeled with tape from an old-fashioned label maker, the kind her grandma had used to organize her stuff in the basement.

She was about to get up to inspect them more closely, but Jonathan stirred. He opened his eyes, and Valentina lifted her head. A tear glittered on her lashes. Jonathan frowned. "Sorry," he muttered. She shook her head and dabbed at her eye with the corner of her cardigan sleeve.

What was that all about? His memories of his brother, maybe, when he'd shared them with Cassie. Valentina was an old friend, so she must have known his brother, too.

Jonathan stood up.

"That didn't take long," Cassie said.

Valentina nodded. "I compress the experiences. Have you ever had a dream that seemed to last a week? It's like that." With a wave of her hand, she indicated the spot on the sofa next to her that Jonathan had vacated. "Are you ready?"

Cassie didn't sit down. "Didn't you get everything from him?"

"No. And we want to make sure you aren't somehow misleading us in your psyche."

Oh, for God's sake. "I wouldn't have any idea how to do that! Besides, if I could fool him, I could fool you, right?"

"Not necessarily," she said at the same time that Jonathan said, "I doubt it."

Cassie sat down, getting a closer look at the coffee table. "Is this made out of Legos?" Plastic bricks, encased in glass, comprised the entire table top, which sat on metal legs. As an eleven-year-old, Cassie would've killed for this room.

Valentina didn't show any interest in discussing furniture design. "Relax."

Jonathan had closed his eyes, so Cassie did the same. She imagined stroking Layla's light mane. Somehow, this idea transformed into the thought of running her fingers over Jonathan's cropped hair. No, this was bad. Valentina would know what she was thinking. She tried to clear her head. After a few moments, she felt nothing, so she opened her eyes to ask what was happening.

Valentina gave her a small, rueful smile. "All done."

"You didn't do anything yet." Why was the woman being nice all of the sudden?

"It actually took quite a bit longer than Jonathan's debriefing, because I don't know you, and because I scanned for psychic ability."

Right. Cassie couldn't remember because she'd erased the time in her head. She'd transported herself into the desert of her psyche, sifting through her experiences, and Cassie didn't even know what either of them had said in there.

Jonathan took a step forward. "What did you find?"

"No Reading capability whatsoever, that I can tell." Cassie could have told her that. "And she's not a ghost talker, an empath, a psychometrist, a projectionist, or any kind of elemental." A sense of failure pricked at her before she reminded herself that she didn't even know what the hell some of those things were. "But there's something. Like the psychic equivalent of a strong will. There's a reason this magic is so strong with her." She gave them both a sweet smile. "It's been a long day for you two already. I know Cassie is supposed to see Dr. Morales, but do you want to take a break? I can make a cup of tea."

"That would be great," Cassie said. She never drank tea, but it would give her time to ask why she was supposed to see a doctor. And it seemed the girl had decided to like her, after all. Cassie didn't know why, but she was glad.

At the kitchenette in the corner, Valentina made tea in a copper kettle. "Are we at war with the Coyote Shifter pack now? That's the last thing we need." She must have reviewed the episode in Las Cruces.

"Not a chance," Jonathan said. "Andre already dug into it. A lot of the Shifters hated the guy Gabi dispatched. He had a few loyal family members, but no other allies. Anyway, they're not like Wolves. Coyotes won't start a war unless they're sure they'll win."

Val arranged two teacups on a tray. "They'll smell mountain lion on the bodies. They're going to think it was Shifters."

"Maybe. But the nearest pack is that huge one in Wyoming."

It was surreal, hearing them talk business.

"Good," Val said. "They won't go to war with that pack, either."

Cassie supposed she should be grateful. She never thought she'd have to worry about inciting a shapeshifter war, yet here she was.

After Val set the tray with two steaming cups on the Lego table, she said she had a headache and was going to go lie down, but that they were welcome to relax for a while.

Jonathan asked, "It's been busy today?"

"Yes, but my head's been hurting ever since I got off the plane from Granada." She frowned. "I should have told you sooner. I saw your father, but I didn't get to talk to him long."

Jonathan shrugged and asked how her parents were doing.

After she left, Cassie asked, "Does she Read people all the time? That's her whole job?"

"Mostly. Everyone gets debriefed after missions. Val has perfect recall of her Readings and writes up reports." He picked up the teacup, tiny in his large hands. "She's also an empath, like Morty, except stronger. She feels what people are feeling."

Oh, great. "You should have warned me."

"Why?" His steel-blue eyes held her in a frank gaze. "What didn't you want her to know?"

That she was very much in lust with Val's good friend, for one thing. "It's just weird." She took a sip of the grayish-lavender tea, and it tasted like flowers. "I'm not sure I like this."

"Whatever it is, it's something good for you." He took a sip himself. "If a Mage makes you a cup of tea, drink it."

She took a big gulp. It wasn't really that bad, and a warm, cozy feeling trickled through her body, like she might get if she saw a bunch of puppies. "Seems like you and Val are really good friends."

"I've known her since we were kids."

"Have you ever been in *her* psyche?"

Jonathan raised his eyebrows. "Yeah. When I was a teenager and still learning how to Read people, I practiced on her and Michael a few times."

"What were their psyches like? Wait, is that private?" The way he screwed up his face made her think that it was. "Forget it. I'm just curious." Were all of them outdoor settings? Maybe some of them were nothing like real life.

"Michael's was... Have you ever been to Bourbon Street, in New Orleans?"

She shook her head, her grip tightening on the cup. What had she been thinking, asking this? It wouldn't be easy for him to talk about. Then again, he could've refused to answer. "I've never been, but I've seen pictures."

"It was kind of a party street, but it smells like it's near the ocean." His wry tone of voice and the affection in his eyes made her smile.

He'd grown up so differently from her. For him, and Val and Michael too, it had been totally normal for him to practice his psychic powers. "Where did you and Val grow up?"

"We weren't always in the same place. Her family and mine were both in Saint Augustine for a few years. Then they moved to

Tokyo, and we moved to Granada—the one in Spain. But when I was a teenager, the Vegas and my parents were both stationed in Cairo."

"Cairo. Wow." Cassie had wanted to go there ever since she'd studied the pyramids in fourth grade. "Why do you guys go so many places?"

"We have more than fifty *guarídas* around the world. This is our headquarters, but at a *guarída*, you'll have anywhere from one hundred to two hundred people." She must have looked confused, because he added, "They're like cells or offices. The only ones in the U.S. are in D.C. and Saint Augustine."

"Where is Saint Augustine?"

"Florida."

"You don't have one in L.A.?" It seemed like they'd want a West Coast office.

He shook his head. "There are so many Knights and Mages here at El Dédalo. We cover a wide territory."

It didn't seem that big to her. "El Dédalo," she repeated carefully. "What's that Spanish for?" It sounded like *dead*, but she knew the word for that was *muerto*.

"Maze, or labyrinth."

It hardly seemed very maze-like to her, but maybe the name wasn't literal. "What's this Dr. Morales going to do to me?"

"Nothing bad. Just a lot of tests."

Fantastic. "Why?"

"They want to make extra sure you're a normal human. And healthy. Plus, there's a chance those animal attacks are the result of a virus."

"Like…a magical virus?"

He nodded. "We've been infiltrated with them before."

"Who would do that?"

"We have enemies that go back hundreds of years."

"You guys are all so weird." Cassie drank down the rest of the tea, and another flush of well-being traveled all the way down to her toes.

"The medical tests are the last thing you have to do today. Then we can relax—if you can relax here," he added.

"You should probably be in bed right now." She set the cup down. "I'm ready."

The doctor's office was small. For an awful moment, Cassie thought Jonathan would stay in the room for the exams, but he told her he'd be right outside. Dr. Morales, a lady about her mom's age, explained that if Cassie became at all agitated, she and her assistant—a large woman wearing scrubs—had shots that would bring down a healthy rhinoceros. Cassie was getting sick of being treated like a dangerous criminal, but she couldn't get too sick of it or she'd prove them right.

They drew blood, made her pee in a cup, swabbed the inside of her mouth, poked at her boobs, and gave her what she supposed was every woman's least favorite exam. After such a dramatic day, all of this left her borderline close to tears, but they weren't done with her yet. An MRI scanned all of her internal organs. An EKG followed, and then she got a brain scan, during which the doctor asked her weird, random questions and had her play a boring videogame while the assistant monitored screens and typed.

"We still have to do blood tests, but everything looks good," Dr. Morales said finally. "That's it."

"Oh, is that all?" Cassie quipped.

She didn't smile. "Get dressed and Jonathan West will escort you to your quarters."

Like Cassie was a child. No, like a prisoner. She guessed it was late in the night by now. When she came out of the office, Jonathan was sitting against the wall, half asleep. It would have been a long time to wait for her, after a very long day, even if he hadn't been injured and jacked up on snake venom. He'd been offered the chance to relinquish the duty to someone else, and the fact that he'd chosen not to humbled her.

He got to his feet. "Hey. How are you?"

Sad. Tired. Wanting to curl up in a blanket. He probably felt the same way. Cassie settled for complaining. "Nobody here thinks I'm funny."

His eyes kindled with sympathy. "At least you're all done now."

As they walked down a corridor tiled in the same marble as the hallway, Cassie asked him something she'd wondered about while Dr. Morales had had her rubber gloves all up in her business. "Did a lot of people grow up in this group, like you and Val did?"

He opened the door to what at first looked like a massive greenhouse. Cassie hadn't seen this glass ceiling and walls from the front entrance. Potted trees and benches, some occupied with people reading or chatting, lined the perimeter of the space. "Yeah, it's a family thing," he said. "That's mostly how Manus Sancti works."

She followed him out to the middle of this huge glass room. "What's Manus Sancti?"

The main part of the floor was also clear glass, showing through to depths below. People rose and descended on glass elevators, revealing moving mechanical parts that made her a little dizzy. Below lay stories upon stories of floors, all transparent, held up and bordered by white girders. People walked here and there, and their footsteps and the sound of the escalators blended into a hum. Cassie's mouth fell open.

Jonathan said, "We're Manus Sancti."

CHAPTER ELEVEN

THEY STEPPED ONTO the elevator, and Jonathan nodded at the woman who already stood there. Her eyebrows rose almost to the top of her purple hijab at the sight of a *sonámbula,* but she merely nodded back. Jonathan pressed the button to go to thirty-two. After the woman got off on level twelve, Cassie said, "I didn't even know you could build something this deep underground. Not in the desert."

It made sense that she'd think of how hard the ground was here, since she'd worked for a mining company. "Most of it was constructed on a natural cave system. But the same architect designed something like it in China. A secret government building."

"I never heard of it."

"Well, yeah," he said.

They stepped out of the elevator. Cassie looked down at the glass floor beneath her feet, and then around at the dozens of full-sized potted trees surrounding the elevator bank. "People must know about this place, though. It's so huge."

As he led her down the corridor, he said, "We're out in the middle of nowhere." He touched the back of her arm, indicating that they needed to turn a corner, and let his fingers rest there a few moments longer than was really necessary. "Some people know this place is bigger than it looks, but they have no idea how much bigger. A bunch of the floors are archives and collections, though."

"Wouldn't it be easier to rent storage units?"

His smiled at the thought. "These are things that need a little more security than that."

She looked up. "Whoa. Mirror ceiling."

"It's one-way glass. It lets light shine through, but you can't see up at people." It caused the light to undulate, the weak shadows bobbing and lengthening. The movement of people walking about them interrupted the light like leaves on a quaking tree.

Cassie paused to look around more closely, and he stopped immediately as well. "What if there's a heavy rain? We always worried about the miners because of that. Or an earthquake?"

"The floors are designed to float a little, and the girders are flexible." He tapped the railing. "And there's a high-tech drainage and dehumidification system. It's more protected from the elements than any traditional building."

"You must save a lot on energy bills, being down here in the ground."

"Yeah, and we have our own power source." Jonathan found himself enjoying the unfamiliar role of tour guide. "Plus part of it's designed to withstand a nuclear blast. If there were a disaster, we could get by down here for several years."

"You guys *are* survivalist nutjobs."

"But we're so much more than that."

She grinned at this, gratifying him. As they walked on, she said, "This place must have cost a fortune to build. I can't even imagine."

"It did. We mostly used workers from India and Bangladesh—that way, no one in this country would be talking about the job later. Officially, they were here to build a casino." The cover story had been a huge effort on the part of the Diviners and the accountants.

"Hmph. I hope you paid them well."

He liked that she thought of that. "Better than average American workers. They finished building about ten years ago."

"But you guys are way older than that, right?" A yawn overtook her.

He yawned, too, because he'd seen her do it. "Our original headquarters were in Granada. We go back to the middle of the fifteenth century."

"West." Capitán Renaud's deep voice came from behind them. Jonathan spun around, touching the heel of his right fist to his sternum in an automatic salute. "Capitán."

Cassie's eyes narrowed, scrutinizing him. In his expensive suit, Capitán probably appeared to her more or less like a CEO of a Fortune 500 company. He was white with thinning hair, more gray than blond. His close-set eyes under the low, pronounced ridge of his brow gave him a feral look. "So this is the woman you brought from Phoenix. Has she been stable since you arrived?"

"Nice to meet you, too," Cassie muttered, worrying Jonathan. This was not the time for her sarcasm.

He answered, "Yes. No problems."

"I look forward to Val's report. Even down here, spiders and snakes are a concern. One incident, I *will* have her neutralized."

"Understood." He was grateful Capitán hadn't wanted it done immediately.

"You give the journal to Dimitriou?"

"Yes, sir." Cassie shot him an accusing look. He'd forgotten to tell her that he'd taken her grandfather's journal to Lucia Dimitriou, as he'd been instructed. "We're meeting with her tomorrow."

"Keep me updated." Capitán Renaud turned and walked away.

"Who has the journal?" Cassie asked, keeping her voice down.

"One of the Scholars. They're the only ones who can help you reverse that spell." They went a little further and Jonathan said, "Here we are." He stood close to one side of the metal door, and a small green light appeared on a panel on the wall. The door slid aside.

"Did you unlock that with your tattoo?" Cassie asked.

"Yeah. They keyed it to me." He followed her inside, and behind them, the door slid soundlessly closed again. Cassie peered around the interior. The brushed steel walls of the small room had rounded corners and a microwave and a television built in. A full-sized bed nestled into the opposite wall, and a partition stood between the sink, toilet, and shower.

"You'll stay here for the night, and then in the morning, we'll talk to Lucia," he told her. "You probably won't run into Capitán Renaud again soon, but if you do, you'll want to…" He searched for the right phrase.

"Not kill him with animals?"

"That, and not be a smartass."

Anger flashed in her eyes. "Don't tell me how to talk."

Damn it. He'd hit a nerve, and he should've known better. There was nothing she hated more than being censored. He didn't blame her. "Believe me, I don't want to. I just want everything to go okay for you."

She sighed and sat down on the only chair, a sleek metal form not far from the bed. "What's his actual name?"

"Victor Renaud."

"He seems like kind of a dick."

Jonathan couldn't help but bristle. "He almost died saving my father's life in Granada."

"Still seems like a dick," she muttered, more subdued. "Were they on a mission together?"

"No. But they were both Knights at the time. It was a coup attempt—very bloody. When Granada was still the headquarters."

"Jesus," she breathed.

"It went on for three days. A faction of Knights and Mages

turned on everyone else, killed the captain and several others immediately, and cast a powerful binding spell."

"Were you there?"

"Both my parents were. Michael and I were just kids. We were at the apartment by ourselves. We didn't know why they hadn't come home."

"Did you call the police?"

Jonathan gave a mirthless laugh. "We were raised to avoid the authorities. I mean, we wouldn't have called the fire department if we were on fire. We tried to get ahold of another Manus Sancti family, but their parents were gone, too."

"You poor kids! What caused the uprising?"

"That's a really long story." He was too tired to explain the intricacies of Manus Sancti politics and the supernatural state of Algeria in decades past. "But Renaud was able to organize this brilliant counterattack in four different places. The traitors were put down. And when my father got hurt, Renaud got hit with a scalding spell blast while dragging him to cover."

"Wow." She gave him a rueful smile. "I'll show more respect."

He sat down on the edge of the bed.

She said, "And your father's in Granada now."

He nodded. "He's the *comandante* there."

"Is Capitán Renaud his boss?"

"Yes, but each *guaría* mostly operates on its own."

She threaded her fingers through her tangled hair. "What did your mom do?"

"Um, she was a Mage. A psychic, like Val. She went on missions, though." He *really* didn't want to go into that.

She shifted in her chair. "I ask too many questions."

"Of course you're curious."

She kicked off one sandal and then the other, scowling down at them as though they'd wronged her. "I'm thirsty. And hungry." She was probably starving.

He got up and pulled at a panel in the wall to reveal the compact but well-stocked refrigerator and freezer. "You should be able to find something."

"Great." She hopped up and came over to survey the bottles of water, green tea, juice, and beer lining the inside of the door. "I wish they had dark beer."

"They have it at the cantina."

"The cantina? This place has everything." She sighed. "I'm too tired to leave the room again. And you must be exhausted."

"Kind of," he admitted.

"Any beer sounds about perfect right now." She grabbed one of the bottles, unscrewed the cap, and scanned the rest of the food on the shelves, selecting an orange and a sandwich on a thick bun.

He showed her the control panel near the bed for the lights, TV, thermostat, and alarm clock. "If you need anything, press this button to call me. And there are spare clothes in here." He touched the duffel bag at the bottom of the bed with his foot.

"Seriously?" She came over, setting her beer and food on the chair, and crouched down almost at his feet to unzip the suitcase. "Oh my gosh, look." She held up flannel pajamas in a vintage cowgirl print. "These are hilarious."

"They look comfortable at least."

"I think I kind of love them." She examined a pair of jeans. "These are exactly my size. Waist and inseam. Whoever packed this must be a genius."

"That would be Nic." Too many of that man's talents were wasted as a mission runner. Nonetheless, his friend's resourcefulness in that role was almost legendary.

She held up a pair of plain white bikini panties. "This is my exact kind of underwear!"

He could imagine peeling them off her. As exhausted as he was, the flash of fantasy woke up his senses and stirred his cock to life. Jonathan closed his eyes briefly and reminded himself that she wasn't deliberately trying to drive him crazy. "I'll leave you alone."

"Yeah. I should take a shower."

The image of her in the shower was almost more than he could take. He nodded and left the room.

As the door clicked and locked behind him, he felt a weary relief and satisfaction. She was safe, unharmed, and at least at the moment, unlikely to endanger anyone else. As he headed back to his own quarters, his phone buzzed, and he took it out of his pocket. She was calling him already? He answered. "Hey Cassie, what's up?"

"Nothing! I didn't mean to call you. I was trying to turn on the bathroom light."

A smile spread across his face. "I forgot to tell you. There's a separate panel for the bathroom lights. On the left."

"Oh! Okay. Thanks."

"Good night, Cassie."

CHAPTER TWELVE

CASSIE DREAMED SHE was back at Mission Minerals, having been out of the office for weeks. Angry emails from neglected clients filled her inbox, and while she struggled to compose an answer to one of them, Ana came to her cubicle to tell her that another group of clients was waiting for her presentation. It was going to be her first presentation ever, since that was usually her boss's job. She went to the conference room and said hello to the visitors while trying to remember what the hell she was supposed to talk to them about.

When she woke up, her first thought was relief: just a dream. Then she recalled why she was in a tiny studio apartment that looked like a spaceship. *Oh, sure. This is a much better situation.*

But strangely, she kind of felt like it was. The dream lingered in her mind, not because of the anxiety, but because the work itself had been so useless, it almost broke her heart. *Mission Minerals*. That had been a joke. Other than helping them wreck the earth for as much money as possible, she hadn't had a mission there at all.

Jonathan came by her room before long, and she went with him to the library at El Dédalo. "Wow," she said when they walked in the door. It was about ten stories tall with clear shelves. Walls of books floated below and above her.

"This is only part of the collection," he said as they walked through the stacks. "They keep the older and rarer texts in the dark."

"In the dark literally or figuratively?"

"Both."

"It's bigger than any city library I've ever seen," she said. "How many people are here, anyway? In the whole place."

"About a thousand, including children."

"Children live here?" she squeaked. She could hardly imagine that. Underground like a bunch of baby moles in a nest.

"Not many. Most families get assigned to one of the *guarídas*. So they live in normal houses and apartments. But there are some. Gabi's kids mostly grew up here."

Cassie stopped walking. "Gabi's a mom?"

"Yes. She and Andre are both pretty needed here at headquarters—"

"Gabi's a mom," she repeated.

He gave her a wry look. "Still yes."

Cassie tried to square the daredevil-driving, rapist-killing warrior she knew with motherhood. "How does she take care of kids when she's running around shooting demons?"

"You can't actually shoot demons. You can block them with metal or stone, but bullets don't affect them. If they possess a human, you can only kill the human."

"That's not the point," she said. "Who takes care of the kids?"

"Andre was always here. And Gabi's sister. But her boys are teenagers now. The older one might go to Athens soon."

He stopped at a red door, rapped on it twice, and waited. A woman in an untucked flannel shirt opened it. Her hair, dirty blond with dark roots, was a mess, and her bangs fell half in front of her glasses. It took Cassie a moment to notice that the woman's eyes were a striking crystalline green. Circles below them suggested a lack of sleep. Although she appeared to be a few years older than Cassie, she also looked something like a college student during a particularly rough finals week.

Jonathan said, "*Salaam*, Lucia."

"*Salaam*." She cast a look of keen interest in Cassie's direction. "You must be Cassandra Rios."

"Call me Cassie."

"Please, come in. Give me a couple of minutes. I need a break and more coffee."

Cassie wondered what kind of accent Lucia had. Dimitriou sounded like a Greek name to her, though she wasn't positive. The Scholar trotted off, and Cassie followed Jonathan inside. Neat stacks of paper lined the huge L-shaped desk, and a big world map covered one wall, stuck with clusters of white pins. Dozens of square photos tiled another wall. Several pictured a handsome man with heavy-lidded eyes, a short moustache and beard, and shiny, coiffed, dark hair. In one, he was kissing Lucia. "Cute couple," Cassie said, pointing to it. "Is he a Knight?"

Jonathan came over to her. "Yeah, that's her fiancé, Samir Hassan. I killed a Black Dog with him in Manchester."

"You killed a what?"

"Not a real dog. A barghest." She must have had a blank expression, because he added, "Something bad."

The people in a few of the photos looked like Lucia's parents and siblings, but most of them seemed to be friends. Jonathan's gaze lingered on a picture of a woman with porcelain skin and bright red lipstick raising a glass of wine toward the camera. Cassie said, "She's pretty."

"We broke up."

Her head swiveled in his direction. "What?"

"Um. That's Sophie Kazakov. She basically broke up with Manus Sancti."

"You used to date her," she said.

"When we were both in London."

Her looks contrasted sharply with Cassie's, with her turned-up nose and fine blond hair in a pixie cut. She looked like a Russian elf model. Did he always date tiny blondes? Maybe Cassie wasn't his type. "How long were you together?" As if that were her business.

"Almost two years."

Pretty serious, then. Cassie kept her voice light as she asked, "Did you ever think about getting married, having kids, the whole nine?"

Jonathan rubbed at his shoulder. "She, uh, doesn't want kids."

Well, this was interesting. "Do you? Is that why you broke up?"

"No." He shrugged. "I mean, we fought about it."

Cassie snorted. "Why would you try to argue someone into having kids? How is that going to end well?"

"She's a psychometrist." For a moment, Cassie thought he said *psychologist*, but he went on to explain. "She can learn things about people just by touching something they touched. It's a rare gift. But a daughter would probably inherit it."

"A daughter she didn't want." Cassie had wanted kids once. When she'd first broached the subject with Rick, he'd wanted to put it off until he got another promotion. By the time he'd done that, things had gotten so bad between them that Cassie hadn't wanted to bring a baby into the mess.

"It wasn't the only thing we fought about," Jonathan said dryly. He walked away from the wall of photos and took a seat in one of the clear acrylic chairs. "We broke up a month before she left."

"Why did she leave?"

"It hardly ever happens." His brows drew together as though he were considering how much to say. "Her cousin was a Knight in London, and he was…killed on a mission by another

Knight." Cassie took in a sharp breath and he looked up at her. "On accident."

This didn't dampen her shock. "How do you kill your partner by accident?"

He closed his eyes briefly. "It's so much easier than you might think. It happened in Delhi last year. In this case, it was also her cousin's mistake that got him killed. We all screw up sometimes."

"But that probably didn't make her feel any better," Cassie guessed.

"She was devastated. He was basically her best friend. She wanted the other guy kicked out, or worse, which didn't happen. *Actus non facit reum nisi mens sit rea.*"

Cassie recalled the gist of the saying. "You're not guilty if you didn't mean to do it."

"Right. I said something like that to her—which didn't help. Capitán Renaud and the *comandante* in London said the same thing. She broke up with me, she was furious with everyone, and she left."

"Jesus." Cassie looked back at Lucia's wall. No one would have guessed, from all of the smiling faces, that they dealt with these kinds of tragedies. "So they let you guys leave if you want to?"

"No. Nobody can find her."

Cassie peered at him. "I would've thought you guys could find anybody."

"Sophie's different. She can hack any computer, get money out of any ATM machine." *Damn.* Why couldn't Cassie have wound up with powers like that? Not that she would steal from people, but still… "Plus she knows all of our tricks. She just disappeared. They looked for a while, and then I think they gave up."

"Aren't they worried she'll go to the media and tell them all about you?"

He shook his head. "They'd think she was crazy. But anyway, she'd never do that. Her family's still with us."

Lucia came back, interrupting Cassie's lesson about how incredible Jonathan's ex was, and set her coffee well out of reach. "Pull up a chair." As Jonathan and Cassie complied, Lucia pulled on rubber surgical gloves, covering up an emerald ring in an ornate yellow gold setting on her left ring finger. "Let's talk about the codex."

Cassie said, "The what?"

She took down Cassie's grandfather's journal from a shelf. With a gloved forefinger and thumb, she flipped through the pages. It struck Cassie as silly. It was an old journal, not the Dead Sea Scrolls. "Here is the page you read aloud, yes?" A guilty, prickly heat rose on the back of Cassie's neck as she nodded. Lucia knew the trouble she'd caused. "It matches no written language in existence."

What the hell? Jonathan leaned forward in his chair as she continued to explain.

"They handed this project over to me because, given your great-grandfather's explorations, it was easy to guess that this was a phonetic transliteration of ancient Mayan. It's a specialty of mine. Well, I began with Egyptian hieroglyphics and moved on to Mesoamerican languages. But this is a different form of the language than any on record." Her green eyes took on a nerdy sparkle. "There are thirty-two modern variations, not all of them formally recognized. But this"—she pointed at the page without quite touching it—"this is proto-Mayan. Maybe twelve hundred, thirteen hundred years old."

Cassie stared at the page. "Holy smokes."

"When your great-grandfather was digging in the Yucatán, he found something very interesting. He makes a reference in his journal to a certain Mayan codex, one lost to the entire world."

Cassie asked, "A codex is like an old manuscript, right?"

"Yes." She pulled a huge black leather book with no title down from another shelf. "How much do you know about the Mayans?"

"Hardly anything. They were native Americans, they knew a lot about astrology, they built amazing buildings. Then the Spanish wiped them out."

"Not exactly. There are seven or eight million Maya still." She opened the big volume. Printed, full-color drawings of hieroglyphs, all in rounded square shapes like keys on a keyboard, filled the page. Looking closer, Cassie could see human and animal faces in the little pictures. Lines and dots separated some of the rows. "Three authentic codices by the Mayans from before the time of Columbus exist today. They contain information about astrology, as you say, and horoscopes, as well as religious rituals and ceremonies."

"I guess most of the books disintegrated, huh," Cassie said.

She looked pained. "Doubtless some of them did. The jungles of Mexico and Central America aren't the best environment for preservation. But the Spanish colonists burned hundreds of books and destroyed countless other objects and artifacts carrying inscriptions. At that time—the mid-sixteenth-century—many of those records were already hundreds of years old."

"My God." Cassie wasn't a book lover the way Lucia was, but this still made her feel ill. "Why? What were they about?"

"Of course, we don't know. The Spanish couldn't read them. But their understanding was that many of them contained Mayan history, religious rituals, and beliefs. Bishop Diego De Landa wrote of one such burning that the books contained 'superstition and lies of the devil'." Lucia pushed her glasses up on her nose. "This is the language of the witch trials."

"What a waste." To lose books forever—it was almost hard to imagine, now that pretty much everything was on the Internet.

"About a hundred years ago, we obtained four letters from a priest employed by Montejo the Elder, one of the Spanish invaders. In one, he writes about a magical spell that caused several soldiers to be unable to raise their swords." Her mouth quirked.

"It's unclear if they referred to weapons or virility. Regardless, the suspected shaman was slowly tortured to death."

"That's a horrible story."

"The point is, we've long believed that some of the destroyed codices contained powerful magic." She took a deep breath. "And that's why your great-grandfather's journal is so exciting. I've come up with a rough translation of this page you read aloud."

Cassie sat up straighter. "Let me see it!"

"As I say, it's still very rough. Essentially, it begins by calling on the privilege of your bloodline."

"My what?" Cassie asked.

"It refers to your family inheritance—a spiritual or magical one."

As smart as this woman was, she seemed to be missing a very obvious point. "I'm not Mayan."

She pointed at Cassie, her eyes dancing with glee. "We'll get back to that. Then it calls on the birds of the air, the beasts that walk the earth, the insects and snakes that creep on the ground, and the fish that swim in the sea to be linked to your heart and to defend you from all mortal and immortal enemies."

Cassie stared at her. Finally, she said, "There haven't been any birds or fish yet."

"Attack fish," Jonathan muttered. "I'd like to see that."

Lucia shook her head in disbelief. "I don't think you understand. Almost all of the Mayan lore was lost. All that knowledge, that insight. And this—" She waved her arms. "A lost codex. A spell from four thousand years ago, at least. And it *works*. This is an astounding find."

It wasn't *their* astounding find. Cassie put her hand on the book and slid it across the table to rest in front of her. Lucia flinched, maybe because she didn't think Cassie was treating it carefully enough.

Jonathan cleared his throat. "How do you know this is from a codex?"

"He refers to it." Lucia reached over and delicately flipped a few pages back. "The word is encrypted, as are some others in his writings, but it's a simple enough code. We're positive he found a Mayan manuscript."

"This does all sound amazing," Cassie said. "But can we go back to the part about how I'm not Mayan?"

Lucia pointed at Cassie again. "But you are. From the buccal swab, Dr. Morales tested your DNA, and it coincides with our genealogical research." She pulled out a piece of paper from a stack and folded it out into a chart. "This shows your family tree to twelve generations back." Cassie looked down at the sheet of paper, stunned and a little excited. No one had ever told her much about her history. "Also, according to his journal, your great-grandfather was deliberately searching for artifacts of his ancestors, based on family stories passed down from generations."

They knew so much more about her and her family than she did. "How did you get all this done already?"

"Jonathan sent me a photo of the journal page you read from a couple of days ago." He must have done it right after they'd retrieved the book from her parents' house. It made sense, but it bothered Cassie that he hadn't told her. "And we have good researchers and good computer programs."

"Still. Don't you ever sleep?"

She apparently regarded this as a rhetorical question. "Look here." She pointed to a name above Rodrigo De La Garza. "Your great-great-grandmother, Jacinta De La Garza. Maiden name Canul, born in Campeche, daughter of Mayan revolutionaries."

"Wow." Cassie felt a glimmer of pride for this ancestor she'd never heard of before this moment. "She sounds like a badass."

Jonathan asked, "Lucia, can any person with Mayan ancestry use the same spell as Cassie?"

"I need to refine the translation, but based on the way it's written and similar spells we've seen, we suspect one has to be a direct descendant. And there's probably more than one spell. I haven't translated the other two pages yet."

Cassie said, "Maybe the other two spells make plants and minerals attack people." Lucia flashed a grin. Finally, somebody thought she was funny. "Did my great-grandfather ever say the animal spell?"

"According to the journal, no. He knew it was a spell, but he was struggling to translate it, so he didn't say the words aloud." Lucia smiled. "Smart man."

"Even if the spells only work for direct descendants," Jonathan said, "with a book that old, there must be thousands of people it would work for."

Lucia nodded. "Yes, even given how thoroughly the Europeans decimated the indigenous Mesoamerican populations. We could track many of them down if we wanted to. There's no one in Manus Sancti. We only have two others with specifically Mayan ancestry, and they have no connection." She tapped the ancestry chart. "As far as Cassie's immediate relatives, they are surprisingly few and far between. Her great-great-grandmother Jacinta had five siblings, all of whom died of typhus, along with her mother. Rodrigo was Jacinta's only child, because her husband was murdered not long after his birth, apparently in connection to their revolutionary activities. Cassie here, her mother, her sister, and her great-aunt in Tapachula are the only heirs we've found so far." Cassie hadn't even known she had a great-aunt.

She put her hand on the open journal. Maybe there would be other spells, like one that made everything one touched turn to gold. Wait, no, that story ended up bad. But maybe a spell to teleport or to make someone fall in love with her. The possibilities were endless.

Or maybe it would be more horrible spells that she'd never

want to utter, and she could just burn the thing. "Do you know how to reverse the animal attacks yet?"

Lucia blew her floppy bangs out of her eyes. "We haven't gotten that far."

"Maybe it says how in this codex. Does the journal say where it is?"

She tilted her head. "I was hoping you could help with that. Does your family have any more of your great-grandfather's belongings?"

Cassie shook her head. "Hardly anything, as far as I know. I found a few things in the basement. A photo of my great-grandma, an old toy army tank, and a key."

"The toy is probably just a memento of the war," she mused.

"Which one?"

"The Spanish Civil War. De La Garza went to fight for the republic. He was already in his late thirties by then."

Did Cassie's mom know about that? Probably. She never told her anything.

Lucia stood up to take a big swig of her coffee before returning it to the shelf. "The key is interesting. Rodrigo made one reference to guarding the codex in a hidden place."

Cassie had tossed all the stuff into her big purse. "It's in my room if you want to see it."

Her mouth parted. "Yes, definitely."

"I have that tank, too."

She shrugged. "We should look at anything that belonged to him. But the key may be, well, the key we're looking for."

"Okay, but I need them back. And I'll take the journal now."

Lucia cast a worried glance at Jonathan. She told Cassie, "I still need to translate the next two pages of Mayan."

"Right." She frowned down at the volume. "I wish I could read it."

Lucia brightened. "I almost forgot. We did translate the rest of it into English, if you're curious."

Cassie blinked at her. "Seriously?"

"Yes. All of the portions that are in Spanish—the journal entries." From the bottom of the stack of papers, she pulled out a blue binder. "Would you like them?"

"Yes!" Cassie grabbed the binder. "I'll read it right here."

Jonathan said, "Actually, you're going to need to go back to your quarters."

"I just came from my quarters!"

"I have to meet with Capitán Renaud."

"Why?" They'd just seen each other in the hallway. But he would have read Val's report since then. "Are you in trouble?"

"Nothing serious," he said, which Cassie took as a yes. She gave an exasperated sigh. Hero or not, his boss seemed hard on people. And as nice as her little spaceship capsule was, she didn't care to live there.

Lucia said cheerfully, "You'll need time to read, anyway."

CHAPTER THIRTEEN

ER GREAT-GRANDFATHER'S JOURNAL began with days of entries about preparing for an archeological expedition. At first, this made her swell with pride, having this ancestor who was so educated and adventurous.

It was strange, too, because she'd always thought of her mom's side of the family as the non-Mexican side. Her dad's grandparents had all been born in Mexico, though both of his parents had been born in the U.S. But on her mom's side, other than Grandpa De La Garza, they were English and German and Irish.

This ancestor in Mexico was impressive, but definitely sexist. One day, he wrote:

I had an unexpected and unwelcome interruption in the form of a lady all the way from Denmark. My correspondent, Mr. Thompson, referred her to me. What possible grudge Thompson may hold against me, I cannot imagine, unless he is still offended by my telling him that there is no possible way the Mayans are the descendants of the lost continent of Atlantis...

This woman, Theska Nygaard—who claims to be a botanist, by which I assume she dabbles in watercolor—has nonsensical theories about plant populations and wishes to join our expedition. I have put her off for now, saying I do not know when or if we will begin, which is not far from the truth.

He at least wasn't so much of a dick that he couldn't listen to his mother. According to her, a site in the Yucatán held the remains of their Mayan ancestors. His mother believed they had possessed magical powers.

Of course. I cannot give credit to any of my mother's or grand-mother's tales of the occult. Such things must be anathema to scientific thought. And yet, I seek above all else evidence of magical beliefs, because they would be invaluable to History and to anyone who studies the mind of Man. These are the reasons for my obsession, and no man of learning could scorn them.

"Liar," Cassie whispered. He wanted the magic.

He begged sponsorship from wealthy patrons, bought provisions, rented mules, hired assistants, and then went to a certain little village in the middle of nowhere, seeking a guide to a site he'd heard of but didn't know exactly where it was. He found a boy in the village who claimed he could take them there. Then his expedition got delayed by torrential rain, and he spent three weeks at the inn, complaining at length about the terrible food and the unexpected expense.

The delay gave him no choice but to talk more with Theska, a professor and the widow of a well-to-do businessman, who finally convinced him to let her come along. Cassie skimmed past pages of muddy slogging and insect bites.

At about three in the afternoon, one of the hired men in front of me shouted, "Over there!"

When I first looked in the direction of his pointing finger, there was nothing. Then I saw it—a column of perhaps seven or eight feet high, so covered in green vines and lichens as to scarcely be distinguishable from the surrounding jungle. And a second one, almost as tall— who knew what the original height had been?—about ten feet away.

I crashed through the brush toward the structures, hacking at a bush in my way. Between the pillars—my heart stuttered in my chest—I could just make out the remains of a dozen stairs. Time and vegetation had nearly turned them into a green slope, but some footsteps—those of the boy and his friends, perhaps—had revealed their shape.

Next, he described how he and one of his men were yanking plants away from a carved wall. Theska Nygaard yelled at them to stop because they were ripping out the rare orchids she'd been seeking. Rodrigo realized that in their hurry, they were also damaging the hieroglyphs they wanted to reveal. Some of the crumbling stone came right off with the vines.

Soon after this, Rodrigo confessed in his diary that he'd developed an "uncommonly warm regard" for Theska. This led to charming old-school flirting. Cassie scrambled for the family tree chart Lucia had given her. Yes, Theska was her great-grandmother.

Cassie kept reading. Rodrigo possessed an inhuman amount of energy, and she wasn't surprised when she came across a reference to his taking cocaine tablets. He'd purchased them at a hardware store. None of his hired men shared his enthusiasm for continuing to dig around in the underground passage at all hours of the night, by the light of kerosene lanterns. Finally, Cassie came to the passage that must have made Lucia's jaw drop.

I have found it—a treasure beyond anything I have ever dared to imagine. See how my hand shakes as I write this—I can scarcely form the letters—and I am grateful for this infirmity, for it lets me know this is real—I am awake. I WILL dare to write of this thing—though where I hide it, I shall not say—and I will not speak of it, certainly not to these hired oafs, not even to my beloved Theska.

I believe this codex to be more ancient, even, than the famous book in Dresden. To translate it will be an arduous task, but I believe it to contain the secrets of my mother's and grandmother's tales. I have no proof of this. But did they not tell me of this place? One might say that this is a feverish fancy, brought on by the jungle—but did the book not call me here? It is dawn, and the men are waking—I will write more later—

"Hey Cassie, it's me." Jonathan's voice was quiet, but she still jumped as it filled the room. "I'm outside your door."

Her imagination dragged itself out of the nineteenth-century Mexican jungle and back into reality. She'd taken off her bra and only wore a tank top with her jeans, but since he'd already seen her go through security, it probably didn't matter that much. "Come on in."

He closed the door behind him. In the artificial light of the windowless room, his face was half in shadow, emphasizing the lines of his cheekbones and jaw. "How's the reading?"

"It's fascinating." She swung her bare feet onto the floor. "My great-grandfather was always looking for that codex—his mom and his grandma told him about it. Those stories in his family must have gone back forever. Can you imagine what it must have been like for him? To find something he always wanted?"

Jonathan dropped his gaze. "It must have been overwhelming."

"And there's stuff in there about him and my great-grandma falling in love. It's too adorable for words." He smiled briefly at this, but said nothing. "I wanted to call my mom and tell her about it, but my phone doesn't work."

"No, yours wouldn't."

His matter-of-fact tone deflated her. The curved walls seemed even closer than usual.

"What's wrong?" he asked. She knew he wasn't an empath like Morty or Val, but he immediately noticed her slight change in mood.

"Nothing." This was a lie, and she shook her head. "I feel like I'm on another planet here. And I'm... I feel so on my own."

He took a few steps to sit on the metal chair next to the bed. "You're not."

Her heartbeat quickened. She shouldn't make more of his

simple words than he intended. "Did everything go okay with your boss?"

He shrugged. "He didn't like me giving you a gun."

"Why did you?"

"I didn't know if your animals would show up or how long it would take. If things went wrong, I couldn't leave you defenseless."

Warmth spread through Cassie's chest and belly. "Did you talk about anything else?"

"I told him what Lucia said about the codex. And he thinks I'm the best person to… Well, to look after you. Val's report said that you had—formed a bond with me." He cleared his throat. "Which she thought would keep you from unleashing your powers here. So that's good."

What was good? That she'd become attached to him? Or that she wouldn't trigger the spell in their cyber-terrarium? She stared at his large hands at rest, his long fingers interlaced.

His gaze on her was steady. "What are you thinking about?"

Shit. She really wanted to kiss him, but he'd pushed her away before. A rejection would be even more humiliating the second time around. "You're the mind reader."

A whisper of a smile crossed his face. "I can't do it without physical contact."

Her heart stuttered. She was almost sure he wanted the same thing she did, but if he didn't… "That's what I was thinking about."

He leaned over and crushed her lips under his in a fierce kiss. Immediately, her mouth parted under his, inviting him to go deeper. Liquid heat poured through her body. Breaking off the kiss, he tugged her lower lip between his teeth, and a small sound came from the back of her throat.

She was still sitting on the edge of the low bed. He stripped off her tank top, wincing as he raised his arms—because of the stitches, she realized. He kneeled between her knees, the better to give and to take. His mouth assaulted hers again, one of his hands cupping the back of her skull, his thumb grazing across her jaw. He hauled her hips to fit against him and through his jeans, she could feel his emphatic hardness.

God, he was making her dizzy. She held on to his shoulders. His teeth scraped her skin on the side of her neck, making her breath shake in her lungs. He buried his fingers into her hair and tilted her head back to capture her lips in an even more ravenous kiss. He acted like an addict with the best drug in the world, and he was making her melt as though in a spoon over a flame.

She pulled off his T-shirt, taking care because of his healing back. He lowered his head to nuzzle his rough, stubbled cheek against her breasts. His tongue lashed over the tip of one. She gasped as his mouth closed over it and sucked, sending rivulets of pure pleasure through her.

He released her, pushed her gently back on the bed, and pulled off her jeans and underwear at the same time, leaving her completely bare. Stretching his half-naked body over hers, one forearm braced on either side of her head, he overwhelmed her with more kisses. He smelled like the desert after rain.

She reached down to pluck at the top button of his jeans. He caught her hand and pinned it above her head as he touched his lips to the hollow of her throat. The dominating gesture ratcheted up her lust. "Jonathan, please," she begged, needing more. He stroked his hand between her legs, and his growl of approval reverberated through her body. She was soaking wet.

As he kissed and nipped at her neck and breasts, his fingers pressed flat against her most sensitive place, circling it. She cried out, pushing herself harder against his firm, insistent hand.

He pulled back enough to watch her as he drove her out of her mind. "God, Cassie." His low voice carried pure reverence. "I've dreamed about you constantly." She was in no state to make a coherent reply. It had been so long, and he felt so good. Not just because of what he was doing, but because he was

Jonathan—heroic, conflicted, beautiful. The tension rose in her, exquisite, maddening, pulling desperate moans from her lips.

And then she came apart, hopelessly and gloriously, crying out his name. Waves of pleasure rocked through her, and he laughed close to her ear, a low sound of satisfaction and delight. It was the sexiest thing she'd ever heard.

He got up to shuck off his jeans and underwear, his thick, veined cock standing up almost straight against his belly. Cassie stared at him, half wasted on orgasm, hazily thanking God or fate or whatever had brought her together with him. He grabbed a foil packet from a pocket in his jeans and tore it open. *Good.* He slid the condom over his length, stretched over her again, and buried himself in her to the hilt. "Ah *God*," he groaned, his voice guttural, stirring her body and heart at once. He slammed deep into her again and again. He was like a wild animal. And she loved it.

It didn't last long. With a low, hoarse cry, he reached his climax. His head bowed, and she ran her shaky hand over his buzzed hair.

He retreated long enough to throw away the condom in the bathroom and came back to bed to stretch out alongside her. His breath still came fast and he closed his eyes. "*Christos.*"

She snuggled into the crook of his arm. Every cell of her body glowed with a primal relief. She hadn't had sex since she'd gotten divorced, and she and Rick had stopped doing it several months before Cassie had moved out. She would've been happy even if she hadn't liked Jonathan so much, and his intensity gratified her to the core. Maybe he was that way in bed with everyone. She was happy regardless. "Do you always carry protection?"

"Ha, no." His voice was lazy. "I picked some up at medical when you were getting all those tests done."

"You sneak," she said, delighted. "So I didn't do *such* a bad job of trying to seduce you before."

He huffed, as though this were the understatement of the

year. "I've wanted you since… Well, since I was in your head. I couldn't stop thinking about it."

"I'm glad you decided it was okay."

He opened his eyes to gaze at her. "I still don't know if this is right. But I couldn't resist. Or I didn't want to."

Leaning over, she pressed her lips against his cheek. "Good thing you don't have to."

She got up to pee and when she came back, he was asleep. He'd pulled the comforter partly over himself, and the small silver crucifix he wore hung askew on his chest. It was no wonder he was tired after their encounter. He was still healing. The guileless look on his face and the way one of his arms was flung over his head made her smile.

It was really too bad her cell phone didn't work. She would have loved to text Ana and her sister Sam, demanding virtual high fives. Instead, she took a shower. Part of her regretted rinsing his scent from her body, which still tingled with satisfaction. After putting on a fresh pair of underwear and a T-shirt, she came over and sat on the bed, watching his chest rise and fall with every breath as she combed out the tangles in her wet hair.

A drop of water splashed him. His body jerked and his eyes flew open. Seeing her, he relaxed. "Didn't mean to fall asleep."

"That's okay." She smiled. "I was just watching you like a creep."

"Creep away." He grabbed her hand and pressed his lips against the tops of her fingers, an impulsive gesture that charmed her.

"I still wish I could mind-read you," she said. "Go into your psyche."

He gave her a sympathetic look. "You can't. Val made extra sure."

"It's not fair," she grumbled. "What's your psyche look like?"

A shadow passed over his features. "Some Mages used to be able to do that, you know," he said, changing the subject. "Bring other people into their own psyche, instead of going into theirs. It's one of the Lost Gifts, like prophecy."

Since she couldn't look into his soul, she let her gaze wander over his body instead. She discovered a shiny line on his upper arm she hadn't seen before and drew her finger across it. "You have a lot of scars."

"I know, I'm a mess," he said matter-of-factly.

"I didn't mean it looked bad." She traced a finger around his back, as far as she could reach, without touching the stitches. "And now you have new ones because of me."

"Worth it." The words warmed Cassie from within. "The stitches are coming out in a few days."

She drew the sheet all of the way aside to look at him. He didn't object. She traced the star tattoo. "Does this mean anything? I mean, the symbol?"

"When they first started using it, there were twelve *guardías*. There were for a long time, actually. So they used a twelve-pointed star."

"How many are there now?"

"Fifty-two."

"Why don't they use a fifty-two-pointed star?"

He cast a dubious look down. "It would look like a hairball."

"Well, a lot of big organizations kind of are hairballs," she said, thinking of Mission Minerals.

"We can be sometimes. And we're not even that big."

"Why'd you guys start getting tattoos? To feel like badasses?"

He laughed. "It's in a place where not everyone's going to see it, but if you needed to prove to someone else that you were really Manus Sancti, you could show it to them."

Her mental picture of this amused her. "Isn't that kind of like showing each other your dicks?"

"No," he said, sounding annoyed, and then tilted his head. "Maybe kind of."

"Where were the first twelve *guarídas?*"

"Mm, let's see if I can remember." He counted them off on his fingers. "There was Granada, where we started. Lisbon, Tangiers, Athens, Rome, Paris, Cairo, London. We were already in Saint Augustine and Mexico City. Buenos Aires. Maybe Moscow? We weren't in Asia yet." He shrugged. "Not sure about the last one."

She nodded and touched the two faint, fine lines on the inside his forearm. "What are these from?"

"Those might fade. They're from bloodletting."

"*What?*"

"Sometimes if you're dealing with an evil spirit, you do a spell, and some of those involve blood. I told you about the one Michael did, on the mesa."

"Isn't it hard to cut yourself?"

"It is at first," he said. "But they're shallow cuts. You practice a few times when you're training. They show you how to avoid a big vein."

"Seriously? That sounds pretty rough."

He shrugged. "Some of the training's a lot worse than that."

"How long does it take you to get trained?"

"Depends. But we never really stop. There's always more to learn. Not just about fighting but things like first aid, dealing with people, undercover work, escaping buildings. And all kinds of magic and lore."

"Can anyone do spells?" She knew she was asking a lot of questions, but he didn't seem to mind.

"Some spells, yes, some no. And we don't always know until we try it."

"That sounds complicated. And dangerous." She touched the scar on his side, the one that had piqued her curiosity from the first time she'd seen it. "Is this one from a bullet?"

"Yeah."

"Ugh." She shuddered. "How did you survive that? Who shot you?"

"It was a mission. Down near Mexico City." She waited expectantly, and he sighed. "Trust me, you do not want to hear my long war stories."

"Trust me, I do." She lay back on the bed.

CHAPTER FOURTEEN

JONATHAN AND MICHAEL had taken one of the gondolas, brightly painted like carnival rides, up the canal to get to Isla de la Muñecas—the Island of the Dolls. Recently, on different days, two male visitors to the island had flung themselves into the canal and, apparently, had forgotten how to swim, though one of them had been a surfer from Troncones.

One might have expected their deaths to scare others away, but even though the height of tourist season had passed, the boat had been almost full. The renewed attention to the creepy locale had attracted American visitors like flies to rotting fruit.

The news stories had indulged in long, panning shots of the trees on the island, from which dangled mostly naked, often dismembered or mutilated dolls, an orchard of nightmare. They retold the old story of the original inhabitant of the island, a hermit who'd recovered a doll from the canal that had belonged to a drowned little girl. He'd hung the child's toy from a tree, where it would be safe from the water. Then, he'd added more, digging through rubbish heaps and squalid secondhand stores in Mexico City, choosing only one or two at a time.

Locals began telling stories of hearing children's laughter among the macabre trees. The Scholars at Manus Sancti believed the man had the ability to sense spirits. Ghosts often attached themselves to dolls or puppets, like substitute bodies when their mortal ones burned away. Neighbors sometimes brought dolls to him, wanting to trade for the fruits and vegetables he grew. Only rarely would he make a deal. He gathered lost souls together, where they could have company.

Occasionally, visitors brought other dolls they deemed to be particularly creepy to string up on one of the branches. In this way, the man's collection grew even after his death.

None of this had ever concerned Manus Sancti. Hauntings were as common as stray dogs. The stories might send chills up some people's spines, but they were almost always harmless. But men drowning for no reason—that was new. Neither Michael nor Jonathan were ghost talkers, but with truly powerful spirits, it didn't matter. Anyone could sense them.

Michael and Jonathan had milled around the island, watching the tourists who giggled, gawped, and snapped photos. The care-taker of the island had watched all of them closely. Most people in town had believed the drownings had been murders.

When the last boat of the day ferried visitors back to town, Michael and Jonathan lagged behind. They both carried the type of expandable batons sometimes used by riot police. The weapons were easy to toss in a backpack, where their guns remained. No bullet affected the spirits of the dead.

Birds trilled and screeched in the lengthening shadows.

Michael said, "So we walk around all night hoping a ghost tells us to drown ourselves?"

"Or throws one of us in the canal and holds us down."

They came upon a store mannequin someone had arranged in a position of crucifixion. "Are you kidding me?" Michael exclaimed when he saw it. "This place. I'd rather be back in Vegas."

"You liked those acrobats."

"They were great! It wasn't their fault they hired a succubus."

They passed a tree of naked Barbies, one of them headless, another one hanging from her rough hair. Someone had lashed a sunbonneted rag doll by her waist to a shrub. Exposure to the elements had left most of the artificial bodies with a layer of filth.

They were looking for one that had been brought more recently, that had housed the malevolent spirit that had almost certainly driven two people to their deaths already. Jonathan grabbed a naked baby boy doll, anatomically correct, by one foot to study it more closely. "Look at this. It looks like someone burned it, or tried to. One of the victims might have done it, if it was driving them crazy."

Michael touched its ear, which had been warped by heat to resemble the pointy ear of a troll. Half of its face had melted. He shuddered. "Too bad we can't burn down the whole island." He pulled up the fine-granular GPS tracker on his phone to drop a pin at the location.

By about two in the morning, Jonathan had begun to wonder if the night would be a bust. It happened all the time. Sometimes, the evil things they tracked were cagey or unpredictable by nature, and it took several attempts to bring them down. On rare occasions, the paranormal happenings just stopped, which unsettled everyone in Manus Sancti.

Then they heard a man's scream.

They ran in its direction through the trees to the edge of the canal. The shining ghost of a little girl in a short dress pulled the caretaker toward the water. A ghost's strength had nothing to do with muscle and bone. Her face was bloated, and muck covered her dress, bare legs, and pale patent shoes. A drowning victim, for sure. He didn't know why the spirit wanted others to drown, and he didn't care. He told Michael, "Help him, and I'll find the doll."

Michael reached the man's side, grabbing his arm, providing more physical resistance against the spirit's pull.

The spirit would react to its artifact being disturbed. With his police club, Jonathan began smashing every doll in sight, like a deranged piñata game. When Jonathan clobbered a particularly ugly one, Michael yelled, "That's it! That's the one!"

The ghost girl stopped to stare over at Jonathan. The caretaker turned and ran into the trees. Jonathan kneeled next to the doll, shining a flashlight on its face. Wooden. Real hair? The arm sticking out of its dress was a bone. *Christos.* A souvenir of a murdered child, made from her parts. No wonder the spirit was angry.

"Jonathan!" Michael shouted. The ghost girl pulled him now. One of his feet was in the water.

Jonathan took out the silver flask of blessed angelica root oil and sprinkled it on the macabre creation as he recited the exorcism spell by heart. He wanted to speak more quickly, but if he didn't pronounce every Latin word perfectly, it would be for nothing. At the final word, a flash brighter than lightning made him squeeze his eyes shut. When he looked over again, his brother was wading out of the water. Jonathan called over, "You all right?"

"Yeah." He reached Jonathan's side and crouched next to him, looking down at the half-charred doll. The wind had already extinguished the flames.

"Human bone, and hair," Jonathan said. He touched the doll's sack-like dress. "And a scrap of the victim's clothing, I'm guessing."

"The murderer brought it here?"

"Looks like." Maybe he'd suffered a pang of remorse. He might have brought the doll to the island in hopes that the girl would find ghost friends. Or maybe he'd thought it was funny. With psychotic killers, it was sometimes hard to know what they were thinking. The object in its indignity was obscene. "We should bury it."

"No, we should get going." Michael stood up.

Jonathan emptied out the rest of the flask of holy oil over the doll. The peppery-musky scent sweetened the air. Michael crouched back down and dug out his lighter. He touched the flame to the sad rag of dress, and the fire once again whooshed into being. Crossing himself, Jonathan muttered, *"Réquiem ætérnam dona ei Dómine; et lux perpétua lúceat ei."* He stood up, and Michael did the same.

Gunfire rang out. Jonathan turned, reaching for his own weapon. Pain seared through his gut. His knees buckled and he fell on his back. Michael fired into the trees. Everything looked blurry. Jonathan heard shouting—not Michael's. His consciousness fuzzed.

Then his brother was kneeling over him, pressing his hand hard against the wound. Jonathan gagged from the pain. Michael clapped his cheek. "You with me?" Jonathan nodded, not attempting to speak. Nic's voice blared into Jonathan's awareness, though he couldn't make out the words. With one hand, Michael answered the phone. "He's shot! In the stomach."

"Shit! Are you safe now?"

"Yes! What do I—"

"Do not move him. I'm sending a chopper." Unlike El Dédalo, the *guarídas* had no hospital wings of their own. The Diviners had set up a hack to give legitimate-looking orders to local hospitals, which included sending medical helicopters. "There's an emergency flare in your backpack. Light it so they can find you. Then keep the pressure on the wound. Jon, listen. You're going to get through this. Keep breathing, *corín.*"

Breathing hurt. Michael dropped the phone, wadded up Jonathan's shirt against the hole in his body, and put Jonathan's hand on top of it. "Press down!" Jonathan tried. Michael rifled through the backpack, found the flare, and lit it. It glowed red in Jonathan's peripheral vision as his life pumped out of him under the black night sky. His brother returned to his side and clamped down on the wound. "Stay with me!" Strain roughened his voice.

Jonathan's insides felt as though they were sizzling in acid.

In desperation, his mind clawed toward God and took hold of a solace that diminished the pain.

Michael's free hand grabbed his. "They'll be here soon," he was saying. "Hang on."

Two days later, Jonathan woke up in the hospital. Michael said he'd become conscious a couple of times before, but he didn't recall it. The damage to the intestine was minimal. He'd received two transfusions, one of Michael's own blood.

The caretaker had somehow convinced himself that Jonathan and Michael were responsible for his almost getting dragged into the canal. He should have been able to see the ghost, since they could, but it wasn't the first time a *sonámbulo* had refused to believe his own eyes. Most sleepwalkers didn't want to be woken up.

It was, however, the first time in a long while that someone they saved had tried to murder them. The caretaker survived the lead that Michael had pumped into his leg, not that Michael seemed particularly concerned about it either way. Manus Sancti smoothed over any awkward questions from the police about the whole affair.

No infection had set in during the weeks Jonathan recovered at the hospital, though between the dosages of the pain medication, he'd hurt like hell. Michael had spent his nights sleeping in a chair in the hospital room, having charmed the staff into not enforcing any visiting hours. When Jonathan had finally been off a feeding tube and allowed to eat, Michael had brought in food from nearby restaurants—soup, horchata, flan—believing the cafeteria fare looked inedible. In three weeks, Jonathan had gone home, though he was still out of commission for a good while longer.

Cassie asked him, "Right after you got shot, did you think you were going to die?"

"No. Michael didn't give me *absolutio*. They're the words you say to help someone die peacefully. And to make sure their soul moves on instead of becoming a ghost here."

She propped herself up on one elbow. "What do you say? Do you have it memorized?"

"It's always different. But you tell the person they did a good job—on the mission, or, you know, in life. If something killed them, you promise to get revenge for them, so their spirit won't try to." He shrugged. "You can say some words having to do with their faith, if you know what it is."

"Wow," she said. "Maybe your brother didn't want to believe you could die. I mean, it sounds like he loved you a lot."

A spark of insight kindled in Jonathan's eyes. Clearly, this hadn't occurred to him before. "Either way, I was very lucky."

"Really? See, I think 'lucky' is when nobody gets shot."

He grinned at that. "The internal damage could have been much worse. One time, a friend of mine got stabbed right here"—he indicated a spot a couple of inches in from his scar—"and part of the intestine bulged out." He paused. "I shouldn't tell you that."

Cassie grimaced. "Next time, I'll ask about a successful mission."

"That *was* successful. The ghost was put to rest, and I healed up fine."

She smoothed her hand over the scar on his abdomen. He squirmed, and the muscles rippled under her touch. Jealousy flowered inside her because he had such an exciting job.

But no, that made no sense. He had a shitty, dangerous job. "Do you ever want to do something different? Maybe do psychic stuff full-time, like Val?"

"Some Mages go on missions regularly. My mom did. But I told you, I don't have enough psychic talent to be a Mage."

"What about something less risky, then?"

"No." When she waited for a further explanation, he said, "For me, once I'd saved somebody, all I wanted was to do it again."

She'd always had daydreams of doing something heroic like that. As a kid, it had usually involved running into a burning building to save a dog or cat. As a grownup, embarrassingly, she would imagine apprehending one of those crazy shooters who decide to fire randomly on a playground or in a mall. Maybe she'd have her gun with her, and she'd shoot him right in the head. Or maybe she'd charge him and wrest the weapon from him. "Did you ever wish you were not in Manus Sancti at all? That you were just a regular person?"

"No. I can't really imagine not being a part of it."

She'd read a book once about Scientology, and a lot of those people said the same thing. She didn't bring this up, though. The people in Manus Sancti seemed to share a bond, and even a culture, that made them closer than normal communities. Maybe that made them like a cult, but she could see a lot of good in it. They knew who they were and what they were meant to do, and they knew they weren't alone.

CHAPTER FIFTEEN

SOMEONE KNOCKED ON the door. Next to Jonathan on the bed, Cassie froze. He couldn't blame her for being jumpy about visitors when she was in a place that was so strange to her. "I'll get it." He put on his jeans and opened the door to Gabi.

When she took in the sight of him shirtless and buckling his belt, the corner of her mouth turned up. She couldn't have been too surprised, he figured, after seeing how he'd acted with Cassie in the car. "Sorry to interrupt," she quipped. "I'm supposed to take your friend to see Val."

Jonathan looked back at Cassie, sitting on the bed wearing only her T-shirt and underwear. "I can walk with her down there."

Gabi spread her hands. "I've got my orders."

Jonathan shrugged and scanned the floor for his shirt.

Cassie turned her back to both of them and finished getting dressed. "Hey, on the way there, could we go to a laundry room or something?"

"Didn't I show you that?" He pushed a wall panel near the door, and a compartment slid out. "This both washes and dries. The soap's down here."

"This place is like a Swiss Army knife." She prodded another panel as if to see what it would do. "Okay, that's just part of the wall."

Jonathan smiled.

"I was hoping to go to Seattle with Tristan and Keiko today," Gabi told Jonathan as they headed down the hallway. "They asked for a another Knight, but Capitán said no."

"Is that the poltergeist?"

"Two of them! Ghosts setting fires together."

Cassie asked, "You think it's a three-Knight job?"

"Keiko's a Mage," Jonathan told her. "Like Val."

"Are most Mages women?"

"Maybe two thirds of them. Women are more likely to have the psychic talent, just like men are more likely to be physically stronger. But some men have it. Of course I have some. And Morty Silva's an empath like Val, and a ghost talker."

"There are plenty of women who are physically strong," Gabi said. "And a lot of fighting is speed and skill."

Jonathan nodded. "And you don't have to be strong to be a sniper, or to taze a guy." They reached the elevator bank, where Gabi's sister was tending to the potted trees. "*Salaam*, Teri." She smiled back at him, and she and Gabi chatted in Portuguese while they waited for the elevator.

After they got on and the doors slid closed, Cassie said, "You all know each other so well."

"She's my sister," Gabi said.

"Oh, wow. Is she jealous of you being a Knight?"

Gabi straightened. "Why would she be jealous?"

"I don't know. I mean…since she just has a regular job."

God knew he was crazy about her, but there was being honest, and then there was being tactless.

"Just a regular job," Gabi repeated.

The elevator doors slid open again, and he gestured for Gabi to get off first. "Gabi, she's a *sonámbula*." The last thing any of them needed was an argument. He caught the flash of hurt in Cassie's eyes.

"The trees are one reason we can breathe down here," Gabi told her. "I'd say that's pretty damn important, wouldn't you?"

Her face flushed. "I'm sorry." Jonathan recalled how Cassie had asked about the treatment of the people who'd built El Dédalo before. It wasn't really as if she didn't respect all kinds of workers. She'd probably been trying to flatter Gabi for being a Knight, and it had gone wrong.

"Every job is important," Gabi told her. "Without clean floors, you get disease. Without food, you starve. It's not hard." She gave Jonathan an aggrieved look, as though he'd brought Cassie here on purpose to piss her off. "Come on."

They passed a group of three Knights in the hallway, and one of them—Zaf, who'd come to El Dédalo from Istanbul over a year ago—looked Cassie over with frank interest. Jonathan moved closer to her, his hand grazing hers, as he met Zaf's eyes. *Don't even think about it.* Zaf looked away. Good.

At Val's office, Gabi banged on the door twice with the heel of her hand.

Val opened the door to them. "Come on in." She held up her palm at Jonathan. "Except Johnny. You're not supposed to stay in here."

"Why not?"

"Capitán Renaud asked me to work with Cassandra and teach her to control the spell. It should be a matter of reining in her temper in the first place."

Cassie snapped, "I don't need anger management class. That's ridiculous!"

"She's off to a good start," Gabi quipped.

"It's good training for anyone," Val said in her soft voice. "Mages all have to learn to clear their heads and control their emotions to do most kinds of magic and psychic work. I can teach you how to do the same."

Cassie sighed. "Fine. But it doesn't happen when I just get annoyed. It has to be real fury." She held her hand over her belly. "It goes all the way from here down through the ground. And I get this metallic taste in my mouth."

"Like blood," Gabi said.

Jonathan said, "I still don't understand why I can't be here."

"She controlled it once against you."

"No I didn't," Cassie complained. "He had to go to the hospital."

Val's long-lashed gaze flickered to her. "After he was attacked by the bear, when you were driving him to Morty Silva's. You became angry with him again when he told you about Manus Sancti justice. He asked you not to get upset, and you managed your emotions."

She was right. Jonathan had forgotten about it, but Val had pulled it up in her memories. "Then she can control it," he said. Cassie's face brightened.

"Against you," Val said. "She could probably do the same around her family and friends. Controlling it against those she doesn't know well, or dislikes, is an entirely different thing."

"I barely knew him then," Cassie pointed out. "And he'd attacked me!"

"True. But you also had…other feelings."

Hearing this warmed Jonathan from within. He touched Cassie's arm. "See you soon." She nodded, her upturned face softening with affection. It didn't seem as though she regretted what had been a rash first encounter. When was the last time he'd felt hopeful like this? Not since Michael's death. No, longer than that.

As he went out the door, Val turned to Gabi. "Maybe you can leave, too? I don't know why there are bad feelings between you and Cassandra, but they're distracting."

Gabi folded her arms. "I have orders to stay."

Cassie didn't feel like she was any threat to Val, but then again, she didn't know what the woman was going to do. Objectively, she couldn't really blame Capitán Renaud for not leaving Cassie alone with anyone who wasn't a Knight.

Val sat down on her furry chair. Today, she wore another polka-dotted dress, but this one was aqua, trimmed with lace, cinched at the high waist, and flaring wide at the knee. White stockings covered her plump calves, and lavender patent shoes shone on her dainty feet. When Cassie sat down on the couch, she realized the polka dots on Val's pastel dress were actually grinning skulls.

"I'm going to talk a little about the anger response, and all you need to do is listen and watch the movement of my hands." She held her hands up, palms facing inward, and began moving them up and down, slowly, fluttering her fingers.

Cassie would have scoffed, except that it was, in fact, relaxing her.

Val's hands lifted upward. "Whether they are very small movements…like the thumb touching the forefinger…or the thumb touching the middle finger…or they are movements that face in your direction…" Her palms turned toward Cassie, the fingers gracefully curved. "Or whether they are simply…fluttering, like the leaves in the lightest of breezes, the gentle motion can bring peace to your heart."

Cassie's brain was sparkling. The sensation traveled down her back and chest, blossoming into a feeling of tingly warmth. It wasn't sexual. Having just been with Jonathan, she could easily compare the two. Tension she hadn't even been aware of released from her jaw and her shoulders.

Val's hands never stopped moving, fluttering, flexing, and waving, utterly fluid. She kept speaking in that soft voice, the kind one might use with a sick child—gentle and filled with love. "When we are angry, we are afraid. We face…some kind of threat. A person's words or actions…may make us fear that we're not loved, respected, or cared for—that we will never be loved, respected, or cared for."

Tears jumped into Cassie's eyes. She didn't expect or want them.

"And sometimes…we become angry because we want to protect someone we love. We can't bear to see them hurt…and so we lash out. To want love and respect…is a valid intention. To want to protect…is a good intention. And with a calm mind…we can begin to realize…that we can want these things…and achieve these things…in peaceful ways."

This went on a while longer. Cassie felt as though she were falling asleep, though her eyes remained open, watching Val's hands. Val talked about breathing deep from the diaphragm and had Cassie practice with her.

"Another thing that can help when you feel yourself becoming angry is to repeat a word in your head."

"I already do that sometimes," Cassie said, though thinking *fuck* over and over had never helped anything.

Val smiled only slightly, making it clear that she expected her to stay focused. "It should be a word you never say otherwise."

Well, *fuck* was out, then. "Like a safe word. Except for your temper."

"Exactly. You can try the word *Shanti*. Have you heard it before?" Cassie shook her head. "Some Americans know it from yoga class. It means 'peace and tranquility.' Because of the peaceful state of mind you're in right now, it'll be especially effective. Say it with me, three times…*Shanti…shanti…shanti.*" She nodded. "We're done for now. Though it may not seem like it, this kind of training can take energy." Her voice was less whispery and sing-songish now, though still high and sweet. "When you came in here, you were already…emotionally charged."

Because she'd been boning Jonathan. As an empath, Val had

probably picked up immediately on the fact that they'd just been together. In a place like this, Cassie felt lucky that she wasn't a more private person.

Gabi said, "I'm supposed to take you back to your quarters."

When they reached the elevators, surrounded by the trees, Cassie said, "Listen, I'm sorry I was stupid about your sister's job. I've done all kinds of jobs. I cleaned out my parents' stables for, like, ten years. I don't look down on any work."

Gabi punched the elevator button. They waited in silence until it arrived.

As they got on, Cassie ventured, "My last job was at a company that was terrible for the environment. And now I'm unemployed. It must be nice for all of you to believe in what you're doing." Gabi stared straight ahead. Well, at least Cassie had tried.

When they got off on their floor, Gabi said, "We're not like most of the world, where a few people make millions of dollars and other people bust their asses and stay poor. My sister has the same kind of quarters and the same pay as Capitán Renaud."

"Really?" Cassie didn't disapprove of the arrangement, but how would that even work?

"Knights and Mages and Scholars have more power," she acknowledged. "But not everybody wants to be them. To become a Knight, you learn how to fight early. Some of us serve in the toughest military outfits in the world, just to train. It's why I emigrated to Chile when I was a teenager. I went into the special forces of the Chilean Army."

"Jesus. You guys are all such badasses."

She smiled, just for a second. "And then when you are a Knight, you're getting yourself almost killed all the time." That much Cassie knew, at least. She could see why some people would prefer to water the plants. "Scholars study so much it's a wonder their eyeballs don't fall out. And Mages can eventually lose their minds, like Jonathan's mother did." Cassie took in a sharp breath. Gabi looked back at her. "You didn't know that?"

Cassie shook her head. He'd only said she'd died. She hoped his mother hadn't killed herself. He'd obviously not wanted to talk about it… *Shit.* She probably had.

They reached Cassie's door. Gabi put her hip close to the panel next to it and it unlocked with a click. "Being a Diviner isn't easy, either. It's no wonder lots of people prefer to be a Steward. About eighty percent of people are. And we need them to keep things running. Mission runners, maintenance crews, doctors, lawyers, investors, you name it." She patted the doorframe. "Don't get all mad, but I'm going to lock you in here now."

"I'm not mad." Gabi was doing what she was supposed to do. And Cassie felt relieved that she was being more or less friendly now. "But I'm kind of going stir crazy in this metal shoebox. Is there any way I could go outside sometime soon? Do you guys ever leave?"

"Everyone here has a few days off every month, if they want to." Who wouldn't want to? Val, maybe. She seemed as at home in her office as a colorful tropical fish in an aquarium. "Not all at the same time. The *sonámbulo*s have no idea how many people are actually down here."

"Where do people go on their days off?"

"Wherever they want, as long as they stay out of trouble," Gabi said. "They can go hunting, motorcycle riding. Into Albuquerque or Santa Fe to shop or eat out. Val always goes to a spa in Santa Fe."

"What for?"

Gabi shrugged. "Haircuts, massages, pedicures?"

"Sounds expensive."

"It's paid for." While this sunk in with Cassie, Gabi added, "I went with her once, but nobody there did black hair. Andre and I usually go out to dinner and the movies and stay at a nice hotel."

It sounded pretty nice, having a big, fat supernatural warrior expense account. Gabi inclined her head, indicating Cassie should go into her quarters. "You could at least go with Jonathan to the shooting range. Work off a little energy."

"There's a shooting range?" It sounded good, but then the obvious occurred to her. "No one's going to let me hold a gun."

"You can use the simulators. And ask Jonathan to take you to *el huerto*. Get some fresh air." Before she could ask what *el huerto* was, she shut the door.

Jonathan came over not ten minutes later.

Cassie asked him, "How did you know I was finished?"

"You have that tracker. I can look up where you are on my phone."

She peered down at her hand. "Can anyone here look me up?"

"Only the security team, and me, because I'm responsible for you."

Cassie bristled at this. "No one's responsible for me but me."

"I am while you're here. If anyone gets hurt because of you, that'll be my failure."

"Well, no one's going to," she said, sounding more sure than she felt.

"How was your session with Val?"

"Weird. But I think it's going to help," she admitted. "And I apologized to Gabi. She's not mad at me anymore."

"Good."

"She said there was a shooting range. With fake guns or something?"

"There is," he said. "I'll show you sometime if you want."

"How about now?"

The shooting range was divided into two parts, one with actual guns, and one with fake ones. Jonathan explained that people mostly used the latter. It didn't waste ammo, and it allowed for more realistic scenarios. He'd led her into a small glassed-in enclosure with a huge, empty, square white room in front of them. She picked up one of the guns, which was extravagantly fake, rendered in bright orange plastic.

He touched a few buttons on the panel on the wall, and the lights dimmed. Two three-dimensional, disembodied human faces appeared, floating in mid-air. "That's your team," Jonathan explained as they flickered out again.

A holographic scene filled the room around them. A bombed-out city, half in rubble. A soldier darted from behind a building, aiming his gun more or less in Jonathan's direction, and Jonathan picked up his plastic gun and fired. Clutching his chest, the computer-generated soldier fell.

Cassie aimed a practice shot in the middle of the screen. After she pulled the trigger, she whipped her head around toward Jonathan. "This feels like a real gun!"

"I know." He attempted a shot with the gun in his left hand and missed. Cassie gave him a curious look. "After Las Cruces, I figure I need to get better with my left," he explained and grazed the next target.

A vibration went through her chest, and Cassie looked up at the screen, startled to see the figure of a triumphant shooter gloating. "Ah, I'm dead. That's so weird."

He restarted the game. On the screen, another soldier ran from behind a pile of bricks, though not in their direction, and Cassie shot him. The whole room filled with bright red light and went dark. "What happened?"

"That was one of our guys. Remember him?"

The faces at the beginning. "Shit."

"It's all right, you'll get it."

"How many scenarios are there?'

"More than a hundred." He switched it to another one in a

thick nighttime forest. "This one's more of a waiting game. It takes forever, and then they come at you when your guard is down."

"What are 'they'?"

"Animated corpses."

"Cool," Cassie said with satisfaction.

"Not so cool in real life."

For all she knew, an animated corpse had killed a buddy of his or something. "I'm always saying the wrong things."

"No, you're not." He put down the plastic gun to face her. "You know, what I said before... I wasn't trying to insult you. I just meant you weren't raised like we were."

She nodded. "What's that word you guys use? Somna-something?"

"*Sonámbulo*. It's, uh, Spanish for sleepwalker. But we use it to mean anyone who's not Manus Sancti. Regular people."

Cassie put her own toy gun down. "It's not very flattering."

"Maybe not," he conceded. "But our whole job is to protect them."

"Why do you guys use foreign words? I mean, even when you're speaking English?"

He squinted as if contemplating how to explain this. "It's jargon. At your company, didn't they have corporate-type lingo?"

"Sure."

"It's kind of like that. There are some words and phrases that everybody uses.

And sometimes we use words a little differently. Just like *sonámbulo* isn't literally a sleepwalker."

"I guess I can see that," she said. "At work, we'd say 'moonshot' for big projects that had nothing to do with the moon."

"What kinds of projects?"

"Boring ones." She peered at the hologram forest of the game. Still nothing. "What other words do you use?"

"Mm, *corín* and *corina*. They're...terms of endearment, I guess?"

"Like, romantic?"

"No, not at all. It's like, uh…my brother, my sister," he said. "But you don't have to be related by blood."

"That's pretty nice. What language is it?"

He shrugged. "It might be just ours. I don't know where it came from."

"Is there a romantic term of endearment?"

A smile played at his lips. "People say all kinds of things. The one that's only ours is *almeris*." He sobered and turned his attention to the fake forest in front of them. "You only say that to someone you're really serious about. It means someone who owns your soul."

"That's dramatic," Cassie quipped and immediately regretted it. His explanation made her uncomfortable, but she didn't really mean to make fun. "Is that one the same for a man or a woman?"

"Yeah."

Branches crashed, and half-rotting people loomed in on them. Cassie and Jonathan scrambled for their weapons, but they swarmed and filled the screen, which went black.

He laughed. "Now we're both dead." He went to the panel to reset it, and then paused and turned to her. "These sims aren't going to make you mad, are they?"

"No! It's just a game." They played a while longer. When they got back to her room, Cassie looked down at their joined hands. "What are we going to do tonight?"

His fingers curled tighter around hers. God, she loved his hands. So large and strong. She wanted him to touch her again, everywhere. He said, "It's Sunday night. I have a…commitment."

"What kind of commitment?" His sudden vagueness unsettled her. She couldn't help but add, "That wasn't a one-time thing, was it?"

He looked bemused, his forehead wrinkling. "You know better than that."

"I guess now I do."

He drew even closer to her. "You know, I'm not... I've only dated, I should say been with, a few people. I told you about Sophie. And I had a girlfriend back in Florida for most of the time I was at West Point."

"Was she in Manus Sancti?"

"Yeah."

"People must hook up all the time here, though," she mused. "You've had two serious girlfriends, but you must have..."

He shook his head. "I dated a Mage in Buenos Aires for a few months when I was outposted there. And that's it." His relative chasteness shocked her. Honestly, after the first time he'd brought her to screaming orgasm, she figured he'd had a hell of a lot of practice, not that she was going to complain. "What about you?"

"You mean, before I was married for five years?" Cassie shrugged. "I had a few boyfriends. Did my share of slutting around." His grin reflected hers. She was glad he didn't judge her for that. She added, "So we're exclusive, right?"

"Yeah." This was the whole reason for the conversation, she realized. To let her know that for him, sex wasn't just a casual thing.

"Good." For her, being with him was nothing close to casual. She doubted anyone else at El Dédalo would have gone near her anyway, between Jonathan's obvious possessiveness and the fact that she was a strange *sonámbula*. But under any circumstances, she wouldn't have been able to think of anyone but him. "Sure you can't stay over?"

His gaze heated. "I can stay a while."

He left her room two hours later, with her sprawled out naked, her body vibrating all over. It hadn't been fast and furious like the first time. His more thorough attentions were a beautiful devastation. She only worried that she hadn't given enough to him in return, though he'd hardly allowed her the chance. The next time they were together, she'd make it up to him.

CHAPTER SIXTEEN

SEVERAL DAYS PASSED at El Dédalo while Lucia pored over the translations. Cassie worked with Val in the afternoons and spent hours every day with Jonathan. They told each other stories from childhood and compared Cassie's high school days in Phoenix with his in Cairo. Jonathan got the stitches taken out of his healing back. They played pool in the cantina.

Cassie also read the translation of her great-grandfather's journal. After she complained to Lucia about not being able to read it in the original language, one that her own father spoke, Lucia loaned her educational videos.

Sometimes Cassie and Jonathan spent the night in his quarters, which weren't much bigger than hers, but with a small closet for a wardrobe that she told him was Spartan—T-shirts, jeans, sweat pants, cargo pants, utility jackets, and one dress shirt, tie, and suit. Intriguingly, though, there was a black robe and a red one, which he said were reserved for rare ceremonies.

One morning, when Cassie emerged from his shower, he looked up from his phone. "They think it's a good idea if you call your mom."

Although Cassie wanted to call her, she frowned at the phrasing. "'They' who? Your boss?"

"And the Diviners." The hackers, she remembered. The ones who'd noticed the animal attacks in Phoenix and figured out that she was the common denominator.

"Okay. Can I use your phone?"

"It's a little more complicated than that."

He escorted her to a Diviner lab, a large, dim room where thirty or forty people sat at rows of computers. Screens lined the walls, some with lit-up graphs and maps, others with blocks of text and numbers. A black man near the back of the room stood up and gestured for them to come over.

She tried to sneak looks at people's monitors as they walked by. What were they all doing? A dingy copy of an old document filled one screen, and wave patterns traveled across another.

Jonathan said, "Cassie, this is Andre Turner. He's Gabi's husband."

"Hey," she said. "Nice to meet you." He had high cheekbones and a narrow face with a closely trimmed moustache and goatee. Casually dressed in a gray Henley sweater and jeans, he stood a few inches shorter than Jonathan.

He nodded in reply and said, "I'll be setting up the call for you." Unlike Gabi, he sounded thoroughly American. He gestured to the empty chairs near his computer and sat down himself. "You told your mother you were in Cancun, right?"

"Yeah." The fact that she'd lied to her mom embarrassed her, even though his wife had ordered her to do it.

He took a swig from his travel mug of coffee with a New Orleans Saints logo. "Did you tell her where you were staying?"

"In Cancun? No." Even if she'd wanted to invent details, she wouldn't have known of any hotels there.

"Good. You'll be calling from this resort." He handed her a brochure, and she stared down at the shiny cover. A huge, sleek white building with a bright blue pool next to a white sand beach. She opened it to a picture of a porelessly good-looking white couple, both clad in white bathrobes, standing on a balcony staring out at the ocean.

"I'm sorry, but this is a terrible alibi. I could never afford this place. I have about one hundred dollars in my bank account."

"You told your mother that Jonathan has a trust fund," he pointed out.

She had. "Holy smokes. You guys don't miss a thing."

He flashed a smile, revealing a slight gap in his front teeth. "'Don't miss a thing' is pretty much the definition of our job. We're going to post these two pictures for you later today. We think your parents will be happy to see you living it up."

In one picture, she was walking along the beach and laughing up at the camera, holding up one hand like she didn't want her picture taken, but with a smile that said she knew she looked cute in a bikini. In the other, she sat at an outdoor table in the shade, making an exaggerated expression of wonder and delight next to a large peach-colored cocktail with a fancy garnish. They resembled no existing photographs of Cassie that she could recall, and they were so flawless, they incited jealousy for her fake self. It would be fun to be on a beach without a care in the world.

Jonathan smiled at the images.

Andre added, "We'll put them up with brief comments about how you really needed a vacation and how delicious the mango margaritas are."

Cassie was both impressed and horrified. "I love mango margaritas." She used to have them at Thunderbird Grill with Ana after work, before she'd gotten fired. Sam had made fun of her for it once, saying it wasn't a real drink. Ana was on Facebook a lot. In the past week, Cassie might have missed a call or two from her, and she might have been starting to wonder where Cassie was. "Fine, you can post them."

His mouth gave a wry twist. Clearly, he hadn't been looking for permission.

Once people had seen those pictures, it would be hard to change her story. If people saw her on a beach in Mexico, and she claimed to have been taken to a secret organization's lair because of her supernatural powers, well. She'd wind up in a psych ward.

Andre handed her a phone like Jonathan's with a blank black screen. "The phone number will come up as yours. When you're ready, press the center of the screen."

"Can I go in another room or something?" Jonathan pressed his lips together, anticipating a fight. "Fine, forget it. Enjoy my private conversation." It was all lies anyway. She jabbed the middle of the phone.

It rang four times, and she thought her mom was probably busy with a customer at the stables. But then she picked up. "Hi!" Her voice projected out of Andre's computer as well as into Cassie's ear. "It's about time you called me back."

"Sorry, I've just been really busy." Wait—that wasn't exactly the right thing to say about a luxury vacation. "I mean, I've been having a lot of fun."

"Is that right?" Cassie could picture the shrewd look on her mom's face. "I can't believe you told me that this David was just a friend. How long have you known him, really?"

"It hasn't been that long. Though things did get intense pretty fast." That was true, at least, in more ways than one. Jonathan's gaze traveled without apparent self-awareness down her body and returned to her face again.

"Well, I hope you're using condoms," Cassie's mom said. Both Jonathan and Andre grinned. Cassie buried her forehead in her palm. Did Andre know that Jonathan and she had hooked up? Gabi had probably told him. "It's probably easy to forget after being married for a while."

"I'm being safe, Mom. Please talk about anything else."

"I'm glad to hear it." She was enjoying Cassie's embarrassment way too much. "What kinds of things have you been doing? Other than, you know."

"Mom!" Cassie's mind raced. What the hell did one do in Cancun? Andre pointed to the third page of the brochure, where another nauseatingly happy couple was exploring something called Chichen Itza. She scanned the description. "Um, we took this day trip to, like, a Mexican pyramid? It's a really old ruin. Chichen Itza? I'm probably saying it wrong."

"Oh, sure. Your cousin Zoe went there once. I bet David was a great tour guide."

"Yeah," Cassie said uncertainly.

"I mean, since that's his field. Archeology."

"Right. He knew all about it." Andre pushed the two fake photos of Cassie forward. "But you know. Mostly I've just been walking on the beach and drinking mango margaritas."

"That sounds wonderful. You deserve it. You know what? You should post some pictures." Andre nodded to himself, looking pleased at how well her mother followed a script she hadn't read. "I'd love to see the look on the faces of those people you worked with. They're at their boring desks, and you're living it up in paradise."

"How are you and Dad? Anything new?" Her mom talked for a while about this and that—an aunt who'd broken her hip, a new gelding who was turning out to be a troublemaker, and how the food bank they volunteered at was looking into buying a bigger building.

An alarm blared through the room and then was silent.

"What was that?" her mom asked. Around Cassie, people had straightened in their seats, looking up at the screens on the walls.

"Um, it was a boat." Did boats make noises like that? She'd never been on one. "I—I've got to go. Love you." She hung up and asked Andre and Jonathan, "What's going on?"

Everyone had turned their focus to a screen full of names, one lit up in red. A woman sitting not too far away from her spoke into her headset. "Sector 18V, 124, Alvaro Limón, cardiac arrest from interrogation resistance training."

Jonathan's blood froze in his veins. The screen flickered, and a live video feed appeared. *No, no, no.* He knew Alvaro only slightly, but this was a disaster.

A Knight wearing a heavy jacket—Portia, he knew her—pulled a hood off a naked man who was bound with his wrists over his head. Alvaro shook as though it were freezing in the room, and his ankles were swollen. Jonathan remembered this experience in his own body. Another man kneeled over a second naked man on the ground, holding paddles from the defibrillator on the wall.

Next to Jonathan, Cassie went rigid. He took her hand as he watched, his right fist pressed against his lips. *God, let him be okay.* The whole Diviner lab was silent, watching. No sound accompanied the video feed, either, but the man with the paddles placed them on the Alvaro's chest and delivered a shock. The second naked guy, having just been freed from his chains, stood side by side with the woman who'd unbound him. The first man removed the paddles and began administering CPR. A medic carrying a steel case rushed into the room, produced a large hypodermic needle, and gave the fallen Knight an injection.

A man in the lab asked, "Kat, any changes?"

On the screen, Alvaro's chest rose and fell. The Diviner who'd spoken before also took a deep breath. "Yes. He's improving." She pressed a button, and the big screen changed to a series of numbers and a heart rate monitor. "I think— I think he's going to be all right."

"Thank God," the man said as Jonathan sagged in relief.

"What the fuck is this? What are you doing to people?" Oh,

no. Cassie was pissed, seriously pissed. Kat looked over her shoulder and punched something into her phone.

Jonathan grabbed Cassie's hand. "Let's take a walk." He cursed himself for not getting her out of there right away. Maybe he could at least minimize damage, taking her off by herself before she decided she was furious at every single person around her.

"That's torture!" she said as he pulled her into the empty hall. "What the hell is wrong with you people—"

"They're volunteers!" He turned to grip her shoulders. "I did it, too."

Her face crumpled. "What?"

He looked down the hall and back at the door to the lab. "I hope to God you didn't trigger an attack."

"I didn't! I—I started breathing like Val taught me." Cassie had been practicing with Val for the past week, and he wanted to believe that was long enough for her to learn some control. "I didn't have the blood taste in the mouth, or the—" She broke off, distress filling her big brown eyes. "Why would you do this to yourself?" Even if she hadn't spurred the spell into effect, she still might get angry about what she'd just seen.

Gabi and Tristan, a huge guy with a full dark beard and an intricate black tattoo on the side of his neck, strode down the hall toward them. Gabi called out, "Kat called for security. Should we be expecting a plague of scorpions?"

"No," Jonathan answered. "We're good."

"I'm positive," Cassie added.

In Spanish, on the phone, Gabi told whoever had called them that there was no immediate threat. Tristan moved closer, and Cassie took an automatic step back. The big Knight probably did look intimidating if you didn't know him. Jonathan hadn't seen him since Michael's death, and Tristan made the salute of respect for the departed, tapping his fist higher up on the sternum, his index and middle fingers extended sideways. "*Salaam*, Jonathan.

I'm so sorry." Jonathan nodded once. They exchanged a brief hug, more of a mutual hard pat on the back.

Gabi gave Jonathan a questioning look, eyebrows raised. He shook his head slightly. "We're going to take a walk."

"Where?" Gabi pressed.

"*El huerto.*" In addition to getting her away from everyone else, it might calm her down to be surrounded by growing things.

Gabi glanced at Cassie and back to Jonathan. "Fine." She said to Tristan, "Go meet up with the others in medical."

"My animals wouldn't go after the guy who got hurt," Cassie snapped.

"Portia and Eli will be there, too," Jonathan said. "The interrogators." He wanted Cassie to know that as brutal as the training was, those who led it had no desire to do permanent harm. He'd hated them right after going through it himself, but that hadn't lasted.

"You're telling her where they are?" Gabi demanded.

"She wouldn't have to know for her animals to find them. But she doesn't think she triggered it."

Gabi muttered. "All right, go. I'll keep an eye on the lab." Although Cassie had assured her no attack was forthcoming, Jonathan didn't blame her for making sure, especially since Andre worked there. Jonathan took Cassie firmly by the hand and led her away.

Even as she was walking with him, she said, "I don't want to go anywhere." Her voice was tight. "We need to talk."

"That's what we're going to do. Away from everybody else." On the elevator, he said, "There's no one on seventeen right now. I think you'll like it."

"I'm not sure I like anything here."

They reached the floor, and the elevator doors opened to the sight and smell of green. They faced a brightly lit open area.

Cassie blinked. "What is this?" She walked closer to an

enormous carpet of lettuce striped with various shades of green and purple.

"This way." He guided her through endless trellises of tomato plants, some flowering, and others bearing fruit, green or ripening red. "How do they grow?" she marveled. "There's no sun. There's no dirt."

"I don't really understand it."

Cassie took a deep breath and let it out. They reached a structure of dozens of plant-covered cylinders, rotating slowly, lit from within. Jonathan sat down on the bench there, and she joined him. "Do all Knights do that torture training?"

He opened his mouth to object to her phrasing, but restrained himself. "Lots of us do."

"Gabi?"

"Yeah, a long time ago." She'd been one of the first, back at the implementation of the training.

"Does that happen often? Cardiac arrest?"

"No! A medical team monitors them so closely…" He shook his head. "That was a freak thing."

"What did they do to you?" Her distraught voice struck him to the heart.

"Nothing that did permanent damage." That probably wasn't much comfort, based on what she'd seen, and he prayed to be able to make her understand. "Demons, *brujas,* certain human groups—they know about us. And any botched mission can get government attention and make them want to know more."

"Our government?"

"For one. Fifteen years ago, one of our Knights in France, Jamal Nagi, was abducted by the CIA and imprisoned in Uzbekistan for four months. Tortured."

Cassie looked sick. "They thought he was a terrorist?"

Jonathan nodded. "Wrong time and place, wrong contact. Wrong religion."

"I never heard about that— I guess I wouldn't have. Why couldn't you rescue him?"

The tragedy pained him again, like an ache from an old injury. "We couldn't find him. He was in an underground cement bunker, and back then, our tracking didn't work that far underground."

"How much did he say about you guys? Is that why you moved here from Spain?"

"He didn't talk."

Her eyebrows rose. "Not at all?"

"Don't get me wrong, everyone has their breaking point. In Nagi's case… Don't get mad."

"I'm fine." Cassie's voice came out dull. "In his case, what?"

"He dropped." She stared at him blankly. *Dropped* was another example of their lingo, one of the few in English, used regardless of the language people were speaking at the time. He shouldn't be telling her this, maybe, but he was in the middle of it now. "You know there are several nanochips in the tattoo." He touched the hip where his tattoo was. "Everyone has their own incantation that triggers an electrical signature from one of the nanochips, which stops the heart."

Cassie remained still for a moment as though stunned. "Jesus Christ. That's so awful. What if someone else says it?"

"It doesn't work then. And it's something you would never say accidentally, in a language you don't speak. Mine is lines from a poem written in Bengali."

"What is it? Fuck, don't answer that!"

He had to smile. "I can tell you what it is in English. "It's like…" He glanced up at the ceiling, finding it difficult to discuss something he guarded as his closest secret, but impossible to keep anything from her. "Well, the whole stanza is, 'You have set me among those without hope. I know it is not my fate to win or to leave. I am here to play the game of my undoing. I will stake all that is mine, and when I have nothing, I will stake myself…'"

He shifted on the bench. "The last line is the drop code—that's the part I would say. It goes, 'I will have triumphed through my utter defeat.'"

Cassie's face had drained of color. "That's horrible."

He felt self-conscious. "I think it's kind of beautiful."

"That's what makes it so horrible! You're not allowed to get captured or tortured, okay?"

His gratitude for her mingled with bittersweet amusement. It was hardly a promise he could make. He intertwined his fingers in hers.

After a short silence, she asked, "How many people know what your words are?"

"My drop code? Me, and the Mage and the Diviner who keyed it. And now you know it in English." Her mouth parted in astonishment. "Any mission runner can also remotely initiate the drop without the code, but that almost never happens."

"You must really trust your mission runners."

"We have to. For lots of reasons." Cassie ducked her head, her hair falling in a curtain that hid her face from him. After a long moment, Jonathan asked, "Are you okay?"

"No!" She lifted her head again, her beautiful brown eyes shining with tears. "Thinking of you going through that training. I can't stand it."

"Hey, come on," he said gently. "I'm fine." He hated to upset her, and at the same time, something inside him received her sorrow on his behalf like a precious gift.

"I don't understand—" She stopped to sniffle. "You've been through all these horrible things, and you let yourself get tortured for practice. How can you still be so kind? And so *open*?"

He wasn't sure exactly what she meant by that last part, but her praise filled him with warmth and light. "Like I said, most Knights go through it." Nobody was looked down upon for choosing not to, though. There were hardly any skills more valuable than listening to your instincts and knowing your own limits.

"What about Mages?"

"Only the ones who go on missions all the time. And some of them can leave their bodies for a while."

"*What?*"

If they'd been talking about anything less grim, he might have smiled at her incredulous expression. "Makes them look unconscious, and they don't feel anything for a while. It can be useful."

"Can Val do that?"

"Yes." Jonathan took out his phone and glanced at it. No new messages. "No attacks so far. If you really reined it in, that was—it was amazing, considering." He loved her fierce protectiveness of others. If it were tempered with control, she'd make a formidable ally.

No. She wasn't going to be an ally at all. In the best-case scenario, she'd return to Phoenix and find a nice, normal job and ride her horse and go out for drinks with her friends and be happy. She deserved a carefree life. No doubt, she'd meet a new man. It would be easy for someone like her… But he couldn't think about that or he'd lose his mind. God knew he probably shouldn't have gotten involved with her in the first place, but he'd never been good at shielding himself from heartache, and he hadn't been able to resist.

Cassie stood up and started walking. Jonathan followed her, not intruding on her thoughts. They came to a vast area of raised beds, where tall, bright green grass grew. "What is this stuff?" she asked.

"Rice."

She fingered the green blades. "That training's so awful. It can't be worth it."

He considered his reply. "For us, betraying the group, or giving up a fellow Knight…nothing could be worse."

"I'm kind of jealous of you guys."

Jonathan did a double take. "What?"

"No, I'm not. You have a horrible job," she amended quickly. "It's just…you believe in what you're doing. You all trust each other so much." She twisted one of the tips of the rice plants, about to break it off, but then she stopped and smoothed it out with her fingers. "I wonder what it's like to have that kind of loyalty."

CHAPTER SEVENTEEN

"IT SOUNDS AS though you came close to unleashing your power," Val said to Cassie the next day. Cassie had come to her office for another anger management session, escorted by Gabi, who didn't seem to especially enjoy the assignment of babysitting a grown woman with a twitchy magical power. Cassie didn't like the arrangement any better.

Val wore a blue dress with a ribbon-laced bodice that showed off spectacular cleavage and lace-trimmed shoes that appeared to have been stolen from Marie Antoinette.

"I controlled it," Cassie said. "You taught me how."

She looked sweetly unimpressed. "We already knew you could control it around Jonathan. Whether you can do it under other circumstances is another question."

Fair enough. "But if I can learn how to not release the hounds, can I also learn how to do it whenever I want? Or call up more animals at once?"

Out of the corner of Cassie's eye, Gabi straightened.

Val asked, "Why would you want to do that?"

"Jonathan's told me a lot about the dangerous work you guys do," Cassie said. "Sometimes you might need protecting."

Val tilted her head. "Or other people might need protecting, right? Friends, family."

"Yeah." Cassie hadn't thought much about that at all. Her friends and family rarely faced mortal peril. She understood why Val said it, though. Cassie wasn't one of them.

The door opened and they all turned around. Jonathan strode in. "Lucia says to come to her office," he told Cassie.

"We just got started," Val protested.

"Yeah, sorry. She says they've discovered something big."

Excitement sparked in Cassie as she stood up and followed him out of the office.

Val called after her. "We have a lot of work to do. Come back as soon as you can."

Cassie found herself jogging to keep up with his long strides. "Slow down." He did immediately. Of course, it was all she'd been doing for a while—running to keep up with her new surroundings and her own life, now that it had become entangled with Manus Sancti.

They passed a couple of men who greeted one another with a hug. Cassie asked Jonathan in a lowered voice, "Why do you all hug so much? Even the guys. The guys I know *never* hug." Jonathan tilted his head, acknowledging the point. "When you were in West Point, and Army Ranger School, did you have to remember not to hug anybody?"

He gave a genuine laugh. "Yeah, you can touch women, but not men. There's a few things like that. You have to act more— casual, I guess? You carry yourself differently."

This fascinated her. "Did you get tired of pretending to be normal? A *sonámbulo*," she corrected herself, proud that she had the term right.

"Of course."

They reached the library. Almost as soon as Jonathan knocked on Lucia's office door, she opened it. "Finally. I mean, *Salaam*."

The Scholar, in a plaid flannel shirt, leggings, and bare feet, smelled like she needed a shower. Actually, she'd smelled a little that way the last time, but Cassie wasn't too sensitive about that kind of thing. Growing up around stables, one got used to ignoring odors. It was less ignorable now, and Lucia's gorgeous green eyes were bloodshot behind her glasses.

Jonathan frowned. "We came straight here. Are you all right?"

Cassie asked, "Did you translate the other two pages?"

She laughed, a little manically. "I did. With help from Javier and Doug. Sit." Cassie's great-grandpa's journal lay open on the desk to one of the pages full of strange syllables in the back. "We've translated both remaining pages. This one describes the location of various wells and talks about the best days and times, according to the stars, to do a ritual to appease the rain gods."

"No wonder you're so excited," Cassie quipped.

Lucia grinned, her bloodshot eyes sparkling. "I'm only getting started." With the same kind of delicacy she'd used before, she flipped to the next page. "This one—we still have more work to do, but it seems to be a famine spell."

Cassie sat up straight. "I could end famine?" No wonder Lucia couldn't sleep. This was it. They were going to solve world hunger.

"Ah, no. This calls down a spirit who *causes* famine. He most likely does not exist."

"Oh." If he did, Cassie didn't want anything to do with him. She leaned back in her chair again.

"Anyway, the codex itself said that the spell probably doesn't work," Lucia added.

"Wait," Cassie said. "How do you know that?"

Lucia held up a finger, as though to say she was getting to that. "We finally turned to studying Rodrigo De La Garza's effects. There's nothing special about the key—mass-produced in a tin factory in Durango, Mexico. No references to it the journal. The toy tank is from Spain, as I suspected. A memento of the war, no doubt. You didn't mention there was anything inside of it."

Cassie exchanged a look with Jonathan. "I didn't know."

Lucia grinned like a madwoman. From a box on a high shelf, she took out the tank and a smaller metal box and set them on the table. They'd rolled the top of the tank back like the lid of a sardine can. "What the hell?" Cassie exclaimed. "I didn't say you could tear it apart."

Lucia froze, alarm washing over her face.

"She's not really angry," Jonathan reassured her in the warm, strong tone Cassie was growing to love. "Are you, Cassie?"

Cassie's irritation burned away. She was going to have to be careful not to scare people. "No. It's all right. What was in there?"

Lucia set the metal box on her lap, and it sprung open with a click. She had a tattoo like Jonathan, of course, with the tiny chips in it that could be programmed to unlock things. After placing it back on the table, she reached in as carefully as someone about to deactivate a bomb. She drew out a small stack of papers, maybe three by six inches apiece, all in plastic sleeves. Her hands shook as she slowly unfolded them on the desk. They connected like an accordion, and she spread them out to about a four-foot length on the table.

Inside their protective casing, the yellow-tan pages were rough around the edges. A rusty ink formed rows of rounded square symbols, smaller than the tip of her little finger. Boxes containing illustrations of monsters or perhaps human-animal hybrids interrupted the text here and there, executed in dingy blue, brown, and a startling bright red pigment.

Jonathan pressed his hands, in a position like prayer, against his lips.

"What is this?" Cassie asked Lucia, although she already knew.

"This is the codex."

Goosebumps rose all over her arms. "Wow."

"There's even more." She took out a piece of glass from the box, holding it up between her fingers and thumbs. "Fragments. Thirty-one altogether. We've preserved each one in a microscope slide." A scrap of the same material as the codex floated between the thin panels of glass.

Jonathan asked, "When will you know if those fragments are from the same text?"

"We've already analyzed them. They're written on the same kind of *amate* paper as the codex, and like the original, it's written in blood."

Cassie drew back. "What kind of blood?"

"Human," Lucia said with a bright smile.

Cassie stared at the rusty glyphs. "That's disgusting."

"It's unexpected. Although there are several European books written in human blood, none of the other Mayan codices are." She shrugged. "Still, bloodletting and sacrifice were fundamental to the Mayans. They're a key part of magic in most cultures, including many of the spells we do here." His brow creasing, Jonathan nodded.

Cassie swallowed and realized her mouth was dry as desert dirt. "How old is this again?"

"It dates to 700 AD."

Jonathan asked, "You're positive this is real?"

"There is no question," Lucia said. "Doug and I did several tests. It's one of our most remarkable finds in, perhaps, fifty years."

"You didn't find it," Cassie said. "You guys remember this belongs to me, right? Actually, to my mom."

"We're not thieves," Jonathan said.

"Well," Lucia countered, a mischievous dimple showing up in her cheek. "That's not strictly true."

"We don't just take artifacts from anyone," Jonathan protested. "Mostly governments and large corporations. They're items that are dangerous in the wrong hands."

"Not anymore," Lucia said cheerfully. "But in earlier centuries, with the Medicis, and the Habsburgs—" She stopped as Jonathan glared at her. "Anyway, there's no use arguing with me. Capitán Renaud will decide what happens to it."

Unexpectedly, the animal of Cassie's rage roared up against its bars. *It's mine.*

She took a deep breath and repeated the soothing word in her head that Val had given her: *Shanti, Shanti, Shanti.*

Jonathan took her hand, helping to calm her further, and said, "Before anything else, we need to find out what it says."

Good point. Cassie asked, "Do you think something in here will tell me how to reverse a spell?"

"Possibly. I've gotten permission to meet with Tom Lorenzo in Aquileia. He's a palaeographist who collects and studies Mesoamerican inscriptions in particular."

"He's one of you guys?"

"No. But he knows us and works with us."

"Kind of like Morty Silva," Jonathan added.

Lucia nodded. "He did important work on our Codex Borgia, which of course was produced much later by the Aztecs."

Jonathan asked, "Is that here? I thought it was in the Vatican Library."

"They have an exceptionally good facsimile of one."

Cassie picked up one of the microscope slides and examined the tiny fragment it held. "You're not actually taking the codex to Italy, are you?"

"The original?" The Scholar laughed. "Oh, no. And I've been asked to keep the trip to see Lorenzo as quiet as possible." She looked to Jonathan. "Capitán says you're my point of contact for the trip. I'll let you know as soon as the arrangements are final."

Jonathan nodded.

Cassie asked, "Where's Aquileia?"

"Northern Italy," Lucia said. "Almost in Slovenia."

It sounded inconvenient. "Couldn't you just talk online?"

She placed her palms on the table next to the codex. "Too risky. No one must know we have this object here."

It was a lot to take in. When Cassie returned to Valentina Vega's office, her thoughts still churned. As soon as she said hello, Val said, "I think you should have some nettle tea."

"All right. Are we supposed to call Gabi?" Even though Cassie didn't particularly like being supervised, she didn't want Val to get in trouble with her boss.

Val shook her head as she made the tea. "Capitán Renaud said she doesn't have to stay for these sessions anymore." This was good. Maybe he'd heard that even after Cassie had seen the horrible interrogation training, she'd kept it together. Maybe even if the codex didn't have a reversal spell, they'd decide she wasn't a threat to humanity anymore and soon they'd decide she could go back to her normal life.

Would that be the end of seeing Jonathan? She'd never believed in long-distance relationships, and managing one with a Knight of Manus Sancti would be a challenge, to say the least.

She shook off the thoughts. They'd found a priceless artifact, and she was thinking about dating. As Val made the tea, Cassie told her about the codex and Lucia's trip to Italy. She felt a little guilty, as though maybe she should be keeping it a secret, but Lucia hadn't instructed her to keep quiet about it.

The door slid open, and Capitán Renaud strolled in.

Val's eyes widened. "Capitán." She set down the teapot and touched the heel of her fist to the middle of her chest. He closed the door behind them by touching the panel next to the wall. Just as when Cassie had seen him last, he wore an impeccably tailored suit.

With a slight gesture, he indicated that Val could sit again.

"Came to see how the training is going. She learning to control the spell?" He clasped his hands behind his back, regarding them like a general reviewing the troops. That made sense when it came to Val, but Cassie didn't work for him.

"She's somewhat volatile by nature," Val said. Cassie felt betrayed by this, even though the Mage only spoke the truth. "But she's learning fast."

Capitán nodded without looking convinced and asked Cassie, "How long have you been here? A week?"

"Eight days." It seemed like much longer. Her whole life in Phoenix, before she'd known about her powers, seemed blurry and somewhat imaginary, like memories from early childhood.

"You couldn't have made much progress."

Anxiety made her breath hitch. He could decide to do any number of things with her, most of them not good.

Val said, "Her response to the interrogation incident was progress. She's extremely empathetic and has a strong protective instinct, but she still controlled her emotions."

Capitán gave a slight shrug. "She was with West. He can talk her down because she's creaming herself over him."

Cassie's mouth dropped open at the casual crudeness of this. Did he always talk this way? Maybe he did. He'd barely spoken to her before now. Val blushed, at least.

He looked Cassie over with studied curiosity. "Not surprised they started fucking. West just lost his brother. She lost her marriage, her job. Whole life imploded. She bonds to her attacker. He feels guilty about attacking. Not to mention turned on—with her bound and helpless. Perfect storm of damage."

Val bit her lip and stared at her pink patent shoes.

Cassie's heart pounded faster. "You don't know anything about me." A lie. Everyone here knew everything about her. "Or about us."

He raised his eyebrows as if pondering this. "You think that's true?" he asked Val. "I think they're two sinking swimmers. Mistaking each other for the life raft."

"It's more than that," Val said quietly.

Cassie's pulse skyrocketed. *I need to calm the fuck down.*

"Interesting," he said. "Well, she'll be here a while. Time will tell."

"How long?" Cassie asked. "You can't keep me here forever." And he couldn't keep her codex, either, though she sure as hell wanted to know what it said.

"I can," he assured her.

"And you're not wiping my memory, either." The idea of this had been tormenting her, especially now that she'd become involved with Jonathan. Would it even be possible to remove Jonathan from her head? Somehow, her body—her soul—would remember.

"If we find a spell reversal, we help you do it. Then clear your memory of us. Return you to your former life. Most logical course of action." He had the weirdest way of talking, in clipped fragments, as though he were reading Morse code aloud.

Cassie planted her hands on her hips. "Maybe I won't do the reversal spell."

He looked bored or amused. "We'll persuade you." The image of the naked man having a cardiac arrest flashed through her mind again. "Of course, if we don't find a reversal soon? We'll put you in a psychic coma. That way, you can't do any damage. We find a counter-spell later, we wake you up."

What if they never found one? Would they even really try, once she posed no threat to anyone? A permanent coma would be worse than being dead.

"Maybe I have more power than you know." It was a stupid bluff, but she didn't know what else to do. "If you hurt me, I might curse you in ways you never imagined."

"The funny thing is, you think you're making idle threats.

They might not be idle." He looked her up and down. "You say you're very dangerous? I believe you. You're alive because of my good graces. Fucking one of my Knights doesn't make it any safer for you."

Righteous anger crashed through her. She tasted the metallic tang of blood, felt that settled feeling, as though she had roots that had plunged right down into the earth so that she could not be moved.

She had to push it back. She closed her eyes and filled her brain with deep indigo silence, as Val had taught her in one of the visualization exercises. It expanded, blotting out and quieting the rage.

"I see you pulling back. Not bad," he said. She opened her eyes again.

Of course. He'd made her angry on purpose.

He stepped on the cushion of Val's couch and perched on the back of it. "Vega, coach Ms. Rios about *focusing* that anger. I'll observe."

Val took a deep breath and let it out. "*Obedezco.*" She went over and sat down in the furry chair and gestured for Cassie to sit on the couch. Cassie hesitated and then settled herself on the very edge of it, with Capitán Renaud hovering right over her like a presidential vulture. Val began talking to her about another visualization, and she tried to pay attention.

Then Val shrieked.

Dozens of black spiders, each about an inch long, marched across the floor in front of them. Val jumped up and stood behind her chair as Cassie got to her feet and took a few steps back. They climbed up the couch, so close together they were like a moving, squirming dark blanket.

Black widows. Cassie recognized them because her family had found a few in one of the stables once. They'd scared the hell out of her dad, because horses were very susceptible to their bites… but so were humans. And humans never faced many at once.

Capitán didn't move. He looked at her. She had to make them stop. God only knew what would happen if she hurt him.

Without knowing what she was doing, she raised her hand toward the spiders. With all her might, she imagined a deep indigo color falling on them, covering and drowning them. Something vital burst out of her, and she recalled the stabbing victim Jonathan had described, with his innards coming out of his skin. The strange force threw her off balance, and she collapsed in the chair Val had just vacated.

The spiders froze. Half of them still waited on the floor, and half occupied the couch, a few a mere inch or two from Capitán's leg. They stood there, like they were in a movie and someone had hit the pause button.

A few turned around and scurried away. Then more. All of them dispersed in every direction, and Val yelped as two of them came toward her, but they passed her by and disappeared into a corner. One spider remained near Capitán's foot. Ridiculously, on sheer instinct, Cassie leaned toward it and yelled at the top of her lungs, "Go!" It ran away, too.

Gulping for air, her brain lit up with panic, she stared at Capitán.

"That was disgusting," Val wailed.

He strode over to the door and opened it. Three people stood there, one carrying a gun, one, a knife, and one, a metal briefcase. They all saluted him, though the armed men both had to put their weapons in their other hands to do so. "You're dismissed," he told them.

The Knights dispersed, but the woman holding the briefcase lingered, asking, "What was it, sir?"

"Black widow spiders. More than we expected. Don't think your antivenin would have helped."

She shook her head. "You take too many chances."

"Dismissed, Navarro." He closed the door and walked back to them.

Val stood on her tiptoes, her eyes scanning the floor. "They're not coming back, are they?"

"I don't think so," Cassie said.

She didn't look reassured. "Where did they come from?"

"Spiders, scorpions, snakes, they stay out of the way of humans," he said. "You would have never known they were around. Had it not been for our *bruja* here."

Fear trickled through Cassie. "Please don't put me in a coma."

"You've got interesting magic. Maybe more than we know yet. And you take action in a crisis. Giving Jonathan the injection. Firing at the Shifter's Jeep. It's rarer than you might think. That bias for action."

He's not going to hurt me. The compliment, from a man who didn't hand them out lightly, made her sound less like an impulsive idiot and more like hero material. He'd only goaded her in order to test her control, and she'd passed.

"Are you getting restless here?" he asked her.

Restless was an understatement. The night before, she'd imagined clawing at the steel walls of her quarters, like a sardine that had somehow gotten canned alive. "Yes."

"Tell West that you and he can go horseback riding tomorrow. There's an excellent stable not far from here. A Steward will give him the details."

Cassie's jaw went slack. She could hardly think of anything she'd rather do, except go riding with her own horse Layla. "I… That would be great. Except he doesn't know how to ride."

Capitán Renaud gave the slightest of shrugs. "You've taught people before."

Her fears about her fate burned away. This guy could be harsh, but he liked her. No, even better, he *knew* her. And he trusted her now, even among a whole stable full of horses—big beasts that could absolutely be deadly, if her magic commanded it.

"Thank you." On impulse, she made the salute that others made to him, the heel of her closed fist touching above the heart. Val's eyebrows rose in surprise, but Capitán Renaud only gave a nod, as though this action were entirely appropriate and expected.

CHAPTER EIGHTEEN

WHEN JONATHAN AND Cassie left El Dédalo in the morning in one of their black SUVs, she was practically bouncing in her seat. "Your boss isn't so bad."

Jonathan cast a wary glance in her direction as they drove out of the gates with the barbed wire coils on top. "I didn't say he was bad."

"You know what I mean. He trusts me. Even around a bunch of horses! I mean, horses are big animals, and they can be dangerous. If a whole stable of them turned on someone..." She stopped herself.

His mouth thinned. "Yeah. It's occurred to me."

"But it'll be fine," she said quickly.

"I trust you. Pretty much." As they drove down the dirt road without another soul in sight, he added, "I figure you'll be extra careful. You don't want me shooting horses."

Cassie recoiled. "I'll be *so* careful. I'm kind of surprised he set this up for us. I know *you* get a few days off every month, but this... It's like it's my birthday."

"I'm surprised, too." Her account of Capitán Renaud provoking her in such a crude way had made Jonathan uncomfortable. He'd assured her that it was completely out of character for their leader, an act designed to test her and nothing more. The fact that Capitán had become involved in setting up a date made him even more uneasy.

After they arrived at the stables, a woman gave them a tour. Jonathan hadn't known that a place where horses lived could look like a giant luxury home with skylights in the high-timbered ceiling. Judging from Cassie's reaction, she hadn't known, either. She said the indoor arena looked perfect, but it was a sunny, clear day with temperatures in the fifties, and she wanted to ride outside. She told the woman, "He's never ridden before. If you've got, like, a really placid mare, that would be great." She darted a quick look at Jonathan, as if she feared he'd be offended.

"Sure," the woman said. "He can take Dicey."

"Dicey," Jonathan repeated. It didn't sound like the best name for a first horse.

"She's white with black markings. Don't worry, she's been walking this same trail for years. Doesn't matter who's on her, she'll plod right along."

As he and Cassie followed her to meet Dicey, Cassie said to him quietly, "Thanks for not acting embarrassed about not knowing how to ride."

"I want the calmest horse they've got. I don't need to be break-ing my arm on a day off."

Cassie chose a gorgeous reddish-brown horse with a white stripe on his head—a quarter horse, they said. Once outside, Cassie showed Jonathan how to get on Dicey. She teased him, saying, "Ooh, you're good at mounting."

"Nice single entendre." He peered down. "I feel like I'm pretty high up here."

She laughed. "You're almost too big for her as it is." She showed him how to take the reins, but as they started on the trail, she made corrections. "Get your hands closer in. Like here, in front of your saddle." He complied. "Bring your elbows in, though—thumbs up, like this. Good. Keep them there. Just relax." She looked up and took in a deep breath. "Isn't it nice to be outside?"

"Yeah." Jonathan leaned forward in his saddle.

"Okay, you're squeezing her with your legs too hard."

He grumbled, "I don't want to fall off."

"I know, but you'll freak her out if you grip too tight." He eased up. "There you go. Just sit up straight." She grinned over her shoulder at him. Her body seemed to move effortlessly with the horse beneath her, and it was clear that she felt like herself, wild and free.

There was no reason why she couldn't stay at El Dédalo with him indefinitely. She could do whatever she wanted. Learn Spanish, go to the shooting range with him, make friends... She urged her horse into a brisker trot, and he envisioned them breaking into a gallop and leaving him far behind.

Cassie was sorry to have to leave a few hours later. They began the drive back to El Dédalo, and with every mile, the worries that had plagued her brain showed up again, like one crow after another coming to rest on a telephone wire. "I wish we didn't have to go back so soon."

His features arranged themselves into a guarded expression. "You really think it's so bad there?"

She was insulting his home. "It's not the place. It's just— I don't know what's going to happen to me. Or the codex."

He trained his eyes on the road. "What do you want to happen?"

"I don't even know. They could buy the codex from me, maybe? And let me go back to my regular life?" She wasn't even sure of that. Her regular life had been kind of sucking prior to all this, and not only in ways that a pile of money could fix. She'd wanted to do something real or important with her life. "They can't release me and wipe my memory. I wouldn't remember to control it. There would be more attacks."

"They wouldn't let you go that way," he agreed.

Her frustration boiled higher. "I have no idea what's going to happen to me here. Am I going to be a prisoner for life?" She squirmed against the seat belt as though it were suddenly binding her fast. "If they found a way to reverse it, then they *could* make me forget everything and take the codex. Because I wouldn't know any different."

Unexpectedly, he pulled the car over to the side of the road and turned off the engine. Cassie blinked at him. What the hell was he doing?

He turned to her. "I'm not letting them wipe your memory."

Before, he'd told her he'd *try* to prevent that. "How can you say that? It's not up to you. And these guys are your whole…everything. Have you ever once not done what they told you?"

"No, never." His gray-blue eyes held hers in a steady gaze. "But my loyalty is to you first. I'm not letting anyone hurt you."

She stared at him in disbelief. He leaned in and kissed her deeply, cupping her cheek and stroking his thumb along it. His tenderness melted her.

He broke off the kiss to say, "Cassie, I love you."

Her heart jumped, a stutter of joy that switched to alarm. "You can't know that yet."

His face, so close to hers, held certainty and devotion, both demanding acknowledgement. "I don't say things I don't mean."

She wanted to believe him, but panic tightened her throat. She and Rick hadn't dated very long before getting engaged. Right away, he'd told her he loved her. She'd said it back automatically and then convinced herself it was true. He'd turned out to be the kind of person who'd said a lot of things—to clients, to friends, to everyone—in order to get what he wanted.

Jonathan was nothing like that. But how could she have earned such an absolute declaration in such a short time? He might be misjudging himself. She couldn't take that chance, not when her own feelings for him were so strong.

A more terrible thought prowled into her mind. Couples who stayed together, even if they loved each other very much, could have vicious fights. The people one loved most could bear the brunt of one's worst behavior. Maybe she shouldn't have gotten involved with him, after all. She could kill him.

She looked away. "It's too soon."

A muscle in his jaw flexed. He wasn't just hurt, but angry. She understood why. They'd grown so close, so quickly. But she wasn't the only one who knew how to control a temper. He only said, "I thought you should know," and then he started the car and pulled back onto the road again.

A heavy weight settled on her chest. She'd ruined their whole day. Or maybe he was the one who'd done that.

"This is embarrassing," Cassie muttered to Val the next afternoon. "You're always calming me down."

"Well, I'm good at it," she pointed out calmly. "Besides, it's okay to get help sometimes. You'll live a lot longer if you realize that."

"You're right. Which is kind of annoying." She gave a small smile.

Cassie's thoughts continued to stomp out an ever-deepening circular path of distress and indecision in her mind. Should she have told Jonathan she loved him, too? Could she even know that yet?

They'd managed to converse about other things before they'd gotten back to El Dédalo—more or less acting as though everything was okay, when it was actually painful and awkward. Neither of them had suggested spending the night together.

She cared about him, a lot. He understood her better than anyone, and every time he touched her, he set her mind reeling. He fascinated her, and his sense of honor and goodness filled her heart. She would do almost anything to make him happy.

"How much can you tell about what I'm feeling?" she asked Val.

"I'd rather not say. It makes people uncomfortable."

"If it bothered me, I wouldn't ask."

She gave a rueful smile. "I don't think that's necessarily true. But I know that you're—agitated. Regretful, scared…and filled with love." Cassie swallowed hard. Val couldn't feel things that weren't there. "And I'm guessing it must be all about Jonathan."

Cassie ran her finger along the Lego table. "You know him really well."

"I've known him forever. His brother, too, of course. Our parents are good friends." Cassie supposed she meant they *were* good friends, in the case of Jonathan's mom. "We all played together when we were little children in Saint Augustine. And when we were older, we were all in Cairo. Our families would get together for dinner every Sunday night. And then sometimes, we kids would watch an American movie on DVD or Japanese anime."

"I didn't know Jonathan was into anime."

Val smiled. "He isn't. I lived in Tokyo before Cairo, and I was always trying to get them to watch these shows I liked. And I didn't usually get my way, since I was younger. They liked some of it, though."

Envy flickered through Cassie because Val had known him for so long. "What was Jonathan like with his other girlfriends?"

She frowned. "What do you mean?"

"Was he nice to them all the time?" Rick had treated her well when they were first dating. After they'd gotten married and he didn't need to win her over any more, things had changed fast.

"I was never around him and Sophie Kazakov," she said carefully. "Or the girl he dated when he was at West Point."

"You probably heard things. I just want to know if he was a good boyfriend."

She straightened in her seat. "I can't help you. He talked to me about you yesterday. I have to keep both of your confidences."

Cassie wanted answers, and she employed her usual strategy: a direct attack. "He told me he loved me yesterday. Did he tell you that?"

She slumped and rested her forehead on her hands. "I was afraid of that."

Cassie knew Val would talk now. "I didn't say it back. It's been a really short time, and I don't know if I can believe him."

She lifted her head again. "You can't tell anyone I'm talking to you about this. Not Johnny, not anyone, ever."

Cassie nodded.

"He made a strong connection to you from the moment he Read you. Walking into anyone's soul is always an emotional experience. And he thought you were beautiful, and courageous, and open with your feelings... He was completely taken with you. Every time he's around you, or talking about you, I feel what he's feeling, and it's this weird mix of domineering lust and...total adoration. And he's not changeable by nature."

Cassie squirmed. Even though she'd asked, the intimacy of the disclosure made her soul feel bare.

Val gave a half shake of her head. "I'm not telling you anything you don't already know. Am I?" This didn't require an answer. The Mage knew everything Cassie was feeling, anyway. "You're in love with him. Otherwise, I wouldn't be telling you this. It never seemed like you were afraid of it. You burn like a wildfire—bright and reckless." Val's talent at describing her emotions unsettled her even more. "Why are you retreating now?"

"All couples have bad fights. I'm scared my animals will hurt him. Aren't you worried about that, too?"

"A little," she admitted. "But you've been doing well around him, and now you've learned how to pull back an attack. And obviously he trusts you."

"He doesn't worry enough about getting hurt," Cassie said, thinking of all of his scars.

Val laughed. "That's it exactly. I told him yesterday he doesn't have his guard up, but he has to remember everybody else does."

Cassie was lucky to be able to talk to someone who knew him so well. "Can I ask you a few more things about him?"

"You can ask. I'll see if I can answer."

"Jonathan told me Michael was his parents' favorite. Is that true?" This had troubled Cassie from the time he'd said it, and it bothered her even more now that he'd offered his love to her and she hadn't returned the favor.

"I can talk to you about that. Friend to friend. Their father was much harder on Johnny, maybe because he was so much like him. Michael was cute and silly and charming, but even as a kid, Johnny was so serious." Cassie could easily envision the child version of Jonathan, and it touched her heart. "If Michael got in trouble, their dad held Jonathan responsible, too, because he was older. He spanked them a lot when they were kids, and hard."

Cassie recoiled. "What the hell?"

"Growing up, I was terrified of him. When they were older, he pushed them really hard in MMA. I do think he loves his sons, but…he could've done a lot better job. He still could. At Michael's funeral, he wouldn't tell Jonathan it wasn't his fault." Her eyes glistened. "When Michael was little, Jonathan was his hero. Then in Cairo, when they were teenagers, they would fight a lot. But by the time they were both here, the past couple of years, they were very close. They worked together so well. And now, it's like a gaping hole in his emotional signature."

Although Cassie hadn't heard this term before, she ached at the description. "He doesn't talk about it all the time. It's easy for me to forget what he's going through."

"We miss Michael so much. I couldn't work at all for a week. I kept drinking cup after cup of lavender and hawthorn tea—it's supposed to help with grief—but it was like I was drinking sadness." Tears welled in her eyes.

Cassie pressed her hand to her mouth. Val had grown up with Michael, so of course his death had hit her hard, too. "Val, I'm so sorry. He must've been like a brother to you."

Val's brow knitted. Instead of directly responding to this, she said, "I'm getting off the subject."

"That's all right." Cassie patted her arm, and Val gave her a tremulous smile.

"I was so glad when I first felt the connection between you two. He deserves to be happy. So do you."

Cassie ducked her head and looked down into her tea. It meant a lot that Jonathan's closest friend approved of her.

"If you don't think you can concentrate on training today, you could probably skip it just this once. You've come so far already."

Cassie smiled. "No, that's fine. We should do it." If she really did want to be with Jonathan for a long time, she'd better get her power under total control.

The session was even more intense than before. Val Read her and plucked infuriating incidents from her past—fights with Rick, an unfair teacher, a childhood incident with a racist man at church. She chose people that Cassie couldn't hurt now, since they were already dead. Val had asked about all of them in her psyche, although she covered her tracks behind her so Cassie couldn't remember her being there.

Then Val asked her about them, one at a time, and she practiced not reacting. Cassie hadn't thought of some of these things in years, and they stirred up fresh resentment that she had to immediately tamp down. Nonetheless, Val could sense her feelings, so she could gauge her control.

As Cassie left the office, a girl of maybe sixteen waited outside the door. She told Cassie, "Capitán Renaud wants to see you."

"Right now?" Cassie whipped around, looking to Val for explanation, but the Mage merely shrugged.

The girl didn't dignify this with an answer. Of course, right now, Cassie realized. When Capitán gave an order, people obeyed. She accompanied the teen to Capitán's office.

"Rios, come in," he said when the girl knocked on the door. She opened it for Cassie, and he said, "You can go, Nara."

The office looked as though he'd moved in just a few days ago. On the large, blocky steel desk, one inbox held a few folders, and a laptop computer sat closed. There was nothing else in the way of furniture, except for his black swivel chair. Guests like Cassie had to stand. It didn't strike her as so comfortable for him, either. Didn't he have any visitors he wanted to relax and chat with for a while? Jonathan had said he didn't have a wife or a significant other.

"I want you to do something for me," he said.

"What's that?"

"Consider becoming one of my Knights."

A thrill of excitement rushed through her—followed by pure fear. Her stupefied mind at least knew how much of an honor he'd bestowed upon her by asking, and she opened her mouth to say thank you, and then hesitated. *Thank you* might be taken for *yes.*

"You have a week to decide." He made a gesture for her to leave the office.

That night, alone in her room, she considered how to tell Jonathan about Capitán Renaud's offer. Or did he already know? She doubted it.

What would it even mean to join Manus Sancti? Would she have to live in this hole in New Mexico for all of her days?

Maybe not. There were dozens of cells around the world; one of them could take her. Could she live somewhere amazing, like Paris? If Paris really was amazing. How would she know? She'd hardly ever been anywhere. She only spoke English, and that would make her a lone hick in an organization full of polyglots. Probably, they'd keep her in the States. How often would she see her family?

Would she go on missions to fight poltergeists, demons, and witches who truly were evil? Maybe she'd learn to fight, like Jonathan and Gabi. But no, wasn't it too late for her to learn how? If Capitán hadn't taken her so much by surprise, she would've asked more questions, about a hundred more, while she had the chance.

Why had he asked her to be a Knight and not a Mage? She had magic. But Val had said she didn't have any of the normal Mage gifts. Sometimes people with a little extra power still became Knights. Jonathan, for instance.

She didn't know martial arts, but she could shoot things, and she could learn to send a jaguar or bear after somebody's ass anytime she wanted to. That second thing, of course, was why he wanted her.

After being rejected by both a husband and a company that were not, by anyone's standards, all that great, being invited to join a secret society full of geniuses, psychics, and super soldiers was an ego boost about the height of Mount Everest. One thought flitted through her mind again and again: *I've been waiting my whole life for this.*

But Jesus, wouldn't she get herself killed?

CHAPTER NINETEEN

ALONE IN HIS room that evening, Jonathan watched television without really following it. He'd told her he loved her, and she didn't feel the same way. He'd honestly believed that she did, or he wouldn't have said anything. Part of him was still sure of it. So why couldn't she say it?

When he'd talked to Val yesterday, he hadn't told her specifically what had happened, but he'd told her his feelings were stronger than Cassie's. She'd said that he needed to give it time, which was exactly what he hadn't done so far, but he didn't know how much time he had with Cassie.

His phone rang, and he looked at the screen. Cassie. What could he say? He'd even told her he'd betray his own vows for her, if necessary, and he wasn't going to walk it back.

The phone continued ringing, and he finally answered. "Hey, what's up."

"Um…do you want to come by?"

He paused. Maybe it wasn't a good idea, but he wanted her like an alcoholic wanted a drink.

"Jonathan?" Her voice was uncertain.

"I'll be there in a few minutes."

Almost as soon as he knocked, she opened the door wearing a tank top and pajama pants.

"Hey," he said, and she gestured for him to come inside.

As the door slipped closed behind him, she said, "Thanks for coming."

He put his hands on her hips and drew her closer.

"I thought you might be mad," she half whispered.

"I know I don't have the right to be."

She peered up at him. "That's not the same as not being mad."

"It's close enough." Her warmth and the sound of her voice filled him with longing, body and soul. He sighed. "Honestly, I didn't come here to talk."

She looked as though she was about to object, but then she said, "Okay. Talking later." Standing on her tiptoes, she offered her mouth to his. He claimed it fiercely. The passion and the connection of their bodies spoke for itself, reassuring Jonathan that he meant a lot to her, even if it wasn't yet as much as he'd hoped. He could live with that.

"Hey." Late at night, she shook his shoulder, waking him up. "There is something I need to talk to you about."

He opened his eyes and half sat up. "What?" Now, maybe, they'd discuss what hung between them. Hope kindled inside him. She might return his confession of love.

"Capitán Renaud wants me to join Manus Sancti."

Maybe he was hearing her wrong. He wasn't awake yet. "What do you mean, 'join'?"

"He wants me to become a Knight."

She's going to stay.

The flame of joy extinguished, stomped out by anger. *No, no, no.* This wasn't how he wanted to keep her here. The thought of her—her spirit, her precious body—undergoing the harsh initiation and training, of rushing into harm's way at every turn, infuriated him. It was sacrilege.

"What," she said.

Christos. All he'd wanted from the time he'd realized she was an innocent woman with a beautiful soul was to keep her safe. How could Capitán Renaud ask this? The answer that came to mind filled him with disgust. "They really want that codex." He got up and began to pull on his underwear and jeans. Where was he even going? To Capitán's quarters, at this hour, to demand an explanation?

"They want *me.* They can have the codex either way—buy it, steal it and wipe my memory, whatever. It's me they want."

He zipped his fly. "You can't. It's insane. You'll get yourself killed."

"Not necessarily—"

"You know what happened to my brother." He flashed back to the image of Michael detonating into dust right in front of his eyes. If something like that happened to Cassie...

"It doesn't happen to everyone. You're still alive."

She could've sounded a little less flippant about his brother's death. And she was naïve—brutally so. "Don't you get it? Even trained warriors get killed. All the time." He'd lost so much already—his brother, his mom. Was it too much to ask that one thing he loved in life wasn't in danger of exploding in his face? "You can't do this kind of work. You have no chance!"

She put her head down on her knees. What was she doing? Calming herself down because she was angry. Why should she be, though, when he hadn't said anything wrong or even untrue? He sat down on the edge of the bed and pulled on a boot.

She raised her head. "You don't think I'm a bit tough."

"I think you're an idiot for even considering this."

"What?"

"You're being used," he growled. "The codex magic is a weapon.

Capitán wants to try it out. You're not some special chosen one. You just happen to be here."

"What does that even mean?"

He pulled the bootlaces too hard and broke one. Fine. "There are thousands of people with your same ancestry. He uses what's in front of him. We all do." He leaned closer. "Tell me you're not considering this."

She said right into his face, "I'm considering it."

He banged his fist on the bedside table, making her jump.

She stood up at the same time he did. "No, you do not get to slam things. You're a big guy; it's not fair!"

He turned away from her, raising his hands in the air. She was right, but he still wanted to smash something.

"I thought you'd be happy I was staying." Her voice was filled with bitterness.

His back was still to her and he set his hands on top of his head. "*Christos*," he muttered, disgusted with himself. If his ill-timed declaration helped encourage her to do something stupid, he wasn't going to be able to stand it.

"Go ahead and leave."

From the sound of her voice, he'd be lucky if a whole family of venomous snakes bit him this time. He spun back around. "Why are you mad at me? I'm the one who doesn't want you to get hurt!"

"You basically said I'd be a worthless coworker." That was too ridiculous to merit a response. "If I don't join, and they reverse the spell somehow, I'll leave, and you'll still be here. Is that what you want?"

"What I want is irrelevant!" He took a deep breath, his chest expanding, and let it out. "We're going to let this go. For now. We're both too mad." Even as he said it, he was choking on his own temper. They were getting too close to her losing control. "Let's not talk about it for a few days."

"I don't want to be away from you that long!"

"That's not what I'm saying!" Belatedly, he recognized that what she'd said was actually sweet, even if she sounded pissed as hell. He stabbed at the inside corners of his eyes with his thumb and forefinger. "Look. I'll see you tomorrow morning. And we won't talk about this." Or about his being in love with her. God only knew what they *would* discuss.

"Fine," she snapped.

He cursed under his breath and left.

"You shouldn't call me an idiot," Cassie told Jonathan the next morning, once they were both sitting down with their breakfasts at the cantina.

He stabbed a piece of chorizo with his fork. "I didn't. I said you were considering something idiotic."

"That's *not* what you said." Even as she pressed the point, her heart sank. She'd had this kind of conversation with Rick before.

"I thought we weren't going to talk about this." He stuffed a large bite into his mouth.

"We're not talking about…that. We're talking about how we fight. I think we should have ground rules."

He met her eyes. "I won't call you an idiot." Well, that was more than she'd ever gotten from Rick. An "I'm sorry" would've been nice, but clearly, Jonathan was still agitated as hell.

"Morning." She and Jonathan both looked up to see Gabi. "Am I interrupting?"

"No," Cassie said quickly, relieved for the interruption, at the same time that Jonathan said, "Join us."

Gabi said she was on her way to the gym after breakfast and teased Jonathan about never going anymore now that he was hanging out with Cassie all the time. Jonathan didn't seem to think it was funny and pointed out that he was just now healing up. He said he'd train with her that morning.

"I'll come along," Cassie said. "I want to see the gym." She did have one set of workout clothes in the bag that had been packed for her. He still owed her an apology, and she probably wasn't going to get it if she holed up by herself in her room.

They both got changed in their own quarters and met up at the elevator bank. Before the elevator arrived, Cassie heard a familiar "*Salaam*." She turned to see Lucia approaching them. "Cassie. Capitán Renaud told me to talk to you about the history of Manus Sancti."

Jonathan stiffened. *Oh, God.* Cassie wasn't up for any more fighting. He said, "She doesn't need to hear any more."

"Excuse me," Cassie said. Lucia gave Jonathan a sympathetic look. "You know you don't get a vote here."

Jonathan said, "Talk to her later. We're going to the gym, and I'm meeting Gabi." Lucia raised an eyebrow. He added, "Cassie wants to see the gym. And I haven't trained in more than a week."

"Yes, you've really let yourself go," Lucia deadpanned. "It has to be now. I'm leaving for Italy in two hours. I'll send you my codes and itinerary." Jonathan scowled. He could hardly argue with this, since Capitán had made him Lucia's contact. "I'll come with you," she said to Cassie. "I can talk anywhere."

The gym took up an entire floor, with a running track around the border, a rough and uneven imitation of a rocky terrain. Several people ran on treadmills through holographic environments. One man loped in a jungle and ducked as a three-dimensional graphic of a knife whizzed toward his head. The woman on the machine next to him alternately walked and sprinted down the streets and alleys of a European city, dodging traffic.

Jonathan grumbled, "I could tell her all about Manus Sancti myself."

"History is the realm of the Scholars," Lucia replied, speaking more to Cassie than to him.

In practice rings, people fought one another, punching and

kicking, but not inflicting serious damage. One man and woman dueled with big sticks. While Cassie watched, another stick flew from the floor straight at the woman's head.

Cassie gasped. Before the woman got brained, it stopped mid-air and then twirled toward the other guy, who used the stick in both of his hands to bat it to the floor.

Her jaw dropped. "What the hell did I just see?"

Lucia grinned. "Telekinesis."

"No fucking way." Cassie whirled to face Jonathan. "Can you do that?"

He made a wry face. "I wish. Samir and Freya are the only ones on the planet, as far as we know."

The two warriors had noticed them watching. The guy's face broke into a huge smile and as he strode over to them, Cassie recognized him as Lucia's fiancé from the photos in the office. He reached Lucia and pulled her in for a quick kiss. "What brings you to the gym?"

"It's not that strange of an occurrence." Cassie had to grin at the two of them together: the magical warrior, and the messy nerd. They were too adorable.

"Please," he said. "You're a rarer sight here than I am at the library." His hooded, dark eyes landed on Cassie. They were framed with lashes so thick it made him look as though he were wearing eyeliner. "This is the *bruja*?"

Lucia reddened. Cassie had figured out by now that for them, *bruja* was an insult—"witch" in the bad way. "Cassie Rios, this is Samir Hassan. Manners aren't his strong suit."

"That's okay," she said. "They aren't mine, either."

"Good to meet you, Cassie Rios," he said. "Even if you're the reason Luci has to abandon me on a quest."

Cassie told Lucia, "I'm sorry you have to go all that way."

Samir laughed. "She loves to travel."

"I've heard Aquileia is lovely," Lucia said.

"She thought *Los Angeles* was lovely," Samir teased, which seemed to Cassie like uncalled-for snark, coming from someone who lived in a giant glass hole in the desert. But still, most of the people here had lived in many places, and the Knights were always getting sent on missions to various parts of the country.

"In its way," Lucia said. "Before Cassie works out, I need to brief her."

Samir had, at least, heard about her invitation to join Manus Sancti. She could tell by the more sober look he gave her. "All right," he said to Lucia. "Find me before you leave, *almeris*."

At the far side of the gym, they met up with Gabi, who wore a black athletic top, matching loose cotton pants, and bare feet. She flashed a smile at Jonathan. "Ready for jiu jitsu?"

Cassie blurted out, "You're fighting *him*?" Crap. She'd probably insulted her. "It's just that he's so much bigger than you. And he does that mixed martial arts stuff." Gabi was also at least fifteen years older, though Cassie didn't think that played into it so much. Hell, Gabi looked like an ad for gym membership or protein powder.

"Not really fighting," Gabi said. "His ground game's rusty, and that's kind of my specialty." She wiped at her brow with one end of her towel.

"Let's do it," said Jonathan. He paused to look back. "Ask a lot of questions," he told Cassie, and then added to Lucia, "Don't lie."

The Scholar straightened. "That's offensive."

Jonathan took in a breath and looked like he might respond with something even more offensive, but instead he said in a gruff voice, "Sorry. I don't like this, but it's not your fault." He turned and walked away toward the far ring. Gabi made a face like, *All righty, then*, and went after him.

Cassie told Lucia, "He doesn't think I should join. We had a big fight about it."

"I'm not surprised," she admitted. "It is a dangerous life."

They sat down in a couple of chairs not far from the ring, where Gabi demonstrated a move for Jonathan.

Lucia asked, "How are those Spanish videos?"

"Good. I love them." Cassie watched Jonathan practice the move Gabi had shown him. "It seems like you can learn about anything here."

Lucia's eyes sparkled. "You have no idea. For a Scholar, there's no better place. Or for a Mage, or a Knight. The resources we have—" She cut herself off with a glance at the practice ring. "But it truly isn't my place to sing the praises of Manus Sancti, only to tell you about its history."

"Jonathan said it started in the fourteen-hundreds." This still sounded incredible to Cassie, but Lucia merely nodded.

"Yes, in Granada, Spain. At that time, the Nasrid dynasty had ruled the city for two centuries. Samir's ancestors, in fact. But they didn't require citizens to be Muslims, and learning was valued.

"Granada developed an intellectual society of Jews, Muslims, Christians, and even freethinkers who would've been condemned in most places as heretics. Scholars, alchemists, philosophers. Besides the Spaniards, Arabs, and Berbers, there were people from Paris, Sicily, and as far away as Egypt and Ethiopia. And all of these brilliant men—fifty or sixty altogether—met weekly to share their theories, translations, and discoveries with one another. It was like a spontaneous university."

"Only men, though."

Lucia gave Cassie a conspiratorial smile. "That soon changed. Manus Sancti was centuries ahead of the world when it came to welcoming women. Much of it was practical—some women had psychic talents that men didn't. But I get ahead of myself. They weren't Manus Sancti yet."

In the practice ring, Jonathan bent halfway over Gabi, who lay on her back on the mats, attempting to pull him down by wrapping both of her legs around one of his. They broke and switched places.

Lucia said, "Among this group of intellectuals in Granada were several men with psychic abilities. Jewish mystics, a Christian priest, and others. Another man had translated old texts with magical spells that, as it turned out, worked. So you see, what we're doing with the Phoenix Codex is something we've done for centuries."

"Wait," Cassie said. "The Phoenix Codex?"

Lucia flushed. "I've been calling it that. There's the Dresden Codex and the Paris Codex, both named after the cities in which they're housed and, well, your ancestors' codex was housed in Phoenix for decades."

In my mom's basement. Cassie shook her head to dispel a sudden sense of disorientation.

"You don't like the name," Lucia ventured.

"What?" Cassie thought about the question. She'd named it after Cassie's hometown, and it seemed like an acknowledgement that it belonged to her and her family. "No, I love it, actually."

She smiled, her dimples flashing. "Good." Cassie felt a sudden affection for the Scholar. Something told her they'd be good friends. Lucia explained that before long, Manus Sancti had begun what they now called missions.

Jonathan and Gabi rolled on the floor with their legs wrapped around each other. Cassie gestured toward them and asked, mostly joking, "Should I be concerned about this?"

"Not in the least. It's just training. And everyone knows Jonathan's excruciatingly monogamous."

"Excruciatingly," Cassie repeated. She didn't know what amused her more—that particular word, or the fact that everyone seemed to know about one another's sex lives. "Okay, go on."

Lucia nodded. She explained that the name Manus Sancti referred to no particular religion, but to the sacredness of their calling to fight supernatural evil. Although they tried to operate in secret, southern Spain had come under Catholic rule, and a Catholic-sounding name seemed like a good idea. Their group spread to Portugal, Morocco, Algeria, Italy, and Greece. "By the dawn of the twentieth century, we were all over Europe and the Middle East, in many parts of Africa, in Russia, the Americas… we'd just started spreading to China."

"World War One must have been awkward," Cassie quipped.

Her forehead creased. "It was terrible." She reacted as though it were her own memory. Maybe Scholars took history more personally.

Cassie wanted to turn to a less painful subject. "Here's something I keep wondering. How in God's name do you all have so much money?"

She laughed. "For centuries, we had people with the gift of divination. They made brilliant investments. And in modern times, we have algorithms and certain inside sources that predict the market quite well."

Cassie nodded. "How many people do you have in total?"

"About ten thousand. A thousand right here, and the rest scattered in *guaridas* across the globe. But most are in supporting roles. We have fewer than eight hundred Knights, and only about five hundred Mages. Real psychic talent is all too rare."

"You must be growing in numbers," Cassie said. "Hardly anyone ever leaves, and you recruit new people like me…" She trailed off at Lucia's pained expression. "You also lose a lot of people."

"Let me be completely clear." Lucia leaned forward, her expression earnest. "The cost is enormous. Mages are prone to psychological breakdowns and have a high suicide rate. And one-sixth of all Knights die on missions before they retire."

Cassie swallowed. It was worse than she'd expected. She looked over at the practice mat where Jonathan and Gabi still writhed on the floor. Gabi had one leg hooked around Jonathan's neck and appeared to be trying to pop his head off in the crook of her knee.

She shuddered and turned her attention back to Lucia, who asked, "Have you decided against joining now?" Her tone suggested there would be nothing wrong with that.

"No. How many people do you recruit a year?" With those odds, many people would probably turn them down.

"Maybe a couple dozen a year, mostly Knights and Mages."

"I didn't know I was so special," Cassie said weakly.

Lucia stared at her. "You're the rightful owner of one of the rarest documents on earth, and you're one of the heirs to its magic."

Cassie gave a half laugh, shaking her head. "I'm an ordinary, unemployed, divorced lady."

"These things are not contradictory."

Lucia hadn't told her everything. Cassie asked, "What else is in the codex?"

The Scholar dropped her head. "It is yours, and you have the right to know. But I don't recommend discussing it with Jonathan, at least not today. It won't make things any easier."

Gabi and Jonathan had taken a water break. Gabi was gesturing as she talked, perhaps describing a defensive move, and Jonathan looked relaxed for the first time since Cassie's fight with him. "Yeah, I'll hold off on that," Cassie promised Lucia. "What does it say?"

"Much of it is devoted to describing an ancestor of yours and his particularly epic ball game."

"Seriously?"

Lucia shrugged. "The ancient Mayans loved their sports. And you already know about the famine spell—which may not work, but we don't recommend your trying it, anyway."

The woman was hedging. "What else?"

"Well," Lucia said, "although you're not exactly what we'd call an earth elemental—someone with a magical connection to the earth or stones and crystals—there may be a spell that allows you to use obsidian to make you immune to any psychic attack, including demon possession."

"Whoa." Cassie had heard enough about their missions to understand how powerful that might be.

"I've written out the spell in English syllables, just as your great-grandfather did with the animal spell. The text is so ancient, it's difficult to know if I'm getting it right. That's why I want Lorenzo in Aquileia to take a look. I would've been unsure of the animal spell, too, except in that case, I already know it works."

"We should try it," Cassie said.

She held up a warning hand. "If I'm reading it correctly, doing the spell also brings up an onslaught of self-hatred that's difficult to survive. According to the text, the spell caused the last person to kill himself on the spot."

"Oh my God." That was a hell of a side effect. "Why? Nothing bad happens to me with the animal spell."

"We're still researching, but I believe it's integral to the working of the spell. The language is something like… *For an hour, conquer the demons within. For a day, no demons may conquer you.*" She gave a rueful smile. "It is, as they say, a feature, not a bug."

Cassie tried to wrap her head around this. "So it wouldn't last forever, anyway."

"A day at most, and maybe much less. We don't recommend experimenting any time soon."

"No. It sounds like things are dangerous around here enough." She considered the mortality rate of Knights and Mages again. "If you only recruit a couple dozen people a year, you guys must actually be getting smaller."

"Ah, well. I was talking about active recruiting. Some people marry *sonámbulos*, and to do this, the outsider needs to join." She smiled. "It's hardly discouraged. We would have a very shallow gene pool if it didn't happen. The *sonámbulos* almost always take a safe, non-specialized job, and of course, some choose to be full-time parents."

Something clicked in Cassie's brain. Was this what Jonathan wanted? For her to stay with him, but out of harm's way? She'd been angry and hurt that he hadn't welcomed the opportunity to keep her near, especially after startling her by declaring his feelings like he had. But maybe he'd seen a less dangerous way to keep her close.

Why hadn't he said so?

Of course he hadn't. Why would he talk about a future together when she hadn't even said she loved him back?

CHAPTER TWENTY

CASSIE TALKED WITH Lucia until the woman finally had to leave for the airport. By that time, Jonathan had finished training with Gabi. Cassie didn't really feel like working out. She had her usual session with Val in the afternoon, and Jonathan came to the office to meet her afterward. When Cassie asked him if he wanted to go to the cantina, he made a noise she took as a yes.

Although she expected him to have a ton of questions about her meeting with Lucia, he seemed to be sticking to their resolution of not discussing the whole issue for a while. In fact, he hardly seemed to want to talk at all. Cassie told him about how Val was training her to focus the energy of the spell, and he made polite but brief responses. He barely even looked at her, which for him was very strange. Tension tightened his shoulders and expression.

As they reached the elevators, he said, "There's someone I want you to meet."

"All right." She looked up at him, waiting for further explanation, but none came.

Apprehension seeped through her when they got off on the medical floor of El Dédalo, where Cassie had gotten her ten thousand tests when she'd first arrived. Jonathan, she'd learned recently, underwent physicals every month—standard protocol for Knights. They'd talked about not needing a condom, since they were both clean and she was on the pill, which the medical department had graciously refilled for her. If she did join Manus Sancti, it seemed, at least the health care benefits would be good.

Cassie couldn't imagine what they were doing here now, though.

The man at the reception desk said, "West. Are you visiting?"

"Yeah."

The man addressed Cassie. "If you're waiting here, there's tea or coffee—"

"She's coming with me," Jonathan said.

They went down a short hallway of closed doors. All of them had corkboards, and in addition to notes, cards, and some oddball items, a few were decorated with *milagros*. Cassie had seen the tin charms before in gift shops and in one old Catholic church in Tucson where people had pinned them to the blanket covering a statue of a saint.

She took a closer look at a cluster of them on one corkboard. Next to a few of the expected forms—a heart, a cross, a praying figure—hung a tin pentagram, a little disc scripted with a word in Arabic, and a couple of discs emblazoned with the Manus Sancti design of Jonathan's tattoo.

"Who's in these rooms?" she asked him in a quiet voice, although he'd stopped several feet in front of her. "People who have gotten hurt in action?"

"And anyone who's sick. Cancer, heart problems, anything."

Impressive—a full-fledged hospital, although a tiny one. They turned a corner, and moaning emanated from one of the rooms. Someone else muttered to himself behind a door that stood ajar. Cassie's heart sped up. What were they doing here?

A man in scrubs approached them. "*Salaam,* Jonathan," he said quietly. "Here to see your mom? She's awake."

Cassie froze. *What the hell?* He'd told her his mom was dead.

No. He'd said he'd *lost* her. Cassie's nerves frayed like wires chewed by rats. She followed him into the room, and he shut the door behind them.

A thin woman with short gray hair perched on the edge of the bed. Her thin cotton robe had slipped off one of her narrow shoulders, and Jonathan leaned over and carefully pulled it back up again before sitting down on a chair. If his mother noticed him, she gave no sign of it. She stared straight ahead.

"Hey, Mom," he said. "I brought someone with me today. Cassie Rios. I told you a little about her before. She's, uh, she's my girlfriend." He sounded so much younger, almost like a teenager.

Cassie realized she was pressing her fingers to her lips and forced her hand back down to her side. Should she say something? "Hello." She felt like she was doing the wrong things even though she was just standing there.

"Capitán Renaud asked her to become a Knight," he said. "I don't think she should." Silence. From outside the door came the muffled sound of more moaning. At least his mom looked clean and neat, well cared for. The room itself, though almost empty, gleamed spotless.

It was only fair, Jonathan pleading his case in front of a mute witness. Gabi had told Cassie that Jonathan's mother had lost her mind because of her work as a Mage. His mother couldn't offer an opinion, but if she could, she'd no doubt agree with him.

"She has magic, like I said," Jonathan said to his mom. Sympathy squeezed Cassie's heart. She was honored that he'd told his mom about her, and stricken that his mom was unable to respond. "And I'm scared I'm going to lose her, like you. Like Michael."

Cassie stared down at the floor. She should've been more understanding and less worried about whether he doubted her abilities. But she'd been hoping for reassurance, because she doubted her own worth.

"Anyway, I thought you should meet her," he said to his mom.

"I'm not going to stay today, but I'll be back on Sunday like usual, all right?" He got up and leaned over to kiss his inert mom on the cheek. God, he was so good, down to the core. She tried not to make any sound as she followed him back out into the hallway and he softly shut the door.

"This is where you go every Sunday." Cassie's voice came out small.

"Let's talk somewhere else."

Cassie took another glance at his mother's door. There weren't many things pinned to the corkboard. A greeting card that looked old, the edges curling up. A couple of *milagros*. Startled, she noticed that both of them were skulls.

Maybe people wished the peace for her that death granted. It was wrong for her to endure in this state of unknowing. Cassie wondered if that was how Jonathan felt, but she couldn't ask.

He took her up to the atrium floor with its triangular glass ceiling where people enjoyed the sun. A few young women sat cross-legged on the floor, crocheting and chatting, and an older gentleman sat alone reading. Other small groups of people gathered around tables. They'd brought coffee from the cafeteria floor. The plants and trees in pots were plentiful enough to emit a green scent. Cassie joined Jonathan on an empty bench.

"I'm so sorry," she said. "And you visit her every week. You're a good son."

He was looking outside. "Once a week, and we live in the same complex. I could do better."

"It must be hard to see her. And you stay for, what, an hour or two?"

He shook his head. "Not that long. I visit her, and then I go to Mass at the chapel."

She'd known he was Catholic, but this surprised her. "I didn't know you were so religious."

He lifted one shoulder in a shrug.

Cassie had to ask. "Do you think you're sinning by screwing around with me?"

"No."

"Good." That made one thing he didn't feel guilty about. "Why not, though?"

"I know what real evil is." He looked her up and down. "When we're together, it feels like the opposite of that."

She interlaced her fingers in his. "It feels that way to me, too."

They sat in silence for a few moments.

"Thanks for taking me to meet your mom." What else should she say? He still treated his mother like a person who could hear and understand things. Maybe that was true. Or maybe it was better for him to do so. Either way, she should do the same thing. "I hope she liked me."

"I wish you could have known her before."

"What happened? Was it one thing, or a gradual…" She was saying this wrong. "You don't have to talk about it."

He looked down at their joined hands. "It was a ghost possession spell. She invited the spirit of a dead Mage to take control of her body because he was the only one who could kill the Rededji." At her confused look, he explained, "He was a witch who reanimated and controlled people's corpses right after killing them."

Cassie recoiled. "Jesus! What the fuck kind of magic is that?"

"A strong kind. My mom thought she could survive the voluntary possession…but too much power went through her, the Mage's and the Rededji's, in the fight. She won, but it burned her out from inside."

Cassie thought this over. "Can you go into her psyche, like you do with other people? And talk to her that way?"

"Nobody can. A few Mages tried… they even had Val try, though she was still so young. I tried it once. Her barriers are impenetrable. You can't tell if there's anything behind him."

"She was a hero," Cassie said. "Like her son."

As Jonathan walked back with her to her quarters, she didn't know what to say. Her imagination roamed to thoughts of kissing him, touching him, making him forget his worries and sorrows for a while. But surely he wouldn't be in the mood, even if it felt to her like energy arced between them.

She asked about Lucia's trip. Was she flying out of Albuquerque? Yes, Jonathan said—they had private jets, but only used them when commercial flights weren't convenient. Regular flights in and out of El Dédalo would have attracted a lot of curiosity. Was it normal for someone to check in every twenty-four hours, like Lucia had mentioned? Jonathan said yes, this was standard.

Once they were in Cassie's room, he set his backpack down and asked, "How did your talk with her go?"

"Good." She tried to keep her voice light as she kicked off her shoes and pulled off her socks. He waited for a more involved answer. More restless than thirsty, she went to grab something to drink. A row of brown bottles with gold labels inside the fridge door surprised her. "Ooh!" She turned to him. "Did you buy this?"

"I asked them to. You said you liked dark beer."

"I love it." She twisted off the cap and took a good drink. The dark, rich taste, almost a little chocolatey, fortified her for whatever conversation was coming next. "Ahh. That was very nice of you."

He didn't answer, just stared at her where she leaned against the wall, barefoot, drinking a beer. She took another swig. At last he said, "My mom's story—that's not unusual. Did Lucia tell you how dangerous it is?"

"She did." After the visit to his mom, he wanted her to say she wouldn't join. That she would stay safe. But hearing about what the woman had fought against only underscored for her how much bizarre and scary shit existed in the world. Someone had to stop it.

Cassie peered at him. "Are you mad at me?"

"No." He stalked over to her, dragged her by the waist up against him, and kissed her hard. She moaned against his mouth and blindly found a spot on a shelf to set her beer.

Maybe she shouldn't have been surprised. More than one of her friends had confessed to having sex right after a funeral. Scandalously, Ana had done it with a cousin her age, one she hadn't seen since childhood, right in the back room at her grandma's house. They'd cleared a big pile of visitors' coats off the bed and onto the floor. Something about being around death and anything close to it made people want to have sex, maybe for comfort and connection, or maybe as a basic biological response, an urge to procreate to make up for what was lost.

As he kissed her, his hand slipped under the fabric of her cowboy shirt, at first caressing the skin below the collarbone, and then lower. She wasn't wearing a bra. Two snaps popped undone as his hand swept down lower, around the outer curve of her breast.

"Understand me," he said when he broke off the kiss. One of his hands rested on the back of her head as though she might turn away from him. "I want you to stay with me. I want that so much it hurts." His thumb swept across her nipple, sending a current of pleasure up to her just-kissed lips, and her breath caught. "But if anything happens to you, it'll kill me."

Her heart lurched. "I'm sorry. I'm... I know I'm so lucky you care about me like you do. And I hate making you upset." She met his eyes. "But I have to do what's right for me."

Jonathan took a step back. His frustration and desire swirled together like poison and wine. He couldn't make her love him, and he couldn't restrain her from rushing straight into danger. These were the two things he wanted most, and they were utterly out of his reach. Another fight with her would be too much to bear. And he wanted her so badly it was almost enough to break him.

"Get undressed." His voice was tight as he tried to mask the desperation and longing behind it.

Cassie's eyes widened. She took off her shirt, favoring him with the glorious sight of her breasts, and shimmied out of her jeans. Wearing only her plain white cotton underwear, she looked up at him, her mouth parted in curiosity or anticipation.

"All the way," he said. She slipped off the underwear and set it on top of her jeans on the floor.

He stared at her. Instead of drawing near, she stood still and endured his hungry gaze as though waiting for him to do whatever he wished. She was completely bare to him, he was still fully clothed, and this woke the fantasies that dwelled in the shadows of his soul. He went over to his backpack, found the handcuffs, and tucked the key into his pocket. He straightened again, fixing her in his gaze. "Do you trust me?"

"Yes," she breathed. No fear registered in her voice or her features.

"Turn around." She did immediately. As he clicked the steel ring around one of her wrists and then the other behind her back, a deep breath shuddered through her. She was aroused, maybe nearly as much as he was, and the realization sent an even more powerful need coursing through his veins. He didn't have her heart, but she trusted him with her body, and that in itself struck him with awe. She was bound to him, safe with him, at least for tonight.

Still standing behind her, he lifted her hair and smoothed it over one of her shoulders, leaving her back and the side of her neck exposed. A fine tremble went through her under this simple touch.

She had such a beautiful back. He pressed a kiss on the delicious place between her shoulder blade and spine, making her arch, and reached around her to caress her breasts. With her hands bound behind her, their tight peaks offered themselves up more blatantly to him. He kissed and bit the delicate flesh of the side of her neck, and she rewarded him with a soft moan. Her pulse slammed at the hinge of her jaw beneath his lips, the life she was all too willing to gamble and he was desperate to protect.

He placed his palm flat on her throat and glided it upward, no pressure at all, and she lifted her chin up high for him in response. The way she yielded to his light caress enthralled him. She was cuffed and obedient to his will, but he was the one enslaved. He raised his hand to her cheek, turning her head to the side, and captured her mouth with his own.

She opened for him and he reveled in the taste of her. His hand teasing her breasts ventured lower, stroking down her belly, which tightened under the caress. When he ended the kiss, a needy sound escaped the back of her throat.

He reached between her thighs, cupping her there hard, a primal move that made her gasp. She was pressed back up against his still-clothed body, and his whole hand was filled with her wetness. *Take her, now,* his instincts urged. It would be so easy to bend her over, then and there, and sink into her willing heat. Instead, he forced himself to go slow and savor this. She might be gone from his life before long, like most of the things he'd ever loved.

"Jonathan," she begged, his own name sounding almost unbearably sweet from her lips.

He delved into the slick folds and settled his fingers right on the place designed to make her lose her mind. "*Christos,*" he whispered. "I can *smell* you." Her scent, her soft sounds, the heat of her body… She flooded his senses. His desire for her rose to the intensity of physical pain. As he worked her clit, he kissed and bit her neck again. He stroked the under curve of her breast, teased the nipple between his finger and thumb, did everything he could to slowly and systematically dismantle her. She gave a soft cry and her head fell back onto his shoulder, wordlessly begging him for release.

Could she ever want him as much as he wanted her?

He spoke in her ear, his voice coming out hoarse. "You want to come like this?"

"Yes," she gasped. He was sure she was a moment away from being undone.

"Not yet," he suggested, withdrawing his hand. She whimpered.

He gently took her by the shoulders and turned her around to face him. God knew if she'd gotten angry with him, if she'd demanded satisfaction, he would've given it to her. But her expression was unfocused, lost in his game.

He cupped the back of her head with the hand still slick from her arousal and his lips took hers again. His kiss forced her mouth wide open, plundering deep into her, as though this were a way he could claim her forever. He didn't touch her anywhere else, leaving her bound body neglected, and she pushed herself closer to him. Releasing her mouth, he stepped back, thwarting her intentions. Softly, he said, "Get on your knees."

She moved slowly, probably taking care because she couldn't use her hands, and kneeled on the smooth, hard floor. Triumph surged through his being that she would do this much for him. He unzipped his jeans and eased down his boxers, his dick springing free. She ran her tongue along the edge of the head, and it twitched in response. Then she took the whole head into her mouth and sucked hard. Intense pleasure engulfed him, and a low growl came from the back of his throat.

She took in more of his length. He could hardly think. With every shred of will he had, he kept himself from shoving himself into her mouth, letting her set her own tantalizing pace. He stroked her cheek, petted her hair. She gagged as he hit the back of her throat and he froze, ready to help her up if she wanted to stop. Drawing back, she rubbed her wet eyes against his thigh, the artless action of someone utterly absorbed, and he almost lost it. *God, have mercy.* She surrounded him with her hot mouth again. His heartbeat roared in his ears. He was close, and she seemed ready to swallow his every drop. He didn't want to finish that way, not before he'd given anything to her.

He buried his fingers in her hair and drew her away from him. She gazed upward, her lips red and wet from kissing and sucking, her eyes watering, face flushed, hair in tangles. She was a beautiful wreck. He'd never seen anything so erotic in his life.

Taking her by the shoulders, he helped her to her feet. He lifted her in his arms, carried her to the bed, and lay her down on her side. She was pliant, allowing him to position her on her knees, her cheek against the mattress, moaning his name. He kneeled behind her, his body half covering hers, and reached around to stroke her.

She ground down against his hand. "Oh God, please…" In only a few moments, she came apart. "Yes!"

Her body shook with her release, and when he drove into her, she convulsed around him. His last frayed thread of control snapped. He gripped her hips and thrust into her hard and fast, and, for a moment, the world whited out, bright, blinding him as his own orgasm overcame him and he pumped himself into her.

Her legs gave way and she lay flat on the bed. He stretched out half on top of her, his breaths ragged, and laid his cheek on the back of her shoulder.

I am going to love her until the day I die. He knew it for a fact. There was nothing either of them or anyone else could do to change it.

She barely moved, dazed and spent. After pulling up the jeans and boxers that he'd shoved down around his knees, he unlocked the handcuffs and set them on the nearby table. She stretched out on her side, and he gathered her into his arms.

"Why do you do these things to me?" Her voice was low, lazy with female satisfaction.

"Why do you let me do them?" He really wanted to know.

"Because it gets me so excited."

He couldn't help a small smile of male pride. "That's one reason why." He could feel her heart beating hard and fast still. The truth tugged at him. "And I want to know how much you would do for me. Because I would do anything for you."

She drew back to look at him, her eyes wide, as if stunned by the honesty of his quiet admission.

Longing filled him, even after all they'd shared, but this was purely spiritual. "Cassie, let me go into your psyche."

She tensed in his arms.

"It won't hurt," he promised. "Not when we're like this."

"Why do you want to?"

"I was only there once, when I attacked you, when I wasn't—"

"That doesn't matter now." Her tone was firm.

"I want to be that close to you." He'd never felt closer to anyone than he felt to her in this moment, and he still wanted more. He searched her face for a response. "When I have a right to be. Please."

"All right," she said. Her acquiescence filled his soul with gratitude. "What should I do?"

"Close your eyes." As she obeyed, an idea occurred to him, something that might make his entrance even easier for her. "I'm going to shut down my own barriers...they're so thin right now, anyway." She probably didn't know what he was talking about. "Okay, here we go."

There was no pressure or pain. Cassie felt his psyche and met and welcomed him in the same way she'd opened many times now to his desire. The walls of her self did not tumble in. They blurred and dissolved. An unworldly feeling came over her, something like goose bumps, though it wasn't physical.

She smelled burning candles. That made no sense. She opened her eyes.

She and Jonathan were both standing, but not in the colorful desert she'd expected. Tall walls surrounded them, many stories high, filled with intricate carvings. A saint with the face of a gargoyle, so hideous she looked down, only to see pages from hymnals or prayer books scattered on the floor, some spattered with blood. She took in a sharp breath.

Dozens of ivory tapers in candelabras sputtered in the niches in the walls, piercing the darkness, throwing shadows that gesticulated like living things. But some light shone down from the tall stained-glass windows, red, green, and blue. She didn't understand the stories they depicted with medieval knights and ladies, but they were beautiful.

Amazing statues, not at all frightening, stood on huge pedestals. Marble, maybe, but so carefully detailed that if they hadn't been larger than life, she would've expected them to breathe and speak. Warriors fought together, back to back. Nude lovers clasped one another, blatantly carnal, yet not out of place in a sacred space. The cord of a vein in the wrist. The fine texture of a lower lip.

A cold wind bit her skin. She was as naked as she'd been on the bed. Turning around, she saw the cathedral was half gone, as though it had been bombed. Beams lay aslant against a remaining wall. One pillar presided over a pile of rubble. Even though light came in through the windows, the open part of the building looked on a benighted forest and a dark sky. But there were stars. The hairs stood up on the back of her neck and arms.

She stared at Jonathan, who stood barefoot, wearing only his jeans. Why had he brought her to this strange place, so grand and so ravaged?

His jaw was slack. He was as shocked as she was. "How did you get in here?" He thought she'd done something on purpose.

"This is you," she breathed, suddenly understanding. "We're in you."

"Val said you couldn't enter people's minds." His voice carried an undertone of accusation.

"I can't! All of this is new to me, remember?" The suspicion faded from his eyes. "You said you closed down your barriers." She wasn't completely sure what that even meant.

He shook his head, dumbfounded. "This should be impossible."

As she looked around them again, new understanding filled her. The carvings of frightening men, of monsters. How many cursed spirits, evil witches, and demons had he faced in his lifetime already? Of course, they'd left their traces. The hymnal pages on the floor, dotted with blood—a sense of guilt, threatening to overwhelm. His every mistake, failure, and fault registered in his mind as mortal sin. Something in her heart cracked at the realization. The huge statues, nine of them, almost glowing in the candlelight—these were all love. For friends, fellow soldiers, family.

For me. She saw now, with awe, that she was the woman in the statue of the lovers. The stained-glass windows glowed far above, many stories over their heads. Vignettes of bravery, kindness, and all of his ideals…so bright, so far to reach.

"What is it?" he asked in a low voice, and she realized a tear traced down her cheek. His voice held fear he couldn't disguise, as vulnerable as he was here, though God knew he'd never been a coward about expressing his feelings. It was one of the countless things she admired about him.

"It's beautiful here," she blurted out. If she hadn't been so emotional, she might've laughed at the look of disbelief on his face. "Look at the statues. No, look up at the windows."

He obeyed, and his expression softened. "They weren't lit up before. When Val Read me. They haven't been in a long while."

He would've remembered Val being in his head, the way Cassie remembered him being in hers. Val had only erased the memory of her Reading in order to make Cassie feel more comfortable, because they'd been strangers at the time. "It's good you're here. You have a right to know about the…the ruined parts."

Jesus. Did he think she was going to run away from him because his mindscape wasn't lollipops and rainbows? Honestly, that would have been terrifying. She had her own damage. He'd seen it: the forest in the distant mountains of her desert, burned black by wildfire. How would he understand her if he had no problems of his own? This place, so troubled and heroic, seemed infinitely precious to her.

"You asked why I let you do…the things you do to me." She smiled. "It's because I want you to know I accept all of you, even the darker parts."

He stared at her like a man visited by an angel. "I don't deserve you," he whispered.

"Don't ever say that again." She hadn't told him she loved him, even though she did, and the wrongness of that pained her. Having messed up her first, best chance, she'd worried about the timing, but she couldn't stand it anymore. She stepped closer to him. "Jonathan, I love you. I love you so much." His whole heart was in his eyes. They'd both been so emotionally raw even before she'd entered his soulscape. She took his hand, enveloping it in both of hers. "I should have said it before—"

"No, I said it too soon. I never feel like I have much time." The statement sent a chill branching up her spine. Why would he think that? "You know I meant it, though."

"Don't you worry about my animals hurting you?"

"You're controlling it." The corner of his mouth turned up. "Anyway, you're worth the risk." He leaned close and kissed her, raising his free hand to caress the side of her face, his thumb grazing along her cheekbone and temple. But in the middle of the kiss, he flickered. For an instant, he wasn't quite there, physically, and then he was solid again. "This might be drawing a lot of energy," he said. "Having you in my head. I don't even know. I should break the connection."

"Do you know how?" A horrible thought flitted through her head, like a crow swooping from one of the high rafters to the other. He wouldn't be able to get her out, she wouldn't know how to extract herself, and it would drain the life out of him. She'd just seen what too much magic had done to his mother.

"I think so." He closed his eyes. She did the same, with a child's logic—if she couldn't see this world, maybe she'd no longer be in the middle of it.

The quality of the air changed. Jerking, she opened her eyes and found herself on the bed again. Jonathan still clasped her against him, perhaps even more tightly.

She breathed, "How the hell did that happen?"

CHAPTER TWENTY-ONE

"JOHNNY," VAL SAID when he showed up with Cassie the next day for their afternoon session. Cassie still wasn't used to Val calling him that, not that she minded. "What are you doing here?"

"We need to talk to you about something."

Her pretty brown eyes flicked to Cassie and back to Jonathan. "I'll make you some tea. I already have the water hot." As they sat down, she pulled things down from the shelves. "Kava and St. John's Wort," she said. "And lemon balm and lavender. You seem like you've had…an emotional time lately."

Cassie wasn't surprised that Val picked up on some aftershocks. After Jonathan had accidentally taken her into his psyche the night before, he'd been lightheaded—a psychic drain, he'd said. The strangeness of the experience and the passion of their whole encounter had taken a lot out of Cassie, as well. She felt elated, but tender and raw, almost as though she needed to grow a whole new skin.

"It's nothing bad," Jonathan assured Val.

When she brought the tea over, she said, "It has an unusual flavor, but it'll do you good."

It smelled terrible. Remembering what Jonathan had told

her before—*if a Mage makes you a cup of tea, drink it*—Cassie took a sip anyway. It tasted worse, honestly like semen, which was actually an okay taste to her in the middle of things, but out of context, it was disgusting. Val knew what she was doing, so Cassie made herself take a second sip.

Jonathan said, "Cassie was in my psyche."

Val blinked. "That's not possible. She doesn't have the gift. I can have Delphine or another Mage check, but I'm sure."

"No, I think you're right. It didn't feel like any other time anyone entered my mind. And she didn't try to get in."

She cast a skeptical glance in Cassie's direction.

Cassie said, "It's true."

Val's expression softened. "People used to be able to do this. Subsummation, they called it—being able to bring someone else into your own psyche, instead of the other way around. How did it happen?"

"I don't know. I was trying to enter *her* psyche." Jonathan took a drink of the tea and looked like he was about to gag. He set it back down.

"Has this ever happened to you before?"

"No!" Jonathan spread his hands. "I've Read, what, maybe two hundred people?"

"Cassie, I assume you were willing this time."

Cassie nodded and then thought of what they'd been doing before the soul-linking. *Willing* hardly covered it.

Val asked Jonathan, "Was there anything that made this time different?"

Well, there was the fact that his dick had just been in me. Cassie felt genuinely curious about how Jonathan was going to explain this.

He massaged his shoulder the way he sometimes did when something made him uncomfortable. "Of course, I hurt her before, the first time. So I wanted to be careful. I lowered the shields in my own mind."

"The way you would do if I were Reading you?"

He nodded. "Except more, I mean—I left it completely open."

Val's pink-lipsticked mouth parted in disbelief. "But how could you drop your defenses while going into another mind? It would be like breathing in and out at the same time! Did someone teach you how to do this?"

He shook his head again. "I was just trying not to hurt her."

"Most people can't drop their defenses the way you do, anyway. Some people can lower them, but you're the only one who can leave yourself completely open."

His brow creased. "You never told me that."

"I didn't think it mattered." Her face lit with wonder. "You have one of the Lost Gifts."

Jonathan looked more wary than pleased. "Why me? I hardly even inherited any of my mother's gifts. Just shielding and the most basic Reading skill."

"Everyone's unique. Let me Read you to see what happened. Experiencing it like you did will give me a better idea of how you did it."

Oh, this could be bad. She might see Cassie handcuffed on the bed. Jonathan cleared his throat. "We can't do that." *Thank God.*

Val looked perplexed. "Why?"

"When I tried to go into her psyche, we were—we'd just been together."

"Then I won't pry." She folded her hands, not looking particularly embarrassed. She'd already said she picked up on Jonathan's lust for Cassie as more or less a constant. God, she probably felt Cassie's, as well. Maybe she wouldn't be shocked by a little respectful domination, but Cassie still preferred to keep it to herself. "Do you think your being intimate with her somehow helped you do this?"

"I...maybe." His eyes darted to Cassie. "I mean we were very close."

Cassie filled the next uncomfortable silence by taking another drink of the tea. It was cooling, which made it all the more gross.

"You have to try it again," she told Jonathan. "See if you can bring someone else in your psyche all the time."

"Debriefing's your job," he protested. "And I've known you most of my life."

"But we have to try this out. Pick someone who isn't psychic, someone you trust."

Within the half hour, Gabi was slouching in a seat in Val's office. "You know I don't like this stuff."

"It won't take that long," Val said. "Cassie, is there anything that you did? To get into Jonathan's mind?"

Cassie shook her head. "I tried to relax. That was it."

"All right." Val nodded at Jonathan. "Let's give this a try."

He reached over and took Gabi's hand. She sighed but closed her eyes, leaning her head back into the stuffed chair. For several seconds, neither of them moved. Cassie felt like she was breathing too loudly and tried to be quieter.

Gabi jerked in her seat, and Cassie jumped, too. Both she and Val leaned closer. Was Gabi in Jonathan's psyche? He straightened, releasing Gabi's hand and opening his eyes. She snapped out of it, too, saying, "Ugh. Thanks a lot."

He let out an exasperated sigh. "I went into her psyche. Sorry. I tried to do it the same way."

"It probably takes practice," Cassie said.

Gabi got up. "Well, no more practice on me."

"Thanks for letting me try," Jonathan said. "Sorry."

She gave him an indulgent eye roll as she left. "Good luck, I guess."

Jonathan said, "I always thought it was the most useless of the Lost Gifts. I mean, teleportation, healing, prophecy, telepathy— I'd cut off my right arm for any of those."

Val leveled him with a look. "Please stop saying how you want to sacrifice yourself for the common good. The Goddess may take you at your word."

"I don't think it's useless," Cassie prodded him. "Stupid me. I thought it was amazing."

He softened at once. "It was. I meant in the bigger scheme of things." He gave a rueful laugh. "And I'm mad it didn't work the second time."

"You'll get the hang of it," Cassie said.

As Jonathan left the office with Cassie, he puzzled over what Val had said. Why would he have a Lost Gift, even one he considered negligible? If only he could've talked to his mother about it. She would've loved it, he was sure.

Cassie interrupted his thoughts by saying, "That tea tasted like jizz."

"It tastes that bad?" He must have had a horrified look on his face, because she laughed at him. They agreed to go to the cantina for coffee to wash the taste out of their mouths. On the way there, the alarm vibrated on Jonathan's phone. He stopped short and whipped it out.

"What's going on?" she asked.

Jonathan frowned at the bright bars and numbers on the screen. "It's Lucia's heart rate. And her breathing."

"You're tracking that?"

"Yeah, I'm her contact." He noted her location as he called her. "She's still at Lorenzo's. It's probably nothing." Physical activity... though he didn't know what that would be. Lucia had checked in with him at the predetermined time yesterday. She and the elderly scholar wouldn't be doing anything but talking and research. Dread rose in him. Lucia wasn't the type to go for a jog.

As the phone rang, Cassie asked, "Isn't it awkward to check in sometimes? I mean, someone could be having sex or something."

"Yeah, well," he muttered. "She's not going to be having sex with anyone who isn't Samir." Anybody who knew the two of them knew that. As he waited for her to pick up, he pressed a button to bring up her complete vitals. He stiffened. "That's a huge adrenaline dump." What the hell was going on? Cassie leaned closer to see the screen. He said, "I'm punching through."

"What?"

He pulled up a keypad and punched in a code. "This makes her phone pick up, turns the camera on, and puts me on a loudspeaker." She probably remembered Nic doing this after the bear attack.

The screen filled with beige, and a woman's scream tore through his consciousness. Cassie jumped. Jonathan shouted, "Lucia, what's happening?"

A man's voice, shouting a question in a foreign language. Nothing on the screen but pockmarked taupe. A ceiling. Lucia's voice, distant but a shout. "Tribunal!"

"No no no—" Jonathan's brain seized up with panic. "I'm sending help—"

"Too far!" she countered. *Oh, God. Lucia.* The face of an ugly, middle-aged man filled the screen, his features both soft and cruel. Cassie let out a little shriek. He stared at both Jonathan and Cassie. Jonathan returned his gaze, memorizing the features of a man he intended to hunt down and kill. A second man said something in the background—he strained to catch it. Then Lucia's voice, yelling but only just audible. "Tell Samir I love him! With all my heart!"

Jonathan bent over and leaned his shoulder against the wall, cradling the phone in both hands. He knew what that declaration meant. He had to be strong for this. The man holding Lucia's phone launched into foreign curses and tried to press buttons, his thumbs obliterating much of the screen. No matter. Lucia could hear him.

"I'll tell Samir. Lucia, listen. You've done so well." He spoke in a loud, steady voice, the way he'd been trained. "You're brilliant. You're loved, by all of us. You leave this world with no debts or cause for regret." Lucia's voice, barely audible. She was saying her drop code. Jonathan continued, "We will take revenge—"

A cracking sound, and the screen went black. The man must have destroyed her phone. Jonathan touched a few buttons with shaking fingers while Cassie looked over his shoulder. Lucia's vitals again: heart rate zero, breathing nonexistent. The bar that read brain activity flared wildly. Then that bar went to zero, and the screen went black.

Jonathan leaned his forehead against the wall, his eyes shut tight. *My fault, my fault.* It had happened so fast. He should've checked in with her again this morning. But she would've called him right away if she were in trouble, or she would've called Samir first. They must've taken Lucia's phone immediately. The Tribunal? A nightmare of history, rising again to life.

Cassie had lowered herself to the floor next to him, sitting on her heels. A couple of people walking by them stopped in their tracks, about to ask if they needed help. Cassie waved them off, angrily, even though they acted out of concern.

"I would have sent Knights from Rome," Jonathan said. He shook his head, trying to clear it. *Do your job.* "I'll send them now." He typed in the message to the *comandante* in Rome and sent it. "I should have told her to hold on. But it might have taken them too long…she knew that."

"She was being tortured?" Cassie's voice cracked. "Or about to be? By who?"

"By the best. Christ help me." Scholars didn't get interrogation training. Lucia would've broken and given information to the enemy. She'd done the right thing. Cassie choked on a sudden sob. Jonathan's hand rested for a moment on her shoulder, an automatic, numb gesture meant to comfort. He made another call.

Davinder Singh, a middle-aged man who wore a black turban and thick eyeglasses, appeared on the screen. "*Salaam*, Jonathan. What do you need?"

"*Obitus.* Samir Hassan. Capitán Renaud. Andre Turner, Gabriela Bravo. And, uh—a Scholar who knows a lot about the Tribunal." The man's eyebrows rose. "And Nic. Dominic Joe. That's all."

The man nodded, his features solemn. "*Obedezco.*" He flickered out.

Cassie sniffled. "What's happening? Emergency meeting?"

"Yeah."

"Am I invited?"

He nodded. "This is *about* you." Her eyes widened in alarm. "They hate us, but they wouldn't murder a Scholar for no reason. They know something about the codex. Besides, you might have heard something I didn't."

"I don't think so. It happened so fast."

"They'll go over the video soon," he said dully.

"You recorded the conversation? Good. They can get the motherfuckers."

Even in his dazed state, he appreciated her spirit. "Everything is recorded."

She sat up straighter. "The guy we saw. He's a dead man. Something's coming for him."

"What?"

"I felt the power come over me," she said. "I tasted the blood."

"An animal attack?" He wished. "I don't think so, Cassie. He's on the other side of the ocean." Spells didn't usually fly so far.

"Right." She shook her head. "I'm not thinking clearly."

"Don't worry," he assured her, grim. "We're going to end them."

"Who are they? Tribunal?"

He drew in a deep breath. "We haven't heard about them in decades. We thought we'd killed them all. That they had no more descendants, no more followers." His phone vibrated, and he answered it. The man he'd talked to before appeared on the screen. "Suyuuf Room, ten minutes."

CHAPTER TWENTY-TWO

CASSIE FOLLOWED JONATHAN into a room shaped like a hexagon. Swords, daggers, and scimitars hung on some of the walls.

Samir stood alone at the other side of the table, his head slightly bowed. He looked up at their entrance, and as Jonathan reached his side, his dark eyes filled with concern. "What's happened? Is Luci all right?"

Jonathan held his gaze. "She's dead, *corín*. I'm so sorry."

Samir flinched and closed his eyes as if he'd been slapped. Cassie's heart wrenched. It was such a blunt way to tell him. Maybe that was intentional. There was no way to misunderstand the words, much as Samir might have wanted to.

Jonathan raised his hand as if to put it on the other Knight's shoulder, but then returned it to his side again. He looked sick, and Cassie's whole soul went out to him. "My fault. I should have asked for someone go with her. You—"

"No one's fault but theirs." Capitán Renaud's loud voice filled the room. For once, Cassie was grateful to him. He entered with two people she'd never seen before. The first one, a woman with an elaborate braided updo, wore a tailored yellow shirtdress and heels and carried a thick folder. Cassie guessed she was the Scholar, though the ones she'd seen so far had been much more slovenly.

The guy was maybe in his mid-thirties, of Asian descent, with dark, wavy hair that hung to the collar of his leather jacket and a short scruff of moustache and beard. *Knight*, Cassie thought immediately. But no, Jonathan had asked for a mission runner. Then she made the connection: Dominic Joe, the one who called Jonathan and Gabi when they were in trouble. Jonathan had called him Nic.

Capitán Renaud added, "No one knew the Tribunal was active."

Horror washed over Samir's face. "The Tribunal. She was tortured."

"I don't know," Jonathan said. "She...I made contact right after her vitals spiked. They must have just gotten there. She told me it was Tribunal. I told her I was sending help, but she said it was too far—and then she dropped."

"She was waiting for you to punch through," Nic guessed, his voice stark. "So she could warn us."

Jonathan looked back to Samir and swallowed. "She said to tell you...she said, 'Tell Samir I love him, with all my heart'."

Samir covered his face with his hand as he turned away. Cassie wished she could think of something to say. God, what if he blamed her? If she'd never shown up, Lucia would have never gone to Aquileia.

"We are very sorry for your loss, Hassan," Capitán Renaud said. After a few moments, Samir raised his head.

Gabi and Andre entered the room. Gabi looked from Capitán's face to Samir's and said, "Oh, no." Andre quietly closed the door behind them.

"Everyone sit down," Capitán said. "West, we'll review the tape later. And we'll hear from Rome in a few hours." Not looking at the video was a kindness to Samir, Cassie realized, giving her yet another reason to feel grateful to Capitán. "But we know it wasn't a random attack."

A wave of dizziness came over her. Not surprising, given what had just happened. She needed to keep it together.

"They're after the codex," Jonathan said. "They must have surveillance in place, tech or psychic, I don't know."

"Unless we have a traitor in our midst," Capitán said.

"It's not me," Cassie blurted out.

Capitán looked bored. "You don't know anything or anyone of importance." It was insulting, but she felt relieved that no one would think this was her fault. He turned to the dressed-up woman with the folder. "Okafor, give us an overview of the Tribunal. My Knights could use the refresher."

She nodded. "That's what I expected." After pressing a couple of buttons on her phone, a woodcut illustration appeared on the screen. It showed a woman being burned at the stake. Dread settled in the pit of Cassie's stomach at the sight. "The Tribunal first formed in the late fifteenth century, not long after Manus Sancti. They were an elite group of Catholic inquisitors, charged by the pope to find, try, and burn heretics and witches."

"By 'try,' you mean 'torture,' right, Hadiza?" Gabi ventured.

"Exactly." The Scholar switched to a map of Europe. A few cities shone with red light. "The Tribunal was based in Rome, with inquisitors in Spain, France, and Germany."

"I'm sorry, I'm confused," Cassie said. She should've kept her mouth shut, but someone she'd liked had just died in a terrible way, and getting a history lesson bewildered her. "Lucia was killed by witch hunters?"

"The Tribunal was an elite force because they had psychic abilities such as Reading. Of course, this was seen as divine favor. They were believed to be living saints." Samir gave a short laugh, raw and bitter.

Nic slouched back in his chair. He kept looking at her in a curious rather than flirty way.

She shifted in her seat as Hadiza continued. "These special

inquisitors became aware of Manus Sancti, then a small society in Granada. In the eyes of the Church, their explorations of the paranormal made them witches and consorts of the Devil."

"Wait a minute." Cassie didn't mean to keep talking, but this was a lot to take in. "How come The Tribunal got to be all psychic and magical, and Manus Sancti didn't?"

"Because Manus Sancti wasn't affiliated with the Church. Not long after they formed, they began admitting women, which was seen as proof of evil. And even at its beginning, Manus Sancti included Muslims, Jews, and even heretics. To the Tribunal, not being Christian equated to being in league with Satan."

Samir was staring at the weapons hanging on the wall. With their ornate details—two even had jewels in the hilts—they looked ancient, but they gleamed as though they'd been made yesterday.

Hadiza turned back to the map. "In 1492, right after Isabella and Ferdinand conquered Granada, the Alhambra Decree ordered the expulsion of the Jews. Along with several Jews suspected of making false conversions, the Tribunal burned thirteen Manus Sancti members at the stake in Granada and five more in Seville." The red lights on these cities pulsed.

"Holy smokes," Cassie said and immediately realized it was a terrible word choice. "Sorry."

Hadiza's brows rose. "That was five percent of the group. The other members in Granada were driven underground—quite literally, in the catacombs."

Interesting. So living underground was truly part of their heritage. Hadiza talked about religious persecution and the emigration of Manus Sancti members. Cassie's eyelids grew heavy, as though she'd been up all night the night before. But she'd gotten plenty of sleep, and she wasn't bored by Hadiza's history lesson. How could she be so exhausted and dizzy at a time like this?

Jonathan touched her arm, frowning in concern. She shook

her head, waving her hand in a reassuring gesture. No doubt she was just emotional. She needed to focus.

The next slide showed the basilica in Rome with sun streaming out from behind it. Hadiza said, "By the eighteenth century, the Vatican saw witch hunting as less of a priority, while the Tribunal had grown too powerful. In 1740, the pope officially decommissioned the Tribunal.

"However, the Tribunal remained an intact group that believed the Vatican had become corrupt. They declared their new goal: to convert the entire world to their brand of religion."

"Lots of groups have that goal," Cassie muttered.

"Quite correct. They continued to torture and murder those they considered heretics, particularly Manus Sancti. Meanwhile, we grew in numbers and spread across the world. The Tribunal saw us as a rival group intended to impose universal worship of the Devil. A new world order, if you will."

"Right, that's us," Gabi said dryly.

"So they think you're, like, the Illuminati?" Cassie asked.

"Yes," Hadiza replied, "if the Illuminati were much worse." She turned back to the screen. "In late eighteenth-century France, the Tribunal infiltrated the Jacobin clubs and sent most of our members in Paris to the guillotine."

Jonathan leaned forward, elbows on his knees. "I never heard about that." Cassie hadn't, either, of course, since all she knew about the French revolution was *A Tale of Two Cities*, which she'd skimmed in high school, and the movie version of *Les Miserables*.

Hadiza went over incidents of violence between Manus Sancti and the Tribunal throughout the nineteenth century and during the first World War. "Finally, in the early 1950s, the Tribunal killed sixty-eight of us at our Paris *guarida* using the Vollum strain of anthrax." Cassie wouldn't have guessed that anthrax existed back then. "Capitán Renaud's mother, Jacqueline Duval, of course, was one of them." Hadiza touched her hand to the top of her chest, her index and middle fingers extended together sideways. Jonathan, Gabi, and Nic did the same, a quick, instinctive gesture.

Samir stared at his hands that rested, folded, on the table. Capitán's expression was stony. How old would he have been when his mother died? A child, definitely.

Hadiza explained that in 1957, Manus Sancti had launched a strike in several cities that had effectively ended the Tribunal. In the early 1990s, the Diviners had come across a few scattered discussions of the Tribunal in Internet chat rooms, but nothing more. She turned off the screen and took a seat.

Andre said, "A few years ago, we came across someone claiming to be Tribunal in the dark web, but it was gone almost immediately, and we couldn't trace it. And no one had heard about them since."

Capitán's gaze flicked from him back to Hadiza. "I need to know who this new generation is. Descendants of our enemies? Psychopaths taking up an old cause?"

"We're on it," Andre said.

Gabi shook her head. "How are we even sure Lucia's captors were Tribunal? Someone could have lied to her."

Samir drew an audible breath and spoke for the first time. "She must have seen something. Luci is a genius. She wouldn't say it if it weren't true."

"She was certain," Jonathan agreed in a low voice. "And she didn't hesitate. She wasn't going to give up a thing."

"Did you—" Samir paused and glanced upward, his eyes glazing with tears, and tried again. "Did you have time to give her *absolutio*?"

Jonathan's frown deepened. "Yeah, I…did the best I could." He looked to Capitán. "What do we do?"

"We hunt them down," Samir said. "*Ultio mea est.*"

"We need to get as much intel from them as possible," Capitán said. "Three Knights in Rome are after them, and I'm sending a psychometrist to pick up any information she can. But none of them can Read a prisoner."

Samir's lip twitched upward in a snarl. "I'm happy to interrogate."

Jonathan darted a worried glance in his direction and said to Capitán, "Send me."

Cassie struggled to keep her eyes open, and her arms and legs felt heavy. She longed to lie down on the floor.

Capitán said to Nic, "We do need someone who can Read people. Who's closer?"

The mission runner glanced up briefly from his phone. "Octavio Zain, in Algiers. He's on a mission now…a necromancer in Tunis." Clearly, he'd anticipated the question. He touched a couple more buttons. "I'm sure it can wait. I'll contact Algiers and put Zain in contact with the team in Rome." He glanced from Samir to Capitán. "Are we sending Hassan?"

"See how fast you can get him there. It's his fight." Samir gave a grateful nod. "Let's discuss final arrangements. Was Dimitriou Orthodox?"

"No," Samir said. "She was an atheist."

Nic said, "Her will says cremation, internment anywhere, memorial here at El Dédalo."

A fresh wave of shock washed through Cassie. They were talking about Lucia's dead body.

Capitán said, "I've sent another Knight to retrieve her body. West, contact the family members right after this."

"I'll call them," Samir said. Cassie expected Jonathan to look relieved. He looked guiltier.

Capitán nodded. "Joe, tell Zain I want every ounce of information he can get. ID every other Tribunal member they know. Let Hassan be the one to finish them. If it's practical."

Andre looked up from his phone. "Um. It may be too late for one of them."

All eyes turned toward him. Capitán said, "Explain."

"Maybe Cassie should explain."

She'd been sagging in her seat, but now she jerked up straight. "What happened?" Was it something with her animals?

"I put a global search on Aquileia news a few minutes ago. Here's something that's already been shared a few times." In a few moments, a photo appeared on the big screen in the room. A man lay in the middle of a street, surrounded by birds.

"What is this?" Capitán asked. Andre pressed another button.

The jerky video flickered in and out of focus. A whole flock of birds surrounded him, starlings, she thought, flying and pecking at whatever vulnerable spots they could reach—his hands, his head. He turned and they could see his whole face. His eyes had been pecked out.

When he opened his mouth to scream, another bird darted in to pull off a chunk of his tongue. Cassie let out a little shriek and pressed her hands to her face. More dived in to peck and yank at his throat. Blood spurted—they hit a vein.

Cassie hid her eyes. "Oh my God." The screaming on the video had stopped.

After a moment, Andre said, "That's the end of the footage. Jonathan, is that the man you saw?"

Cassie lifted her head again. Jonathan stared in awe at the now-blank screen. "Yeah, no question."

Samir's eyes sparked with vicious satisfaction while Hadiza's expression reflected frank horror. Capitán Renaud's eyes half closed, like a cat after it knocked a water glass off the table.

"I—I thought this would happen," Cassie said. "Not birds, but…" She trailed off.

Capitán said, "From the other side of the world. Impressive display of power."

She felt dizzier than ever. "I was…very angry."

"Resourceful, too," Capitán added. "Such an ordinary bird. But with enough of them—immediate retribution."

"Wasn't…choice," she murmured. The room spun.

Samir turned to her. "I'm in your debt. If I can ever repay you, I will."

Relief. He wouldn't come to hate her for what had happened. But no, she didn't deserve thanks. "I'm not…" she started to say. The edges of her vision sparkled. "I won't going…" Jonathan moved closer and put a hand on her arm. She tried again. "I wanted maybe my…" The connection between feelings and speech had snapped in her. Everything went black.

CHAPTER TWENTY-THREE

JONATHAN SAT IN the darkened room in the hospital wing next to the bed where Cassie lay unconscious. Everyone said she just needed to sleep. The doctor and nurse had gone away. Once they had, Jonathan had tried to wake her up anyway, to reassure himself that she was okay, but she remained dead to the world.

Should he pray for her? It probably wouldn't do any good. As a teenager, he'd prayed every night for months for a miracle for his mother. Since that time, he hadn't asked for any healing, though he often asked for strength and wisdom. Those requests hadn't always been answered, either, but maybe that was his fault.

He sent up a prayer for the peace of Lucia's soul. She hadn't believed in God, but he didn't believe in a God that punished people for things that harmed no one. Lucia had worked night and day trying to figure out the codex and help Cassie. Had Jonathan ever even remembered to thank her? No, he hadn't. He remembered his irate tone with her when she'd just been following orders by debriefing Cassie on Manus Sancti. His only consolation was that Lucia probably didn't care what he thought of her since he'd never gotten to know her as well as he should have. Sophie had been better friends with her when they'd all been in

London and he'd still been dating Sophie. It was strange to think that Sophie wouldn't even know about Lucia's death, but leaving Manus Sancti had been her decision.

Lucia's heartrending scream at the other end of the phone echoed in Jonathan's consciousness. At the end, she'd been so brave, hanging on until he contacted her, laying down her life rather than endanger the group. Samir should be very proud of her. But Samir had always been proud of her, and now she was gone.

Jonathan said a brief prayer for Samir, as well, wishing him comfort and strength. It seemed pointless, though. Samir and Lucia had been engaged—planning their wedding at Anantara, the beautiful estate in Saint Augustine, and their married life together. What comfort could there be for Samir?

Footsteps sounded behind him, and Val sat down in the chair next to him. She'd left a few hours earlier, and he suddenly realized how tired he was. She set one of the biodegradable containers from the cantina on the table. "I didn't know if you'd gotten a chance to eat."

He hadn't. The spicy smell of the food, whatever it was, revolted him. "Thank you."

She slipped her hand in his. "You know she's going to wake up, right? All the tests say she's fine."

He could tell her what he'd kept thinking when the doctors had assured him of this. "They thought my mother would wake up."

"They hoped. But it was different since no one could Read her."

Jonathan had refused the doctors who'd asked him to go into Cassie's psyche. They'd needed to do it to make sure everything was normal, but in her state, he was afraid he'd accidentally hurt her or make things worse. They'd brought Val in to do it, which hadn't worried him, because Val could drift into another psyche so lightly. She'd assured everyone that there was no damage. "I didn't tell you this with the doctors here, but Cassie's psyche is more beautiful than ever." Val squeezed his hand. "She's fine."

A dark suspicion still clung to his mind.

"What?" she asked.

"Michael and now Lucia. I feel like I'm cursed on missions."

"Neither one was your fault! You've saved so many lives. I've seen you do it. Cassie thinks you're about the last thing from a curse. Maybe she hasn't told you she loves you yet, but—"

"She did." It lit a small hope in him, shining in the darkness.

Val smiled. "The bond between you two is so strong."

Did he catch a note of wistfulness in her voice? As far as he knew, Val had never dated anyone. To him, she was simultaneously a child and a Mage of formidable power, although he supposed the first thing wasn't true anymore. Relationships were so difficult for strong empaths that they often remained alone. The thought made him appreciate even more how lucky he was to have Cassie.

After a little while, Val left him again, and he looked at Cassie where she lay in serene, deep sleep. They could have the things Samir and Lucia had wanted, things many people wanted: a wedding, a shared life. A family, maybe—the thought of it filled him with longing. If Cassie were a fellow Knight, they could always be together, or at least as long as they lived.

The idea of her becoming one still scared the hell out of him. After seeing what she was capable of, though, it was almost hard to imagine her doing anything else. And if she were a Knight, she'd know how to defend herself in more ordinary ways, as well.

No matter what one chose, there were no guarantees of safety. Maybe that was all the more reason for them to do what they wanted most and to get as much joy out of their lives as they could.

Cassie woke up in a hospital bed with Jonathan lying next to her. Panic sent her heart into overtime, and she grabbed his shoulder. "What happened? Did I hurt you?"

"Cassie! Hey." She'd woken him up. "No, no you didn't." Tenderness filled his voice.

She remembered Lucia. Then the attack of the birds. "Oh my God." In her disoriented state, it was too much, and her throat tightened with sobs. Jonathan pulled her close to him. Someone had put her in a hospital gown, but he was wearing a T-shirt and jeans—he wasn't a patient. She sank into the blessed comfort of his strong, warm body.

"You passed out," he said. "At first, we thought it was a stroke. The way you were glitching."

She frowned, remembering her babbling. "And Val was in my psyche." Or had she dreamed that part?

"She didn't erase the memory of her being there?"

Cassie shook her head. Maybe it meant she and Val were friends now. "She said you all had to make sure nothing was damaged."

"They did an MRI, a bunch of tests. You're completely fine."

They had time to do all that? She drew back to look at him. "How long have I been out?"

"A little more than a day."

"God." She rubbed her eyes.

"They say you burned up too much energy with the animal spell. Controlling something across the world…" He gave a wondering shake of his head. "You told me, but I didn't believe you."

"I didn't know for sure."

He stroked back a strand of hair that had fallen into her face. "How are you feeling?"

"I think I'm okay. I'm sad." The shock of Lucia's death had settled somewhere deep in her bones. She hurt all over. "How are you?"

"The same." He grabbed her hand and kissed it, a quick, impulsive gesture familiar to her by now. "But a lot better, now that you're conscious." She'd given him a scare on top of everything else.

"Wait. Were there any other animal attacks?" Maybe her spell had found the other men who attacked Lucia.

"Andre's team was watching for them, but no."

"What about the Knights in Rome? Did they track any of them down?"

"No. I've been getting updates on everything on my phone." Had he been here the whole time? His face settled in grim lines. "The Knights went through Lorenzo's apartment—the palaeographist who got killed. Lorenzo had started helping Lucia on her translation of the codex, but the Tribunal took Lorenzo's computer and ransacked his books and papers."

So strange that a group of humans would exist for centuries, trying to bring Manus Sancti down. Or maybe it wasn't any stranger than Manus Sancti itself. "They think you're like the Illuminati," she said.

"Yeah."

"Well?"

His brow puckered. "You're asking if we want to secretly take over the world? Don't you think I would have told you?"

"No," she said. "Because it would be secret."

"Well, there's nothing like that." He looked beyond weary. "I'll always tell you anything you want to know, I promise. And probably some things you don't."

She kissed him on the cheek, and they were quiet for a minute. Her mind returned to the codex. "So they have the translation." They could find someone else who could use the animal spell. She gritted her teeth at the thought of those monsters using her magic.

Jonathan shook his head. "Lorenzo and Lucia wouldn't have used the computer. Lucia wouldn't have trusted it for security. She mailed the latest translations to our safe house in Taos, tucked in a big stack of Italian fashion magazines." Damn, that was clever. "We're sure they didn't get anything from Lucia about the codex or about us. She dropped too fast."

Cassie's stomach felt like a lead weight. "Did they find her body?" Jonathan barely nodded. "Did they do anything to her?"

He gave her a pleading look. "You don't want—"

"You have to tell me!"

He'd just told her he'd never keep secrets, but he looked like he was about to be sick. "They gouged out one of her eyes. They must have done it immediately."

Oh no. Oh God. Her hands flew over her mouth.

Jonathan pulled her close again. "I know."

Hatred coursed through her veins. "I'm going to kill them," she whispered. "Why didn't my animals get to all of them?"

"We talked about that, too. It seems like you have to know what someone looks like." That sounded right to her. "I'm so glad you didn't," he added with soul-deep sincerity. "Multiple long-distance attacks… That much power might have broken you."

"Maybe it would have been worth it." She wanted them torn to shreds.

The corner of his mouth turned up in a rueful half smile. "It's no wonder Capitán wants you with us."

"Right," she said, cautious. Her heart couldn't take another bitter fight, not now.

"Does knowing what happened with Lucia… I wonder if that changes your thinking about it." He didn't want a fight, either. She could hear it in his voice.

"It does." She looked in his eyes—beautiful eyes the color of the sky before a rain. "Now I know I want to join." He said nothing. "They killed Lucia because of me." Jonathan began to object, and she cut him off. "I never even heard of them before, and they killed her and some old guy I never met over my codex. And I hear about your guys' missions. There are bad people and bad things out there, and I can help fight them. I want to." He still didn't say anything. That drove her crazy. "Are you mad at me?"

"No. God, no." He let out a harsh sigh. "I know it's your

choice. I'm scared for you, and at the same time, I'm…very proud of you." He shook his head. "And I can't help it. I'm so glad you're going to be here with me." His forehead creased. "Not that you're committed forever. I mean whatever happens, I'll always be your friend—"

"Shut up," she interrupted him. "You know I love you."

He cupped the side of her face and kissed her like he was drinking the words from her mouth.

CHAPTER TWENTY-FOUR

"I WANT TO join," Cassie told Capitán Renaud in his office. Excitement shone on her face, and Jonathan, standing mutely next to her, felt another pang of misgiving.

"Good," Capitán said in a hearty tone and then turned to Jonathan. "I'm curious. West. How do you feel about this?"

Giving a complete answer to that question would've taken all day. "She's a powerful force to have on our side."

Cassie ducked her head. "I don't have a bunch of training like him and Gabi."

"You'll never have anything close to their fighting skill," Capitán agreed. "But you can learn some basics. We can develop your marksmanship even further. And you have magic. Even more than you've used so far."

Jonathan cocked his head. "What do you mean?"

"Did Dimitriou tell you?" Capitán asked her. "The codex includes a spell for immunity to psychic attack."

What? Cassie nodded. How had she not told him this? "Any psychic attack?"

Capitán nodded. "It's temporary, but yes. Anyone trying to enter the psyche. Demon possession, mind control spells, you name it."

"That's fantastic." If it worked, her risk on missions went down dramatically.

"But it might kill me to do the spell," Cassie mentioned. "So that's kind of a drawback."

Jonathan went from feeling hopeful to wanting to punch a wall. Why the hell were they even talking about it?

"It's challenging," Capitán acknowledged. "But promising. Our enemies would've loved to have had it."

It would be a long time until Cassie would be a Knight going on missions, Jonathan reminded himself. There was no sense getting mad about it yet.

Cassie asked, "How did the Tribunal learn about the codex?"

"Val and a few other Mages are Reading everyone at El Dédalo, looking for a mole," Jonathan told her.

"Everyone?" she exclaimed. "That's going to take forever."

"They're halfway through," Capitán said. "Everyone's clean so far. Vega may meet with you at odd hours as a result. She'll oversee your initiation."

Val was going to be exhausted. And Jonathan never would've expected Capitán Renaud to put her in charge of Cassie's ritual. That was going to be hard on her…though not as hard as the ritual would be on Cassie. And there would be nothing he could do to help her.

Capitán added, "Samir Hassan will be your mentor for training."

"I can be her mentor," Jonathan said without even thinking.

"You know it doesn't work like that." He did know, of course. Family members, lovers, and even close friends were too emotionally invested. Capitán was probably giving Samir the job to distract him from his grief. Jonathan couldn't fault the logic. He'd have to assume that Samir would be able to focus enough to give Cassie the training and knowledge she needed to survive. Maybe, having lost Lucia, Samir would be all the more determined to do so.

Cassie asked, "Will I always be here at El Dédalo?"

"You'll be wherever we need you."

This would probably be in the States, since she didn't speak anything but English. Either here, or in Saint Augustine or D.C. She was working on Spanish, though, with videos Lucia had given her, and she'd told Jonathan she wanted to learn Arabic, too. Just as well, if she were going to join them.

The whole topic of her deployment disturbed him. If they'd been engaged or married, Capitán would have never ordered them to serve in different *guarídas,* but he didn't make any special dispensations for those who were merely dating. It would've been impossible to accommodate all relationships like that. At least, in the short term, she'd be here, since Samir would be her mentor.

Cassie asked, "How often will I get to see my parents?"

"You'll get a few days off every month. You can do anything with that time."

"That's not so bad."

"We won't separate you from your family," Capitán said. "But we do want to keep them safe. And us, too. Go meet with Andre. He has your cover story and a communication plan. It'll start with a call to your parents." Capitán's eyes flicked to Jonathan. "Rios is no longer your responsibility. She's shown herself loyal to us. She's controlling the animal magic. If she fails in the future, that's on her."

Jonathan nodded. Cassie didn't need his supervision, and he should be glad that his Capitán trusted her.

"However," Capitán added, "feel free to keep following her around."

Cassie's mind was a tangle of thoughts as she and Jonathan walked to the Diviner lab.

"Samir will be a great mentor," Jonathan admitted. "He'll

push people, but he won't humiliate them. And he's the best warrior we have."

"I thought that was you," she teased.

"Ha, no. Telekinesis makes you very hard to fight. And Samir was raised as a Knight pretty much from the time he was born, because he had it. He and Freya both were. 'Course, he can't teach you to throw things with your mind." He crooked a grim smile. "He's a big fan of your animals, though.

"I don't think he'll want to start right away," she said.

"No." The expression in his eyes dulled. "Lucia's service is tomorrow."

Cassie had heard they'd returned her body to El Dédalo. She and Jonathan got on the elevator.

"Are you sure you want me in the meeting with Andre?" he asked. Maybe Capitán Renaud's comment about him following her around had affected him.

"Definitely. You're going to see my mom again. And meet my dad. I want you to have the story straight."

They found Andre in the same spot as before, in a room full of computer geeks, but he took them to a side room and shut the door behind them, He gave Cassie a binder full of papers. "Here's your story. You can go over it in detail later, but today, you'll be telling your parents that you've taken a job at Freemont Mining Corp. in New Mexico."

She'd heard of the company. "But I told them I was glad I was getting out of mining."

"Oh, people who get fired say lots of things," he said easily. "Now you have a high-paying, high-pressure job that'll require a lot of travel. You also have government contracts that you really can't talk about."

"That's pretty good," Cassie admitted. They'd probably be proud of her. "But what if they want to visit me? I have to tell them no?"

"You put it off," Andre said. "If it's unavoidable, we do have a few very nice properties set up nearby, which you can claim as your own for a weekend or so." He flipped to the next page. "We've made a basic call script." A series of boxes in a flow chart outlined statements and responses. "Make it sound as natural as you can."

Cassie knew it was for their protection as much as Manus Sancti's. Still. "You guys have no idea how weird this feels."

"Actually, I do," Andre said. "My parents in Mobile think I work for a federal laboratory."

She gaped. "You were recruited. How did you wind up here?"

"My thesis project at MIT got their attention." He handed her a phone that looked like Jonathan's, a solid black rectangle. "That's yours to keep, by the way. Your parents' numbers are already in there. I took the liberty of putting in a few other numbers, as well—Samantha, Ana Quintero, Jonathan, Valentina Vega, and Samir Hassan, since he'll be your mentor."

Having a phone full of contacts in her hand pleased her more than she would've expected. "Can I get yours and Gabi's, too?" As soon as she asked, she felt embarrassed. Maybe he would tell her they weren't really friends.

"Sure thing." He took it back, input the information, and returned it to her. "Whenever you call your parents, your old cell phone number will show up for them. Let's get started. We'll be listening in." He put a silver disk in his ear and handed one to Jonathan.

At first, the call went smoothly. Cassie told her mom about the new job, and then she made Cassie wait until she got her father on the other line so she could fill him in, too. "Good for you, Cassafrass," her Dad said. Jonathan smiled at her childhood nickname.

Cassie mentioned that she was house hunting in Albuquerque. "So honey," her mom said, "Are you and David breaking up then?"

"Uh, no." She looked to Andre, who shrugged with an expression like, *You're on your own.* "I think we're pretty serious, actually."

"You should bring him for Christmas dinner. You're still coming for Christmas, aren't you?" her mom added. "Sam will be home on the twenty-second. You know she doesn't get that much vacation."

"I…" Cassie looked to Andre, who nodded. "Yeah. I'll see if David can come, too. I don't know what his plans are."

"Oh, and tell him to bring your grandpa's journal back," her mom said. "I don't want to lose track of that."

They held Lucia's memorial service in the library. After Jonathan got dressed in the same suit and tie he'd worn to Michael's funeral, he met Cassie outside the library doors. She was wearing a black dress and pumps that one of the Stewards had procured for her. He'd never seen her dressed up before, except for the party he'd seen in her memories, and even though it was a modest outfit, her appearance stunned him. When she turned and saw him, her eyebrows rose. "You look very nice," she said quietly when he drew near. Obviously, the occasion left her subdued.

"I was thinking the same of you." She'd never worn any jewelry in the short time he'd known her. Would she like some? Her ears were pierced. Maybe he could give her emerald earrings. People often gave them to lovers because the earth elementals considered them the best love-stone. Earrings like that might be impractical for days spent training, but maybe someday they'd have a positive reason to get dressed up.

Like a wedding. He pushed the stray thought out of his mind. It would be a long time before Cassie would ever be able to consider that, given that her first marriage had been a disaster.

Rows of chairs filled the big open space in the middle of the library, surrounded above and below by the clear shelves lined with books. Because it wouldn't be a religious ceremony, several people who loved her would say some words—Lucia's family, Samir, a couple of the Scholars. Then there would be a full minute of silence, followed by a ceremony in which her name would be written down in a large ancient book filled with the names of Manus Sancti members killed in action over the centuries.

The library was already crowded, some people in their seats, and others standing in little groups. The sight of the gathering brought Michael's memorial rushing back to him, blurring his consciousness. He closed his hand around Cassie's to guide her to the front. The contact brought immediate comfort to his battered heart.

Samir sat next to Lucia's parents. As they approached, Samir turned around and stood up. Jonathan made the symbol of respect to the dead and then hugged Samir, willing the Knight more strength. He asked in a low voice, "How are you holding up?"

Samir looked about ten years older than when they'd seen him last, teasing Lucia at the gym. "I'm not," he said bluntly.

The answer didn't surprise Jonathan. "She was lucky to have you, Samir. You made her happy."

Samir closed his eyes briefly and nodded.

Jonathan shook hands with Lucia's father and mother, saying, "It was my honor to work with Lucia. She was brilliant and very brave." Next to him, Cassie squirmed. The day before, she'd told him that she was afraid they'd blame her for the codex that had gotten Lucia killed.

"I'm Cassie," she said to them, her voice pitched higher than usual. "I'm new here. I didn't know Lucia long, but I really liked her. I'm so sorry." She choked on the last word. Jonathan's chest ached with love and tenderness for her.

Lucia's dad pressed her hand, nodding.

As they took their seats a few rows back, she murmured to

Jonathan, "That was nice, what you said to Samir. About him making Lucia happy."

"People want to know that they did well." At Michael's service, he'd wanted someone to tell him he was a good brother. When he'd told Cassie the story of Michael's death, it had been almost her first response. He knew she didn't think of herself as someone who said the right things, but when it really mattered, she did.

Afterward, when people were milling around and talking, Samir approached them, touching Cassie's shoulder. "I understand I'm going to be training you."

She blinked. Jonathan doubted she'd expected to discuss this now. "I'll try to do a good job."

"So will I," Samir said.

CHAPTER TWENTY-FIVE

L UCIA'S DEATH DELAYED Cassie's initiation into Manus Sancti. Samir went on leave from El Dédalo to spend time with his sister and her family. Because he would be Cassie's mentor, he would play a role in the ceremony.

She was glad he could get away for a little bit and be with people who loved him. Without asking, she knew Jonathan hadn't gone anywhere after Michael's death. His best support would have been here.

A few times, she went to the gym with Jonathan, who showed her a little about weight training. She'd never taken an interest before, but he'd told her that working with Samir would include becoming physically stronger. They went to the shooting range a couple of times, where Jonathan continued to practice shooting left-handed. Cassie focused on simulations that featured evil spirits and demons, and ones that posed the challenge of telling the good guys from the bad.

One night, she watched a movie in Jonathan's quarters with him, Val, and a Knight Cassie had seen around named Tristan Münter. It was a tight squeeze with Jonathan wedged between Val and Cassie on the bed, while Tristan, a big, quiet guy with a dark beard, sat on the floor basically at Cassie's feet. She was growing accustomed to the fact that no one at El Dédalo had much of a sense of personal space.

Jonathan and Val enjoyed the film more than Tristan and Cassie did because it was in Arabic with no subtitles.

"I thought everyone in Manus Sancti spoke Arabic," Cassie murmured to Tristan.

"No, we all speak Spanish and English. Some people speak Maghrebi—Moroccan Arabic—and some speak Egyptian Arabic like this." He pointed at the screen.

"But you all have a few Arabic words you use," Cassie pressed. "And sayings."

"Yes. And Latin."

Cassie glanced over at Jonathan and Val. They didn't seem to mind that she and Tristan were talking through the movie, but she lowered her voice again anyway. "I get why you all speak Spanish. You started in Spain. But why do you speak English?"

He raised his eyebrows, which were thick and angled, one with a bare patch in the middle from a scar. "Why does everybody speak English?"

Not quite deterred, she asked, "Why did the headquarters move here?" She'd intended to ask Lucia when she got back from Italy.

"It's a big country. Nobody pays attention. And you leave people with guns alone."

It didn't sound particularly complimentary. Cassie doubted he'd been raised in the States. "Do you speak anything besides English and Spanish?"

"German and Maori." At her confused look, he explained what Maori was, with considerable grace, considering he was part Maori.

Ordinary life at El Dédalo was kind of like living at a college dorm full of much more grownup international students and nobody puking in the hallway. Cassie was beginning to feel at home there.

While Samir was still away, Capitán Renaud assigned Jonathan and Gabi on a short mission, Jonathan's first since Cassie had arrived. Nic, the mission runner, briefed them over breakfast at the cantina while she listened, not feeling like a hanger-on because she was supposed to be learning about how things worked now.

"Basic ghost banishing in Amarillo," Nic said. "The American Quarter Horse Hall of Fame and Museum."

"There's a horse museum?" Cassie was sick with jealousy.

"Tell me the ghost isn't a horse," Gabi said.

"No. Supposed suicide, but pretty clearly a murder victim. Three people injured so far, no casualties."

"What do you need both of us for?" she asked. "It's four hours away."

Nic shrugged. "It does seem like an easy one, but we always send two for ghosts. You remember what happened in Sligo."

Gabi half closed her eyes in annoyance. "You may as well send Cassie. A child could do this job."

"Hey," Cassie objected half-heartedly.

"You've done enough dangerous missions for two careers," Jonathan said to Gabi. He'd told Cassie before that Gabi was way past her twenty-year obligation and lucky to still be alive and whole. Now he paused, taking a bite of his *huevos rancheros*. "Maybe you should quit while you're ahead. Marc and Luis are growing up, they might have kids before long—"

"Before long?" she snapped.

"A long time from now," Jonathan amended.

"You think I'm too old?" she pressed him. "I'm as good as I ever was."

Jonathan glanced up at the ceiling. "You know I know that."

"You'll have plenty to handle soon enough," Nic told Gabi. "Capitán wants you for a *comandante*."

Jonathan's and Gabi's heads swiveled to look at him.

She demanded, "What makes you think that?"

Nic shrugged. "It's obvious. Taveres in Athens told a few people he was stepping down within the year. Capitán sent you there to command the Furies mission last year, when Taveres was getting treatment. And he encouraged Marc to go to Athens instead of Sao Paolo." Jonathan gave a huge grin.

Gabi's eyes narrowed at Nic. "You think you know everything that goes on."

"There's a good reason why I think that."

Cassie asked Jonathan, "Do you want to be a *coman-dante* someday?"

Nic and Gabi both stiffened. Apparently, it was a tactless question, but Jonathan was probably getting used to those from her. "No. I mean—as long as we're together, I couldn't."

She would hold him back somehow? She didn't like the sound of that. "Why not?"

He spread his hands as if this were obvious. "Because I can't give you orders."

"Yes you can!" she snapped. Nic and Gabi exchanged an amused look. "Work is work," she clarified. "Unless they have rules against it." Maybe they did. At Mission Minerals, a person couldn't date a direct report.

"We don't," Gabi said.

Jonathan folded his arms. "Still not an option." He had thought about this before. The realization humbled Cassie. His father was a *comandante*, and he'd probably at least imagined following in his footsteps.

Nic said to Cassie, "Yeah, it would never work. He couldn't risk you. You'd have missions to, I don't know, go find Girl Scout cookies."

She grinned. "Hopefully, they'll cover that in my training."

Gabi said dryly, "Well, it wouldn't be much more dangerous at the horse museum."

Nic pushed the black file folder toward Gabi. "Cheer up. Maybe something will go horribly wrong."

"It's been known to happen," Jonathan said, more grim.

Sometime after midnight, Jonathan texted Cassie to let her know they'd persuaded the ghost to move on. It had been just as much of a milk run as Gabi had expected, but still worth doing, since malevolent ghost activity tended to escalate. It satisfied Jonathan to accomplish a simple mission again, even if it felt a little strange that Cassie was at El Dédalo without him. He and Gabi returned late the next night, as did Samir. The day after that, Cassie and Jonathan met with Samir and Val in her office to discuss the ceremony.

Samir wore jeans and a white T-shirt damp at the collar from his wet hair, as though he'd just taken a shower. The light had gone out of his eyes. Lucia's emerald ring hung on a chain around his neck, and Jonathan felt a stab of sorrow at the sight of it. "The initiation is much different from full Knighthood," Samir told Cassie. "Right now, you're only indicating your intention to begin training."

"I'm not promising to complete it?"

He shook his head. "For all we know, you may not be able to."

Cassie's jaw set, the expression on her face saying, *the hell I won't.* Jonathan doubted there was any chance she wouldn't complete it…assuming she made it through the initiation. Every time he thought about it, his gut twisted. If she didn't complete the ordeal, she'd be crushed. Either way, it was going to be brutal.

Samir went on to say, "You'll promise to never betray Manus Sancti, and that pledge holds for life. And as long as you're an initiate, you're expected to obey orders—from Capitán Renaud, from me, and from any other Knight if you shadow them on a mission. But you can choose to end your training at any time."

"Fair enough," Cassie said.

"The ceremony is old-fashioned," Val told her. "It may seem strange to you as a *sonámbula*."

Cassie sighed. "Are people going to call me that forever?"

"Not after this," Samir said.

"I'm a little nervous."

"I'm nervous, too," Val said. "I haven't overseen a ceremony before. I'm surprised Capitán asked me to do it."

Jonathan's pulse sped up, although he kept his face neutral. *Nervous* hardly captured what Val was feeling. The night before he'd left for the mission in Amarillo. Val had sought him out, breaking down into tears.

Should he tell Cassie what to expect? It might make it easier on Val, too. But if he broke his vows like that, he had almost no chance of getting away with it. Val wasn't the only empath, and someone might notice that Cassie reacted like someone who expected an ordeal. Any one of a couple dozen people in El Dédalo could Read him and prove he'd warned Cassie ahead of time. People who grew up in Manus Sancti knew about the rituals, but outsiders needed to prove themselves. This rule went back a few centuries. Breaking the silence could lead to a long sentence at Solemore, Manus Sancti's only prison. That might make Cassie lose control of her animal spell, and what would happen to her then?

The ordeal served other purposes beyond a test of courage and determination. It gave initiates more confidence in their own strength and more commitment to Manus Sancti, and it gave their new Manus Sancti brothers and sisters loyalty to them in return. But none of that seemed worth it when he thought about Cassie being in pain.

Maybe she wouldn't withstand it, and Jonathan would never

have to worry about her launching herself into danger again and again as a Knight. But he couldn't bring himself to hope for her failure. Maybe she'd refuse to do it completely. Probably, she should.

"You'll do great," Cassie told Val. Her kindness and obliviousness tore at his heart. "Do you have to memorize anything?"

"Yes, and so do you." Val gave her a couple pieces of paper.

Cassie took a deep breath. "That's going to be hard."

Samir gave Jonathan a grim look. The grieving warrior wasn't taking Cassie's initiation lightly, which Jonathan deeply appreciated.

"What?" Cassie said.

"It'll be a challenge," Val told Cassie. "But I know you can do it."

CHAPTER TWENTY-SIX

A WEEK LATER, Cassie stood outside the auditorium on level seven. She'd thought she wouldn't be scared.

She walked alone into the huge space filled with people wearing scarlet robes. Ordinarily, El Dédalo was high-tech, all sleek surfaces and white-noise hum. Here, only the flames of dozens of torches, burning in sconces along the walls, lit the large unfamiliar space. Everything flickered.

"Old-fashioned," Val had said. It looked like a graduation ceremony in hell. Panic washed over her. *What the fuck am I doing?*

Then she saw the faces of familiar people—friends. Val and Samir, standing on the dais at the front of the room. Gabi, the warrior she'd come to like and respect, with her husband near the front of the crowd. Jonathan stood next to her, his beautiful face solemn. His eyes met Cassie's, and the love in them went straight to her soul and propped up her confidence. Lengths of black braid draped at the front of both Jonathan's and Samir's robes. Because they were mourning, Cassie guessed: one for a brother, and one for a lover. These were good people at Manus Sancti, who'd risk anything to protect the world from the evil it didn't even recognize. And she was going to join them.

She wore a white robe that reminded her of being a child and playing the angel in a Christmas pageant. Her feet were bare. She reached the dais and stood in front of Val. On a side table, next to a carved stone box, lay a bundle of red fabric, the robe they'd soon drape over her.

Val said in a voice loud enough to carry, "We are here to witness the initiation of Cassandra Rios, descendant of the scholar Rodrigo De La Garza, descendant of the freedom fighter Jacinta Canul, brave ally to our Knights, and heir to ancient magic."

Well. That sounded a lot more impressive than Cassie believed herself to be. The brave ally part particularly surprised her. Val said a few sentences in Latin, which everyone but Cassie seemed to understand, and then switched in English to say, "Let the initiate come forward, discarding her old life and preparing herself for the new."

Now Cassie was supposed to take off her white robe, a symbol of her pre-Initiate life and the innocence it entailed. Val had told her that for most initiates who'd grown up in Manus Sancti, this part of the ritual signified a coming of age rather than a transition into a whole new life. All of them had been initiates, in a matter of speaking, for their whole lives. None of them had been raised unaware of the supernatural evils that plagued the world.

For an outsider initiate like Cassie, however, it resonated more powerfully, not the least because she still had her conventional shyness about her body. Nonetheless, she unfastened the two hooks holding the front of the robe together, slipped out of it, and let it fall to the ground.

She was standing naked in front of hundreds of people. Hadn't she had nightmares like this? But fine. It was done. As Val said more in Latin, the mortification of it burned away. Everyone had a body. There was no shame in that.

Val switched to English again to say, "The Initiate will speak her vows."

Though Cassie didn't have much practice at memorizing

things—the Gettysburg address in grade school, a Shakespearean sonnet in high school—she'd been over her oath so many times that she didn't even worry about screwing up. She kneeled and raised her left hand, palm out, as she'd been instructed. She thought this was weird, since most people were right-handed like she was, but Val had been clear on this point. There were no microphones, and Cassie spoke as loudly as she could without actually yelling. Val had asked her before she'd learned the vow about her religious beliefs, because Manus Sancti had alternate wordings for certain faiths and for atheists, but the standard one was fine with Cassie.

"By the Divine, who goes by a thousand names,

by my own highest principles,

by my soul, and the souls of those I love the most

in this world and the next,

I offer my open hand.

Fill it with knowledge, virtue, and power,

so that it may be sanctified.

I pledge my loyalty and discretion,

upon the loss of my life."

She let her hand fall to her side again. With a shake of his head, Samir reached down and lifted it back into position again. *Oops.* She expected him to give her a reassuring smile, the way a priest at a wedding would if the best man fumbled with the ring. But Samir looked somber.

While Val asked the whole crowd ritual questions about guiding her, she held her hand there in the same outstretched position. They answered in unison, and she felt humbled and vulnerable, hearing people promise to look after her while she kneeled naked. No doubt this was the intended effect.

Val said, "Now I will explain and administer the initiation ordeal."

This wasn't part of the script as she knew it. Only pride kept her from whipping her head around to look at Jonathan. Instead, she glanced up at Samir, who gave an almost imperceptible nod.

Val looked different from any time she'd ever seen her before, her pretty round face pale and hard. Cassie's hand trembled because she'd been holding it out for so long, and she anchored her elbow against her side.

Val said, "Cassandra Rios, coal is a symbol of hidden knowledge, and a burning coal symbolizes this wisdom being revealed." She didn't sound like herself. Her soothing voice, to which Cassie had become so accustomed, had been replaced by something almost robotic. "In this part of the rite, you will show yourself willing and able to accept this knowledge, and the sacrifices that come along with it."

Samir picked up the carved stone box from the side table and removed the lid.

From a pocket in her robes, Val produced small silver tongs. She said, "I will place a burning coal in your palm, and you will grasp it with all of your strength as you repeat words after me. You will not let the coal drop or even open your hand until I command it, or this rite is forever forfeit."

Cassie froze. *Jesus Christ. They're serious.* Terror short-circuited her brain. This was wrong, deeply wrong. *They're a cult. A sick cult.* Val reached into the box with the tongs and drew out a glowing orange coal. *No. Fuck these guys.* Now was the time to get up, grab her robe, and walk away.

But she didn't pull back her hand. She didn't want an ordinary life. She never had. In her heart, she yearned more than anything to fight with them and be one of them. She had come this far.

Val placed the coal in her palm, and she cried out as it seared her skin on contact. *I know you can do it*, Val had said before. No. She couldn't stand this for three seconds.

Fuck it. I can stand anything. She gripped it tight.

Val said, "With the wisdom of a thousand generations, my hand is filled."

Repeat. I'm supposed to repeat. "With the—" *Fuck.* What had she just said? "With the wisdom of a thousand generations, my hand is filled." The agony from her palm throbbed through her whole body like a second, torturous heartbeat.

"With the knowledge of a thousand worlds, my hand is filled," Val said.

"With the knowledge of a thousand gen—worlds, my hand is filled." Cassie's voice ended on a whimper as the coal continued to burn her, somehow hotter now than when she'd first grabbed onto it. The smell of her own searing flesh sickened her. Light flashed behind her eyes. If she passed out, would she fail?

"With the power of a thousand spells, my hand is filled."

Cassie got the sentence out. Her hand seemed fused to the coal now, and tears bathed her cheeks. *They're monsters.* In desperation, she offered the pain up to God or Val's Goddess or whoever might be there. Not that any deity enjoyed her suffering. But she had nothing else to give, and maybe it could be transformed into something good. The corners of her vision dimmed.

"Cassandra Rios, open your hand."

Her hand sprung open as if on its own, and Val lifted the coal from it. Her stomach roiling, Cassie stared down, bracing herself for the sight of oozing or charred flesh, exposed bone. Her palm was smooth and unblemished. Now that the coal had been taken away, she felt no pain.

A magical illusion. Her soul sobbed in relief. She closed her eyes and took a deep, shuddering breath through her mouth, because her nose was running.

Val said, "Cassandra Rios has completed the Initiate ritual with honor."

A touch on her shoulder. Samir handed her a clean white towel, exactly like one might get at a nice gym. As Val said something else in Latin, Cassie cleaned her face with it, blew her nose, and dropped it on the floor. She was gross. She didn't care. Val looked pale, as though she'd gone through an ordeal herself.

Samir handed Val the red robe. She said, "Rise, Cassandra Rios, and receive your initiate distinction."

Cassie's soul swelled with pride at the words. *This is it. I did it.* Samir held out a hand to help Cassie up, which she appreciated, because her knees had gone numb. Val shook as she helped Cassie into the garment without meeting her eyes. Wordlessly, she took Cassie by the shoulders and turned her to face the crowd.

When she did, they erupted into applause. Fresh happiness sprang into Cassie's heart, and her eyes teared up again. *I belong.*

As voices and cheers still echoed around him, Jonathan bowed his head and closed his eyes, willing his shaking body to still. It was over. He would have taken any pain for Cassie, and he'd been able to do nothing but stand by and witness as she suffered. Michael's and Val's initiations had both gutted him, but they'd both known the trial was coming and that it wouldn't do permanent damage.

Gabi squeezed his shoulder. He lifted his head and met her knowing and sympathetic gaze. On the dais, Cassie wore the red initiate robe she'd so bravely earned, and she was smiling now, her eyes sparkling with tears of joy rather than pain. Samir hugged her, which clearly took her by surprise.

Jonathan took a step toward her when Val came rushing by him, her face the color of ash, bleak misery in her unseeing eyes. He took hold of her shoulders. "Val! Are you all right?"

She blinked, finally seeing him, and her face crumpled. "I'm sorry, please don't hate me." Her voice strained high.

Empaths could swing all too quickly to dangerous depths of despair, and although she was practically family to him, he'd never seen her like this. He tried to catch her gaze, and he spoke as unequivocally as possible. "I love you, *corina*, you know that. Nobody hates you."

"Cassie will never forgive me." She tried to pull away from him. "I need to get out of here."

"Call me if you need me. Promise?"

She nodded, and when he let her go, she rushed to the exit. He'd ask someone to go look after her.

He looked back at Cassie, who was watching him with her lips twisted in annoyance, no doubt wondering why he wasn't already at her side after what she'd been through. His heart overflowed with pride in the warrior he loved, unpracticed but fierce. He strode over to her, took her face in both hands, and kissed her, drinking deeply of her triumph, offering himself as reward. He still cupped her face as he told her, "You did so well. I'm so proud of you."

"I didn't know that was going to happen—"

"I couldn't tell you. I'm so sorry." He stroked her hair. The hatred he'd felt toward all of Manus Sancti—himself, first and foremost—was subsiding somewhat now that she was all right.

"But it's fine." She held up her palm. "It didn't hurt or anything as soon as I let go of it. What the hell was it?"

"The Jaizkibel Stone. Made by a Basque witch, centuries ago. The burning is an illusion."

"It was real enough," she muttered.

"I know." He took her left hand and caressed the palm that had caused her so much pain. "It was so much worse for you. You had no way of knowing it wouldn't do permanent damage."

"How would anyone know that?"

"If you'd grown up Manus Sancti, you would've been told beforehand. With outsiders, they make sure of their conviction."

She nodded. "Do you guys always use the burny coal thing?"

He shook his head. "There are different ways to do it." The dread that had dogged him before cast a shadow over his thoughts again. "Are you mad I didn't warn you?" She'd just made a vow of secrecy herself, so maybe she'd understand.

"No," she said firmly. "I proved myself like everyone else."

He took in another cleansing breath and exhaled. "It was horrible to see you go through that. I've been through interrogation training, but…" He shook his head. This had been worse. He glanced back at the entrance through which Val had made her escape. "Val hopes you don't hate her."

"She was just doing her job."

"It was hard on her." He hadn't meant to talk about everyone's pain except Cassie's. He raised her hand and pressed a kiss in her palm. "Not nearly as hard as it was on you."

Cassie's brow furrowed. "I should go talk to her."

She was so good. "I'll text Delphine to check in on her. People will expect you to celebrate."

She blinked. "What do you mean?"

Hadn't they even told her about this? "Everyone's going to the solarium level to party. There's going to be food and drink like you won't believe, and dancing, and every single person will want to congratulate you personally."

"Wow," she said. "Okay, I'd better go change."

"No. We stay in our robes."

She pulled her own robe more tightly around her. "But no nudity?"

He laughed. "I can't promise that." An initiation party usually involved a lot of high spirits and alcoholic spirits. "But you can keep your robe on." Taking her hand, he led her to follow the crowd.

"Okay. As long as it's not an orgy."

"I told them you didn't want that."

She darted him a look and then grinned, realizing he was kidding. It was no wonder she had to make sure, since he didn't joke around with her often. She was one of them now, officially a part of their world, and the selfish part of him exulted in that.

"I wouldn't mind a really exclusive orgy," she said. "Like, only one other person."

"I can arrange that later."

CHAPTER TWENTY-SIX

J ONATHAN HELPED CASSIE move out of her rental house in Phoenix. She packed up the quilt her grandma made, her gun, some pictures, and a few clothes. Everything else went to Goodwill.

They had dinner with her parents, where Cassie asked them a lot of questions about relatives and friends in order to avoid talking about the vacation in Cancun that she and Jonathan had supposedly enjoyed and the new job she'd supposedly taken.

The fake stories weren't the only things making her nervous. Her mom, of course, already loved Jonathan, but she didn't know if her dad would. He'd never liked Rick, even at the beginning when her mom had been trying very hard to see the good things in him.

Cassie didn't need to worry. His innate, respectful attitude toward his elders would have been hard for any parent to resist, and he asked her dad intelligent questions about running the stables, dug for cute and embarrassing stories about Cassie as a child, and just listened when her parents talked about people he didn't know. It didn't hurt that he kept saying complimentary things about Cassie, which he didn't seem to be doing on purpose. Basically, her dad adored him.

While they were in town, Cassie bought a bunch of new clothes from the mall and the army surplus store, including a couple of cargo vests, a utility jacket, and black work boots like Gabi's. If she was going to be a Knight, she might as well look like one. It all went on Jonathan's credit card, to be billed to Manus Sancti. When she asked him if she was spending too much, he laughed at her. "I'm pretty sure Val spends this much on clothes every week."

They moved in together at El Dédalo. The new place was like a small one-bedroom apartment, but after Cassie's tiny room, it seemed almost spacious.

"You don't mind if I decorate this ledge?" she asked him. She was arranging her framed photos and her great-grandpa's toy tank—now empty, of course—which she'd more or less repaired.

"No, that's fine."

She turned around to look at him where he sat on the love-seat. "Do you have any pictures you want to put up here? Of your family, maybe?"

He looked thoughtful. "Yeah. I have some." He rummaged through the unpacked box in the corner, found it, and then handed one to her.

His whole family stood on a dock, blue sky and ocean in the background. "Where is this?" Then she answered her own question. "Must be Florida." The laughing woman, plump and sun-burned in her bright floral dress, bore little resemblance to the hollowed-out patient she'd met in the medical wing. "Your mom is beautiful."

She'd never seen even a picture of his father before. Tall, with a receding hairline, he had narrow blue eyes and an angular face, a serious man trying to smile for the camera. "Whoa, you look so much like your dad."

"I know."

Jonathan was maybe seven in the picture, with a thick shock

of very blond hair, squinting up seriously at the camera. His little brother had been caught in the middle of springing up from a crouching position, laughing, his arms spread wide. He was so adorable it made her heart hurt, even though she'd never known him—or maybe because of that.

She hesitated before saying, "Val told me your dad was pretty strict when you guys were growing up."

His eyebrows rose, and then his face assumed a nonchalant expression. "You know how sensitive she is."

"She said he spanked the hell out of you," Cassie persisted. "And forced you to do that cage fighting."

He sighed, obviously realizing he wasn't going to get out of this conversation. "I think he wanted to make sure we'd grow up, you know, strong. And with good morals. The way Knights ought to be." He shrugged. "I think we did."

Obviously, he had, but he deserved most of the credit for that. Cassie looked back down at the innocent faces in the picture. "So you think that's the right way to raise kids?"

"No. I'd never be like that." Her head snapped up again at his sharp tone. He added, "Children should always know they're loved." Although he'd defended his father's behavior, it sounded as though he'd thought long and hard about not replicating it. Cassie must have had a questioning look on her face, because he spread his hands. "I'm just saying I don't feel sorry for myself."

"Right, because God forbid," she said, touched and exasperated. She got up and put the picture in the middle of the mantel.

Jonathan watched her place the photo of her and Sam next to it. "I know this isn't what you'd call a home," he said. "You might get outposted to Saint Augustine or D.C. sometime. Then you could have a real house."

She smiled. "I'm learning Spanish *and* Arabic now. Pretty soon, they could send me to Mexico City, Buenos Aires, Cairo, or a bunch of different places." But they wouldn't necessarily send her and Jonathan to the same place, because they weren't pledged or married. *We should do something about that.* "Right here is fine for now. You're here. That makes it a home." The affection and joy in his gaze warmed her down to her toes. She crouched down to look at his box of belongings. "You have any other pictures in here?"

"Yeah, a few."

She pulled them out. The first one showed him and a few others in very fancy uniforms, yelling and throwing graduation caps and fists into the air. "What is this? Oh, it's West Point!"

He sat down on the floor to look at them with her. "That was a good day."

"Do you ever see any of them on Facebook or anything?"

He gave her a dubious look. "I'm not on Facebook. What would I say?"

"'Super tired after killing those zombies'," she suggested. "Or I know, 'Check out this ghost photo'!" She flipped to the next picture. Jonathan and a man who was clearly his brother, drinking beer with a couple of women. Sometimes, she had the worst timing. "You and Michael—I'm an idiot."

"You're fine."

Jonathan's ex-girlfriend, the sexy Russian elf, sat next to him in the photo.

"I can get rid of that one," he said.

"Don't be ridiculous. It's a great picture of you and Michael." She didn't need to worry about exes. Jonathan never stopped giving her reasons to believe in his devotion.

His eyes widened. "If it were the other way around, I'd want you to throw it away."

"Well, you're a jealous idiot," she said sweetly. The other woman in the photo, also blonde but chubby and bosomy, hung on Michael's arm and made a silly face for the camera. "Who's that?"

"Ha, no idea actually. Probably someone he met that night."

She flipped to the last picture, a wedding photo of his parents. "Ah, that is wonderful." Jonathan didn't say anything, and when she looked up, his expression was intent. "What?"

He shook his head, a smile ghosting across his face. "Nothing."

The phone in her back pocket vibrated. She'd never been good about keeping her phone charged and handy, a fact that sometimes led to her getting texts along the lines of, *Answer me, damn it.* Somehow, Manus Sancti phones never lost their charge, and she kept it on her person at all times, like everyone else at El Dédalo. Jonathan took his out at the same time she did.

She read, "1450, Victoria Room, 22 J189." 1450 was the time—about a half hour from now. She scrolled down. "We're both in this meeting. They must have tracked down some Tribunal." The religious psychopaths couldn't stay in the wind for long. Andre and other Diviners had been scouring the dark web, and the Knights in Rome had been questioning everyone they could think of, trying to ferret them out.

Jonathan shook his head. "If it were Tribunal, they would have called in Samir."

Cassie looked back down at her screen. "I'm supposed to bring a guest from the *entrada*? What the hell?"

Jonathan stood up from the table. "Same here. I guess we go together."

"I'm an initiate," Cassie said as she followed him out. "Why'd they ask me?"

CHAPTER TWENTY-SEVEN

WHEN THEY GOT to the security checkpoint, Jonathan found himself staring at the backside of a heavyset man walking through the body scanner and saying, "God, I hate you guys." Morty Silva. At Jonathan's side, Cassie laughed, but she looked away while Morty finished the body scan and got dressed again.

When he spotted them, he looked more surprised than pleased. He strode right past Jonathan to put a hand on Cassie's shoulder. "How you doing, babe? You kill anybody with wild animals lately?"

"Yeah, but they started it," she offered, smiling at him.

"Huh," he grunted. "Fair enough." In a lower tone, though still audible to Jonathan, he asked, "They treating you okay here?"

"Definitely."

Morty gave her a keen look, and Jonathan wondered what his empath abilities were telling him.

He cleared his throat. "Hey, Morty."

Without smiling, Morty shook his hand. "Hey, Ace. How's that back of yours?"

"Healed up. Thanks. Why are you here?"

He harrumphed. "I was hoping you could fill *me* in. You may as well just take me wherever you're taking me." As they started walking, Morty explained more. "Two of your goons showed up and invited me here." He put an ironic emphasis on the word *invited*.

"That was voluntary," Jonathan said quickly, for Cassie's sake. "You're never forced to help."

"In theory," Morty allowed. "But they seemed very determined. Someone named Chance, and a big, bearded guy with a tattoo on his neck."

"Tristan Münter," Cassie said.

"You one of them now?" Morty asked her. She nodded. "Can't say I'm happy to hear it," he said. "Though don't get me wrong, this one's a good kid. God knows he'd do anything for you."

Jonathan snorted. "Are you talking about me right in front of me?"

"I'm saying good things, so don't be a moron." Morty turned his attention back to Cassie. "But this group?" He waved his arm in a vague gesture that encompassed all of their surroundings. "They do good things—hell, great things, sometimes. But there's something wrong here."

"I used to work for a mining company," Cassie told him. "You know what they do to the earth?" He didn't answer, and she said, "If there's a perfect employer out there who wants me, you let me know, and I'll go work for them." Jonathan smiled to himself.

"Every group's got their issues," Morty agreed grudgingly. "But this is different. I don't know what it is, but I can feel it. And I *can't* feel it. I get close to that leader of theirs, and I get nothing."

Jonathan couldn't let that pass. Cassie had just pledged herself to Manus Sancti, and Morty was trying to cast doubt. "Val says Capitán Renaud keeps his emotions under control. In his position, he has to."

Morty held up a hand as though Jonathan had proved his point. "In an organization with this kind of hierarchy, this unquestioning allegiance, there are going to be problems. Look at any cult. Any fascist government."

Jonathan's temper snapped. "We're not fascists! Or a cult," he added as an afterthought.

"They've had the same leader—the same dictator—for twenty years," Morty told Cassie.

They came face-to-face with Renaud.

Jonathan made the automatic closed-fist salute. "Capitán."

Cassie eyed him, as if considering whether this was maybe a tad bit fascist, after all.

Morty met the leader's gaze and said in a loud, genial tone, "Good morning." Jonathan had never before heard *Good morning* sound so much like *You heard me, asshole.*

"*Salaam,* Dr. Silva." Capitán gestured to the open door of the conference room with easy grace. "We're all waiting for you."

Gabi, Val, Dominic Joe, and a Scholar named Doug Smith sat around the table. Doug's appearance was anything but intimidating: he was a short, stocky, middle-aged white man with graying hair and horn-rimmed glasses, wearing a sweatshirt advertising an old television program about outer space. He looked like a nerdy *sonámbulo* dad. Nonetheless, his presence unsettled Jonathan, reminding him of his last mission with Michael.

Capitán said, "Let's make introductions."

The Scholar spoke up first. "Doug Smith. I'm assigned to the Urraca Mesa demon called Dakos."

So this was about Dakos? How could it be? Cassie gave him a horrified look, and Morty's lips pressed together in a hard line. Others introduced themselves, directing their words toward Morty. When it was Cassie's turn, she floundered. "I'm Cassie Rios, and I'm going to be—right now I'm an initiate."

She shouldn't be here. Nothing about this meeting was good. Jonathan sat hunched in his seat, the knuckles of his fist pressed against his mouth. Capitán nodded at Doug to begin.

"This week, several dozen Boy Scouts have been at Philmont Scout Ranch on Urraca Mesa as part of a winter camping program," he said. "A few hours ago, police responded to a call from a Scout leader. One of the boys had murdered another one by driving a sharpened stick through his throat."

Next to Jonathan, Cassie cringed.

"The boy dragged the corpse into the brush and dismembered it with an axe used for firewood. The Scout leader noticed the child was missing and sent the other Scouts out in pairs to look for him." Doug pushed up his glasses. "The murderer didn't join the search, and it was discovered that he was roasting pieces from the victim's corpse over the fire."

Jonathan's soul crumbled into dust. *My fault. All my fault.* He was supposed to be a Knight, a protector, and instead, he left a trail of dead in his wake.

Cassie pressed her hands to her face. "Oh my God. How old was this kid?"

"Fourteen," Doug said. "But it wasn't the kid—it was definitely our demon. Police interrogated the child, and he spoke in a cold, wooden way—no remorse. Fifteen minutes into the questioning, he suddenly started speaking normally and crying. He has no memory of what he did."

"That poor kid," Gabi said. Jonathan knew she was thinking of her sons. "Do you think we could try Palimpsest? Andre thinks they're ready."

Cassie's brow puckered with confusion. Jonathan would have to explain it to her later. Andre and a team of Mages and Diviners had been working on a protocol to obliterate not only an individual's memories, but the world's recollection of an event. It was incredibly complicated, involving the planting of a new narrative and sweeping up every last crumb of the truth. Even the name of the project, Palimpsest, had been chosen to keep them from getting too cocky. A palimpsest was a manuscript written on an erased page, on which remnants of the earlier writing showed through. No matter how perfectly they executed it, traces would remain.

Capitán considered the question. "This is a good test case. Not too big. Let's do it."

Nic and Gabi exchanged a gleeful look. So many people had wanted to try this for so long. Andre and his team would be thrilled if it went forward.

Knowing that the possessed fourteen-year-old might not have to live with this horror, and that the parents of the deceased child might be granted a more natural cause of his death, was some comfort to Jonathan. But he still burned with shame. "I never knew for sure if we got him. If I got him. I finished the spell after he killed Michael, but it wasn't like other banishments. There was a flash and a force that knocked me out cold. And he was just gone." He looked around the table as if at a convicting jury. "If I didn't send him back, he might have done more damage than we know. There could be skeletons stacked up in someone's barn—"

"No," Doug interrupted. "There's not one missing person in the area. And no one saw the blue lights on the mesa until a day ago. The boy who went cannibal reported seeing them."

"Cannibal Boy Scouts," Cassie said and let out a slightly hysterical laugh. Everyone stared at her. "Sorry," she said. Nic inclined his head, acknowledging that yes, this was pretty messed up.

Jonathan asked, "But if we didn't send Dakos back to the other realm, why hasn't he been active? All the lore says he has an insatiable appetite for human flesh, getting stronger the more he feeds." Morty nodded at this.

Doug said, "Our best guess is that your spell was incapacitating but not lethal. He needed time to heal."

Morty half raised a hand. "Question. Why am I here?"

"You studied with Francine Notsinneh," Doug said, and explained to the rest of them, "Notsinneh is a professor of anthropology at New Mexico State University. She's a Jicarilla Apache and specializes in native American mythologies."

"She's an underpaid adjunct," Morty said. "I only spent one long weekend with her, interviewing her about local lore—Apache, Navajo, even urban legends. We talked a little about the Urraca Mesa portal, but this was last year. There hadn't been any demonic activity in centuries." He spread his hands. "Fran said it was a cannibal demon. She heard that the shaman who warded him off buried cat totems made of malachite, and used burned magpie bones in the ritual. That's all I know."

Doug said, "If that's true, that's more than we knew. I'll have to consult with one of the elemental Mages about whether this might strengthen our banishing spell."

"Call Agnes Goldberg," Nic suggested. "She charged the stones for that Oregon cave thing."

Morty looked troubled. "Why not bring Fran in? She's the expert. And she could use the money."

Capitán made a steeple of his fingers. "We're at a heightened security risk. Not bringing in any new consultants."

"Huh." Morty cast a shrewd look in Cassie's direction. "You were happy to sign this one up, though. What's she got that you want?"

Doug passed one of his folders to Morty. "This is a facsimile of a Mayan codex that dates back to 700 A.D." Jonathan recalled that Doug had helped with the translations. But Cassie couldn't be any part of this. It was unthinkable. "Cassie has inherited magic from her ancestors written down in this codex, including an animal spell—"

"Yeah, I know all about that one," Morty peered at the first page of the binder. "You sure this is authentic? Just because the magic works doesn't prove anything."

"None of us could believe it ourselves at first," Doug said. "But we've put it through every test."

Morty let out a low whistle. "Well, you guys would know better than anyone. 700 A.D. Can you even read the thing?"

"We think we have a good translation."

Lucia's voice on that final phone call, shouting out to Jonathan, came into his head. Something twisted in his chest.

"And that didn't come cheap," Morty muttered. He must have felt Jonathan's sadness, and maybe that of others, too. "Any other spells in there?"

Doug glanced at Capitán. "We're only talking to you about it because you studied the Ora Fragment. But it's highly sensitive information. Our enemies have killed for it."

"I gathered." Morty flipped another page. "What have we got?"

"The spells are ancestral. They work for Cassie because she's a descendant of the author of the Codex. There's a spell to cause famine that we believe to be useless, at best, but there's also a spell that could render her immune to possession—or any psychic attack."

No. Jonathan's literal worst nightmares were converging. The demon who killed Michael. Cassie in danger. His fear rose until it threatened to suffocate him.

Morty looked up again, his eyes wide. "Completely immune?"

"It's temporary, but yes."

"So this is your play—Cassie makes herself immune, and then she and Jonathan re-try the banishment after you've made some tweaks?" He shook his head, looking appalled. "She's a neophyte. If the immunity spell doesn't work, she's done for."

Thank God someone besides him was saying it. Jonathan's horror swung to fury. Cassie looked at Capitán and then at Doug, as if waiting for one of them to say that no, this wasn't the plan. Neither of them did.

As Jonathan got to his feet, he clenched his hands into fists at his sides. He wanted to throw a chair or smash something, and that wasn't going to help. "The immunity spell itself is too dangerous. Lucia told Cassie about it. The psychic blowback can make a person destroy herself."

Val and Gabi both tensed.

"West," Capitán said quietly. "That's enough."

Adrenaline coursed through his veins, his body begging for a physical fight, but he kept his voice as calm as he could. "Sir. I can do the banishment on my own. If I'm not covering for someone else, I'll be strong enough." He had to argue this from Capitán's point of view. "Cassie's a valuable asset, and we don't want to lose her by sending her before she's ready."

Capitán looked bored. "Since when do I send people to fight demons solo? You get possessed, who takes you down?"

Cassie's mouth parted.

Val told Jonathan in a quiet voice, "That spell is too complicated for one person."

Jonathan bit back a response, feeling utterly betrayed by her.

"It is," Capitán said. "And this immunity spell could be a powerful weapon. I need to know if it works."

Cassie still hadn't said anything. She crossed her arms, rubbing her hands on her forearms. Even though she liked the idea of fighting evil creatures, this plan had to come as a shock to her. They'd told her she'd have months of training.

Gabi must have been thinking the same thing, because she said, "She is only an initiate, sir." Jonathan felt a rush of gratitude toward her.

"Refresh my memory, Bravo," Capitán said. "Your very first mission, when you helped wipe out a band of kobolds in the gold mine in Tolima. What was your status? How old were you?"

"Initiate," she admitted. "I was eighteen."

"And did you protest? Your boyfriend at the time?"

Gabi shook her head.

"I'll do it," Cassie said. Jonathan's heart dropped to his feet as all eyes turned toward her. She said, "I just— I wish Samir were here." He had taken a short trip to visit Lucia's great-aunt in Crete, who hadn't been well enough to attend the memorial service, and bring her a rare book Lucia had bequeathed to her. Jonathan's throat tightened. Soon, they'd ask Cassie about her final wishes.

Capitán said, "You can do this, Rios. Silva, work with Vega and Goldberg to improve the banishment spell."

"Goddamn it," Morty muttered.

"You'll be handsomely compensated. As always."

Jonathan didn't know why he kept emphasizing how much they would pay Morty, who never expressed any interest in it. The ex-priest's face settled in grim, weary lines. "I'll help, because you'll move forward either way." No doubt Morty didn't love the option of letting a cannibal demon terrorize northern New Mexico, either.

Capitán said, "Joe, you're mission runner. Rios and West, you leave by car for Urraca Mesa twenty-four hours from now."

Jonathan sat down again, dazed by his own despair. He had lost. The only thing he could do was keep Cassie safe on the mission, by any means necessary.

Nic said, "I won't be able to track Rios's vitals since she doesn't have the tattoo yet, but I assume she's got a temporary tracker in?" Both Jonathan and Cassie nodded. "I'll get the code from security. And they could use a driver."

"You drive," Capitán said.

Nic talked as he typed things into his phone. "Smith, Mr. Silva, and Vega, you can confer about the spellwork tonight in Vega's office with Goldberg. Let's say an hour from now—give Mr. Silva a chance to eat dinner. I'll procure the same materials as last time, with the addition of the burned magpie bones and malachite totems, which I'll get Goldberg to charge. If you need any additional supplies, contact me immediately—I'll be up all night." He put the phone down. "I'm thinking a zero-seven-hundred meeting to review the completed spell. That way, if you need anything else, I'll have time to get it. Any conflicts? Good."

Cassie blinked, no doubt taken aback at this onslaught of organizational efficiency delivered in such a casual manner.

"West and Rios, we can leave at fourteen-hundred. We'll meet at the *entrada*." He flipped to another view on his phone. "Dress warm. It's going to be close to freezing on the mesa. West, you'll want your gun and your knife. I'll give you an extra Glock for her—you can give it to her after the immunity spell is in effect but before you summon the demon."

As Nic asked Doug and Morty about the ritual requirements, Jonathan, Cassie, Gabi, and Val left in a little group.

Gabi said, "He really wants to test out that spell."

Jonathan stalked a few steps ahead of them, still taut with anger that had no means of release. "He shouldn't be so careless with Cassie, even if he doesn't care about her. He loses her, he loses the magic."

"That's not exactly true," Cassie pointed out. "It's like you said before. There would be thousands of descendants, and he could recruit another one."

Gabi said to her, "Maybe he wants to test you, see how you are in the field."

Val shook her head. "I don't think it's Cassie he's testing. He wants to make sure Jonathan can let Cassie be a Knight."

He whirled around, still angry with Val for what she'd said in the meeting. Hadn't she been worried about Cassie before? How could she have spoken up in favor of this mission? "I don't have a choice. She's chosen this for herself. And she has the right mindset, I admit it. Where most people freeze up, she fights." Cassie smiled, as though he'd spoken sweet, romantic words to her. "But this immunity spell sounds like serious power."

"I think she can handle it," Val said.

"You don't know that!" She flinched at his tone. "We don't know if anyone can survive it!"

Gabi's thick brows snapped together. "That's no way to talk in front of her, when she's going to try. What the hell are you thinking?"

She was right, though he wasn't about to admit it. The last thing Cassie needed right now was someone undermining her confidence, and that was exactly what he was doing.

Christos. He'd have to make it up to her, let her know that he believed in her in no uncertain terms. Later, when they succeeded at the mission and she was safe at home again, he could indulge in being angry.

"We're going over the spell tonight." Val employed her soothing, feathery voice to full effect—for Cassie's sake rather than his, Jonathan guessed. He knew Val had supported the idea of Cassie going because she truly believed it was even more dangerous for Jonathan to try it on his own. Her concern for him should've lessened his bitterness. It didn't. She said, "Cassie has…a certain kind of strength. I felt it the first time I touched her mind. She can do this."

CHAPTER TWENTY-EIGHT

TWENTY-FOUR HOURS, CASSIE thought as she walked with Jonathan back to their new quarters. She'd go on her first mission in twenty-four hours. That wasn't enough time to somehow transform into a new person who could kick demon ass. It was barely enough time for anything. At her side, Jonathan was silent.

In the meeting, she'd almost said that no, she couldn't do it. But what if she could? Her immunity spell might enable them to succeed. Knowing what this demon had done to a child and to Jonathan's brother—and to Jonathan, for that matter—she couldn't help but try.

"I'm sorry for saying that about the spell," Jonathan said after he closed the door behind them. Clearly, he'd taken Gabi's reprimand to heart.

"It's all right. You didn't jinx me."

He let out a tense half laugh. She got a beer out of the fridge and dug around to find the bottle opener in a drawer.

"You heard what Capitán Renaud said. If I get possessed—"

"I know my job." She didn't want to hear him say the rest. Her hands shook. She fumbled the bottle opener, got a good grip on it again, and popped off the cap.

He drew nearer and his eyes bored into hers. "You can't hesitate. It would be one of the best things you ever did for me, I swear. I'd sooner burn in hell than let a demon use me."

"You wouldn't go to hell!"

His mouth twitched. "I'm just saying nothing could be worse."

Cassie took a long drink of the beer and hoped it would help her get some rest. She didn't want to be exhausted for tomorrow, but her nerves stretched so thin they felt like they might snap.

Jonathan rubbed at his shoulder. "And I don't want to die like Michael did, either. People should have something to bury."

She nodded. Never in her life had she expected to have such a grim conversation, but she'd signed up for this, and she wasn't going to back out now. "You have to do the same for me." She didn't want to go up to the mesa fearing she'd turn into a cannibal.

"I know." The look in his eyes was as bleak as a winter storm.

She put the beer down and took his hand. "But that's not going to happen. Because I'll be with you. You're a strong warrior, and you know this demon now."

That broke through the ice. He looked at her for a long moment and then cradled her face in both hands to kiss her, soul-deep, with so much tenderness she thought her heart might break.

Heat poured through her like a triple shot of tequila. This was terrible timing. Surely he didn't want to wear himself out on the eve of a battle. But God, she ached, and she wanted his hands on her already tingling skin.

He ended the kiss but still held her face in his hands, leaning his forehead against her, blocking off everything in the world besides his love. "You've got that wrong, though," he murmured. "We'll survive because of you. You're strong with your ancestors' magic. You'll contain it here…" He ran his hand over her head, stroking back her hair. It felt like a blessing. "And here…" He laid his hand flat against her hard-beating heart. Leaning even closer, he whispered in her ear, "And all through your perfect, precious body." He caressed one of her breasts and glided his hand down to the curve of her waist, as though his touch could strengthen her and protect her from harm. His lips pressed against the sensitive place behind her ear. Then he continued to murmur into it, even as he unbuttoned her shirt. "You have magic no one else has. And I knew from the moment I met you how brave you are. I believe in you."

Cassie drew back long enough to strip off his T-shirt and then kissed him again, plunging into his mouth. Her hands smoothed across his mostly healed back. She needed to touch him everywhere. When she stroked his ridged belly above his belt, a growl emanated from his throat. Reaching around her back, he attempted to unfasten her bra, and his hassled sigh made her laugh. She undid it herself, tossing it on the floor.

His large, gentle hands encircled her breasts, and he lowered his head to suck hungrily at her nipple. He teased the other one with light, circular caresses. Wild sensations traveled through her body as though along invisible meridians of pleasure.

He unzipped her jeans and crouched down to peel them off her, along with her underwear. She stepped out of them, completely naked now, warmed and enveloped by his love. Instead of standing again, he shifted to a kneeling position. One of his hands spanned her hip and the other caressed her ass. He scattered kisses across her tightening belly and licked the flesh just inside her hipbone, where her Manus Sancti tattoo would soon lie. He lightly bit her there, and she squeaked, taking hold of his shoulder. His hand delved into the wetness between her legs, and she thought she would lose her mind. "Jonathan, please."

He groaned. "You don't know what it does to me…hearing you say my name like that." He brushed his thumb over her clit, and she gasped, almost losing her balance.

In response to her unsteadiness, he pressed her back gently, the flat of his hand on her stomach, to lean against the wall. When he nudged one of her thighs, she breathlessly obeyed the unspoken command, spreading herself for his gaze and his touch. She couldn't get enough of him. Two of his fingers thrust inside her as his thumb massaged her clit. Pleasure spiraled through her, but then a terrible thought intruded on her bliss. What if this were the last time?

His tongue darted across her heated flesh, and everything else went out of her head. He gripped the sides of her hips and feasted on her. "Yes! Please yes," she implored. Her whole body flushed with heat. He pressed a third finger into her and sucked on her swollen clit, sending her senses spinning. Her climax crashed over her, and she cried out.

He released her heated bud but kept stroking and nibbling at her unbearably sensitized flesh. Her legs were shaking. She should reciprocate, or at least, he'd want to be inside her now, and she began to pull away.

He captured both of her hands in his and held them against the wall on either side of her, fixing her with an implacable look. "More."

Panting, too overcome to argue against her own pleasure, Cassie let her head fall back against the wall and surrendered to his skill. He tasted her, teased her, delved into her, and she writhed as the sensation became almost too much to bear. Without stopping, he released her wrists and took hold of her hips, keeping her still to take everything he had to give.

She touched the side of his face with shaking fingertips. God, she loved the way he loved her, deep and dark and thorough, demanding much and giving much more in return. She was coming apart, unable to bite back her wordless rising cries. He paused long enough to groan, "God, yes. Give it to me." He took her into his mouth again, and she screamed as ecstasy shattered her.

The aftershocks pulsed through her body. Stunned, she swayed on her feet. Immediately, he stood to support her, his face glistening and his eyes filled with adoration. She wrapped her arms around him and lay her head on his shoulder, trying to catch her breath.

He murmured, "You're so beautiful when you come. You have no idea." She smelled herself on him, and it gave her a primal sense of ownership and satisfaction.

Wanting to finally reciprocate, she unbuckled his belt and unzipped his jeans, pushing them partway down, along with his boxer briefs. She ran her hand up his sleek, hard length, and he flinched with pleasure, his reaction filling her with delight. Inspired, she reached between her legs, slicking her hand with her own abundant wetness, and took hold of him again, stroking hard.

He moved her hand away with a half-choked laugh. "You're going to kill me." Grabbing her by the hips, he hauled her up off her feet, her back still up against the wall. She sucked in a breath. Roughly, he adjusted his grip under her thighs and drove into her.

Oh, God. The conflicting sensations of being off her feet, yet supported, sent her mind reeling. She circled her arms around his shoulders and wrapped her legs around him. "Don't drop me," she whispered.

"I've got you." The low, sensual rumble of his voice sent shivers across her skin. He filled her with one slow thrust and then another, a rhythm that mirrored his steady devotion. His breath against her neck was ragged, either with the physical strain or from the effort of keeping himself in check. He hit a spot deep within her that made her see sparks. Suddenly, she didn't want him to hold back. She locked her ankles behind him and rocked against him.

He responded to her wordless bidding, serving her with faster strokes. *Yes.* She squeezed her muscles tight around him, and his pace grew wild. Hanging on for dear life, she reveled in his strength. Her pleasure escalated, up and up, until it overcame her. A low cry escaped his lips as he climaxed, pumping into her.

For a moment, he rested his forehead against the wall.

"Oh, God," she breathed, stunned. He lifted her up off him, carefully setting her on her feet. Then he kissed her between her breasts, right where her heart beat wildly. The strange, ardent gesture brought sudden tears to her eyes. No matter what happened in the future, this moment existed: their intimacy, their love. It could not be unwritten.

"We should lie down." His voice came out hoarse. He yanked his jeans up and zipped them.

"I don't think I can walk."

He picked her up and carried her to the bed. After laying her down, he stretched out next to her, taking her into his arms. "Thank you," he murmured.

"I should be thanking you. *Jesus*." His cheek rested close to her lips, so she kissed it. "I hope you haven't worn yourself out for tomorrow."

His low, easy laugh reassured her. "You give me strength."

Warmth coursed through her veins at the words. "Well, you've exhausted *me*."

"Good." He smoothed back a damp strand of hair that had fallen in her face. "Then you can get a good night's sleep."

Already, her body and mind were succumbing to it. Her last thought was, *Really, what stands a chance against us?*

When Cassie had fallen asleep, Jonathan got up quietly from the bed and took a quick shower. The muscles in his arms and legs were fatigued, and he'd be sore by this time tomorrow. His senses still thrummed from her passion and his, the sound of her soft moans, the taste of her. She didn't wake up when he returned, and he sat on the edge of the bed.

Although he hadn't prayed for a specific thing in years, it wouldn't hurt to do it. He closed his eyes, took a deep breath, and exhaled.

God, you know I don't usually ask you for favors. Please keep Cassie safe. Help her contain the spell. Make me able to protect her. He thought of Michael, and it stabbed his heart. *Help us put this thing down for good. It's brutalizing innocent people. Children. You know I would give my life freely. If it takes a sacrifice to defeat it, let it be mine.* He opened his eyes briefly to look at Cassie again. Her brow was smooth, her body slack in what appeared to be a deep, dreamless sleep, the kind that would give her energy for the mission ahead. For that, at least, he was grateful. He finished his prayer, repeating himself. *Please keep her safe. In Christ's name, Amen.*

CHAPTER TWENTY-NINE

THE NEXT MORNING, Cassie woke up before Jonathan. She got dressed in a pair of jeans, a tank top, and a long-sleeved Henley over that, and then laced up her new black boots over wool socks. Nic had said it would be cold up on Urraca Mesa. She didn't want her hair blowing in her face when she was in the middle of a demon-summoning spell, so she pulled it back in a tight ponytail. After she put on the jacket she'd bought in the Army surplus store in Phoenix, she sized up her reflection in the mirror. To her, at least, she resembled a Knight.

"Hey." Jonathan propped himself up on one elbow. "You look great." He got up and got dressed himself. As he attached the Glock in a concealed carry holster to his belt and tucked a folded knife in the front pocket, he avoided her eyes.

When they got to the conference room, Doug, Morty, and Val were already waiting.

Morty said to Doug, "Should we go over the summoning spell first? That's the easiest part."

"Yes," he said. "Jonathan, you're already familiar with this one. We didn't make any changes."

Jonathan nodded, his face hard, and took a seat. Cassie listened carefully. Jonathan would be in charge of painting the complex sigils. "Did Nic get a bone from the latest victim?" he asked. "We'll need it for the ink."

"We still have powdered bone from the victim in Taos," Val said. "It should work."

Cassie would do the immunity spell only after they got to the mesa, since they weren't sure how long it would last. Once she was supercharged, they'd complete the summoning, which would include her reading an incantation while Jonathan did some bleeding and setting things on fire. Before Manus Sancti, she'd always thought of magic as meaning something easy. It was the way everyone talked: *it appeared like magic. It worked like a charm.* This was exactly wrong, she knew now. Magic was complicated, uncertain, and it could cost a lot.

Doug talked them through the banishing. "We've made additions based on Morty's talk with the local lore expert and looking at other texts. Cassie, you'll read the incantation. Jonathan will place magpie bones at the four compass directions near the portal."

"Wait," Cassie said. "Where do we get those?"

"Dominic Joe already got them," Doug said. "And he got an ancient malachite carving from this area that should also bolster the spell."

"Wow. How does he find these things?"

"We have whole floors that are storehouses," Jonathan said. "But it's still not easy to find stuff sometimes."

"He's good at tracking things down," Doug agreed.

"What do we do with the carving?" Cassie asked.

Val said, "Well, Agnes cleansed and charged it, and Jonathan will bury it at the portal after you say the incantation."

This sounded like a lot of stuff to do at once while a demon tried to turn one of them into a murdering cannibal—or exploded them into smithereens. She tried to ignore the cold dread in her gut. "Can't Jonathan bury it before we summon the demon?"

"He can dig the hole beforehand," Morty said. "But if it's like other banishing spells I've done, actually burying it will need to go last."

Adrenaline skated through her body. She tried to remain still. "How am I going to remember all this stuff? And what if I read the wrong spell at the wrong time?"

"Nic's putting booklets together for both of you," Val assured her. "All the incantations will be there in order. It'll also have the ritual directions. All you have to do is follow along." It sounded like a church bulletin, except for something that would end in demon banishment or tragic death instead of coffee and cookies in the fellowship hall.

Val said, "Now we need to talk about the possession immunity spell from the Codex." She darted a nervous glance at Jonathan.

"It's okay, *corina*," he said quietly. "I'm not going to yell at you."

She opened her glittery notebook. "It's a straightforward incantation like the wild animal spell."

Cassie said, "I guess my animals won't do any good here?"

"If the demon's possessing a human, they can attack that body. Otherwise, no. Now with the spell, the only other thing you'll need is obsidian touching your skin. Nic has a necklace for you. You'll read the transliteration out loud, like you did with your great-grandfather's journal." She looked up at Cassie. "How much did Lucia tell you about the effects of the spell on you?"

"She said it would bring up a bunch of horrible thoughts about myself that would make me want to kill myself or something."

Val nodded. "A torrent of negative thoughts and feelings. Since they might tempt you to self-destructive thoughts or actions, you can't have any weapons on your person. That's why Jonathan will do the bloodletting part of the summoning spell."

After a moment of silence, Cassie said, "It's a hell of a side effect."

"We think it's how the spell works," Doug said. "It engenders a massive internal psychic attack. All your defenses rise up to fight it. These defenses then make it impossible for anything else to break through. Even a demon can't find its way in."

"It's like a vaccine," Jonathan said.

Morty grunted. "A vaccine with enough virus in it to maybe kill you." Doug shot him a remonstrative look. He said, "She's got to know what she's dealing with."

Doug said, "The good news is that the defense this spell raises should be much stronger than one any person could raise by will alone. Holding one's defenses up, the way Jonathan will be doing, takes a great amount of energy. With this spell, they should remain without effort. If the person survives the initial psychic blast."

Cassie asked, "How long does this shield or whatever hold?"

Morty nodded. "That's a good question. And the answer is, we don't know."

"Lucia made her best guess from the context of the passage," Doug said. "It's true that we don't know for sure. But she guessed several hours, at least."

"That's a big window," Jonathan said, looking hopeful for the first time.

Cassie put her palms on the table. "Okay. Tell me how to not lose it after saying that spell."

"The way you've trained your mind against anger should also help against despair," Val said. "Resisting the unwanted emotions and repeating your mantra word."

Cassie nodded. *Shanti, shanti, shanti.* Val's mantra method seemed dumb and simplistic but actually worked. One thing she'd learned in life was that if something did the job, you went with it.

"You'll also want to mentally argue with the thoughts that come up, if it's possible," Val said. "It says one thing, you say the opposite."

Jonathan's hand came to rest on Cassie's knee. "I can help with that. Right?"

Val frowned. "I'm not sure."

"You'll need to fight like hell, babe," Morty said soberly. "Don't underestimate the threat of something just because it's all in your head."

"I won't," she promised. "But here's what I don't get. Where will all of these negative things come from?"

"Your own mind," Val said. "Guilt, shame, depression. I do think you're in better shape to survive the spell than most. You don't carry as much as some people do." Cassie suspected that by *some people*, she meant Jonathan. He had grief to spare, and he blamed himself for everything: his brother's death, Lucia's death, this demon running wild, and even her being at the table that morning.

"I'll handle it," Cassie said.

Morty stood up and walked over to her, drawing a vial of something out of his pocket. "Let me give you a blessing before you go." He tipped the vial against his thumb and made a criss-cross on her forehead with the oil, saying a few words she didn't understand. It smelled like pepper and wood.

Feeling awkward, Cassie said, "You're just like them, speaking Latin."

"Aramaic, but close enough. You too, Jonathan." She didn't think she'd ever heard Morty call him by his actual name before.

Jonathan didn't register any surprise, closing his eyes briefly as Morty administered the blessing. "Thanks, Morty."

Nic drove the SUV, Jonathan rode shotgun, and Cassie sat in back. A four-hour drive lay ahead of them, and she felt desperate for distraction. "Hey Nic, I have a question for you," she said. "When I first came to El Dédalo, were you the one who packed that bag for me? With the clothes and the toiletries and things?"

"That was me," he said. "Why do you ask?"

"No reason. I really liked the cowgirl pajamas."

He chuckled. "Figured you would."

She was tempted to ask him how he'd gotten her correct bra and underwear size, but maybe it hadn't been difficult. They knew everything else. Instead she asked, "How long have you been a mission runner?"

She thought it was an innocuous question, but Jonathan tensed up.

"A while," Nic said, casual as he completely avoided the question.

"When I first saw you, I thought you were a Knight."

"He'd be a great Knight," Jonathan growled. Nic said nothing, staring over the steering wheel. Cassie knew she was missing something here, but the upcoming demon smackdown kept her from thinking too hard about anything else.

Nic switched on the radio and flipped around, making a sarcastic comment about a preacher on one station and a sports talk guy on another. When he got to a news story about the cannibalism incident at the Boy Scout camp, he turned it off. "They're trying Palimpsest tomorrow."

"Yeah, what is that?" Cassie asked.

"Rewriting the world's memory after a trauma. If it works, the family of the boy who was killed will believe he died of a congenital heart condition—his body's already been cremated, so there's no evidence of anything else. The boy who was possessed will believe he had nothing to do with that death. And there won't be any newspapers, radio shows, or websites to suggest the contrary."

Cassie's jaw fell open. "That's not possible. *How* is that possible?"

Jonathan said, "It's a mix of science, hacking, psychic work, and magic. There's a team of over a hundred people, not just at El Dédalo. Andre's the main architect. If it works, it's going to be amazing."

She loved the idea of the possessed boy being able to live a normal life. At the same time, it seemed like too much power. "Are you worried that someone will mess with your own memories?"

Jonathan shook his head. "They've done experiments, and deep in the psyche, the original memories don't change. If you Read somebody, it's still there. We have too many people with psychic ability for it to work on us."

"That's why it's called Palimpsest," Nic added. "The traces are still there."

They rode in silence for a while. Cassie asked, "How far is this place, anyway?"

"We're about three hours out now. If you get done early enough, we can go into Taos. There's a new Japanese restaurant, great sushi."

"Cassie doesn't like sushi," Jonathan said. They'd talked about this before. Cassie felt like sushi was cute and all, but it ought to be cooked.

"Yeah, maybe something other than Japanese. No offense," she said to Nic.

"Do I look like a sushi chef? And I'm not Japanese."

"What are you?" Cassie regretted the words as soon as they were out of her mouth. "Sorry, that was stupid. I know you're American."

"I'm not. Well, a couple of my aliases are. My mom was Chinese and my dad was Korean. I grew up in Seoul and D.C. And Paris," he added. "I only mentioned sushi because Jonathan likes it. Though Michael was the one who *really* liked eating sushi."

"Stop," Jonathan said.

She looked from one to the other. "What am I missing now?"

Nic grinned. "That was Michael's favorite euphemism for going down on a woman. And according to Michael, he loved eating sushi."

Cassie laughed. "Well, I guess—" Jonathan cut her off with a look.

"What's that?" Nic asked, an amused glint in his eyes.

"Nothing." She'd been about to say that Jonathan liked it pretty well himself.

"Tell you what, *chica*," Nic said. "You kill this demon, and I'll get you some tacos."

She snorted. "Very funny."

"You don't like tacos?"

"Actually, I fucking love them," Cassie admitted. Who didn't? "Wouldn't eating tacos work as a euphemism, too? Or maybe it would be singular."

Nic shrugged. "Might be plural on a good weekend."

Jonathan said, "It's like I'm working with children."

"Lightening the mood," Nic said. "Just one of the many services I offer."

By the time they got to Colfax County, the sky was purpling to black, but thin patches of snow covered the rough ground like broken plates. They passed a sign that said the Scout camp lay a couple of miles ahead. Instead of continuing in that direction, Nic turned onto a side road.

The wheels ground against the gravel.

"We're in the middle of nowhere," Cassie said.

"No, but we're coming up on it," Nic answered. Instead of feeling remote, the bumpy road felt all too familiar to Jonathan, as though they were driving through the wreckage of his own life. When Knights and Mages had an unsuccessful mission, the task almost always fell on them to make it right. *Mi derrota, mi deber.* You make a mess, you clean it up. It was the first time Jonathan had been sent to fix his own failure, and he fought to believe that it wouldn't result in even more disaster.

Nic made a detour around the yellow bars announcing the road's dead end and plowed on over open terrain. They climbed steadily. Cassie watched out the window as though the demon might come screeching out of the scrubby pines. After a mile or so, Nic glanced at the GPS on the dashboard and came to a stop.

They got out. The slamming car doors echoed in the silence. A cold wind cut through his jacket, and he caught a faint smell like rotten eggs or garbage, out of place in a wintry chaparral.

"I hate it here," Cassie said.

Nic opened up the back of the vehicle. "Cassie, here's your script." He handed her a booklet and a flashlight. "And you can add this to your jewelry collection."

He moved behind her and brought her hair forward on one shoulder. Jonathan flashed back to one of the times he'd made love to Cassie, and before he even knew it, he took a step forward.

Nic gave him a look of disdain. "Seriously?" The mission runner was right, of course. Jonathan knew he needed to calm down. Nic added to Cassie, "I'm putting it on you because the clasp is high-tech. This won't come off you accidentally, no matter what." He fastened it with a click. The smooth, oblong stones on Cassie's neck reminded Jonathan of leeches. From the trunk, Nic pulled out a black backpack and handed it to Jonathan. "You've got everything you need in here for the spell work. And water. Jon, you've got a knife?" Jonathan patted his front pocket and nodded. "Good. The portal is a half mile this way, south by southeast." He pointed.

"I remember," Jonathan said.

"I'll stay here with the car, beyond the perimeter. Call me if you need extracting. Go get him." He made a gesture, holding his hand up, all fingers extended except for his ring finger, held down by his thumb. *Good luck.*

CHAPTER THIRTY

JONATHAN SLUNG THE backpack over one shoulder, and Cassie followed him on the trail up the mesa. If there even was a trail—she couldn't pick it out by flashlight, and she was usually pretty good at tracking. The needles on the ends of the pine branches spreading across the path looked sharp and cruel.

To keep up with his long strides, she had to occasionally jog, but she didn't mind. She hadn't really thought about it taking time to hike in, and she wanted to get there as soon as possible. Large rocks jutted out here and there, and she pointed the flashlight toward the ground right in front of her to keep from tripping.

Despite her best efforts, he got several paces ahead of her, and after a long while she called up to him, "Do we have much farther to go?" It embarrassed her to ask, like she was a little kid hoping to get to Disneyland soon. But instead of the Happiest Place on Earth, they were going to the Most Hellish Place on Earth, or at least one of the 1,001 Hellish Places to See Before You Die.

Jonathan stopped. "We're pretty close." He dug a titanium water bottle out of his backpack and brought it over to her. She took a long drink, and he downed a swig, too, before putting it away again.

Behind them, a tree branch cracked. They both jumped and

turned around, saying nothing, staring into the dark. Cassie expected to see a glowing pair of eyes. As nervous as she was, if a baby bunny had hopped up, she probably would've considered it a harbinger of death.

After several moments of silence, Jonathan muttered, "Guess it was nothing."

They trudged on, reaching a flat and less wooded plateau, and then made another short climb up to a higher level, sharp enough that they had to use their hands to grab onto rocks. Once they were both on the plateau, Jonathan said, "This is it."

No moon shone. Cassie had never walked out into a wilderness this dark. The rotten, garbage-y stench assaulted her nostrils again. "Do you smell that?"

"It's a bad place," he said in a low tone. He pointed. "The portal's right there." She could barely make out the black hole, like a little cave, and the silhouettes of a stack of stones above it. Jonathan's makeshift memorial to Michael. It was still there. Sweat trickled down her back and under her arms, despite the cold. Would either of them get out of this alive? Would someone else add two more stacks to mark their passing?

She pulled out the booklet Nic had given her and hunched her shoulders against another gust of wind. "Anti-possession spell first. All I have to do is say it."

Jonathan shifted his stance, planting his feet wider. "How can I help?"

"Just stand by me." She tucked the flashlight under her arm to flip to the first page, and then shone the light on the text. Her mouth felt dry and she was glad she'd taken a drink of water earlier, when she hadn't especially needed it. She began reading, taking care to pronounce each syllable correctly and to raise the pitch of her voice where the type indicated.

She finished and waited. Nothing.

"I don't know if I said it right," she said.

The rocks below her feet whispered, *You do everything wrong.* A feeling like bitter acid poured down her throat and then her spine.

"Okay," she said. "It's happening."

Jonathan stiffened as though ready for an ambush, though there was nothing for him to fight.

Why are you telling him? He doesn't love you. He likes fucking you. The bitter acid in her burned. She gagged on it and bent over, her hands on her knees, as if she could vomit out the negativity.

That's how stupid you are. Not only the rocks, but also the trees and air spoke. *You're too stupid for this group, too selfish, too ugly, too weak.*

Val had told her to argue against it. "I'm not weak." Her throat was so constricted that it came out a whisper, making the statement a lie. Jonathan's arm was around her shoulders, and he was saying something to her, but it sounded like he was underwater. Fiery pain ran through her brain, spine, and every inch of her nerves. She fell on her knees.

Pushing back his rising panic, Jonathan crouched down next to her. A strangled sound came from the back of her throat as she covered her head with her arms, rocking back and forth. "Cassie!" He pulled one of her arms away to look her in the eyes, and she struck out blindly, landing a solid punch to his face.

"Leave me alone!"

She thought he was attacking her. He lifted his hands. "Cassie, it's me!"

Fear and despair filled her wide, unseeing eyes, and her lips formed soundless words. Did she even know he was there? "Disgusting," she whispered. "Loser. Your family hates you." Jonathan froze. His father might hate him. *Focus.* Had the spell turned Cassie against him? She said in a small, broken voice, "Manus Sancti hates you. They sent you here to die." *Christos.* She wasn't talking to him, but herself, caught in the spell's self-loathing. "*He hates you.*"

This went straight through Jonathan's soul. "Cassie, no!" He took hold of her shoulders, leaning close to her. "Listen to me—"

Quick as a rattlesnake strike, she pulled the gun from his side holster. His heart stopped. In two seconds, he grabbed her wrist, wrested the weapon out of her hand, and tossed it out of her reach. He pushed her down to the ground on her side, straddled her, and took hold of her right arm, pinning it across her body. As she attempted to struggle, he took in a breath and let it out. She had no chance of escaping, and he could keep her like that as long as he needed to without hurting her.

She went limp. "You're a mistake," she sobbed. "You're the universe's biggest mistake." He ignored the urge to let her out of the restrictive hold and take her into his arms, though his heart was breaking. They never should have let her try this spell. He should have stopped it. With his free hand, he touched her hair, and she jerked her head away. Without even thinking about it, he'd been attempting to shield her psyche, even though he couldn't protect her from the internal threat. In the edge of his awareness, her very being shuddered under the strain of the spell, and he realized that even if she wasn't able to physically harm herself, this could still destroy her.

God, please, no. He bent down close to her ear. "Cassie, remember who you are." Even though his spirit quaked in fear, he kept his voice strong. "The love of my life. An initiate Knight." He recalled her words about her family. "A beloved daughter. A beloved sister."

With another strangled sob, she thrashed against him. She couldn't hear him at all, and she'd have to fight this alone.

The struggle was exhausting her. All she had to do now was give in. Everyone would be so happy if she did, if she were gone from their lives. She'd be so relieved. A bonfire burned behind her eyeballs, charring the optic nerve. The pain. It reminded her—

The initiation ritual. The red-hot coal. She'd gotten through that.

It was fake! half of the cells along her spinal column and her brain yelled. But not all of them.

It was real. It proved she was strong.

You're stupid. No one loves you.

She shook her head against the malevolent hiss. Another voice came to her, kind, almost too faint to hear. *Love of my life. Initiate Knight. Beloved daughter. Beloved sister.*

It brought her a glimmer of daylight. Her brain still screamed for her blood, demanding an execution. *No one loves you—*

Even if no one did, there would still be her. She was someone. She mattered.

The Universe's mistake.

With every bit of strength she had left, she fired back. *The Universe's plan. I was created on purpose because I was a good fucking idea.*

The pain behind her eyes receded. She gasped in a deep breath and let it out. Her throat ached.

She saw a shadow. Heard, "Cassie please, come back to me."

She jolted in response to the voice. Stared at a face. Pieces came together like a broken mirror repairing itself. "Jonathan."

"You can see me." He was straddling her where she lay on her side and holding her arm across her body, as if they'd been grappling, like him and Gabi at the gym. "Is it still happening?" She shook her head, dazed. "Are you all right?"

"Yeah." The destructive force inside her was gone, leaving her light and free. She gave a shaky laugh.

He released her from the restrictive hold and pulled her close enough to him that she could feel his pounding heart. "Thank God." His gun. She'd grabbed it. That must have scared the life out of him. She was half drowning in saltwater and snot. He gave her his bandana, and she blew her nose. "Are you all right?" he asked again.

"Yeah. That—" She shook her head. "That really sucked."

"But you did it," he said. "I couldn't help. You couldn't hear me."

"I did hear you!" she exclaimed, suddenly realizing. He'd been that other voice. "You did help. And you kept the gun out of my hands."

"You should be immune now." He looked at her with a kind of wonder.

"I am," she said without even thinking. She could feel the protection covering her like a hard shell. "Let's get this demon to come out and play."

He scrambled to his feet and offered a hand to help her up. She found her dropped booklet on the ground.

A growl nearly shook the earth, and a dark shape bounded toward her. White teeth glinted in the dark.

Cassie shrieked, turned, and sprinted, forgetting she was next to the ridge. The ground beneath her feet gave way to nothingness. As she landed hard, her ankle twisted and her weight jammed down on top of it.

Then gunfire. She struggled to an upright stance. Another shot. When she put weight on her foot, pain lanced through her. "Fuck!"

"Cassie!" Jonathan scrambled down to reach her side.

"I sprained my ankle."

"Sit. Let me take a look." He guided her to a seated position on a rock, unlaced the boot in a few seconds, and eased it off her foot. As he gently removed the sock, as well, he asked, "Did you hear or feel a crack?" She shook her head. He ran his fingertips lightly over the bones of the ankle and the foot. "I don't think it's broken."

"I don't think so, either." She pulled her sock on again. "What was that, a bear?" She peered up at the plateau.

"Yeah, I shot him in the head. Then shot him again to be sure." Jonathan picked her up to carry her back up the ledge.

"He was coming right at me," she said. "My animals never hurt me." Her thoughts swirled. "The bad thoughts. I was angry at myself."

"Suicide by bear attack," Jonathan grunted. "They could have warned us." On the plateau, he said, "Okay, you can sit on the ground." He set her down close to the large, flat stone. She stared at the huge bear carcass not too far away, pitying it.

He was looking down at her foot. "Listen, Cassie, we've got to finish this. I'm sorry."

"Fuck yeah, we've got to finish this," she agreed. "I'm not spraining my ankle for nothing."

He gave her a relieved nod. "How bad does it hurt?"

"I'm okay if I don't move it." Adrenaline was coursing through her veins, which might have helped. He dug into the backpack, found a flashlight, and handed it to her. The wind picked up. "Shit. Where's the booklet?"

After searching around wildly, he spotted it bouncing along on the ground, retrieved it, and brought it to her. "When I start sprinkling blood on the sigils, you start the incantation. All right?"

She flipped to the page that was helpfully titled SUMMON-ING INCANTATION. "Got it." Jonathan gave her the spare gun, and her chest tightened as she stuck it in her belt holster. She asked, "You're sure you can protect your mind and do this at the same time?"

"Yeah. I've got my shields up." His face was composed and controlled as he pulled the silver bottle out of the bag.

He held his flashlight with one hand, and with a short brush, he painted complex symbols, one after another, from memory. Oddly, it soothed her to watch. The sigils formed an arc and then a circle on the stone. Another gust of wind made him put up the hood of his jacket. He retrieved two sticks of fatwood from the backpack and crossed them in the center of the stone. Cassie shivered where she sat.

From another bottle, he sprinkled oil on each of the symbols in turn. The fragrance that rose up reminded her of Mass when she was little, a welcome counterpoint to the stink of the place. As though for good measure, he shook the bottle empty over the wood. He rolled up his left sleeve, got out the knife, and slashed a gash in his forearm. "Okay."

As he sprinkled the blood over each sigil, she read the incantation. Latin was easier than transliterated proto-Mayan. She glanced up when he stood and lit a match. The hood partially shadowed his calm features, and the flame danced over them. He looked like a beautiful monk. He set one after another of the symbols on fire and then the fat sticks in the middle as she pronounced the last word.

A thick rope of blue lightning stabbed into the ground not far from them. Cassie let out a scream and dropped the flashlight as her hair flew against her cheeks. Bright blue clouds roiled into being over them, much lower than clouds could be.

Jonathan stood tall beneath them. "Cassie, next page! Read!"

With shaking hands, she picked up the flashlight and scrabbled to the next section, the banishing spell.

A shadow like a man, but twice as tall, faced Jonathan. No, not a shadow, but nothingness, a black hole in a human shape. Dark, terrible laughter echoed in her ear. She froze and then pushed a thought against it: *Fuck you, asshole. You can't hurt me.*

Jonathan grabbed the burned bones and placed one along the edge of the stone. "Read!" *Shit.* If he had to keep yelling at her, his control would slip. She read as loudly as she could, because she wanted him to be able to hear her. The long arm of the human-shaped void reached out and rested a hand on Jonathan's head. He stopped what he was doing.

No! Keep going! she shouted in her mind. If she said anything aloud, she'd have to start the incantation all over again. His shields must be crumbling. But if she hurried… She read another line. He placed the rest of the bones at compass corners slowly.

A boom and a flash of blinding blue lightning knocked her on her side on the ground. When she looked up, the hand of Dakos was sinking into Jonathan's head.

Fuck, fuck. What could she do? She dragged herself over to him and grabbed his hand. Her vision filled with light. She blinked. They were both standing, clinging to one another. She didn't hurt, and she was warm. "What happened!"

"We're in me." He laughed, a strange sound and sweet after so much terror. "It worked."

Cassie stared around them, dumbfounded. A golden aura surrounded his cathedral. It was difficult to tell which part of his church was bombed out and which was whole.

"When you grabbed my hand, I brought you inside me. This is you," he said, gesturing toward the light. "I have your immunity."

"Oh my God," she breathed. "How did you know that would work?"

"I didn't." He pointed as the dark, giant shadow swam and dived beyond the golden nimbus. "See? He can't get in."

Cassie shook her head. "You did it so fast."

"My shields were already gone." He took a deep breath and let it out. "I just needed a break."

The dark shadow swam closer, bumping against the shell of protective light.

"What do we do now?" Cassie asked.

"We finish it. The summoning spell doesn't hold him there. As soon as he's bored, he'll move on."

"Are you going to be okay?"

"Yeah, I think so. I feel stronger again already. I'll bury the malachite. You finish reading." She nodded, and he pulled her to him and kissed her hard. "Read fast."

They were on the cold ground. The demon's hand hovered over Jonathan's head, trying again to get inside it. Cassie scuttled on her hands and knees for the booklet, ignoring the pain in her ankle. Jonathan got a small shovel out of the backpack as she read as fast as she could. Two or three shovelfuls of dirt, that was all he needed.

Two lightning bolts slashed down to the earth, making her jump, the electricity lifting the ends of her hair. She resumed reading, and Jonathan set the carving in the hole. He threw dirt back over it as she shouted the last word.

The huge dark shadow screamed. It was cursing, but in one hundred voices and languages at once, impossible to understand, and the sound pierced through her. Cassie dropped the booklet and covered her ears.

The portal sucked at the bottom of it like the world's most powerful vacuum cleaner. The demon's legs disappeared. It lashed around with alarming motions that, in her freaked-out state, reminded her of one of those tall, skinny blow-up figures dancing out in front of car dealerships. *Come on. Let it be gone.*

An arm lengthened and flashed across the short distance to Jonathan. It captured his hand and dragged his body toward the small cave that led to the demon realm.

"Jonathan!" Cassie shrieked and ran over on her bad ankle, excruciating pain jolting up her leg with every step. He was scrambling to pull free. She flung herself on the ground and grabbed his arm, trying with all of her strength to keep him in the world of the living. It wasn't helping. Now they were both being dragged.

Jonathan's eyes locked on hers, visible in the sickening blue glow of the low clouds above. "Let go! I need my gun!"

The demon had his right hand, and he couldn't get at his

holster with his left hand because she was hanging on to him. But what was he thinking? He couldn't shoot a demon. They were close to the portal to the other dimension, a black maw eager to swallow Jonathan whole. Maybe if she got a better grip on him, pulled harder...

His eyes blazed. "That's an order!"

Sobbing, she released him and scuttled backward.

Jonathan drew the gun, pointed it above the portal, and fired.

The rock at the bottom of the cairn exploded and the rest of them tumbled down, nearly blocking the entrance to the small gateway. One landed on the demon arm, and suddenly, nothing held on to Jonathan because the arm was contained in the portal. A piercing, unholy scream faded to silence. The blue clouds above exploded in a loud sonic boom that shook the ground.

Jonathan blinked. *It's finished.*

"Oh my God." Sobs fractured Cassie's voice. She half lay on her side, propped up on an elbow. "Did that work? Are you okay?"

The poor thing. His love for her filled his whole being. He scrambled over to kneel next to her and pulled her up into his arms, hugging her hard against him. "I'm all right. It's done."

She clung to him. "I didn't want to let go. I thought you were going to get sucked in." She sniffled. "I didn't know what you were doing."

"I wasn't sure, either, but I thought if I could block it..." He shook his head. "Glad it worked." He'd been moments away from initiating the drop code rather than getting pulled into the demon realm. "How's your ankle?" She'd been *running* on it. Just thinking of it made him feel sympathetic pain in his own body.

"It hurts. That was a hell of a shot. With your left hand." Her voice had become steadier. No doubt the terror of the last few minutes was burning away.

He kissed the top of her head. "I've been practicing."

She frowned at the portal. "Do you want to stack those up again?"

"No, it's okay." The humble memorial he'd made for his brother had saved him. "This is going to sound crazy… Never mind."

"What?"

"I felt like…his spirit was there, just for a second. When the demon got sucked in." He didn't know how else to explain it. The presence had brought a deep, restorative peace to his heart. He didn't care any more about the earthly marker.

"I bet he was," she said softly, and he could tell she wasn't just humoring him. She pulled back to meet his gaze. "Everything's done now, for sure?"

"No question. That's how it's supposed to look." Without the sickly blue clouds above, it was harder to see, but he could see her smile.

"What the hell was that?" Nic demanded on speakerphone. Jonathan hadn't heard him trying to call. "Tell me that was a demon sent back to wherever he came from."

"Yeah, it was."

"Cassie?"

"She's fine," he said and then darted her a guilty look. Cassie had teased him before about using the word *fine* to mean *not actively dying*. "She's got a sprained ankle, and she's in a lot of pain."

"Ouch. Give her a Percoset. Front pocket of the backpack."

"Great. I'll carry her out."

"I'll meet you halfway," Nic said.

After Cassie washed down a pill with water, Jonathan picked her up. As he started down the trail, she leaned her head against his shoulder. Warmth spread through his chest. He kissed her on the temple, just a brush of the lips. "You were amazing. I was in awe."

"Sorry about my stupid animals, though." Her body was lax

in his arms, as though she were exhausted, and he wasn't at all surprised. He carried her in silence so she could rest, and with every step, he exulted in the safety of his beautiful warrior, the one who owned his soul. She dozed until they met up with Nic on the trail.

"I can take her," he said, and Jonathan hesitated. "Don't be stupid, you're tired." Nic gathered Cassie into his arms, and she didn't appear to be embarrassed, probably because she was worn out, too. "How was the immunity spell?"

"It was bad," Cassie mumbled.

Although Nic was a few inches shorter than Jonathan and leaner, he didn't strain under the burden. Even though he'd given up his Knighthood years ago, Jonathan knew he still trained like one, at odd hours when almost no one was at the gym. Nic peppered him with questions about the banishing.

Jonathan's phone vibrated, and he took it out of his pocket, saw who was calling, and answered. "*Salaam*, Samir."

"Why wasn't I told about this?" Samir didn't even bother to greet him back. "What were they thinking? She hasn't even started to train!"

Jonathan smiled to hear his own sentiments echoed so perfectly. "Believe me, I know. But ready or not, she kicked its ass."

CHAPTER THIRTY-ONE

A CHANGE IN the vehicle's speed and direction jolted Cassie awake. As Nic pulled onto an exit ramp, Jonathan, in the back seat next to her, stirred and rubbed his face. "Hey, what are you doing?"

"We're not going far." Nic pointed ahead on the left, at a small restaurant called Joey's Tacos. "I ordered takeout."

Cassie laughed. "No way. You're like the dad who takes the kids out for ice cream after the ball game whether they win or lose."

Nic pulled into the restaurant parking lot. "Well, if you'd lost, you'd be dead. And then I'd have way too many tacos."

The grubby little cinderblock building looked sketchy as hell, but like any Southwesterner, she knew great tacos often came from hole-in-the-wall places. She didn't even care if they were great. She could probably eat about twelve of them.

He parked and got out, saying, "Be right back."

"Hey, Nic," Jonathan called after him. Nic stopped, looking over his shoulder. "Give us ten minutes." Nic nodded.

Jonathan wanted time alone with her. It made her smile. As Nic walked away, Cassie felt light and glowing inside, and not only because the painkiller had kicked in. "I hope I get to go on more missions with you. Do you think I will?"

His forehead puckered. "Hopefully, you'll do all your training before they send you out again." She couldn't disagree with him there. It would be nice to be better equipped. There was probably nothing like doing one mission to convince a person to work as hard as she could at her training. "But I don't know why not. We're obviously amazing together." His rare look of cockiness made her smile. "How's your ankle?"

"It's not bad now. Don't you get tired of worrying about me?"

"Never." The affection in his eyes made her melt. He took both her hands in his. "Let me go into your psyche."

"What, now? Why?" He looked as though he didn't know how to answer that, and she felt strangely reluctant to press the point. "Okay. Be careful, or I'll wind up in you."

A smile ghosted across his lips and then he bowed his head to concentrate. She felt no pain, only a jolt. The welcome smell of creosote and ozone surrounded her. She opened her eyes.

It was the same landscape as before, and yet not. The mountains stood in the same places. The wild herd of horses grazed, closer than before. But purple carpets of wild verbena and clouds of yellow brittlebush bloomed.

Jonathan, holding her hand, stared around in frank wonder.

"I've never seen a spring like this," she told him. Scarlet stars bloomed at their feet. Indian paintbrush. "This is the high desert," she realized aloud. The plant didn't grow near Phoenix, except in carefully xeriscaped yards. "The elevation's changed." The air was cooler and softer. It rained more often here.

"And I thought it was amazing before." Jonathan's low voice held awe. The trees near the mountains were no longer burned out, but a healthy forest that looked like it had been there forever. Their scent came to her on the breeze. Ponderosa pine.

"It's because of you," she said. He gave her a gentle kiss that sent warmth all the way down to her toes. "Why did you want to come here?"

"I wanted a minute alone with you in a beautiful place."

God, she always wanted to be with him. Would they get married? Have children, even? Maybe in a couple of years, once she was absolutely sure her powers were under control. Once, she'd imagined that kind of life, and maybe it could be hers after all. "We should… We should talk about the future."

"We will. I promise." Steady commitment reverberated in his voice, and joy lit his eyes. "Not now. You're tired, you're hurt, and you're on painkillers." He traced her cheek with a light fingertip. "I want it to be perfect."

"I'm with you. It's already perfect." Her voice quavered.

He placed his palm flat on his heart, a gesture she hadn't seen before, different from the salute to a superior. "*Cor meum tibi offero.*" Strangely, with him in her psyche, she understood the words with no trouble—*my heart I offer*—and their significance in Manus Sancti. It was a pledge of lasting love, a precursor to a proposal. "I'm yours as long as you want me."

Her eyes filled with tears. "That might be a while, *almeris*— Did I say that right?"

"You did." He pulled her close in his arms. The kiss started out light and sweet, but he deepened it, parting her lips under his. She'd never in her life felt so cherished or desired.

She was luckier than any person on the planet deserved to be. At last she knew what she'd been called to do in this life, and she'd do it by the side of the Knight she loved. More than ever before, she knew she was home.

THE END

Thank you for reading THE PHOENIX CODEX. If you enjoyed the book, please support the author with a review.

If you'd like to read a sneak preview of the second book in this series, THE EQUINOX STONE, read on! But beware: it contains spoilers and a cliffhanger.

THE EQUINOX STONE

BOOK II, KNIGHTS OF MANUS SANCTI

He stood naked in the wilderness at night, shivering in the cold wind. How long had he been here? He started moving again. He must've been walking before, though he couldn't remember it.

Most likely, he'd staggered away from an accident that had left him dazed. That didn't explain the lack of clothing, though. He felt over the surface of his head and found no soreness or injury. As far as he could tell, he wasn't hurt in any way, although he might literally freeze his dick off if he didn't find help or shelter soon. Rocks cut into the numbing soles of his feet, and he could barely distinguish the ridges of the short mountains on the horizon from the sky. There had to be a road, a house, something in this soulless landscape.

The wind picked up with an almost human wail, and he cowered, covering his private parts with his freezing hands, utterly bereft of dignity. After a minute, the wind subsided. His feet were bleeding now, and he wanted to lie down and curl up in a ball. That could mean death. He had to keep moving. If he'd had a phone, he could've called 911 or a friend.

What friend? He couldn't think of one. Loneliness and profound abandonment cut through him like another bitter gale.

Light in the distance. Headlights. He broke out into a run, his heart thudding hard in his chest. "Hey!" His voiced sounded strange to his ears, deeper and more growly than he'd expected. "Over here!"

The vehicle came straight at him, bumping over the rocky terrain. He stopped still in his tracks. It pulled up close enough that he took a step back, shielding his eyes with his forearm against the blinding glare of the headlights. Two figures exited the black SUV, leaving the engine running and one of the back doors opened as they advanced.

Both men held guns. *Shit.* He raised his hands in the air. In the headlights' beams, he could see them clearly. The one who'd been driving had shoulder-length dark hair and wore a black leather jacket. His face was taut, observant. The other guy was taller, with a buzzcut, his eyes blazing with hostility.

"Hey, easy," he told the gunmen. It was hard to sound casual with chattering teeth. A woman emerged from the backseat of the vehicle with a few awkward hops. "Just trying to get a little help here."

The hostile guy's mouth curled back in a snarl, and he raised the gun. *Christos.* The leather jacket guy said, "Don't shoot!" Almost at the same time, the woman shouted, "Read him first! Make sure!"

The hostile guy closed the short gap between them. *Disarm him*, he thought. He could envision the quick moves it would take, but if he succeeded, would the other man shoot him? The hostile guy grabbed his arm.

Something cracked his skull like a walnut. The pain extracted a guttural cry out of him, and he squeezed his eyes shut. The coldness disappeared. *I'm dead.* No, he was still conscious, because his head still pounded. He opened his eyes again.

They both stood on a city street lined by three-story buildings under a violet twilight sky. Neon signs, no people. The unmistakable, vaguely sexual scent of the ocean. *What the hell is going on?*

The other man looked wildly around him, his mouth parted, breathing hard. "What..." His eyes glossed over with unshed tears. "How are you here?"

He's crazy. Maybe we both are. Carefully, he asked, "Where are we?"

"You're confused. It's okay."

Everything dimmed, and cold air surrounded them again. He was back in the other landscape, the guy still gripping his arm. The man in the leather jacket and the woman stood closer to him now. She balanced on one leg, a hand on the hood of the car for support. She had big brown eyes, a prominent nose, and dark hair pulled back into a tight ponytail, though a few strands had escaped.

The guy who'd somehow ripped him to a different dimension and back shoved the gun back into his belt. "It's Michael." His voice came out rough, and he swiped a hand across his eyes. "I don't know how, but..." Suddenly, the guy threw his arms around him and pulled him close. "*Christos, corin.* How are you here?"

He stiffened in shock. The man's breath shuddered against his body. First, he'd threatened him and hurt him, and now he was embracing him like a long-lost friend? While he was naked, no less. The wrong word or move might swing the stranger into violence. He was probably mentally ill.

The man released him partially, still gripping him by the shoulders. "I'm sorry. It was all my fault. I—" A wave of pure amazement washed over his features. "You're really here." The guy in the leather jacket had a similar expression, and the woman covered her mouth with her hand, tears standing in her eyes.

They couldn't all be crazy, could they? He gave an awkward laugh. "Look man, I'm sorry," he said to the guy who'd hugged him. "I have no idea who you are."

3 1901 10065 2645

CPSIA information can be obtained
at www.ICGtesting.com
Printed in the USA
LVHW111531050921
697041LV00001B/124

9 780996 715249